P9-DIY-324

"This addictively readable thriller marries a breakneck pace to a complex, multilayered plot. . . . A roller coaster ride of adrenaline-inducing plot twists leads to a riveting and highly satisfying conclusion. Exceptional characterization and an intricate, flawlessly crafted story line make this an absolute must read for thriller fans."
—*Publishers Weekly* **(starred review)**

NO MERCY

"*No Mercy* grabs hold of you on page one and doesn't let go. Gilstrap's new series is terrific. It will leave you breathless. I can't wait to see what Jonathan Grave is up to next."
—**Harlan Coben**

"John Gilstrap is one of the finest thriller writers on the planet. *No Mercy* showcases his work at its finest—taut, action-packed, and impossible to put down!"
—**Tess Gerritsen**

"A great hero, a pulse-pounding story—and the launch of a really exciting series."
—**Joseph Finder**

"An entertaining, fast-paced tale of violence and revenge."
—*Publishers Weekly*

"No other writer is better able to combine in a single novel both rocket-paced suspense and heartfelt looks at family and the human spirit. And what a pleasure to meet Jonathan Grave, a hero for our time . . . and for all time."
—**Jeffery Deaver**

STEALTH ATTACK

A JONATHAN GRAVE THRILLER

JOHN GILSTRAP

PINNACLE BOOKS
Kensington Publishing Corp.
www.kensingtonbooks.com

PINNACLE BOOKS are published by

Kensington Publishing Corp.
119 West 40th Street
New York, NY 10018

All Kensington titles, imprints, and distributed lines are available at special quantity discounts for bulk purchases for sales promotions, premiums, fund-raising, educational, or institutional use. Special book excerpts or customized printings can also be created to fit specific needs. For details, write or phone the office of the Kensington sales manager: Kensington Publishing Corp., 119 West 40th Street, New York, NY 10018, attn: Sales Department; phone 1-800-221-2647.

First printing: July 2021

10 9 8 7 6 5 4 3 2 1

ISBN-13: 978-0-7860-4554-9
ISBN-10: 0-7860-4554-X

Printed in the United States of America

Electronic edition:

ISBN-13: 978-0-7860-4555-6 (e-book)
ISBN-10: 0-7860-4555-8 (e-book)

To Christopher John Gilstrap

Chapter One

Roman couldn't stop staring at her. Ciara Kelly, for God's sake. Hanging out with him at a swimming pool while everybody else from Northern Neck Academy was touring some old fort and an art gallery. Maybe an old Mexican church if there was time. There'd be hell to pay when they rejoined the group, but even if Dr. Washington sent him home, this moment in the sun would make all the crap that followed be worth the price.

He lay half naked on a fake beach in the middle of the desert next to Ciara and her thong bikini. Unlike Roman, whose body development seemed stuck at age twelve even though he was about to turn fourteen, she could have passed for . . . well, she had boobs.

This escape had been her idea. Ciara had asked *him*. Not the other way around, as if he could in a million years screw up the courage to ask her to do anything, let alone skip out on a field trip with the rest of the *Tribune* staff.

This Texas adventure was all about attending a journalism conference at the University of Texas at El Paso. As editor of the *Northern Neck Middle School Tribune*, Roman had finally landed on something he was good at. He wrote as Roman Alexander even though his last name was Pennington because his father was a piece of shit who'd disappeared before Roman knew enough to form a memory of him. As far as he was concerned, Mama Alexander was his grandma, and his mom's boss, Mr. Jonathan, was as close to a father as a kid could have. And put Father Dom D'Angelo on that list, too.

Then there was his mom. She was going to go into orbit when word got back to her about this trip to the Shady Sun Water Park, but so what? She went into orbit about just about everything these days.

"What are you thinking about?" Ciara asked him, poking his ribs with her finger. "You look so serious."

"I'm thinking about how close that driver came to killing us."

Ciara laughed. "Oh, my God. Our driver must have been drunk." On the way here, their RoadRunner driver ran a red light in front of an 18-wheeler.

"We're too young to be road pizza," Roman said. "I almost pissed myself." As the moment passed, he fell more serious. "Do you think we'll get expelled?"

Ciara laughed. "Not with what our folks pay to put us there. We might get kicked off the *Tribune* staff, though."

Roman wished he could say that prospect didn't bother him, but it really did. He'd finally found an extracurricular activity that he liked. It bummed him out that when he moved to the Neck's upper school next year, he'd be bumped all the way back to beat reporter. "Maybe we need to start heading back. We've been here two hours."

Ciara flipped her dark brown hair from one shoulder to the other. He'd have sworn she did it in slow motion. "If we're going to be a couple, I need a better tan than this. Next to you . . ."

"I'm black," he said and instantly felt stupid. "Wait, we're a couple?"

She looked hurt. Was she faking? "Don't you want to be?"

"Well . . . sure." He'd never thought about it in those terms. He wasn't even sure what it meant. Would other people know? Because that would be freaking *awesome*. Luke Eadie would be *so* pissed.

"You're a cute guy, Romey. You're nice and you're smart. Why do you look so surprised that I want to go out with you?"

"Please don't call me Romey. I hate that name."

"You're not answering my question."

His ears grew hot. "You're right."

He sat up on the blanket and pulled his feet in under his thighs. The Shady Sun Water Park had to be at least fifty years old. Lots of trees—the only concentration of green that he'd seen since they'd landed in El Paso—provided shade from the blistering Texas sun, and he supposed that was why people flocked to the place. The water rides, though, were all in some stage of being broken. The slides had barely enough flow to keep the foam pads from getting stuck on the way down. The wave pool was better called a ripple pool, and the water reeked of chlorine. Corrosion caked every exposed plumbing connection.

Roman didn't like the way the ticket taker at the peeling entry station was looking at him. No doubt a carney in a previous life, the zitty teenager had redneck written all over him, with long greasy hair tied back behind his neck. He appeared to be glaring straight at Roman from twenty yards away. As if to remove any residual doubt, Carney Kid peeled his shades away from his eyes to make it clear that Roman was the source of his interest.

"He's not staring at you, if that's what you're thinking," Ciara said. She'd rolled to her side, her head supported by her angled hand.

"Yeah, he is," Roman said.

"No, he's staring at *us*. I told you I needed a darker tan." She laughed.

Roman didn't. He'd heard stories of racist goobers in the Deep South, but he'd never encountered one himself—at least not without an adult backstop nearby. Northern Neck Academy—the Neck—was the kind of school that attracted diplomats' kids, so students there were pretty much color-blind. Throughout Fisherman's Cove, everybody knew he was Mama Alexander's grandson, and nobody dared to cross her, so racist bullshit didn't happen.

"That guy really doesn't like you being with me," Roman said.

"Did we ask his permission?"

"We need to get going."

"I'm not running away from that asshole," Ciara declared.

"Don't think of it as running away," Roman said.

"Think of it as a last chance not to get sent home. If we can beat the bus back to the hotel and be waiting for the others when they get back . . ."

"That's brilliant!" Ciara declared. She popped up to a sitting position and planted a kiss on Roman's cheek, following it with a big hug.

He didn't know what to do.

"That'll piss Pizza Face off," she said. "Meet at the gate?" She stood.

He stood, too. "Sure. Five minutes?"

Ciara reached out and twisted his nipple. He yelped and covered them up.

"Don't keep me waiting," she said.

Holy shit, what was happening? *Could* this even be happening? To him? Holy, holy shit.

As Roman walked toward the crumbling locker room—essentially a pole barn with a half wall and a moldy gang shower with corroded heads—Zit Face never took his eyes off of him. It was a scary glare, but Mr. Jonathan and his ginormous friend Mr. Boxers had told him thousands of times that you never let yourself be stared down by a bully. It might trigger a fight, and you might lose that fight, but at least you'll lose it with honor.

Mr. Jonathan was funny about honor. In his world, nothing was more important.

When Ciara had thought up this escape, she'd thought of pretty much everything. She'd warned him to put a bathing suit and a towel in his backpack, and she'd even brought the five-dollar locker rental fee for him. Five bucks for a dented school locker seemed outrageous, but everything about this shithole was outrageous.

Holy shit, Ciara Kelly pinched my nipple!

Roman used the rusty key to open the rusty lock to reveal his blue backpack. He wrapped his towel around his waist for modesty, stepped out of his bathing suit, then into his underwear and shorts. The Washington Nationals T-shirt came next, and he was ready to go. He wrapped the damp suit in his towel, then shoved it all into his backpack and zipped it up. He didn't need anything close to the agreed-upon five minutes.

When he stepped out of the locker room, Zit Face called, "Hey, kid."

Something tightened in Roman's stomach. "Yeah?"

"Come over here."

"Kiss my ass." More advice from Mr. Jonathan: go big or go home.

"Be happy to," Zit Face said. "Bring it on over here."

"I don't want your leprosy face infecting my butt," Roman said. He knew he was crossing a line here. It was Mr. Boxers who'd warned him not to let his mouth write checks that his ass couldn't cash.

He didn't want this to escalate to a real fight, so he turned his back on Zit Face and walked toward the sidewalk.

"That's it, pussy," Zitface said. "Walk away."

Roman turned and took a step closer. "What is your problem?"

"You are my problem. You and that girlfriend of yours. You don't belong together. That's my problem."

Roman forced a laugh. "Oh, well, if you don't approve, I guess we'll just have to break up." Bold talk for a guy who didn't know until a few minutes ago that he was in a relationship.

"How about I kick your ass instead of kissing it?"

Time to double down. Roman threw his head back and forced a loud laugh before turning back to the sidewalk. By then, Ciara had cleared the ladies' locker room. "What's wrong?" she asked.

"Keep moving," Roman said.

"The ticket guy?"

"We got into it a little. I don't want it to go to a fight. This is his turf."

Ciara laughed and hip-checked him. "Did you say *turf*? Like some gang thing?"

Now he felt stupid.

"Do you actually know how to fight?"

He had a black belt in karate, but he didn't talk about it much. First of all, there were a gajillion levels of black belt above his, and sparring wasn't really fighting. "Can't you see how everybody cowers in fear when they see me?"

As they walked to the curb and Ciara pulled her phone out of the little bag that Roman supposed she called a purse, a gray BMW SUV approached from their left and slowed.

"Did you call RoadRunner already?" Roman asked.

"No, not yet. Do you think the zitty kid called the cops?"

"Awfully nice car for cops. Besides, it's too soon."

Another car, this one a black sedan, turned toward them from the intersection ahead of them and stopped before reaching them.

"Let's walk," Ciara said.

Roman followed, but he wasn't sure that it was the smartest move. This didn't feel right.

The BMW raced forward, past Roman and Ciara, and jerked to a stop. A man in a suit climbed out of the shotgun seat and buttoned his jacket. He definitely looked like a cop.

"Can I talk to you for a second?" he asked. Roman wasn't good at identifying accents, but English was not this guy's primary language. The man smiled, but there was nothing friendly in it.

Ciara froze. "Guzman?"

"Hello, Ciara."

She backpedaled. Roman stayed with her. "Why are you here?" she asked. She looked scared.

"I thought we could spend some time together." Something behind the guy's eyes unsettled Roman's stomach.

"I–I can't," Ciara stammered. "Not today. We have to get back."

Guzman—whoever the hell he was—continued his slow advance as Ciara continued her slow retreat. Roman stayed with her step for step.

"And who is this?" Guzman asked.

"A friend." It was not lost on Roman that she did not offer his name.

Guzman beckoned to a guy from the second vehicle. "Well, Ciara's friend, you wouldn't mind if she spent some time alone with her Uncle Cristos and me, would you?" A man emerged from the second car and strolled their way.

Roman didn't know what was happening, but he knew they were in danger.

"Stay back!" he yelled. Really, truly *yelled*. He wanted to draw as much attention as he could. He pushed Ciara behind him and dropped down into his fighter's crouch. Weight evenly distributed left to right, back to front.

"Get out of the way, kid, before you get hurt."

"What are you doing?" Ciara whispered.

"Leave us alone!" Roman shouted.

Both men were beginning to look nervous with the shouting. A couple of faces gathered at the fence, looking out at them from the waterpark.

"You're about to overcommit, kid," Guzman said. He rushed forward, taking a swing at Roman, but the boy squatted below the punch and launched one of his own, squarely into the man's solar plexus. Guzman's knees buckled, but he didn't go down.

As the second guy rushed in, Roman launched a powerful kick that caught him in the knee. He didn't go down, either, but Roman had bought them some time.

"Come on," Roman said. He pushed Ciara in front of him and kept his hand in the middle of her back until they were both sprinting past the cars and down the sidewalk.

Running in flip-flops took precious time off every stride, but the concrete sidewalk was about a million degrees, so running barefoot was out of the question.

"Right at the corner," Roman said, pointing ahead. As if there were any other choice. Behind him, he heard a car's engine rev and a brief squeal of tires as the men came at them.

The BMW raced up on their left and swung the turn wide, driving the front wheel up onto the sidewalk about ten yards ahead, blocking their path completely.

"Other way," Roman said, grabbing Ciara's arm and pulling her back.

The guy called Guzman had recovered, and when he peeled himself out of the door this time, he looked pissed as hell.

Roman and Ciara reversed course and sprinted across the two-way street toward the desert that seemed to stretch forever out in front of them. When he heard the footsteps approaching from behind, combined with the sound of the big BMW turning around, Roman knew that they couldn't win a foot chase.

When they got to the sidewalk on the other side, he said, "You run. I'll slow them—"

Before he could finish the sentence, one of them caught up and delivered a massive shove between Roman's shoulder blades, sending him sprawling face-first into the blistering sand. He tried to find his feet, but a heavy shoe caught him squarely in the balls and his world exploded in pain. His whole body, from his knees to his chest, seized up in a giant cramp that stole his breath.

He was vaguely aware that Ciara was yelling, but he didn't know what she was saying. All he knew for sure was that his mouth was full of sand and that he couldn't see anything.

"Let go of me!" That was definitely Ciara. Then she went quiet.

Roman rolled up to his hands and knees, hoping to stand, and then hands were on him. "Okay, tough guy," an adult male voice said. "You're in this, too."

He was half-carried, half-dragged toward the car, one hand squeezing his neck in the front and another lifting him by the waistband of his shorts. When they got to the car, hands patted his thighs hard, causing him to raise his legs. He couldn't survive another shot to his nuts.

The guy took Roman's cell phone from his front pocket and shoved him into the backseat.

"Where is Ciara?"

"Hey, kid."

Roman turned in time to see a bright red light flash behind his eyes.

Chapter Two

"**R**oman is missing!"

Jonathan Grave's head jerked up from the administrivia on his desk to see Venice Alexander trembling in the doorway to his office, her eyes red and wet. Melting mascara streaked her face like a mime's tears. She was on the edge of a meltdown. Everything about her screamed terror.

"What does *missing* mean?"

"It means that he didn't report back to the bus by the designated time," she explained. Other than the movement of her lips to speak, her body remained locked in place. Frozen.

Jonathan rose from his chair and stepped around to the front of his desk. Behind him, in the marina beyond the double window, the masts of million-dollar yachts swayed against the crystal springtime sky.

"Come in, come in," he said as he approached with his arms out, either to embrace her or to catch her as she collapsed. "Tell me what's going on."

Venice Alexander (pronounced "Ven-EE-chay" because long story) had been a part of Jonathan's life since the day she was born. Her mother—Florence, officially, but known to the world as Mama—had been Jonathan's family housekeeper when he was a boy and had morphed into the role of surrogate mother when little Jonny's mom died young. That made Venice his ersatz little sister, with more than a few years separating their ages.

Roman Pennington was her everything. A living monument to his mom's bad taste in men, Roman had been hit hard by adolescence. For the past few months, he'd been exploring the dark corners of young teen assholery and had made himself impossible to be around.

Jonathan gently grasped Venice's wrist and elbow. "C'mon, kid," he said. "Let's sit you down before you fall."

Venice walked with a hesitant gait. In a different setting, she might have looked drunk. Jonathan guided her to the seat closest to the fireplace, the dark-green leather sofa. Normally, he would have put himself in the William and Mary rocker that was easiest on his back, but he chose to sit next to her on the couch, instead, so close that their thighs touched.

Rapid knocking drew his attention back to his office door, where Gail Bonneville stood breathless in the opening. She was a key member of Jonathan's team. "I just now saw your text," she said. "Oh, my God, Ven, what have you heard?"

Did I get a text? Jonathan wondered. He gestured to

the sofa opposite them. "We're just about to get to that," he said. Then, to Venice: "Start at the beginning."

Jonathan watched as Venice struggled to reel in the emotions that had leapt well past her ability to reason. He'd give her all the time she needed.

"He was on his trip," she began, but Jonathan interrupted her.

"What trip?"

"The school trip to El Paso," she explained.

Jonathan shot his hand to her knee. "Wait. El Paso, *Texas*?"

Venice looked startled.

"Did I know about this?" he asked. Then, to Gail, "Did *you* know about this?"

"I knew he was going on a field trip," Gail said.

"So did I. But I didn't know it was to El-friggin-Paso." Jonathan's mind reeled. As far as the Mexican drug cartels were concerned, El Paso was just an extension of their local market. "Holy shit, Ven," he blurted, immediately regretting his tone.

Gail's eyes shot lasers. "Digger!"

Okay, he wasn't doing much to defuse the angst, but Jesus. "You know what I do for a living, right?" he said. "You know that we've blown major chunks out of northern Mexico. El Paso is literally an inch from Mexico."

"Come on, Dig," Gail tried again. "She's already scared to death."

"This is the newspaper thing, right?" Jonathan asked. Roman loved his role as editor, and this trip was one of the few things Jonathan had seen him excited about in a long time.

"Multimedia journalism," Venice corrected.

How can that distinction possibly matter? "I thought that was at Arkansas State."

"It was, but that fell through. Something about budgets for summer programs."

"Aren't there a couple hundred other journalism schools that aren't in war zones?"

Gail had had enough. "Digger, stop!"

"The conference is at UTEP," Venice said. "University of Texas at El Paso. Dr. Washington is an alum. Oh, my God, Digger, what do you think might have happened?"

Jonathan resigned himself to moving on. "It doesn't matter what *might* have happened," he said. "I don't yet have a grasp on what *did* happen. What do you know?"

Venice explained, "Dr. Washington called me about fifteen minutes ago. The kids had free time this afternoon to look around the city, but they were supposed to be back to their bus by three o'clock to go on to their next event. Dinner, I think. Roman and another student were the only ones not to return."

"Who is the other student?" Gail asked.

"Sarah somebody, I think." Venice said. "I didn't recognize the last name, but Roman had mentioned her before."

Three o'clock Texas time meant four o'clock Virginia time. Jonathan looked at his watch. Seventeen-ten. "He took his sweet time making the call."

"Who is Dr. Washington?" Gail asked.

"Everett Washington is the headmaster of Northern Neck Academy," Jonathan explained. Jonathan had spent twelve miserable years as a student at the Neck before he escaped for college. He thought of the place as a prison for overprivileged rich kids.

"So, where does it stand with Washington now?" Jonathan asked.

"He told me he's got the police involved. The other children are back in the hotel for the night. Everyone is saying prayers."

"Good," Jonathan said. "Thoughts and prayers. That's always the best way to go." He didn't know if his irony shined in his words, and he didn't much care. "How many kids are on this trip?"

"Ten or twelve, I think," Venice said. "The entire newspaper staff."

"We have to stay positive," Gail said. "Chances are, this is nothing at all. Some prank."

Won't they have an interesting story to report? Jonathan didn't say. He stared at the dark fireplace as he catalogued what he'd just been told. The police wouldn't do jack to track down a couple of thirteen-year-olds who'd been given permission to wander off. There'd be a picture on cops' duty sheets, and they'd be urged to keep an eye out for them, but there'd be no priority on it.

"Can you get the other student's name?" Jonathan asked.

Venice swiped at her eyes, worsening the mascara disaster. "I don't know. Probably." Her lip trembled. "Oh, Digger, please don't tell me you think that anything bad has happened to him. I don't know what I'd do if . . ." She didn't finish the sentence.

"I don't think anything yet," Jonathan said. Honesty was the best strategy at this point. "But we can't rule anything out, either."

Venice stared at the floor as she hugged herself and rocked gently.

"Hey, Ven?"

She looked up.

"I gotta ask a hard question," Jonathan said. "How have you two been getting along?"

"You already know the answer to that," she muttered. "It's been horrible. He's angry all the time. Nothing I do or Mama does is ever good enough. He wants to be left alone, but when we leave him alone, he stops studying. He doesn't do anything. There's something not right there. What's your point?"

Jonathan sat back in his seat. "No point to be made," he said. He kept his words barely audible so Venice would have to lean in to hear him. "But that's one of the questions the police are going to ask you."

"Okay. So?"

"So . . . Do you think he might be doing drugs? He and this friend?" He expected to be severely admonished by Gail for asking the question, but he saw in her eyes that she was way ahead of him.

"No!" Venice exclaimed. "Absolutely not! Roman? You've known him as long as I have, Dig. Do you see him as a druggie?"

The truth of it was no, he didn't. Jonathan knew Roman to be a good kid with a big heart and a quick sense of humor, and he knew that for more than a few weeks, that heart and humor had evaporated. Wasn't that the story every parent and close friend tells when they find out their kid has gone to the dark side?

"I'm just saying it's something they're going to ask. If you say no, then the answer is no. Regardless, they're likely to assume that the kids are being kids. That kind of assumption is likely to get in the way of a good investigation."

"What are you suggesting I do?" Wired like a spring, she was ready to launch at the slightest provocation.

"Not a thing," Jonathan said. "I'm just thinking out loud at this point. The one thing I absolutely want you to do is answer any questions they might ask truthfully."

"Why would I lie?"

Jonathan looked to Gail for some help.

"They *are* going to suspect drugs," Gail said. "It's their default assumption. When they start asking you questions about Roman's attitude and actions recently, it'll be easy for you to try to shade facts to draw them away from that."

"Roman is *not* taking drugs!" Venice insisted.

"And we're not suggesting otherwise," Gail said. She leaned forward to grasp Venice's hands, but Venice wanted nothing to do with the gesture.

"Police are creatures of habit," Jonathan explained, hoping that he'd be making things better. "When there's a homicide, the person who finds the body is assumed to be the murderer until evidence points otherwise. The guy left standing after the fight is over is the aggressor."

Gail said, "When kids in general, boys in particular, go missing, the default assumption is that they're off to find drugs."

"Or get laid," Jonathan added. Frankly, having recently caught a glimpse over Roman's shoulder of what he was watching on his phone, off to get laid was the more likely scenario.

"The point," Gail said, "is that when the time comes for the police to interview you, you need to truthfully answer the questions they ask and not try to get ahead of them."

Jonathan said, "If they think you're not being forthcoming, they'll focus even less on the search to find them."

Venice's features had locked into an angry glare. "Are you both finished? When was the last time I ever lied to either of you?"

"Never," Jonathan said. He launched the word quickly.

"That's exactly right," Venice said. "I sure as anything am not going to start now."

It was time to move on. With more disturbing thoughts. Jonathan prepared himself with a deep breath. "You know how I feel about coincidences," he said.

"You don't believe in them."

"I believe that they're dangerous to believe in." In his mind, there was enough of a coincidence to require a re-statement. "El Paso is literally one step away from Mex-ico, and I've got a lot of enemies in Mexico. We've done a lot of damage down there, and if the Mexican army or their national police force got wind that someone who's close to me was so close to them . . ." He didn't finish the thought.

Venice's face registered panic. "Do you think they kid-napped Roman?" She turned her gaze to Gail but got no relief.

"Again, Ven, I'm not to the point of *thinking* anything. Am I worried that might be the case? You bet your ass I am."

Venice stood. "We have to go down there," she said. "If the police aren't going to handle this seriously—"

Jonathan stood, too, and pumped the air with both hands. "Whoa, whoa. Let's do this one step at a time." He kept his hands out, palms exposed as he ran the permuta-tions through his head. If Roman had taken off to enjoy a few hours out of adults' eyesight, there'd be hell to pay when he got home, but the danger was minimal, and there was no need for anyone to go anywhere from Fisherman's Cove.

If Roman were the victim of street crime, or if he'd gotten lost, or if he'd fallen off a bridge, the locals would eventually handle it, and what would happen, would happen. Jonathan had no role to play.

But if this was a cartel play . . .

In the absence of evidence to the contrary, he had no choice but to assume the worst.

"Okay," he said. "I'm going to Texas. Get Boxers on the phone and tell him to meet me at the airport as soon as he can get there."

Gail rose from the sofa and reached out to Venice, then thought better of trying again to grasp her hands. "Try not to worry," she said. "We'll get this all straightened out."

Venice looked startled. "Why does this sound like a goodbye? I'm going with you."

Jonathan caught Gail's eye and with a quick flick of his head invited her to leave them alone.

As Gail approached the office door, Venice said, "I'm serious, Digger. I'm going to Texas with you."

"Let's sit back down."

"No. I don't want to sit back down. I want to go find my son."

"Then that puts us all on the same page," Jonathan said. "With any luck at all, we'll find out that Roman is fine, and we'll get the news before we're even wheels-up out of Manassas."

Venice said, "But if he's in trouble, I need to be—"

"Here," Jonathan said. He softened his tone even more. "You need to be *here*, Ven."

"He's my son."

"And that puts you too close to it all. You have to see that."

The tears came in earnest now. "I am not just staying back in Fisherman's Cove waiting for the phone to ring. I need to do something."

"And what skills do you bring to El Paso?" Jonathan asked. "Look, I don't want to be an asshole here, but seriously. What in your skill set makes you think that you would make our time on the ground in Texas more productive?"

"Well, it's a good thing you don't want to be an asshole. What do you call this?"

"I call this being practical. And if you think about it, you know I'm right. You are our eyes and ears, Ven. Do what you do and what only you can do. Find out everything you can. Start with everything you can find out about this Sarah Somebody kid and her family tree. Use those computer skills of yours to make the internet afraid."

His words found their mark. He could see it. "I don't know that I can do that," she said. "How am I going to be able to concentrate?"

"How are you going to be able to think about anything else? You can stew and worry and cry and be in the way, or you can stew and worry and cry and be useful. Find out everything you can about everybody on that field trip. Tap into the security cameras at the hotel they're staying in. Hell, find out what they had for lunch and what they're thinking about in their spare time."

She wiped her eyes with her fingertips. He could see the wheels beginning to spin in her head.

Jonathan continued, "When we're wheels-down, if we haven't already gotten good news, I want to be ready to roll with our own investigation. I want to know more than the FBI, and I want to know everything the El Paso PD knows."

"It's sounding like you have a plan," Venice said through the slightest trace of a smile.

Jonathan winked. "I do," he said. "I'm going to find your baby boy, and I'm going to bring his ass home so that you and Mama can take turns beating him blue."

Jonathan caught up with Gail as she arrived at her desk. "Can I talk with you for a second?" he said.

"Sure."

"Not here."

Jonathan led the way down two flights of stairs to the first floor of the converted firehouse that served as both his home on the first two floors and the headquarters for Security Solutions on the third. They stepped out into the bright sunshine, then he buttonhooked to the left and punched in the code to open the front door to his residence. As commutes went, this one was pretty damn easy.

Jonathan pushed the door open and stepped aside to let Gail enter first. Here, as in his office, his decorating palette ran toward dark woods and leather. Lush oriental rugs adorned the floors. Jonathan had spent a ridiculous amount of money converting the four-bay firehouse into his home. Having spent so much time as a youngster hanging out here with the fire crews, he still recognized much of the original architecture, but those details would be invisible to a casual observer.

"What's with the secrecy?" Gail asked, still standing in the foyer.

"It's not secrecy," Jonathan said. "It's that I'm about to piss you off. I need you to stay behind for Mother Hen. This is a lot for her to take, and I don't want her here alone." The request struck right at the heart of a long-standing wound. Gail had come up through law enforcement, not the military. A lawyer by training, she'd been an FBI agent and the sheriff of Samson, Indiana, before joining on with Jonathan's team. Her view of the world was more nuanced than his—and a world away from Boxers'—and her contrarian views had often chafed, leaving her to feel sometimes that she was less than an equal part of the team. Jonathan got it. He didn't think it was true, never even for an instant, but he understood how she might think that way.

And now he was asking her to stay behind.

"Why me?"

"Big Guy has to fly the plane. And I think we can all agree that I'm nobody's first choice for providing comfort."

Gail clearly wanted to argue. He could see it in her stance, the way she'd crossed her arms. But he could also see that she understood his point.

Jonathan went for the close. "There'll likely be leads to follow here anyway, and I don't want Ven to feel compelled to become a field operator. Especially not when she's as spun up as she is."

Gail's jaw muscles tensed. "You know I don't like this," she said.

"Yeah."

"Are you guys going to do anything stupid while I'm not with you?"

"Probably." He flashed a smile as he stepped closer and folded her into a hug. She hugged him back.

"I won't say it," she whispered.

"Good." Jonathan considered wishes for good luck or to be careful to be fundamentally damaging to a mission. The desire for either could get a team killed.

"But you will, right?"

"I'm going to bring Roman home."

Chapter Three

Venice stood there in front of the sofa in Jonathan's office for what might have been two minutes. She didn't move. She couldn't think. The enormity of what she'd just learned was incomprehensible. Her baby was missing.

Was Digger right? Had she been irresponsible to let him go on the trip to Texas?

She felt a flash of anger. If it was such a dangerous thing to do, why hadn't Digger spoken up before? She knew for a fact that she'd told him about the trip. It was typical of him to tune out any information that wasn't specifically about him.

"Settle down," she said aloud. Things were spinning out of control, and what she was doing—this panic—accomplished nothing.

I'm the master of electrons. That's what Digger called her, anyway. How many times had she saved their butts by working miracles over the internet? Now it was time to turn her skills on finding Roman.

Venice spun around, strode out of Digger's office and across the Cave—the secured inner office that housed the workings of the clandestine side of Security Solutions. A renowned private investigation firm that served some of the most recognized corporations in the world, Security Solutions specialized in obtaining the kinds of information that sometimes could not be requested in official settings. For the overt side of the company, which employed a team of supremely talented investigators—many of them disabled vets to whom Jonathan Grave had given a chance when so many other companies would not—discretion was perhaps their most valuable commodity.

But there was a covert side to Security Solutions that the investigators who toiled in the Fishbowl—the outer office on the third floor—knew nothing about. And if they suspected, they knew not to say anything. Again, discretion.

This side of the business had no official name, but its focus was unique among private investigation firms. Nominally specializing in freelance, extralegal hostage rescue—resolving kidnappings without the burden of due process—the team was frequently called upon by Uncle Sam, usually the FBI, to accomplish tasks that governments were not permitted to perform.

Three levels down, a reinforced concrete underground bunker spanned the width of the parking lot and more, with disguised entrances in the basement of the firehouse on one end and the basement of St. Katherine's Catholic Church next door on the other. The bunker housed all kinds of weaponry, from small arms to explosives—the tools of Digger's trade. Venice hated going down there and avoided it whenever she could, which was pretty much always.

The covert side of the business occupied maybe one-quarter of the entire floor space on the third floor, and it resided behind a locked and guarded door. Known colloquially as the Cave, the space housed offices for Digger, Brian Van de Muelebroecke (a.k.a. Boxers), and Venice Gail worked out of the Fishbowl to serve as a management influence and resource for the investigators.

Venice beelined to the War Room, the high-tech teak conference room and mission control center. From there, she had access to resources that would make NASA blush. She couldn't access nuclear launch codes, but in all fairness, she'd never tried. Her latest technological acquisitions had come to her direct from the National Security Agency, entirely without their knowledge. There had to be a way to find one boy in El Paso.

As she settled in behind her computer screen, she logged in and went straight to work. The first step would be to find Roman's cell phone signal. Roman would be furious if he knew how much software Venice had loaded onto his phone while he slept. The kid thought he'd disabled the tracker, and she had no intention of setting the record straight. Given their progressively more open warfare as he struggled with adolescent angst, she figured the more he thought he was winning, the better off they'd all be.

Everybody else was going to think he ran away, but that didn't make sense to her. As much as Roman hated her these days and as much as he might want to make her squirm, he would never hurt Mama. He was her everything, and he knew it. He'd never in a million years do anything to make her worry.

It took all of five minutes for Venice to navigate to the cell towers in and around El Paso and from there to initiate her search for his smartphone. Nothing. Certainly nothing in the downtown area or around the university.

She widened the search and still got no response. Worry began to blossom large. That boy *never* turned his phone off. Even if it *was* turned off, she should still be able to find his SIM card. Even if he knew how to remove it, why would he possibly want to? He thought he was invisible in the first place.

The phone was gone. Nowhere to be found. The worry became fear and bloomed larger.

"Come on now, think," she said. She decided to hack into his call history. All of the numbers she found were from Virginia. The most recent was an incoming call from a 757 area code. The number traced to Dennis Kelly. A bell rang in her head. Roman hadn't run off with Sarah Somebody. It was Ciara Kelly. That couldn't possibly be a coincidence.

Venice entered Ciara Kelly's number into the tracking program, and it likewise was nowhere to be found. It took a little longer to hack into Ciara's phone list, but it was well within Venice's skill set. Sure enough, there was Roman's phone number, number two in her list, and with the corresponding time stamp.

Correlation is not causation, she reminded herself. The stakes were too high to allow herself to jump to conclusions. Maybe they were in some weird kind of dead spot where phones were invisible.

She needed to see if other phones had become invisible, too.

"What's that boy's name?" she asked no one. There was one classmate who had been Roman's friend since their early years at the Neck and also was on the trip. *Come on. He's been to the house!*

Luke Eadie. That was the name. Luke Eadie. Nice kid, deeply into martial arts. That's how he and Roman became friends.

Again, it took a few minutes to funnel through all the possible Luke Eadies to find the right one. Venice narrowed the choices down dozens at a time at first, then one at a time, until she found the one and only Luke Eadie in El Paso whose phone carried a Northern Neckphone number.

And there it was, pinging a tower downtown.

"Damn," she said. Hearing the word made her feel uncomfortable. Venice did not like cussing, whether from herself or from others.

Commotion from out in the Fishbowl, beyond the security door, drew her attention away from her computer.

Annoyed by the interruption, she pushed herself away from the computer, exited the War Room, and moved to the security door. When she opened it, she saw a very angry Mama Alexander and a very frightened Rick Hare. A former Special Forces operator with too many years in the Sandbox to calculate, Rick was a hard-as-mahogany member of the office security team. Venice had seen him stare down some very scary people. But Mama was Mama.

"What is going on out here?" Venice demanded.

"Venny, you and me are gonna have words," Mama said. "And you." She thrust a stubby finger toward Rick Hare. "You're lucky she saved your sorry backside."

Venice opened the door wider. "Please come in, Mama. We can talk in here."

She led her mother past the War Room, where there were too many gadgets and widgets that she had no business knowing about, and back to Jonathan's office.

"Have a seat, Mama." Venice gestured to the leather sofas.

"I don't want to sit."

"Well, I'm not going to talk to you while you're yelling at me," Venice countered.

"Is it true that Roman is missing?"

"Mama, please sit down."

Her eyes showed that she didn't want to, but Mama rounded the coffee table and lowered herself into the nearest end of a green leather sofa.

Venice took the leather chair closest to her. Reached out and grasped her hand. "We don't know what happened to Roman, Mama. All we know is that he didn't show up to a place he was supposed to be."

"Why didn't you tell me?"

"Because I just found out myself. We're still piecing the details together."

"Is he all right?"

"We have to assume that he is. There's no reason to assume that he's not." Venice wished that she could bring herself to believe her own words.

"Well, what happened?"

Venice caught her up on the details of his going missing from the field trip. She left out Digger's embellishments about El Paso.

"Roman wouldn't do that," Mama said. "He's not that kind of boy."

"I mostly agree with you, Mama. But you know as well as I that he's been acting out."

"He's not that kind of boy," Mama repeated. "If he wandered off, it wasn't his idea."

Venice didn't see how that could matter, so she didn't reply.

Mama's features hardened as her eyes turned red. "I saw Jonny heading down into the basement. He looked very serious. Was that about Roman?"

Venice's breath caught. There was no way Mama could be allowed to know what the team was doing. "I, uh . . ."

"Don't you lie to me, Venny. You know I'll know, and I don't want to be insulted with a lie."

"Then I won't answer," Venice said. "I can't tell you."

"Can't or won't?"

"Pick the one you're most comfortable with."

"You're going to sass me at a time like this?"

"I don't mean to," Venice said.

"Why was Jonny so serious if there's nothing to worry about? If there's no reason to assume that he's not all right? Those were your words."

When Mama Alexander wanted information, she was like a dog with a bone. She'd keep gnawing until she got what she wanted.

Venice settled herself with a sigh. "Digger and Boxers are going to fly down to El Paso to help with the investigation."

"There's an *investigation*? Oh, my God."

Venice held out her hands to stop the panic. "No, no, no. Not like that. We're concerned that the police aren't going to take the disappearance seriously. They're going to assume that they just ran off to be teenagers."

"They?"

"Roman is with a girl. At least we think that. They're both . . . Both of them failed to report back on the field trip." She didn't want to utter the word *missing*.

"So, Jonny is gonna spend all the time and money to take his plane down to Texas *just in case* something is bad?" Mama's jaw had set. "That don't make no sense, and you know it, Venny."

Venice had no words.

"You look here, Venice Alexander." Mama pronounced her name as if it were the city in Italy. She'd never bought into the "Ven-EE-chay" affectation. "I don't know what you all do back here behind your closed doors and security guards, and I'm pretty sure I don't want to. But I see the bruises on Jonny when he comes back from trips. I see them on Gail, too, and that giant bag of scary they travel with." Boxers and Mama had never gotten along very well. Neither had he and Venice, for that matter.

Mama continued, "I suspect that you cross legal lines and bring violence to people. I won't ask you to confirm that, and please let me believe that you only hurt people who need to be hurt."

Venice prayed that her poker face was holding fast.

"If something has happened to Roman. If, God forbid . . ." Mama's voice broke. She brought her hand to her eyes and struggled through the moment. Her shoulders settled and her hand came down. "If that's the case, I'm depending on *you* to make sure that awful things are done to anybody who lays a hand on that boy."

Venice wasn't prepared for the flood of emotion that erupted from her own soul. She dropped her face into her hands and let the tears flow. "Oh, Mama, I'm so frightened."

Mama placed a hand on Venice's knee. "Hey."

Venice looked up, surprised to see Mama fully recovered from her own emotional break. In fact, her eyes were stony.

Mama stood. "You don't have time for that," she said. "No tears. No anger. You get to work doing what you do and bring our boy back."

Mama left the Cave and never looked back.

Chapter Four

Jonathan and Boxers were airborne in record time, less than two hours after the news had broken in Fisherman's Cove. The Beechcraft Hawker 800 executive jet resided at Manassas Regional Airport in Prince William County, Virginia, in a hangar leased to a fictitious company that Jonathan owned for the specific purpose of being untraceable. A maintenance team retired from the 160th Special Operations Air Regiment doubled as a security team, taking care not only of the aircraft and physical plant but also the munitions that were stored there. The TSA administrator would fall over dead if she knew what kind of cargo the Hawker carried.

One of the benefits of hiring former Special Forces soldiers and operators was their appreciation of the importance of keeping secrets. As for nosy neighbors at the airport, Jonathan wasn't terribly concerned. The closest operation to his own possessed a lot of unmarked white aircraft with meaningless tail numbers. It tried to be low-key, but as far as Jonathan was concerned, they might as well have painted the CIA shield on the vertical stabilizers.

Bottom line: this corner of the Manassas fixed-base operation was as safe a neighborhood as any airplane could find.

Boxers drove the airplane while Jonathan sat in the copilot seat. In a nightmare scenario, Jonathan knew enough to get the jet on the ground, so long as the autopilot was on and the control tower had someone on hand who could talk him down.

Once airborne, Jonathan placed a call to Fisherman's Cove Police Chief Doug Kramer. Doug and Digger had grown up together, and Doug felt like part of the family. "Where the hell are you calling from?" Kramer asked. "You sound like you're in the middle of a highway."

"We're airborne," Jonathan said. "On our way to El Paso." The chief listened while Jonathan filled him in on the details of Roman's disappearance.

"You probably already know this," Kramer said, "but you're not going to get a lot of interest from boots on the ground in El Paso. Teenagers stepping off together—"

"Yeah, I know," Jonathan said. He didn't need to hear the resistance another time. "That's why we're headed down there."

"What do you expect to accomplish?"

"We're going to help the police with the investigation they're not going to want to do."

"How?" Kramer asked. "On whose authority? Does Texas have some kind of reciprocity agreement with Virginia private investigators?"

"I have no idea," Jonathan said. "And you know me well enough to know how little I care."

"You're only half of that equation, Dig. I imagine they're going to care a lot."

"That's where you come in," Jonathan said. "We're hoping that you can call someone. You know, chief-to-chief. Explain a little of what we're trying to accomplish and maybe get them in the mood to cooperate with us."

"I can try," Kramer said. "I'll be happy to make the call, but just so you know, I don't have any connections down there."

Boxers asked, "Is Thor still attached to that BORTAC task force?"

"Good question," Jonathan said.

Kramer laughed. "So, you guys are on a first name basis with the God of Thunder?"

"He's a DEA agent we've worked with a couple of times," Jonathan explained. "Real name is Harry Dawkins. Tell you what. I'll reach out to Harry and see if we can scare up the police chief's name. Get back to you in ten, fifteen minutes?"

"It's your phone bill."

"Rog," Jonathan said. He clicked off, then scrolled through his contacts list till he landed on Dawkins's number.

The call connected on the third ring. Over the speaker, Dawkins's distinctive voice answered with "Miss me?"

"Like a genital rash," Jonathan replied.

"Is Big Guy with you?"

"I never leave home without him."

"How ya doin', Big Guy?"

"Livin' the dream."

"What can I do for you?" Dawkins asked.

"Are you still resting your head at night in El Paso?"

"I'm still in the drug business, Dig. Gotta be where the action is."

"Is that a yes or a no?" Boxers snapped.

"Whoa, Big Guy's cranky," Dawkins teased. "Stake out a goat for him to stalk and eat." As a jokester, Dawkins showed a lot more courage from afar than he did from close in. "But yes, it means yes."

"Good," Jonathan said. "You remember Venice, right?"

"Mother Hen? How could I forget?" Venice detested her radio handle, but Jonathan refused to change it.

"Okay, well, we got a bit of scary news," Jonathan said. "Her thirteen-year-old—almost fourteen now—was on a field trip in your fair city—"

"Who the hell brings kids to El Paso for a field trip?"

"Don't get me started. There's some thing going on at UTEP. Anyway, he's gone missing."

"Holy shit."

"Yeah," Jonathan said. "We're winging our way down there on the theory that we're not going to get a lot of love from the local flatfeet."

"EPPD has a lot of good folks," Dawkins said.

"I'm not questioning their professionalism," Jonathan said. "I just don't think this is going to be high on the list."

"You think—what's his name?"

"Roman Pennington," Jonathan said. "Probably goes by Roman Alexander, though. Long story."

"Are you thinking Roman's disappearance has something to do with your . . . shall we say *interaction* with the cartels?"

"That's the fear."

"And you can't clue the EPPD into the concern because you can't afford to be identified as the guy who blew up Mexico."

"We weren't alone, as I recall," Boxers said.

"I'm proud to have been part of the effort," Dawkins said. A while ago, Dawkins first met Jonathan and the team while naked and being tortured south of the border. A bit of violence followed in that adventure. "How can I help?"

Jonathan explained how he wanted Doug Kramer to soften the opposition in advance of their arrival. "Do you have any connections?"

"I know one of the assistant chiefs," Dawkins said. "His name is Chester Gill. Good guy. He's my liaison with the department. This is a bit out of his line."

"I just need a name," Jonathan explained. "Doug's going to do a kissy-kissy cop call and see what he can work out. We just want more access than they'd likely give to other outsiders."

"All right," Dawkins agreed. He shared the assistant chief's phone number, and Jonathan wrote it down.

Dawkins said, "While you're contacting your chief buddy, I'll give Chester a call myself and tell him to expect to hear from . . . Kramer, right?"

"Doug Kramer."

"Hey, listen, guys I hope all this works out. I'm praying for the best."

"Much appreciated, Harry." Jonathan clicked off. "Hey, Big Guy, how long before we touch down?"

The El Paso police were going to need a current picture of Roman. And Venice couldn't find one.

Couldn't find a picture of her only child. What kind of mother was she?

School photos were optional to the kids these days, and, of course, Roman wanted nothing to do with any of that. Thus, the most recent formal portrait she had of him was two years old, and he'd grown into encroaching manhood since then. Back then, he wore his hair cropped close, with a part cut in by the barber. Now, he sported an Afro, and his face was shadowed by wispy sideburns and a poor impersonation of a goatee—really, just hairs on his lip and chin, but they were important to him.

But there were no pictures.

Venice hacked into his Facebook account and found that it had not been updated in ages.

Facebook is for old people.

How many times had she heard that from him?

She knew that there was a grab bag of other social media options that were more popular among kids these days, but she had neither the time nor the desire to chase down those rabbit holes and reverse engineer Roman's credentials. For now, all she needed was a picture.

A simple picture.

Luke Eadie. Friends were always snapping pictures of each other. Maybe Luke would have a current shot that he could share. She dialed his number into the landline at her command chair and waited.

"Hello?" The voice sounded young. Tentative. He didn't know who he was talking to.

"Hi, this is Mrs. Alexander," Venice said. "Roman's mother. Is this Luke?"

"Is Roman okay?"

"We hope so. We haven't been able to find him yet. I'm sorry for calling so late. Can you tell me what happened? What you know?"

"I don't know anything. Just that he disappeared with Ciara Kelly."

"Did he say anything about where he might be going?"

"No, he was real secretive. I knew he was up to something, but he wouldn't tell me what it was."

"Any detail could help. Anything at all."

Luke hesitated, a sure adolescent sign that he owned information that he didn't want to share.

"I'm his mother, Luke." Venice heard the crack in her voice. "He's my only son and he's missing."

"Hold on a minute," Luke said. Sounds of movement, some muffled voices. Thirty seconds later, his voice returned, but barely above a whisper. "Are you still there?"

"What do you need to tell me, Luke?"

"Ciara Kelly is a troublemaker, Mrs. Alexander. I think she's got a thing for Roman, and he's really changed. He doesn't hang with anybody else anymore, and she's mean."

"Are you saying you think Ciara might have hurt Roman?"

"Oh, no, nothing like that. I think she talked him into sneaking away. On the bus riding from the airport I think they were planning something. Just from the way they were keeping to themselves and ignoring everybody else. Plus . . ." He fell silent.

"This is important, Luke."

"Well, he had a swimsuit in his backpack. I saw it when he opened it."

"Why is that important?" Venice asked.

Luke cleared his throat. "Well, first of all, the hotel doesn't have a pool. But more than that, I wondered why he had it in his backpack instead of in his duffel bag with all his other stuff."

Venice thought she saw where he was going in is logic, but she wanted to hear him say it. "Why did that seem important?"

"I guess maybe it didn't until after they didn't show back up," Luke said. "But looking back, I think they had a plan. You see, we knew that our rooms wouldn't be ready yet. They told us that we'd put our bags in the lobby and then we could go and look at stuff around town."

"Alone?" Venice heard the shock in her own tone.

"Well, with a buddy, you know? Roman was supposed to be my buddy, but, well, Ciara happened."

"They were buddies, then?"

"Right."

"Did you tell Dr. Washington?"

Silence.

"Luke?"

"I don't want to the one to get him in trouble. Roman never would have done something like this before Ciara. It's really all her."

Venice prayed that one day she might understand the priorities of young people. "I'm not looking for anyone to get in trouble, Luke. You can keep this just between us. I won't tell Dr. Washington."

"Really?"

"Really." She'd sure as heck tell Digger, though. "Hey, listen. Do you have a recent picture of Roman?"

"I think so. Do you want one of Ciara, too?"

Luke Eadie sent three pictures in total. One showed Roman laughing at something that wasn't obvious from the framing of the photo. Another showed Roman standing with Ciara. They were both wearing bathing suits, Roman in knee-length blue board shorts and Ciara in a bikini that Venice would never have allowed if she'd had a daughter. It was no wonder that Roman was distracted by her. Long dark hair, an infectious smile, and an adult's body. Did her parents not understand the risks that outfits like that posed for young girls? It was all part of the sexualization of young people that Venice did not understand.

The third picture was the one that would be most useful to her. Facial recognition software worked best when features were flaccid. This third shot caught Roman in a pensive pose, perhaps paying attention in class. This was the one she would load into the software purloined from the National Security Agency.

As she scanned the photo into the system, she turned back to the kids' phones. Both had turned off their tracking feature, but she figured that the way boys and girls lived on their phones these days, there had to be some bit of useful data in there. The swimsuit in the backpack was important, she knew. Maybe they'd done an internet search for the best places to go swimming in El Paso. A different hotel, maybe?

As she scrolled through Roman's hacked account, she

found nothing that seemed important. She switched to Ciara's account.

Wait. Could it really be that simple? Could she already have seen the clue she needed?

Ciara's call to Roman's phone was the *second* most recent number dialed. The most recent number was an El Paso area code.

"Oh, please, please, please," she whispered absently as she entered the number into her computer. The phone was registered to Luis Alvarez, and she got his home address. He had a police record, but the charges were all related to theft, the most recent being five years ago. No hint of violence.

Luis Alvarez was the divorced father of two daughters, both of whom were enrolled in San Pedro Catholic School. His credit score hovered at 643, which meant he wasn't the best money manager. He lived in the Sam Houston Mobile Home Park, where he was current on his rent.

"Come on," Venice urged her machine. "Give me something useful."

How about work history? That was a little harder to dig into because it meant accessing files that typically were guarded by more advanced security and encryption devices. Enter the NSA once again.

A while back, Venice had fallen in love with an extraordinarily talented hacker who was employed by the Puzzle Palace at Fort Meade, Maryland. He understood some of what the covert side of Security Solutions was into, and he bought into the importance of the mission, holding hope that he would one day become part of the team. In one of the most tragic moments of Venice's life, Derek Halstrom died while trying to save her from attackers.

But the toys he brought all remained.

Luis Alvarez had worked a number of menial jobs over the years, mostly as a store clerk. His terms of employment averaged out to be about two years, so that indicated to Venice that he must have been trustworthy, at least to a point.

"So, what are you doing for a living now?" she asked.

When she saw her answer, she knew she'd found her solution.

Chapter Five

The Hawker's engines were still spinning down when Venice called. Jonathan connected, and she was talking before he had a chance to say hello. "I know where he went," she blurted.

Jonathan switched the phone to speaker mode. "You know where Roman is?"

"Not what I said," Venice snapped. "I know where he *went*. I pray that he's still there, but I don't know that." She explained about the cell phones being turned off. "But the last number in Ciara's phone log was to a man named Luis Alvarez, a RoadRunner Rideshare driver."

"Why would she *call* a RoadRunner driver? Isn't there an app for that?" Jonathan was not a ride share kind of guy.

"Mr. Alvarez told me that the kids were not at the official pickup spot, so they called to tell him to pick them up on a different corner."

"Do we know where he took them?" Boxers asked.

"To a place called the Shady Sun Water Park. It's just a few miles outside of El Paso proper."

"Did you check with the park?" Jonathan asked. "Were they seen?"

"They said they had hundreds of customers today. And as the jerk on the phone put it, half of them were boys and half of them were girls. When I suggested that maybe the differences in skin color between them would make them more memorable, he said, and I quote, *The Shady Sun Water Park neither notices nor judges our guests' racial backgrounds*."

"Damn," Boxers said. "Where are the racist assholes when you need them?" Big Guy had an uncanny ability to misjudge his audience. When he saw that his attempt at humor fell flat, his smile evaporated.

"I want you guys to go out there and talk to those people personally," Venice said. "Look around. Maybe they're still there."

Jonathan and Boxers exchanged glances. She wasn't usually the one to be giving orders. "Will do," Jonathan said. "Have you checked for security footage you might be able to tap into, see if maybe you can find pictures of them?"

"Of course," Venice said. "Once I knew what to look for, I was able to find images of them waiting for their RoadRunner and then climbing into the car—an old model Ford, it looked like. And then I was able to trace the Ford as it took them toward the water park. Then, there's nothing to find. Apparently, this park is out kind of in the middle of nowhere."

"And the park itself?"

"If they have security, it's not connected to the internet."

"Okay, then," Jonathan said. "You keep working your end, and we'll keep plowing the dirt here." He really didn't want to ask his next question, but he didn't know how to avoid it. "I know you've been going in a million directions, but—"

"Your car is a white Suburban," Venice replied, nailing what he was going to ask her. "You found the parking spot I reserved for your plane at the airport?"

Jonathan looked to Boxers, got a nod. "Yes, ma'am."

"Don't you *ma'am* me. Have I ever let you down?"

"No, m . . . Venice."

"You go and get done what you need to get done. I'll worry about my job, while I'm worrying about your job. It's what I do." She clicked off.

"A little spun up, I'd say," Boxers commented.

"Her son is missing," Jonathan said. "This is a big deal, cuts way too close to the bone, and it pisses me off. Let's get this thing done and bring Roman home."

"Okay, then," Boxers said. "Let's go visit a water park. But I forgot to bring a suit."

As shitholes went, the Shady Sun Water Park was shitholier than most. In desperate need of maintenance and landscaping, it looked more like a Route One miniature golf park than a place anyone would want to swim. It was nearly ten o'clock, and the place was still hopping, but to Jonathan's eye, was about half the lights were burned out. The parking lot itself—big enough to hold probably a thousand cars—hadn't been paved in years.

Some of the potholes were eight or ten inches deep. Jonathan didn't understand how that could even happen when the temperature never dipped below freezing for more than a day or two every year.

"What a special treat for the family," Boxers muttered. "Come to the Shady Sun and get mugged in the dark parking lot."

"Only after you've broken your leg in the craters."

They'd armed up for this in the plane—just pistols— but they had big stuff in the back of the Suburban if they needed it, covered with a tarp to hide it from prying eyes.

As they climbed out of the truck, the stench of chlorine hung like fog in the humid air. "Damn," Boxers said. "I bet you can smell that from a mile away."

"Two," Jonathan said.

"How do you want to handle this?" Boxers asked as they started across the parking lot. "We look very cop-like."

They did, indeed, dressed as they were in matching tactical khaki pants and shirts. This being Texas, they saw no reason to conceal their pistols.

"Are we playing our FBI cards again?" Boxers asked. Several operations back, when they were doing the bidding of Irene Rivers, the director of the FBI, they had been granted mostly real credentials as agents, each identifying fictitious people with ridiculous names.

"Not now," Jonathan said. "Doug is vouching for us with the locals. I don't want to make anything difficult for him. I say we just take our badass selves into the park and look around."

Boxers laughed. "If Roman is still there and he sees us, he's going to turn to Jell-O."

Jonathan laughed, too, but he didn't think there was a chance in the world of him still being there.

Jonathan used his Mini Maglite to illuminate the route across the parking lot. As the stench of chlorine got stronger, the noise from the park got louder. Whatever was going on in there, it was a hell of a party. And no one was leaving, at least not in this direction.

Above them, mounted atop a large pole, a neon sign displayed most of the outline of a breeching dolphin—the dorsal fin was burned out—and in flickering light advertised Sʜ ᴅ S ɴ ᴀᴛᴇʀ ᴀʀᴋ.

When they were within fifty feet or so of the fence, the pavement transformed into dirt, through which a few hearty tufts of grass were making a valiant effort to sprout. Poor things didn't have a chance.

The sidewalk leading to the ticket counter was little better than the parking lot. No potholes, but rebar showed through crumbling concrete in a few places.

"Can you imagine walking here barefoot?" Jonathan mused aloud.

The entryway to the park was supposed to be a cut-away porthole, Jonathan figured, most of a circle with faux rivets protruding out of the concrete, forming a photo-op archway. Best guess was that the rivets were once yellow and the edge of the porthole itself was once blue. Inside the adjacent ticket booth, a skinny kid with an unfortunate complexion appeared to be closing out for the evening.

"Excuse me," Jonathan said. He had to shout to be heard over the booming music.

The kid looked up, then jumped a little. "Whoa. Who

are you?" When he gauged the size of Boxers, the kid's body language read, *and* what *are you?*

"We're here to look for somebody," Jonathan said. "A boy and a girl, thirteen, fourteen years old. We know they were here a few hours ago."

"A few hours ago, that described half the people in here."

Boxers added, "The boy is black, the girl is white."

"You mean as a couple?" the kid asked. "No. And that kind of thing would stand out here, if you know what I mean." Jonathan saw the twitch in the kid's eyes, something subtle. One day, he'd be a good liar, but he wasn't quite there yet.

"What's your name, son?" Jonathan asked.

"I'm not your son."

Boxers stepped closer. "Okay, what's your name, *asshole?*"

The kid wanted to fire a retort—his face showed that, too—but then he did the math. "Rocky."

"How long you been working here?" Jonathan asked.

"Two years."

"How about today?"

"Since about one-thirty. I go to eleven. I'm closing tonight."

Jonathan slid his phone out of his pocket and opened the picture of Roman and Ciara that Venice had sent to them. He turned it so Rocky could see. "And you're sure you've never seen these two?"

"Positive."

"I know you're a lying sack of shit," Jonathan said. "But experienced sacks of shit at least pretend to look at something before they say *no.*"

Rocky made a show of opening his eyes wide and leaning in close to the screen. "Is this good enough?"

Boxers struck fast, smacking the side of the kid's face and bouncing the other side off the wall of the ticket booth. He growled, "You can show some respect, or you can walk with two canes for the rest of your life. Choose."

Jonathan clicked his Maglite back on and shined the beam into the kid's face. No blood that he could see, but the lump was already beginning to grow.

"That's gonna hurt in the morning," Jonathan said. He looked at his watch. Ten-fifteen. "Mind if we look around?"

"With a ticket."

Okay, the kid had balls. You had to admire that. Jonathan and Boxers bypassed the turnstile and entered the park.

In its heyday, the Shady Sun Water Park had probably been a nice place. With three water slides of varying heights and two massive swimming pools, it must have provided great respite from the desert heat. Hell, it still did, Jonathan supposed, but it was hard to get past the fact that the landing pools at the base of the slides were an opaque green. He didn't know much about swimming pools, but he knew that he'd never go into one of them without a tetanus shot.

They split up to wander among the revelers. If you didn't look at the swimming apparatus, the place had a certain charm, Jonathan had to admit. People had brought in grills to cook dinner, countless coolers provided hundreds of gallons of beer—cans only, no bottles—and if he wasn't mistaken, weed was the herb of choice. Up on a makeshift stage next to a paper-mache version of the breeching dolphin mascot, a DJ was spinning songs that to Jonathan's ear weren't songs at all, but rather just a heavy bass line with rhythmic shouting.

Two of the patrons called Jonathan a pig—testament to his tacti-cool look, no doubt—and one asked if he'd killed any innocents today. He didn't respond, but he did keep an eye out for any flailing, flying kids that Big Guy might have launched had any dared to speak to him that way. Turned out that the current generation was smarter than some would lead you to believe.

Jonathan saw no signs of Roman or Ciara, and given the sobriety status and emotional state of the partiers, it seemed like a waste of time to ask around.

He met back up with Boxers near the front gate, far enough away from Rocky that they wouldn't be overheard. "Any sightings?"

Boxers shook his head *no*, adding a thumbs-down for emphasis.

"Did you show the pictures to anyone?"

"No one would care," Boxers said.

Jonathan looked around. Venice was certain that Roman had been here. He couldn't tell her that they'd struck out unless he was sure he'd swung at every pitch. He pointed with his chin toward a bored-looking lifeguard in her elevated chair, reading a book in her lap. Twelve people could have been drowning, and she'd have had no idea.

"Let's check with the rest of the staff."

They walked single file down the concrete sidewalk where faded signs made it clear that neither running nor horseplay would be tolerated. The lifeguard looked up as they approached. Her posture stiffened, and she swung the paperback behind her back, out of sight. Very smooth.

Jonathan approached and Boxers hung back. "Excuse

me," he said as he closed within hearing range. "Can we ask you a few questions?"

"What did I do?"

Jonathan flashed the smile that he'd calibrated over the years to melt hearts. "Nothing that I'm aware of. But if you'd like to confess to something . . ." She clearly thought he was a cop, so why let the truth get in the way?

The lifeguard looked terrified.

"Seriously," he said. "You're not in any trouble. We just need some help finding a couple of kids."

"A boy and a girl?"

Jonathan felt his back stiffen, and Boxers took a step closer. "Yes," he said.

The guard cast nervous glances over both shoulders, then turned and climbed backward down the short ladder to join them on the deck. "I get in trouble if I'm not in the chair," she said.

Jonathan presented his hand. "My name's Neil," he said, using the pseudonym from the FBI credentials he'd chosen not to use. "What's yours?"

"Abigail. What took you so long to get here?"

Jonathan cocked his head, waiting for the rest.

"They were shoved into those cars hours ago. What took you so long to get here?"

"Did you call the police?"

"I didn't, but I told Rocky to."

Boxers seemed to inflate. Jonathan used a gentle shooing motion to tell him to back off. "Did he?" he asked. "Call the police?"

"I think so. He said he would."

"Did you hear him make the call?" Jonathan asked.

Abigail looked suddenly uncomfortable. "Well, no, I

didn't *hear* him make the call. But I saw him pick up the phone. I had to get back to my chair."

"Tell us what you saw," Jonathan pressed.

"I was walking over there near the fence." Abigail pointed toward the road. "I needed to check the pH levels in the kiddie slide. I heard this noise out beyond the park, on the sidewalk. It was hard to see all the details through the trees, but I saw a boy and a girl—"

Jonathan pulled up their pictures on his phone and presented it to Abigail.

Abigail's face lit up, and she pointed to the screen with her forefinger. "Yes! Yes, that's them. Who are they?"

"What time was this?"

"Two o'clock. That's when I check the kiddie slide."

"Continue with your story, please."

"Well, two cars had pulled up—a silver SUV, BMW, I think, and a regular sedan—and two guys got out. One from each. They looked like they were cops, too. Wearing suits, except now I don't think they were cops, not with the way things went down. It started out okay, but then it went bad really fast."

"What does *went bad* mean?"

"Well, at first, it looked like they wanted to talk, but stranger danger, you know? The kids backed away. Then one of the guys sort of lunged at the girl."

Jonathan's ears perked. "Lunged at the girl?"

"Yeah." Abigail was becoming more animated as she told the story. "But the boy got in the way, kind of pushed her behind him. Then a fight started. The boy looked like he knew karate or something. He put up a good fight. Got one of the men with a kick."

Jonathan felt a swell of pride. He liked that Roman had fighting skills and knew how to use them.

"That bought them a little time," Abigail continued. "They took off running that way." She pointed toward the far end of the park, away from the parking lot. "It got hard to see from there because of the trees and stuff, but I know they got to the corner of Thirty-eighth and Herbert, right there, just beyond the fence. But by then, the guys were back in their car, and they caught up with them."

"Abigail!" It was Rocky. "Get back in your chair. It's not your break time."

She looked terrified. "I–I was talking to the police here about—"

"They're not police," Rocky said. "Get your ass back up in the chair where it belongs." He pointed a finger at Jonathan. "Did you tell her—"

Rocky dropped hard onto both knees as he passed Boxers, no doubt from a punch that was so fast that Jonathan didn't even see it. From the way Rocky was gasping for air, he figured it had to have landed on his solar plexus. Big Guy feigned concern as he knelt on one knee and put a hand on his shoulder. "Are you all right, sir?"

Jonathan turned back to Abigail, who now looked totally lost. "What happened at the corner?"

"Is Rocky okay?"

"Do you really care?"

The question seemed to amuse her. The hint of a smile stretched the corners of her mouth. "Did that huge man just hit him?"

"I honestly don't know," Jonathan said, and the answer was more true than false. "What happened next, Abigail?"

"The men put the kids into the cars and drove off." Her

voice started to quaver. "It looked like some kind of kidnapping to me."

"When you say *put them in the cars* . . ."

"Shoved them, really. One into the SUV and one into the car. They didn't want to go."

"This is bad," Jonathan mumbled. "Do you remember which kid went into which vehicle?"

Abigail looked sad. "No. Who were they?"

Jonathan whirled on her far too aggressively. "Are," he snapped. "Who *are* they, not were. No past tense."

Tears breached Abigail's lower lids. Her lip trembled.

Jonathan dialed it back. "I'm sorry for that," he said, meaning it. "That young man is very dear to me."

"I–I'm sorry, too. I don't know why Rocky . . ." She couldn't finish the statement.

Jonathan lowered his voice to barely a whisper, drawing Abigail in closer. "Rocky is an asshole. You don't know me from a stranger on the street, but I'll tell you this. If you quit this shithole right now, you'll feel proud of yourself. If you're still here tomorrow, you'll hate yourself." He gave that a few seconds to sink in. "I really am sorry about snapping at you."

"What's his name?" Abigail asked.

Jonathan didn't understand.

"The boy. What's his name?"

"Oh," Jonathan said. It was hard to believe that he wasn't prepared to answer that question. "Roman. Roman Pen . . . Roman Alexander." As an afterthought, he added, "The girl is Ciara Kelly."

"Roman is a nice name. I hope . . ." She struggled with her voice again. "I guess I just hope." Abigail started to climb back into her chair but stopped. Balanced there in the middle of the ladder, she seemed lost in thought. Abruptly, she reached under the arm of the guard chair, snatched her book off the seat, and climbed back down the ladder.

"This just isn't right," she said as she passed Jonathan on her way toward Big Guy. Boxers saw her coming and rose abruptly and stepped out of the way. When she got to Rocky, he was still trying to find air to breathe. "Why didn't you call the police when I told you?" she shouted.

Heads turned. It wasn't the kind of attention that Jonathan wanted to draw.

"I told you that two people had been kidnapped, and you didn't do anything!"

"Oh, pound it," Rocky said. "Get back—"

With a loud shriek, Abigail grabbed Rocky's ponytail in both hands and yanked.

"Hey! Ow! The hell you doin'?"

Abigail never stopped. As she pulled, Rocky tried to find his feet, but she was dragging him across the rough concrete, toward the water.

"You're fired, bitch! I swear to God—"

At the edge of the pool, she started to swing him around by his hair the way you'd swing a kid around by his arms. He was too heavy to get that kind of momentum, but she was strong enough to get him partially on his feet and entirely unbalanced. She let go with one hand and smashed her fist into his nose. As his nostrils erupted, she shoved him with both hands into the water.

"I'm not your bitch!" she screamed. "And I quit, you pizza-faced cocksucker!"

The crowd erupted in applause. Jonathan and Boxers stepped back to give her room.

As she stormed away, she stopped in front of Jonathan. "That felt good."

The crowd was still applauding as she made her exit. Boxers said, "Can we hire her?"

Roman Alexander had lost all track of time. After shoving him and Ciara into the vehicles, the guys in the suits drove only a few blocks to one of those low-rise office parks where every storefront had a garage, but not every store fixed cars. For the entire ride, he'd been pressed face-first into the floor of the backseat, something heavy forced into the small of his back. He assumed it to be the attacker's knee, but how could he know?

Once they stopped, the guy on his back said, "You have a big decision to make here, kid. What's your name?"

"Roman." He couldn't think of a reason not to share the basics. "Roman Alexander."

"Okay, Roman Alexander. I know you're scared shitless, and that's good, because you should be scared shitless. You're being kidnapped. That's kind of a traumatic thing. I get that."

As awful as the words were, and the message they delivered, the guy's tone didn't sound threatening. He might have been explaining the answer to a math problem.

"So, here's your decision. Clearly, you've been trained in some fighting skills. You caught me by surprise back there. If you try that again, I promise you that I will take a sledgehammer to your knees and both your hands. Not only won't you ever fight again, you'll be lucky to ever walk again. Am I making myself clear?"

Roman nodded, scraping his cheek against the rough carpet.

"Say it."

"Yes."

"Yes what?"

There were two ways to go here. Roman decided to try both. "Yes, sir. You made yourself clear."

"Are you going to behave yourself?"

"Yes. Sir."

"You can drop the *sir* shit. This isn't the military."

A million questions flooded Roman's head, but he figured this was not the time.

"Here's your test, Roman Alexander. I'm going to let you up."

The pressure lifted from his back, and his T-shirt drew tight across his neck as the guy pulled on him. He heard the door click open and felt the car shift as the guy stepped out, still tugging on Roman's shirt. Roman got his hands up on the seat so he could rise to his knees, then he worked his way backward toward the door.

"Doing good, kid," his captor said. "Keep it up. Come all the way out."

Roman got his feet on the concrete floor.

"Watch your head as you stand up."

Just like that, he was out of the car, surrounded by the guys in the suits, plus three more. And Ciara. She had a bruise under her eye that seemed to be growing. She'd been crying.

"*Quien es este?*" Roman had taken two years of Spanish, and he got this one. *Who is this?* The guy who asked it seemed to be the youngest in the room, and he was not happy.

The answer came in a flurry of Spanish that Roman didn't have a chance in hell of understanding. It became

an argument between the suit with the knee in his back—
Guzman—and the young guy.

It ended with the young guy pulling a silver gun from
somewhere and aiming it at Roman's forehead.

"Who are you!" the man yelled. His English sounded
perfect to Roman's ear.

Roman took two steps back till he impacted with the
side of the BMW. He put his hands up. As if they could
stop a bullet. "Don't!"

"Answer my question! Who the hell are you?"

"Roman Alexander! Honest to God, don't shoot me."

"Why are you here?"

"What? You kidnapped me! I have no idea why I'm
here!"

"Why were you with Ciara?"

"Because she asked me to. We skipped school to go
swimming."

"But you don't live here."

"It was a school trip," Roman said. As if that made a
difference. "We skipped out on a *field trip* to go swimming. Is that better?"

Pistol Man moved to smack Roman across the cheek,
but the boy got his hand up too fast. He blocked the blow
without thinking.

"Remember what I told you," Guzman reminded from
off to the side.

Roman put his hand down and allowed himself to be
smacked. The blow wasn't very hard, but it didn't need to
be. The shame of letting it happen hurt more than any
slap possibly could.

"Your attitude is not appreciated here, Mr. Roman."
Pistol Man turned to Guzman and spoke in Spanish. Pis-

tol Man was not happy, and Guzman appeared apologetic.

Then Ciara joined the conversation, rattling off fluent Spanish. This was news. Roman didn't know Ciara spoke any language other than English. In school, she was struggling to learn French. At least, that's what she'd told him.

Whatever Ciara had to say stopped the others from sniping at each other and brought all the attention around to herself. Then the heads turned in unison toward Roman. A chill launched from his tailbone to his brain. This couldn't be good. He tried to take a step back, but the car still blocked his way.

Pistol Man's whole demeanor changed. He holstered his gun and smiled. "Let us start over," he said.

Roman jumped when the man extended his hand in greeting. "My name is Cristos Silva," he said.

Roman didn't know what to do. He ended up staring at the hand.

"Please do not show me disrespect," Silva said. "We have discussed this already."

Roman took the man's hand, expecting to be hurt. But it was a friendly handshake.

"Please come over to the table and have a seat." He pointed to a folding card table surrounded by six folding metal chairs.

Roman looked over to Ciara, whose smile seemed genuine. Encouraging. Guzman had a similar smile.

"Sit right there, Mr. Roman," Silva said, patting the back of the closest metal chair.

This felt so not-right. It felt lethal. The seat they wanted him to sit in faced the wall, his back turned to the rest of the room—to Guzman and another guy who hadn't bothered to introduce himself.

"You come, too, Ciara." He patted the seat next to Roman's.

Roman watched her eyes as she watched the men who stood around them. Where there used to be some familiarity, now there was a hint of fear. His spine launched another lightning bolt. When she was seated, Roman reached for her hand, but she pulled away.

"Now, Mr. Roman Alexander," Silva said. "Tell us all about your father."

Roman's jaw dropped and his stomach tightened again. He didn't know what to say.

Silva's head cocked to the side. "I'm trying very hard to be nice to you now. Please don't look at me that way."

Roman looked to Ciara, who nodded vigorously. "You need to tell him."

He didn't know how to form the words. "I–I don't know what to say. I haven't seen my father since I was little. I mean, *really* little. I don't even know what he looks like."

Silva's face grew angry as he shot a glare toward Ciara.

"Don't lie," Ciara said. "Tell him about the money."

"What money?" Roman said. As panic bloomed, he shot a pleading look to Silva. "Honest to God, Mr. Silva, I don't know what she's talking about. For all I know, my father is dead."

"What about the guy who gave a mansion to the church?" Ciara said. "The guy who gives all the money to the school."

"He's not my father," Roman said. He heard the indignation in his own voice. "He's my mom's boss."

"You talk about him all the time."

Roman didn't know if that was true, but he supposed it could be. "That doesn't make him my father." Again, to Silva: "He's white. Look at me."

Silva didn't look convinced, but he looked like he was close. "What is this man's name?"

Roman didn't want to say. It didn't feel right to say, plus his mom had told him a thousand times to keep their personal business personal. And there was the *thing*. That's the way Roman thought of the secret that no one ever talked about. He didn't have a clue what it was, but he knew that Security Solutions was more than what it pretended to be. His mom spent too many late nights that she couldn't talk about, and Mr. Jonathan walked around with too many bruises he wouldn't talk about.

And there was the attack on their house. The one that shot the place up and got his mom's boyfriend killed. Derek. He was kind of an asshole, but Mom really liked him. Really mourned for him.

"Do I need to hit you again?" Silva asked. "Is that the only way to get conversation out of you?"

"No, sir," Roman said. He didn't see a way not to answer. "His name is Jonathan Grave."

"And what does Jonathan Grave do for a living?"

"He runs a company. He's a private investigator."

Silva's eyes narrowed. "Private investigators are not rich."

Roman didn't now how to answer that, so he said nothing.

"Is Mr. Grave a rich man?"

"I suppose. He's got a lot of nice stuff."

Silva's eyebrows drew closer together as he thought about something. "How often do you see Jonathan Grave?"

"I don't know." Roman said it as a space holder as he tried to figure out how to answer. "He's, you know, my mom's boss. The office is just down the hill from our house. It's a small town."

"What is the name of the town?"

"Fisherman's Cove."

"Look," Ciara interrupted. "This guy—this Jonathan Grave—might not be his father, but he's got tons of money. The way he talks about the guy, you'd swear he was his father."

"This man cares for you?" Silva asked.

From the way he formed the question, Roman saw what was in play. "What are you going to do with me?"

Silva smiled. "Well, Mr. Roman, I will let you decide. Until Ciara here spoke up and told us about this Jonathan Grave, I was going to shoot you and get rid of your body. You weren't supposed to be here at all. You are a burden and a threat."

Roman felt fear boiling in his stomach. It was entirely possible that he was going to barf on them all.

"But then Ciara saved your life. These are your choices, Mr. Roman Alexander. You can work with us to gather as much data as possible to give Mr. Jonathan Grave incentive to pay us a great deal of money to get you back. Or, I can kill you. Worse, I can ask Mr. Guzman here to kill you. He has a wonderful talent with hammers. He said he mentioned that to you."

"You want me to be your prisoner so Mr. Jonathan will pay you money." Saying the words aloud made them seem real.

"You are already my prisoner," Silva said. "Your mother's boss will pay for your release, or I will mail you home in ten different boxes."

Silva's eyes shifted to something behind Roman, and he nodded.

Roman sensed the movement before he could see it, and he found his chin locked in the crook of someone's elbow.

Ciara screamed at the same moment Roman felt the needle plunge into his arm.

Chapter Six

Jonathan called Gail first and asked her to make an excuse to be near Venice in a few minutes. No, it wasn't going to be tragic news, but it was going to upset her.

While they waited in the Suburban with the lights off and the windows down, Boxers' shadow leaned forward. "You okay, Dig?"

"I've been better. This is going to tear Venice apart."

"It's not bad news yet."

"I don't need a pep talk, Box. I know what it is. And you know how much she has lost in the last little while. This is a parent's worst nightmare."

Boxers took a breath, but Jonathan cut him off. "Don't say it. Second worst nightmare."

Jonathan closed his eyes and took a deep breath as he pressed SEND on his phone. Venice answered on the first ring. "Why did you send Gail to sit with me? Is Roman okay?"

"We have no reason to believe he is not," Jonathan said, but he hated how evasive the words sounded. "It's pretty clear that he and Ciara were picked up by bad guys."

"Oh, God."

He could hear the panic on the edge of her voice, and he wanted to take her away from that. "Yeah, I know it's scary, but at this point, that's the end of the bad news. We know that they were snatched very close to two o'clock on the sidewalk outside of the Shady Sun Water Park outside of El Paso, right where you thought they might be."

"I've scoured all of the cameras I can find in that area," Venice said. "I can't come up with anything useful."

"But I have more information," Jonathan said. "First of all, in addition to the time, we know from a witness that one of the cars that picked them up was an SUV. I think that's pretty reliable. The witness guessed that it was a silver BMW, but I'm less confident about the make and color."

He remained silent while Venice processed the information. "It gives me something to look for, for sure."

"I've got something for Gunslinger to track down, too," Jonathan said. Gail hated her handle, but it so perfectly described her skills with a firearm. "Is she there?"

"What've you got?" Gail asked.

"Okay, the witness said something very interesting. Her name is Abigail, by the way, and she's a lifeguard for the water park. In case you need to know that. I don't have a last name for her. Anyway, she seemed to think that Ciara was the focus of the attack on the kids."

"I don't understand."

"I'm not sure I do, either," Jonathan confessed. "I'm just repeating what Abigail told me. She said that the guy who got out of the vehicle—dressed in a suit, by the way, looked like a cop—went for the girl, but Roman intervened. Fired a kick that bought them some time to run."

"Roman did that?" Venice sounded proud, too.

"Chivalry in action," Jonathan said.

"But they didn't get away, right?" Gail asked, bringing them back on point.

"No, they got as far as the corner before the car stopped them again."

As he spoke, two El Paso police cruisers rolled up to the front of the water park.

"I'm not sure I'm seeing where you want me to go with this," Gail said.

Jonathan explained, "When I came down here, I was convinced that if Roman had been taken, it was because of me—us—and our previous operations in Mexico. Maybe I was wrong. Maybe this is about the Kelly family, and Roman is just collateral."

"Would that be good news or bad?" Venice asked.

"Let's assume it's good. Without a vendetta to settle, maybe he'll be in less danger." What Jonathan didn't mention was that not being a principal also made him a burden and a potential witness.

Outside, the cops moved slowly, clearly not on alert as they strolled through the faux porthole toward the ticket booth. Jonathan wondered what story Rocky had conjured to make himself anything but the dickhead in that altercation.

"We've got to click off in a minute. El Paso's finest is here, asking questions about us, I think."

"What did you do?" Venice asked the question with the tone you might use for a dog that'd messed on the floor.

"Big Guy might have gotten a little too much lip from an asswipe manager," Jonathan said. His phone buzzed, showed a DC area code. "I've got another call. Let us know if you dig up anything interesting."

He dumped one call and answered the other. "Hi, Thor. Hang on a second."

He pointed ahead through the windshield. "Let's get out of here. Those cops don't know what we're driving." Boxers dropped the transmission into gear and drove out through the far end of the lot, away from the cop cars. To Dawkins: "Okay, Harry, whatcha got?"

"Have you been to the cops yet?"

"Haven't had time."

"Don't bother, then. Not tonight. Everybody who can make a decision has already gone home. We can catch them in the morning, first thing."

"We?"

"Sure. You know how cops are. A familiar face opens a lot of doors."

"Don't you have other work to do?"

"Nah," he said. "You guys are too much fun. Whatever you're up to, I'd like a piece of it, if you don't mind."

Thor was a good operator, but he was notorious for not making a commitment. He liked his government job and the benefits that came with it. Plus, there was security in having a badge. He'd been helpful enough to Jonathan over the years, though, that they'd worked out an unofficial part-time gig for him when he wanted it.

"I don't mind, but I also don't know where this is going."

"Do you have a place to stay?" Dawkins asked.

"Not yet, but we have one more thing we have to do tonight."

"When you're done, if you're not all shot up, come to my place. I got spare bedrooms and good scotch. How can you do better than that?"

Jonathan turned to Boxers. Big Guy said, "He had me at good scotch."

As they turned right out of the lot something in the street caught Jonathan's eye. "Wait, wait," he said, pointing past the windshield. "That thing in the road near the curb."

Boxers brought the Suburban to a stop.

Jonathan jogged through the beams of the headlights to go and pick Roman's flip-flops up off the street.

Finding a vehicle through computer software on unintentional loan from the NSA was more difficult than finding a person—people were unique, after all—but it wasn't impossible. The trick was to endure the fire-hose flow of information while paring down the data to a manageable size.

"*Silver BMW sports utility vehicle*" sounds specific until you factor in the number of styles and model years. In the current model year, the company produced the BMW X4, 5, 6, and 7, each of them classified as an SUV. But to a commoner's eye, the X1, 2, and 3 might also look like an SUV. The fact that it was silver helped some, but silver looks a lot like gray or even soiled white.

Plus, not all the security feeds captured color, so Venice needed to weed those out.

Using a commercial mapping site, she determined the search area around the water park to be roughly ten blocks square. She considered searching only on the main streets but decided that to be counterproductive. Any search that begins with the notion that you know what you're looking for and where is doomed to failure. You let evidence drive assumptions, not the other way around.

Even when you're looking for your little boy.

Forty-five minutes evaporated from Venice's world as she manipulated the parameters, working every angle she could find to locate the suspect vehicle.

While Digger's witness swore that the encounter happened at two o'clock, people never knew what real times were. Anywhere from 1:45 to 2:15 was routinely rounded to straight-up at the hour. Especially when the testimony came from someone who was supposed to be at a certain place at a certain time. Accordingly, Venice set her initial search to the sixty minutes that began at 1:30.

"Thank God I'm not looking for a Chevy or Dodge pickup," she mumbled. She'd have never been able to winnow the number down.

She bolted upright in her chair as a thought smacked her out of nowhere. How did they know to grab the kids at the water park? Roman and Ciara weren't supposed to be there at all. How did the kidnappers—she could bring herself to call them that now—know to lie in wait at the Shady Sun?

She quickly saved what she was searching, then shifted her focus back to camera-rich downtown El Paso. Back to 11:43 A.M., the last pictures she had of Roman and

Ciara as they climbed into Mr. Alvarez's RoadRunner car.

How long had she stared at this scene before, without ever seeing anything but Roman? Even Ciara had been invisible to her. Now she saw that there were other pedestrians on the street. An old guy on the corner appeared not to have any legs, and he seemed to be panhandling to passersby who made a point of not seeing him. A bus hovered around the top left of the screen. Venice wondered if that was the bus where Roman's classmates were gathering with no one noticing that he was gone.

Ciara was standing inappropriately close to Roman, she thought. Were they holding hands? He was not quite fourteen, for heaven's sake. Way too young for an unaccompanied date.

What about the other cars on the street? There were SUVs and pickups everywhere, but all she could see by toggling in and out with the zoom were American brands, plus one big Toyota.

Less than a minute into the video feed, Luis Alvarez showed up with his all-too-familiar Ford, driving right-to-left on her screen. He stopped at the curb, the kids got in, and the Ford drove away.

And there was the BMW. Only five seconds after the Ford left the screen, a silver SUV cruised through. She froze the image. The mounting bracket for the license plate was clearly visible, but the angle was wrong for the numbers. She progressed the video slowly, hoping that the image would clarify, but by the time the BMW cleared the frame, nothing came into focus.

Now she was on familiar turf. She'd already tracked Alvarez's Ford through the streets of El Paso and the surrounding area. She knew exactly which cameras to switch to in order to keep the RoadRunner car in the frame. Now, she just needed to wait a little longer before switching. Had she not known already to look for the Beemer, she would not have been able to tell from the video that it was pursuing the kids. It was too straight a shot down at-grade roads that had no curves.

No, scratch that. The RoadRunner pushed a yellow light to get through, then the BMW raced through a red to keep up. Definitely the action of a vehicle in pursuit. Venice stopped the action repeatedly to try to get a read on the license plate, but it never worked.

New camera. Once again, the Ford with Roman and Ciara rushed a yellow light. This time, the light wasn't even pink when they went through. Luis Alvarez plowed straight through a deep red light. And nearly got hit by an eighteen-wheeler that was rushing a left turn ahead of them. She imagined horns blaring.

But the BMW got cut off. At the top of the screen, Venice saw the Ford make a turn onto a side road, but there was no way the Beemer could have seen it.

The question remained, then: How did the kidnappers know where to find their prey?

That was obvious, wasn't it?

She picked up the phone and pressed the speed dial for Digger.

Chapter Seven

Gail rapped on the heavy glass door to the War Room, and Venice beckoned her to come in. Gail took a seat at Venice's right. "Patrick Kelly is a cipher," she said.

Venice moved to close the lid on her laptop but didn't. "Talk to me."

"From what I can tell, he just sort of left a hole in the ether." Gail opened the speckled notebook that had been her version of a personal digital assistant for as many years as she'd been in law enforcement. "I scoured the internet for the guy, and I went into some of the off-book sites that you've given me. He owns a bunch of companies, but the companies don't seem to do anything."

Venice shifted her gaze back to her laptop. Good thing she didn't close it. "Give me some names."

Gail ticked off the names of three companies.

"That's enough to start," Venice said. "Do you have

EINs?" Employee information numbers were the corporate equivalent to Social Security numbers for tracking IRS data. They were also public record.

"I didn't think to get them."

"Not a problem." As Venice typed, the commands and results were projected onto the 106-inch screen on the far wall to Gail's right. In under a minute, they were inside the IRS tax records database.

"How did you do that?" Gail asked.

"Would you understand if I told you?"

"Good point. Isn't this illegal?"

Venice gave her a look. Another good point. Security Solutions rarely colored inside the lines of the law.

Once inside, Venice took her time perusing the tax returns on the screen. After ten minutes, she said, "Give me the others you have. The other companies."

Gail read from her notes. Eight companies in total. With that done, she sat quietly and waited for Venice to work her magic.

"Okay," Venice announced with a final flourish of a keystroke. "Between the eight companies, Patrick Kelly makes seventy-three thousand dollars a year. Less than sixty after he pays his taxes."

"If I read correctly, all of the companies are some form of consulting firm, right?"

"Yes." Venice rocked back in her Aeron chair and folded her hands behind her neck. "Care to guess what I pay for Roman to attend Northern Neck Academy?"

Gail waited for it.

"Sixty-three thousand."

Gail's jaw dropped. "A *year*?"

Venice arched her eyebrows. "And because Digger's on the board, I get the friends and family rate."

Gail regarded the screen again. "Kelly can't afford that."

"Not even close. Not from real business dealings, anyway. Maybe a different Patrick Kelly? It's not exactly a unique name."

"It's unique at the address where he lives," Gail said. "I already searched for others. Can you tap into the records of the Academy to see how he pays his bills?"

Venice shook her head. "Sadly, no. They are doggedly old-school. All records are manual. They don't even have an email address, other than for marketing purposes. All communications are done the old-fashioned way."

"Why on earth would they do that?"

Venice opened her arms to the screen on the wall. "Because of people like me. The Neck attracts students from many different backgrounds. Kids whose parents don't relish publicity. When you think about it, keeping manual is kind of a smart strategy."

"So, what—"

"Wait!" Venice lurched forward in her chair, and her eyes widened. "The application process for the Neck is pretty arduous. The administration is paranoid about getting jammed for tuition, so you have to submit all kinds of financial data. It's almost like qualifying for a mortgage."

"But all on paper."

"In person," Venice corrected. "It's part of the interview process. The Neck keeps all the records."

"But they're in file cabinets. "How are you going to get access?"

It was Venice's turn to wait for Gail to connect the dots.

Gail gasped. "Burglary?"

"You've done it before, haven't you?"

Gail coughed out a humorless laugh. "Oh, my God, Ven. Seriously?"

"He's my son."

The number of reasons why this was a bad idea stacked up like dominoes in Gail's head. Start with the fact that the school was in their own community. And that one of the chief benefactors was her boss. "What about security?"

"I can get past that," Venice said. "Their electronic security is only slightly more advanced than their online record keeping."

"Don't they have a physical security guard, too?"

"You and the boys deal with that kind of thing all the time."

Gail brought her hands to her head. "We can't immobilize some old guy making minimum wage in a school."

Venice hesitated. "We?"

"Hell, yes, *we*. If this is the way we have to go, I'm sure as hell not going to do it all on my own."

Venice shook her head. "I'm not a . . . what does Digger call it? I'm not a *tradecraft* kind of gal."

"Then think of another plan. If I'm going to do something stupid and against my better judgment, I sure as hell am not going to do it alone. Your idea, your burglary. Call it." It was too easy for people with no skin in the game to command others to—

"Okay, I'll do it."

Suddenly, it felt as if there wasn't enough air in the room. "What do you mean?"

"How many meanings to *okay, I'll do it* are there? I'll break into the school with you. It'll be exciting. I've never done fieldwork before."

Her words triggered a new pang of anxiety in Gail. She hadn't thought Mother Hen would call her bluff. It was true. Venice had never done fieldwork before, and she'd had no training for it. There were nuances to entering and leaving a building in a way that left no traces that anyone had ever been there.

"When do we go?" Venice pressed. She looked genuinely excited.

The more Gail thought through the details, the more concerned she grew. "First of all, we can't just go in there blindly. We need *some* form of intel. Whatever we can dig up."

"I already told you I can knock out the security alarms."

"I don't worry about electronics," Gail said. "I know you can take care of those like nobody's business. It's the human element that I worry about." She thought for a few seconds. "What do we know about the staff?"

"I know the names of Roman's teachers."

Gail scowled. "That's not going to help."

"The headmaster?"

"We already know him. Washington, right? And he's still in Texas."

"What are you looking for?"

"Ideally, I'd like to know who the security guards are," Gail said. "Can you imagine what would happen if someone tried to burgle our offices? They'd be shot to pieces."

Half a second after she'd asked the question, Gail wished she could take it back. The reason they had the heightened security was because of an attack against Venice.

"Sorry."

Venice literally shook it off. "You meant no harm," she said. "For what it's worth, I've seen their security people.

They are not a polished group of tactical operators. They're guys in blue uniforms and clipboards. I don't even think they carry guns."

"But they carry radios and cell phones."

"Who are they going to talk to? During the day, a secretary in the main office is on the other end of the radio."

"Maybe they have two guards at night," Gail suggested. "Do you even know where the financial records are kept?"

Venice turned back to her computer and typed. "Watch the screen," she said.

The projector blinked, and the image of a grand stone edifice filled the wall. Built to resemble an antebellum mansion, the front of Northern Neck Academy featured tall pillars supporting a roof that provided cover for an ornate set of stone steps that led to carved double doors.

"This is what expensive tuition buys you," Venice said. "The administration trolls for diplomats' kids, and that's largely what they get. I guess this is what the world envisions when they think of America."

Gail didn't mention that the school building actually looked a little smaller than the mansion that served as the headquarters for Resurrection House, the residential school for the children of incarcerated parents that was anonymously endowed by Jonathan. and also served as Venice's home.

The image blinked again, and they were inside an equally grand circular lobby that was dominated on the far end by a curved double staircase to the second floor. An elevated desk sat in the foreground on the right— more lectern than desk, really.

"That's where the security guard sits," Venice said, pointing with the arrow on her mouse.

"What's that on the walls?" Gail asked. Someone had painted a giant mural, but she couldn't tell what it depicted.

"That is the history of the Commonwealth in pictures," Venice explained. "From John Smith to the Cold War, when I think the thing was painted."

"Is it ugly up close?"

"As sin."

"Where are these images coming from?" Gail asked.

"This is their marketing literature. The finance office is at the top of that staircase and to the right. See those double doors on the ground floor? Beyond those is the lower school, for the elementary-age kids. There's another set of doors just like it on the second floor that leads to more classrooms for the little kids. The middle school and high school are in different buildings beyond this one. As far as I know, those are strictly academic buildings. All the administration works out of the main building."

"And the headmaster? Where is his office?"

"Top of the stairs to the left. The office is amazing. Fortune Five Hundred CEOs work in closets compared to Dr. Washington."

Gail chuckled. "Again, high tuition put to good use." She scowled and leaned in closer to the screen. She pointed. "Click on that *Information* icon in the top right."

Venice clicked it and a menu dropped down. Headings arranged horizontally, superimposed over a riding ring and three horses. ABOUT. ADMISSIONS. ACADEMICS. CAMPUS LIFE. SUMMER. SUPPORT.

"Click *Support*," Gail said.

She'd hoped that the menu item would show support

staff, but instead, they got a list of links to ways to donate money to the school.

"Nope, not it. Try *Academics*." Security guards weren't teachers, but she couldn't see any other heading where she might find faculty and staff.

A waterfall of subheadings dropped down. Second on the list, just below ACADEMIC OVERVIEW, there it was: FACULTY AND STAFF.

Venice clicked the link. Administrators came first, then teachers and teaching assistants. Athletics got top billing over liberal arts and science, with security guards holding the rear.

"There they are," Gail said, pointing to pictures and short job descriptions. "Cameron Castro works days, Carlos Palma's on nights. I'm not sure what Desmond Pryor does as a *contingent*."

"It says *and weekends*," Venice pointed out. "He must work the off-hours and fill-ins."

Gail leaned back into her chair and inhaled deeply. An idea was forming. She clapped her hands together once. "Okay," she said. "We need to know everything we can find out about Carlos Palma and Desmond Pryor."

"Not the other one?"

"We're not going to go in during the day," Gail said.

Venice smiled. "So, we're really going to do this?"

Gail pointed to the computer. "Do what you do."

For what Gail had planned, Desmond Pryor was a potential problem. He lived alone in a mobile home park in a unit that he rented by the month. He'd only recently moved to the area from Oak Brook, Illinois, and his only debt was a reasonable car payment and his rent. His credit score was better than most, and he had no criminal record.

"I've never seen anyone with so little to leverage," Gail said.

"Well, he *is* the long shot," Venice pointed out. "Carlos Palma is the one who *should* be on duty. Let's see what we can find."

The results for Carlos were far more encouraging. Married and a father of three, he'd defaulted on three different car loans over the years, and his credit score was among the lowest Gail had ever seen. Eight months ago, he and his family were evicted from their apartment for nonpayment, and he'd moved into his mother's house in Colonial Beach. That house was paid for, but Mom had been sent to a nursing home just after he'd moved in. That's where she resided now, and according to visitor records, Carlos spent time with her at least three times per week.

"How do you get all of this stuff out of the internet?" Gail asked.

"You just have to know where to look," Venice said with a grin. "It also helps to have really advanced technology. But really, no one takes firewall security all that seriously. As more and more people *work from home*"— she used finger quotes—"companies are dropping their guards even more. The fewer barriers there are to entry into the system, the less work the technical services department has to deal with."

"But a nursing home is a medical facility."

"True enough, but it's a medical facility primarily for old people," Venice explained. "The patients are technologically clueless, so their case management turns to their kids or caregivers, who don't know what the heck they're doing, either. Hospital systems are generally a lot harder to break into. Not impossible—I mean, I've done it—but their tech people are better than most."

"But the visitor records?"

"Okay, that was a gift," Venice admitted. "I wanted to know how much of a mama's boy Carlos was, and I got lucky that the visitor records are in the system." She took a few seconds to gloat in the glow of her success, then asked, "So, what's next?"

"You can pull up the security cameras in the school lobby, right?"

Venice clacked the keys, and the screen filled with a view of the lobby. The image was grainy and black-and-white, but the detail wasn't awful. The man at the security desk looked exactly like the website's picture of Carlos Palma, right where he belonged.

"Ready when you are," Gail said.

Chapter Eight

Luis Alvarez lived in a single-wide trailer, dead center in the middle of the Sam Houston Mobile Home Park. In Jonathan's experience, such parks were often less than well maintained, but here at night, in the middle of the desert, it was hard to tell. Scalloped ankle-high wire fencing defined the edges of Alvarez's front yard, such as it was, where stubby cacti rose above sand and gravel. No grass that he could see, but, well, it was the desert. Orange flagstones marked a path to the front door, which stood open, protected from the elements by a storm door.

Boxers cruised the Suburban past the home, drove to the end of the cul-de-sac, and then turned around. "How are we doing this one?" he asked.

"Let's be FBI," Jonathan said. He pulled his counterfeit badge from his pocket and clipped it to his belt.

"Oh, man, I hate that," Boxers grumped as he fished

out his own badge. Just a little under seven feet tall, Big Guy had a not-unsubstantial gut that was made of stone. The tiny FBI badge looked like a toy when he clipped it to his waistband.

It was the nature of Jonathan's relationship with Irene Rivers that no favor was ever bestowed without a thumb in at least one eye. That's how Boxers' federal alias became Xavier Contata. Jonathan survived pretty well with Cornelius Bonner, a name that was easily reduced to Neil. Xavier was a bit more problematic. Big Guy had tried several alternative aliases to cushion the embarrassment, but the rest of the team wouldn't let him get away with it.

It was too much fun to mess with him. Until you went too far. A pissed-off Boxers was a frightening creature.

As they approached the walkway, Jonathan twisted the knob on the portable radio that was likewise clipped to his belt and fitted the transceiver bud into his ear canal. "We'll keep it on channel one. PTT, just in case." Push-to-talk, not to be confused with VOX, which would mean voice-activated transmission. "Just to be safe, go around to the black side and let me know when you're in place."

A thousand years ago, before Jonathan and Boxers had served in the Army's First Special Forces Operational Detachment-Delta, a.k.a. the Unit, someone had decided that buildings shouldn't have fronts and backs, but rather white sides and black sides, along with green sides (left) and red sides (right). Modern Unit operators had moved past those to numerical designations, but Jonathan saw no reason to adapt his system to theirs.

As he waited in the street for Boxers to get into position, Jonathan kept an eye out for interest from the neighbors. The presence of badges in a neighborhood brought notice. While most were just curious, others got nervous. He and Boxers posed zero threat to anyone on the street, but the people on the street didn't know that.

"Hey, Scorpion," Big Guy said in his ear. "I'm in place. There's a back door, but it appears to be blocked from the inside. All the windows are closed."

"Roger that. I'm heading to the door." The short wire tripping hazards continued running parallel to the flag-stones all the way up to the one-step stoop. When he got to the door, Jonathan glanced inside and saw a young man in a wife beater sprawled in a puffy chair in front of a television. If he wasn't mistaken, the guy was watching one of the old Adam West episodes of *Batman*.

Jonathan rapped on the glass with the knuckle of his second finger. When the guy didn't respond, he tried again, a little harder. The guy jumped awake, spilling the bottle of beer he'd had balanced on his knee into his crotch.

Jonathan kept his features neutral as the occupant rose from the chair and walked bowlegged to the door, doing his best to brush away the wet spot as he guzzled what was left in the bottle. Jonathan keyed his mic. "You can come back around," he said to Boxers.

The occupant of the trailer was nearly to the door when recognition hit. He must have seen the badge. For a brief second or two, he considered running. It was written all over his face, emblazoned in his eyes. Then, maybe he remembered that he'd blocked his back door. The man's shoulders slumped as he closed the distance and opened the storm door.

"Good evening," he said.

"Are you Luis Alvarez?"

"You know I am."

"I'd prefer to hear it from you."

"Yes, I'm Luis Alvarez."

"Are you here alone?"

"What's this about?"

"Can you answer my questions, please?"

Alvarez folded his arms across his chest and shifted his weight to one leg. "After you answer mine," he said. "Look, this ain't my first rodeo. I don't have to—"

"Did you sell out a couple of kids to some bad guys this afternoon?"

The question hit Alvarez hard. Color drained from his face. Maybe it had something to do with the fact that Boxers had just stepped into view.

"You were about to tell me whether you're alone inside," Jonathan prompted.

"Yessir, I am."

The *sir* was not lost on Jonathan. People always show a little more respect when they're frightened.

Alvarez pivoted his body to let Jonathan enter. "Please, come in. Your friend, too." As Boxers passed, Alvarez craned his neck to track his progress.

"What, you pissed yourself already?" Big Guy asked, noting the beer stain.

Alvarez said nothing.

The guy didn't ask for identification, so Jonathan didn't bother to introduce himself. "Tell me about the men you talked to."

Alvarez's eyes twitched as he worked the angles. "Do you mind if I sit down?" He started back toward his chair.

Boxers stepped in his way. "Yeah, we do mind. This doesn't have to take long." Somehow, he made himself even taller. "Or, we can stretch it out all night."

Alvarez puffed up a little. "Are you *threatening* me?"

Boxers kept his lips pressed together as they pulled back into a smile.

"Yes, we are," Jonathan said. "Well, I'm not, but my colleague most definitely is."

Alvarez turned back to Jonathan, and his shoulders sagged again. "What do you want to know?"

"The whole thing," Jonathan said. "Word for word, front to back. Start with when you dropped the kids off."

"You mean at the Shady Sun, right?"

The guy was stalling, and he wasn't very good at it. "How many kids did you betray today?"

Alvarez objected, "I didn't *betray* anybody. I didn't know they were going to hurt them."

"Who said they were hurt?" Boxers asked from above and behind.

Alvarez pivoted to look up at Big Guy but came back around to Jonathan. "You're here, aren't you? Throwing around the word *betrayed*? How big a stretch is it to guess that they were hurt?"

"Everything that happened from when you dropped them off," Jonathan prompted.

"Do you have anything to do with the lady who called earlier about this? Constance somebody?"

"Not that I know of," Jonathan lied. Constance DuBois was Venice's FBI alias.

"Why is there so much interest in this one fare?"

"Why don't you just answer the questions we ask so we can let you get on with your night?" Jonathan countered.

"Okay. I picked the kids up at a hotel. On a side of the hotel where we don't normally pick people up."

"How old did you think they were?" Boxers asked.

"I don't know. Fourteen, fifteen, maybe?"

"And that didn't give you a moment's thought?" Boxers pressed. "Kids that young calling for a car to take them away from a hotel?"

This time, Alvarez did turn, and he addressed Big Guy as eye-to-eye as was possible. "Don't you try to paint me as some kind of perv," he said. "People call, we pick them up. I'm not even allowed to ask questions. If they've got a service llama with them, I gotta take them. That's the way the system works. Whatever happened, whatever this is about, is no way my fault, you get that? I'm just the goddamn driver."

"You knew that the guys who asked where you dropped the kids off were probably up to no good," Jonathan said. "I'm not casting blame on you, but let's not paint an overly rosy picture."

"Fine. I picked them up and took them to the Shady Sun Water Park. They got out, and I drove off. When I was headed back into town on Route 85, this Beemer SUV pulled in behind me in my lane and started flashing its lights. I looked in the mirror, and they were waving me over to the side of the road."

"You pulled off?"

"Onto Prickly Pear Avenue. You know, to get out of traffic."

"You weren't concerned?" Jonathan asked. "Someone asks you to pull over, and you just do it?"

"I thought maybe something was wrong with the car, you know? Or, maybe it was one of you guys. A cop."

"Why would a cop be pulling you over?"

"It's what they do. I'm on parole, you know? I get rousted all the time just because they're bored. It sucks, but it goes with the territory. One of the reasons I like to cruise the same areas is that the cops have learned that I'm okay to leave alone."

"So, you pulled over, and they came to your door. What did they look like?"

"Mexican, I think. Not white, not black. Dressed well. They were wearing suits. Even more why I pulled over." His eyes brightened. "You know what? I bet I have pictures of at least one of them." He started to move, then stopped. "I need to get my phone."

Jonathan nodded to Boxers, who stepped out of the way. "Your phone better not look like a weapon," Big Guy said.

Alvarez hurried to the chair where he'd been sitting and lifted a smartphone from the table next to it. "These days, you've got to be careful, you know?" he said. "I keep cameras in my car. There's the one that everybody knows is there—the one that sees the passengers in the back—but I've got a hidden one, too, that watches me the whole time." As he spoke, his thumbs danced over the screen of his phone.

"Why do you do that?" Jonathan asked.

Alvarez stopped typing and shot Jonathan a look. "Remember, you asked. It's because of shithead cops who pull me over. When you're a parolee, you can get jacked up for anything. Jacked up because it's, like, Thursday, you know? The camera makes a record, and the fact that it's hidden keeps the assholes true to their instincts."

Jonathan didn't say anything, but he thought it was a damned good idea, for the same reasons he believed in body cameras for cops. When you're on the job, there's no reason not to record yourself doing the right thing.

And if you're forced one day into an altercation, it's always good to have proof that it wasn't your fault.

"The camera records to the cloud, whatever that is," Alvarez continued. Once he got started, he seemed to enjoy talking. "I got an app that lets me get to it and watch it."

"Do you do that a lot?" Boxers asked.

"Only after some asshat stops me. I live for the time one of them steps way out of line and I can get his badge. Sorry."

Jonathan gave a noncommittal shrug. What did he care?

"So, while you look for the picture, tell us what—"

"Here it is," Alvarez said, and he handed the phone to Jonathan, who quickly pulled up the share function, typed in a phone number, and hit SEND.

"Hey, what are you doing?"

"I sent the picture to my office."

"I didn't say you could do that."

"You didn't say I couldn't." Jonathan handed him back the phone.

"I hate you people," Alvarez said.

"Now we have the pictures. Will we have the audio, too?"

"It's all there, yeah."

"Excellent. That much less for you to have to worry about. Just for the record, though, and in case the video doesn't work, what are we going to see when we play it?"

They watched the video in Harry Dawkins's apartment, a short-term rental for the remaining weeks or months that he would be assigned to DHS's JTF—joint task force—focusing on illegal immigration, drug smuggling, and human trafficking. Together, they watched as the camera caught a brief glimpse first of Ciara Kelly and then Roman as they slid into the backseat from the driver's side. The images were surprisingly clear.

The angle of the camera was such that virtually none of the backseat was visible, and the audio was likewise configured to focus on sound from the front half of the vehicle. With the sound cranked up, they could hear snippets of adolescent chatter, but nothing of substance. Yet they stayed with it for the entire drive, all of about twelve minutes. Alvarez pulled to the curb, presumably let the kids out, and then he was on his way again.

With the car empty now, Jonathan fast-forwarded to the point in the video when Alvarez clearly was reacting to something in the mirror behind him. They rode with him as he turned right and stopped.

Alvarez rolled down his window, and as he waited, he cast a glance over to the camera, presumably to make sure it was working.

"Good afternoon," a voice said from off camera. A torso appeared framed in the window, a shirt, tie, and sport coat, and then its owner bent at the waist and looked inside the vehicle.

"That's our money shot," Jonathan said, pointing. "Mark the time stamp."

"Got it," Boxers said.

"What's going on?" Alvarez asked.

"Those kids you picked up," the visitor said, standing straight again. "Where did you drop them off?"

Alvarez hesitated. "Why do you want to know?"

"When you talk to me, it's never a good idea to answer a question with a question."

Jonathan heard the sound of knocking, and Alvarez spun in his seat to cast a frightened look out through the passenger side window.

"Don't worry about him," said the man in the driver's window. "He's my partner. Look at me."

Alvarez returned his gaze back to his window.

The man said, "We saw you pick up the kids at the hotel, but we lost you in traffic."

"I thought I saw you following me," Alvarez said. "I lost you at a light, right?"

"Shouldn't've done that. That's why we're having to have this chat here."

"Why are you looking for a couple of kids?"

Window Man thumped Alvarez's left temple with the heel of his hand. "Don't lose focus, friend. Where did you drop them off?"

"At the Shady Sun Water Park."

"Not lyin' to us now, are you?"

"Why would I do that?"

"If we find out that you did, we'll find you and hurt you."

Dawkins clicked the remote and paused the video. "Not a lot there to go by," he said.

"Bet you a hundred bucks that guy in the window has a record," Boxers said.

"Sucker's bet," Jonathan said. "And if he does—*since* he does—Mother Hen will be able to nail down an identity."

Dawkins rose from his chair, a scratchy beige-plaid Danish modern monstrosity with arched wooden arms. "I'm getting a beer. Want anything?"

"You promised scotch," Jonathan reminded.

"None of that super-smoky expensive shit you drink, but I've got a blend. Passport, I think."

Boxers made a retching noise.

"What about gin?" Jonathan tried.

"Again, nothing expensive. Beefeater."

Jonathan beamed and shot to his feet from his own Danish modern monstrosity. "Vermouth?"

"I can make you a martini, if you want," Dawkins offered.

"No, you can't," Jonathan countered. "I'm the only bartender I know who doesn't screw up the recipe for a martini."

Chapter Nine

Security Solutions operated a small fleet of nondescript cars with current registrations and inspection stickers, ones that could not be traced back to any real person or company. If pulled over for some reason, the driver would present the registration to the police officer. If pressed for something more, there was a stash of business cards in the center console.

Tonight's chariot was a three-year-old brown Nissan, and Gail drove.

Northern Neck Academy boasted on its website of being set on "forty pristine acres of forests, fields, fun, and adventure." While that was technically true, those forty acres were surrounded on all sides by private homes and subdivisions.

Gail parked at the end of an undeveloped cul-de-sac in the Potomac Plains neighborhood. She'd pre-sited the parking spot with the help of a commercial satellite program that wasn't in the least bit proprietary. It wasn't necessarily current, however, so she'd double-checked through real estate records to make sure that the spot hadn't been built on since the satellite photos had been taken.

"Where's the school from here?" Venice asked.

Gail pointed across Venice's nose. "Through those woods. We'll have some hiking to do." Gail opened her door, noting with pleasure that the dome light did not come on. "Don't slam the door," she said. "We want to draw as little attention as possible."

Gail got out and stood at her open door for ten or fifteen seconds, scanning every compass point. Dressed all in black, including black gloves, she hoped she was invisible against the tree line.

"What are you looking for?" Venice asked as she scanned, too. She likewise wore black-on-black, but her coveralls clearly belonged to someone else. At least she had good outdoor shoes on.

"Anything," Gail said. "If somebody's walking their dog, we might want to wait a few seconds before we kit up. Or, maybe we'd need to relocate. A lot of this business is just taking your time."

"You're not bringing a gun, are you?" Venice didn't like guns.

"I never go anywhere without a gun." Her choice had long been a Glock 19. Chambered in nine millimeter with a fifteen-round magazine capacity, it was easy to conceal and soft to shoot.

"Why? Do you expect to shoot someone?"

Gail had no idea that Mother Hen was so far separated from the operations side of what they did. "If I thought I was going be in a gunfight, I'd be carrying something a lot bigger," she said. "I carry for what you might call an abundance of caution."

Convinced that she'd chosen a secure parking spot, Gail opened the Nissan's back door and unzipped a range bag. "Come around to my side," she said.

Working by feel, Gail found two folded bits of fabric. She handed one to Venice. "It's a balaclava," she explained. "Pull it over your head, leave only your eyes exposed."

"My God," Venice said.

Gail donned her own balaclava, then reached back into the back for night vision goggles, or NVGs. For herself, she chose a four-tube array that provided a much broader range of visibility but cost about fifty thousand dollars more than the two-tube array that she'd brought for Venice. After she slipped the headband in place and settled the lenses in front of her eyes, she turned to face Venice.

"Ever used night vision?"

"I've seen YouTube videos," Venice replied.

"Close enough." Gail slipped the cradle over the crown of Venice's head and adjusted the two lenses so they were over Mother Hen's eyes. "It'll take a minute or two to get used to the tunnel vision," she explained, "and things will feel a little two-dimensional till your eyes adjust."

"A simple flashlight wouldn't do? How are we going to explain all this if we get caught?"

"The trick is to *not* get caught," Gail said. The sharp tone in her voice was intentional. Always presume success. "One of the reasons to use the night vision in the first place is to see complications before they can become problems."

"I didn't mean to anger you."

Gail was beginning to think that it was a mistake to bring Venice along. She was projecting a troubling scaredy-cat vibe. But it was too late now. This was the op they'd planned, and now it was the op they were stuck with.

"When do we call the guard?" Venice asked.

"Not until we're in position to see how he reacts." Gail reached back into the car, pulled out her pack of burglar tools, and shrugged it onto her shoulders. "Don't forget your laptop," she said.

Venice snatched up a satchel of electronics. "Got it."

After locking the car, Gail said, "We're all set. Stay close behind, and if you need to stop or if you get stuck, let me know. Otherwise, we need to be as quiet as possible. Watch where you put your feet."

Not waiting for an answer, Gail stepped off into the woods. Past the first lines of trees, the undergrowth thinned out quite a bit, making her wonder if perhaps maintenance crews kept the creepers and bushes under control. She'd studied the topography as well as she could, using satellite photos and public source maps from the U.S. Geological Survey. She knew that the woods would give way to a creek and that a pretty little arched bridge spanned the banks up and to the right. The bridge would take them to more woods, which would then give way to the most concerning part of the evening's journey—the wide-open athletic fields. The fields themselves were sunken, probably thirty feet lower than the level of the driveway and the school building to which it led. Access from one level to the other was gained via steep concrete steps.

They were blessed with clouds over a tiny sliver of moon, so their shadows would be minimal, but there'd still be a wash from the lighted driveway up to the school. If this were a different op, she'd have started by killing the power to the school, granting them the advantage of true darkness, but this was supposed to be an in-and-out with no signs of forced entry.

When they finally broke through to the fields, Gail led Venice to the base of the bleachers and stopped. "How're you doing with the NVGs?"

"They're a lot clearer than I thought they'd be. Clearer than what you see on YouTube and the news."

"Good. Okay, here's what I need you to do." As she spoke, Gail gestured out to the fields with a bladed hand. "We have to cross this. Your instinct is going to be to run—or at least to move quickly—but you need to resist. If anything, we're going to move more slowly than normal."

"Because the human eye detects motion in the dark?" Venice asked. Then she added, "Digger's talked about that a million times."

It was time to go.

Perhaps Gail's words of warning were better targeted at herself. Moving slowly, without any cover, was agonizing. She felt as if she might as well have been wearing neon. The fact that she could see the world so clearly through the NVGs intensified the feeling of vulnerability. But she kept her instincts in check.

Four minutes later, they were at the base of the concrete steps, and she dropped to a knee. Venice did likewise.

"Lift the NVGs out of the way," Gail instructed as she lifted her own. "The streetlight up on the driveway would wash out the images. Here's what we're going to do. You stay here at the base of the steps. I'm going to go to the top and scope out a shadowed spot where we can call from. When I find it, I'll come back and get you. Keep your eyes on the top of the steps. I don't want to have to come all the way back down for you. Any questions?"

Now that Venice's eyes were visible, the fear in them was clear. She shook her head *no*.

"I'll just be a minute," Gail said, and she was off. This was probably their most exposed moment of the entire plan, the black figure against the white backdrop of the steps. She considered climbing the hill itself, but it was very steep, and a fall would make more noise than her footsteps, and the difference in cover wasn't all that great. Sometimes, you just needed to roll the dice.

She counted thirty-five steps to the top of the embankment. Once there, she could clearly see the circular driveway that served the next set of stairs—the grand ones that led to the inside. The driveway coming from the street was every bit of a quarter mile long, and it, too, was a giant loop, up to the school on one side, away from the school on the other. The design created an island that was well landscaped with firs and dogwoods. The firs in particular cast sharp shadows in the dim glow of the streetlights. She'd found the place where they'd stage for the next phase.

Gail looked back down to the bottom of the steps and beckoned for Venice to join her. Mother Hen acknowledged with a wave and made the climb.

With them together again, Gail explained the plan. They crossed the driveway one at a time and hunkered down behind a fir tree that towered over its neighbors. This had to be the one they decorated for Christmas. It would have been a sin not to.

"Okay," Gail said. "It's time for you to shine."

Venice reached into her satchel and produced her laptop and a velour blanket that they'd brought along to cover themselves so light wouldn't leak out. Shoulder to shoulder with Gail under the cover, Venice opened the lid and let things boot up. The screen showed two images, a phone app on the left and the security camera view of the school's lobby on the right.

"Where is he?" Venice asked. The desk that was supposed to be occupied by Carlos Palma was empty.

"Shit. On rounds, maybe? We saw him earlier."

"Two hours ago. Maybe he saw us, and he's coming out to get us."

Possible, but not likely, Gail thought. "If he saw us, dressed as we are, he'd be crazy to come out on his own. He'd call the police."

"Oh, my God."

"But then he'd stay at his monitor, wouldn't he? That's what I'd do. Concentrate on the plan. Are you going to be able to spoof the call?"

Venice went to work on her keys. "His caller ID is going to show a call coming from the Washington's Rest Rehabilitation Center." She placed her Bluetooth transceivers into her ears and typed in the number for Carlos's cell phone. But her finger hovered over the touch pad.

"What's wrong?" Gail asked.

"I feel terrible about doing this."

"How do you feel about finding Roman?"

Venice clicked SEND. It took long enough for the call to connect that Gail began to worry that he didn't have his phone with him. When the call finally did connect, Gail could hear only Venice's side of the conversation.

Mother Hen affected a sweet Southern accent. "Hello. Is this Carlos Palma? The son of Consuela Palma? . . .

No, I'm sorry to say she is not . . . Consuela took a bad fall just a little while ago . . . I'm afraid I can't say because I'm not a doctor, but the ambulance crew seemed to suspect a hip fracture . . . No, sir, we use a private ambulance service . . . They also seemed concerned about *why* she might have fallen. Was it her heart? A stroke? We don't know . . . No, not here. They took her to Mary Washington Hospital in Fredericksburg . . . About twenty-five miles . . . No, I'm sorry I don't have their names, but they were both EMTs . . . You're very welcome, Mr. Palma. I'm just so sorry I had to make this call."

Venice disconnected the call and turned to see Gail. "I feel like I need to go to confession."

"I have it on good authority that Father Dom's heard a lot worse." Gail chuckled, but Venice did not. "Let's watch now and see."

Less than two minutes later, the security feed showed the double doors at the back of the lobby, under the stairs, burst open and a distraught Carlos Palma beelined to the desk, his phone pressed to his face.

"Can we find out who he's talking to?"

"Easy," Venice said. "But let's keep watching this."

Carlos shoved some items into his pocket, fiddled with something on the desk that was out of view, and hurried out of the frame toward the front door.

"Keep watching your screen," Gail said. "I want to watch real time."

Taking care to minimize light spillage, Gail rolled out from under the blanket and took a position where she could watch the front door. Carlos damn near took a header down the main staircase as he hurried down, grabbing the rail in the center to save himself at the last moment.

"He's out of the building," Gail said.

Carlos disappeared around the green side of the building, on his way to the rear, where Gail knew there was a parking lot. Thirty seconds later, she could hear an engine rev, and just a few seconds after that, a white Toyota pickup truck screamed down the side of the school building and past her hiding spot. He didn't even pause at the stop sign before cutting the wheel and heading left at the bottom of the driveway.

"Okay, Ven. Time to go to work."

Venice pulled the blanket away and started to fold it. Apparently, she'd already put her laptop back in the satchel. "I might have some bad news," she said.

Gail waited for it.

"That call he was on? It traces back to Desmond Pryor."

"Why does that name sound familiar?"

"He's the third guard. The *contingent*. We figured him to be the swing shift filler-inner."

"Calling him in to work?"

"I didn't have time to tap into the call itself," Venice said. She sounded apologetic. "But that's my guess."

"Damn. Well, we're in this deep now."

"I'm not leaving without what we came here for. I already killed the cameras."

"Then let's get to it."

With the security guard gone and the cameras neutralized, the concerns about fast motion evaporated. Together, they hurried up to the front door, where Gail unslung her rucksack and placed it on the stoop. She opened the flap to the main pocket, but then paused.

"Do me a favor," Gail said. "Check the door to see if it's unlocked."

Venice gave her a look but thumbed the latch anyway and pulled. The door opened. "How did you know?"

"I watched him leave," Gail said as urged Venice inside with a hand on her shoulder, then scooted in behind her and closed the door. "This is an old building, and typically, this kind of lock needs to be locked from the outside with a key. Our friend Carlos didn't do that."

"I must have really unnerved him."

For good measure, Gail corrected the guard's mistake. If Desmond Pryor had, in fact, been summoned, she didn't want him to be suspicious. "You did great," she said, then straightened and scowled. "No alarm warning?" She hurried to the guard's desk and looked at the annunciator panel. Everything showed green.

"It makes sense, I guess," Venice said. "Why would he set the alarm when he has to come in and out all night? He forgot all the protocols, I guess."

"And the Academy Award goes to Constance DuBois for best actress in a burglary scam. It's time for you to lead the way. You've been here before."

They climbed the right-hand sweep of the stairs to the closed door that led to the staff wing. Unlike the main entrance, this door was locked.

Venice stepped out of the way to make room for Gail to take care of the lock. Despite the glare from the nightlights down in the lobby, Gail swung her NVGs back into place for a clearer view of the lock. Completely oldschool pin-tumbler job, probably the original from back when the school was built. She used a Y-shaped tension bar to put pressure on the pins and inserted a rake, which she moved vigorously back and forth in the keyway. The cylinder moved a touch but didn't release entirely. She put the rake back into her burglar pouch and replaced it with a half-diamond pick. She felt for the recalcitrant pin, found it, and pushed it out of the way.

"We're in." She almost dropped the burglar pouch back into her ruck, but then realized that she might need to use it again.

With the door to the staff wing closed behind them again, darkness returned, and Venice dropped her own NVGs back into place. "The finance office is down to the right. Third door, I think."

Finally, a door that at least pretended to take security seriously. Made of all-wood construction and mounted in what appeared to be a steel frame, it was secured with a hasp and a combination padlock.

"Can you do one of those?" Venice asked. "That looks like a substantial lock."

Gail smiled. "Watch this." She brought the burglar pouch out again. "People don't think this stuff through. You've got all this hardwood and steel, but ultimately, it's mounted in standard Sheetrock construction. I'll bet you a thousand bucks that if I didn't mind making a bigger mess, I could kick a hole through the wall of the adjacent office and just enter the finance office through the hole I made. I call this security theater."

"But you're not going to do that, right?"

"Won't have to," Gail said. "Because it's just this simple." Opening combination locks by conquering the combination itself was a tedious task that could eat up serious amounts of time. But most padlocks purchased by consumers required nothing like that.

A padlock pick looked a lot like a long, thin fingernail on a metal stick. Gail opened her stance so Venice could watch. "This thin piece is shaped to match the dimension of the lock's shackle."

"That's the loop?"

"Right. Some people call it the shank." She shoved the tapered end into the lock on the outer edge of the lock face. "This is a little tighter than most, but that actually works to our benefit. Now, watch this." Holding the lock steady with her gloved left hand, she used her right to twist the fingernail around the circumference of the shackle, where it physically pushed the locking bar out of the way and allowed the lock to pop open.

"It's that easy?"

"Makes you wonder why you lock your doors at all, doesn't it?"

The inside of the finance office was little more than a desk, a chair, and file cabinets. "Do you want the left side or the right side?" Gail asked.

"When in doubt I always go left," Venice answered.

"Good for you. But wait, I have a present for you." Gail reached into an outside pocket of her rucksack and unclipped a penlight, which she handed to Venice.

"What about the windows? People will see the light."

"These are infrared flashlights," Gail explained. "They work just like regular flashlights, but only for people wearing night vision."

"How cool is that?" Venice clicked the light, and a green circle of illumination hit the cabinets on the far wall. "What are we looking for?"

"Anything that looks like it might tell us where Patrick Kelly gets his income. We need to know who this guy is and whether someone might feel compelled to kidnap his daughter."

Gail couldn't remember the last time she'd filed a piece of paper. When important papers came to her, she scanned them and trashed the originals. At the office, the individual investigators dealt with their own paper piles.

Another sweet victory for the good guys: the individual file cabinets were not locked.

The first cabinet Gail opened was packed with stuff, all crammed into hanging files, all of which looked overloaded. Lots of memos, some printed-out emails, and more than a couple of school yearbooks. She closed that one and moved to the drawer below, where she encountered more of the same.

"You're a hacker," Gail said. "This kind of thing is up your alley. Any idea what the system is here?"

"You're right," Venice said. "This is a lot like hacking. Social engineering. Filing is a very personal thing and often makes sense only to the filer. That's why it's always traumatic for a company when a senior administrative assistant quits. Not only can't the new person find anything, she starts her own that makes sense only to her."

Gail hadn't really intended for Venice to take the question that seriously.

"You know, I think that's what we're working with here. I bet we're seeing decades of many different filers. I haven't even found a financial record yet."

Gail paused, her hands hovering over the files in the second drawer of the first cabinet. Maybe they were going about this the wrong way. She turned away from the cabinets along the walls and turned back toward the desk that sat in the center of the room.

Financial files were the ones that a finance officer would reference most frequently, right? She wouldn't put those frequent files in the cabinets that were farthest away, she'd keep them close to her chair, maybe even in her desk.

Gail closed her current drawer and scanned her light over the other cabinets, the ones deeper in the room. She felt a smile blooming as she noted the change in the labeling of the cabinets. TAXES. FUNDRAISING. COMMUNITY. SWIMMING POOL. LANDSCAPING. Some of the labels were for individual drawers, but some were for entire cabinets.

"I found it!" Gail announced. Except *it* wasn't quite right. *Them* was more appropriate. Three cabinets stood side by side directly behind the desk chair. The labels across the top of each read TUITION AND APPLICATIONS. Below, the labels on the individual drawers were marked alphabetically.

"We're not alone anymore," Venice said.

Gail looked out the window in the direction Mother Hen was pointing. A set of headlights was approaching up the driveway toward the school building. "That was fast," Gail said. "How close does our friend Desmond live?"

"I never thought to plot that out," Venice said.

And it didn't matter, did it?

The *K*s didn't begin until the top of the second cabinet. Gail pulled the top drawer open and finger-walked across the tops of the folders as Venice added her light beam to Gail's.

"Kelly, Kelly, Kelly . . ." Gail spoke aloud as she searched.

Venice reached back farther into the drawer and pinched the top of a file. "Here," she said. She pulled it out of the drawer. "Kelly, Charles. Wrong one."

As Venice put the file back into the slot from which she'd drawn it, Gail looked out the window again. The headlights were no longer visible. "Our clock's ticking."

Venice stayed focused. "Kelly, Madeline. Kelly, Gregory. Apparently, alphabetical order goes only so far."

"You keep going," Gail said. "I want to peek out and see what our status is. When you find what you need, take a picture and get it back into the drawer."

Aware for the first time of how creaky the old floor was up here, Gail eased back to the office door and pulled it open a crack. The hallway was empty. That was a good start. She opened the door all the way and turned left, back toward the doorway that separated the staff wing from the central stairs.

She stopped at that door and pressed her ear against it. She didn't know what she was listening for, but that didn't matter either, because all she could hear was the pounding of her own pulse.

Right now, the only data point she had was that they were not alone in the school. Beyond that, she was situationally blind. That couldn't stand. She held her breath as she rocked the NVGs back out the way and gently pushed the door open. Wood scraped against wood as the door cleared the jamb. She'd have sworn that there hadn't been any noise when they'd entered.

She took her time. A five-one-thousand count just to peer through the crack, then she opened it farther. Six inches. Twelve. Eighteen. She saw no shadows, sensed no movement.

"Where is he?" she whispered to no one. Easily five minutes had passed since she'd seen the headlights, maybe even seven. Why wasn't he inside? And if he was inside, why wasn't he making noise?

At times like these, whenever the dots didn't connect

logically, the danger scale shot up. *No such things as co-incidences.*

She dared a step out onto the balcony, where she craned her neck to peer down to the security desk. Sure enough, it sat abandoned.

Were those sirens in the distance?

Of course they were.

And as soon as Gail realized what was happening, she could see blue lights through the front windows, strobing against the trees out on the main road. Whatever dim hopes she'd harbored that maybe this wasn't about their burglary were dashed. The strobes stopped, and two police cruisers headed up the driveway, one on each leg of the circle, presumably to block egress.

It was time to go.

Gail spun on her own axis and scooted back into the staff wing, closing the door behind her.

With her NVGs back in place, she hurried back into the office, where Venice had placed a file folder on the desk and was using her phone to take pictures of every page—a blast of white light in the otherwise dark space.

"Stop!" Gail shouted at a whisper. "Police are here."

"Oh, God."

"Yeah."

"But I haven't finished."

"Yes, you have," Gail said. She slid the file folder over, straightened the pages, and closed it. "We're out of here, now."

"But what—"

Gail stuffed the folder into her rucksack and closed the flap. "We'll take it with us."

Downstairs, the front doors opened. She could hear

voices, but couldn't make out words. A dog barked. A big bark, the kind that comes from a big dog.

"Oh, shit, a canine unit!" Gail hissed.

"How are we going to get out?"

"Not the way we came in." What came next was all raw instinct. No thought, no strategy. They needed time. Not a lot, but enough to get out of the building and back to the car. Gail scanned the desk for something heavy she could throw. The best she could find was a stapler—one of those industrial jobs that probably weighed the better part of a half-pound. She lifted it from next to the blotter-style desk pad and heaved it through the window. In the silence of the night, the noise was startling.

"What are you doing?"

Gail didn't answer. Instead, she drew her Glock. Standing away from the window opening, she settled her sights on the base of a distant tree and fired four shots.

The response was both loud and instant as the officers scrambled for cover and dragged the dog out of the building.

"Gail, are you crazy?"

"We bought time," Gail said. "With shots fired, if they're like every other police agency in the country, they'll pull back and wait for backup. Follow me."

"Now they're going to shoot us if they see us."

"They won't see us if we hurry."

As Gail stepped back into the hallway, she looked left at the glowing exit sign on the far end, but opted against going that way. That exit was too close to the front of the building—too close to arriving cops. She turned left, instead, and headed back out toward the main stairway balcony.

"We'll be out in the open," Venice said.

"Stay on me."

Gail didn't have time to explain and wasn't even a little bit sure that she wasn't being stupid, but this close to the time of the gunshots, the cops would still be in disarray, hoping to find cover as they tried to figure out where the shots were coming from. Since it was nighttime, they had no way of knowing that she'd shot a tree—had no intention of endangering officers. She was rolling the dice on them not watching the interior right now. They'd have eyes on the windows.

For the time being, the cops didn't have enough manpower to cover the exits and watch for more shooting, but without a doubt, every cop from every conceivable jurisdiction was screaming toward them, as was every air asset.

Back out on the formal breezeway, among the mural of Virginia's antebellum history, Gail led the way to the double doors that opened to the second floor academic wing.

"Are you going to tell me what we're doing?" Venice asked.

"No," Gail said. It was the real answer, and she didn't have the time to explain that, either. If Venice kept up, she'd know exactly what the plan was. If they executed it with speed, they might actually succeed. If they paused to discuss it, they'd have plenty of time to fill in the details in the paddy wagon.

Beyond the closed doors now, they could run. No lights were on, save for the red exit sign on the far end of the hallway. Gail hadn't seen any diagrams of the building's interior, but she'd committed the exterior footprint to memory. There were no annexes to the building, so that far door should lead straight to the outside.

Besides, they needed a break.

Gail didn't slow as she approached the door, turning sideways at the last stride to throw her hip into the crash bar and launching the door into the fire escape railing with a bang that sounded nearly as loud as the gunshots.

She threw a glance back over her shoulder and was pleased to see that Venice was still with her, keeping up step-for-step.

The fire escape stairway was more a cage than a stairway, screened by expanded metal vertical mesh screening, presumably there to keep children from jumping to their deaths while escaping the flames. Two long flights took them down to the parking lot at the rear of the building, where suddenly it felt as if they were onstage. The lot was illuminated by twice as many streetlights as the front driveway.

"We can't get back to the car in this light," Venice said.

She was right.

And Gail had a solution. It was a massive overkill—on the scale of the proverbial shotgun to kill the proverbial fly—but Gail had no intention of going to jail tonight. She had no doubt that in the future, she'd look back on this entire op as a colossal mistake, but that didn't change the here and now.

"Stay put and lift your NVGs. This will only take a minute."

"Do we have a minute?"

"Ask me in two minutes."

The main electrical feed for the campus fed into a transformer that sat atop a pole on the edge of the parking lot, about ten yards away. From there, the main traveled down the length of the pole to a massive locked breaker cabinet that sat at about chest level.

As Gail moved toward the box, she unslung her rucksack. If there was one thing she'd learned during her time with Jonathan and Boxers, it was that you never knew when explosives might come in handy. While Big Guy was routinely burdened with pounds of the stuff, Gail allowed herself a single GPC—general-purpose charge. Consisting of a small block of Compound C4 with a tail of detonating cord, GPCs offered a lot of flexibility, but in very unsubtle ways.

Gail's hands trembled a little as she let the paper wrapper from the C4 drop to the ground and she slapped the malleable block into the base of the rat's nest of electrical inputs at the top of the breaker box. Next, she pulled an assortment of detonators from a different pocket in her ruck and fingered through them until she found the one she wanted—OFF, old-fashioned fuse, the kind you light with a match.

She jammed the detonator into the block of explosive, then cut the fuse to what she eyeballed to be fifteen seconds. She stuffed the excess back into her ruck, then produced a Zippo lighter. It took three cranks of the wheel to produce a flame, but the dangling fuse jumped to life the instant the fire kissed it.

Keeping low, she turned to rush back to Venice.

"Freeze! Don't move!" A cop had rounded the corner from the building's green side and had lit her up with the muzzle light from his pistol.

"Get down!" Gail yelled to both Venice and the cop as she closed the distance to the school building.

"I want to see your hands!" the cop yelled. "Don't make me shoot you!"

As Gail dropped to her belly, she pointed to the plume of smoke rising toward the breaker box. "Explosives! Get down!"

The cop's face showed nothing but confusion.

"I'm not kidding—"

The rest of her words were lost in the sound of the blast.

The world went dark.

Chapter Ten

Gail grabbed a fistful of Venice's coveralls and pulled her up. "We need to go. Now."

The pressure wave of the explosion was big enough to knock the cop on his ass, but not big enough to do any harm. Gail couldn't completely dismiss the possibility of fragmentation injury, but she hoped that he was smart enough to be wearing body armor. He was still struggling to find his feet when Gail dashed over to him and pushed him over onto his side. She ripped the pistol out of his hand and tossed it into the parking lot.

As the cop reached for the radio mic clipped to his epaulette, she ripped it away, epaulette and all. Acting purely on instinct and fear, she drew the pepper spray canister from its holster on his belt, stepped back, and let him have four or five seconds' worth.

That would hold him.

"Goggles down," Gail said, and she pushed Venice forward, toward the edge of the parking lot that would lead to more woods but would keep them away from the front part of the athletic fields.

"You hurt that officer," Venice said as they ran.

"*Shh.* We can talk later."

Gail had done more than just hurt the cop. She'd committed a felony, and by taking a weapon away from the officer—two, actually—she had justified the use of deadly force against them. The sky would soon be filled with helicopters, the woods with dogs, and the airwaves with breathless reports of the burglars' assault on a police officer.

They needed to be somewhere else. Anywhere else. And quickly. Like, now.

The darkness of the night was blessedly black, and she told herself that they alone were equipped with night vision, but she had no idea whether or not that was true. All she knew was that the window of opportunity to get away whole was closing with blistering speed.

The slice of field they decided to cross on the way out took them straight to the horse corral and the stables beyond.

At the fence, Gail said, "Squeeze through, don't try to climb," and Venice complied. To climb presented a risk for a fall that might injure, but more importantly, climbing over the top would change the silhouette of the structure of the corral, if only slightly. At this point, there was no such thing as a superfluous detail.

Gail was right behind Mother Hen as they ran at a low crouch through the churned grass and horse shit past the open doors of the stables. A few horses acknowledged their presence with whatever you call the equine equivalent of a growl, but for the most part the occupants of the stable remained silent.

On the far side of the corral, they squeezed again through the fence rails, and Gail had the sense that maybe, just maybe, they'd made it.

They made no effort to avoid the creek this time, splashing through the knee-deep water as quickly as they could without falling. Venice almost went down once—she'd later blame it on a submerged rock—but she got her hand out in time to grab Gail's shoulder for support.

"You okay?" Gail asked.

No answer. No need for one, really.

On the opposite bank now, they scrambled up a much steeper slope, and the woods went on for longer than Gail thought they should.

"Stop for a second," she commanded.

"Where's the car?"

"Right where we left it," Gail said. "But we're not where we're supposed to be." The new path they'd taken to return had caused them to overshoot the cul-de-sac. If Gail's sense of direction wasn't totally wrecked, they needed to pivot to the left and feel their way through this patch of woods. In the best case, they'd emerge directly in front of their vehicle.

In the worst case, they'd emerge in someone's backyard.

What was it about worst cases that there always turns out to the even more terrible outcome that you never thought of?

They emerged in the backyard of a house with a big noisy dog that took its guard responsibility very seriously. The beast came at them at a dead run, making homicidal noises at 100 decibels. Cujo meets the Hound of the Baskervilles.

"Oh, God. Ohgodohgodohgod . . ." Venice stood frozen in place.

Gail shoved her. "Get going. That way." She pointed.

"You're not supposed to run from—"

"Go!"

The dog's yard was surrounded by a fence, but under the circumstances, it seemed far too low and far too fragile. Running was still the best option as far as Gail was concerned.

The fence held, but that seemed to piss Cujo off even more.

After a dozen strides or so, Gail finally saw the Nissan in the distance. They'd overshot it by way more than she'd expected.

"There it is," Venice said, pointing.

"Got it."

Thirty seconds later, they were almost home.

"Take off the NVGs," Gail said as they closed the distance. She thumbed the button on her key fob and heard the locks click. "Balaclava, too." She tore the door open.

Gail moved quickly, sloppily, as she stuffed the gear into the bag and zipped it closed.

The coveralls were next. She unzipped the long zipper, shrugged out of them, and marched free of the legs. On the other side of the car, Venice was doing the same. "Be sure to stuff the coveralls into the duffel. We don't want anything in the open."

Within a minute, they looked like civilians again. Like regular people. They scooted into the front seat. Venice's door was still closing when Gail cranked the ignition. She backed away from the curb, swung a U-turn, and turned her lights on.

"Oh, my God, that was close," Venice said, bringing her hands to her head.

"We're not out of it yet," Gail said. At the end of the cul-de-sac, she navigated her way out of the neighborhood, then turned left onto the main road.

"Wait!" Venice said. "You're headed *toward* the school."

"Yes, we are, Special Agent DuBois," Gail replied. "You did bring your badge like I asked, right?"

"I brought it, but I don't know what to do with it."

"Just have it ready in case you need it."

Venice moaned. "Please don't kick a hornets' nest."

"We have to," Gail replied. "I don't know if it will pay off for us in the future, but I know that it could be trouble if we don't."

"I don't understand."

"You will." Gail eased off the gas pedal as she approached the school. As she expected, a cop car sat across the road in front of the entry gates, blue lights flashing. Two police officers wearing Victoria County uniforms stood at either end of the vehicle, M4s battle slung across their body armor and their attention focusing at the approaching Nissan. The muzzles were pointed at the ground, but their hands looked tight on the pistol grips.

"Are you out of your mind?" Venice said.

"Get your badge ready. Follow my lead." Gail had her own badge in her left hand. She rolled down her window and held it out in hopes that the cops could see its gleam in her palm. She also turned on the dome light and killed her headlights. It was the universal message to the police that you had nothing to hide. "Hold your badge out your window."

Venice did as she was told.

As added reassurance, Gail stuck her empty hand out the window, too.

The two cops exchanged words. After a few seconds, the one on the right approached the Nissan. He moved hesitantly, clearly uncomfortable.

"We're federal agents!" Gail called out the window. "FBI! Would you like me to get out of the car?"

"No. Just keep your hands visible." The officer continued his approach, but kept his distance, getting just close enough to lean forward and take Gail's creds case out of her hands. As he opened his stance, she saw the name tag that was Velcro'd to his vest. Blake.

The cop handed the creds case back but continued to keep his distance.

"Do you need Agent DuBois's credentials, too?"

Officer Blake bent lower and scowled through the windshield. "She your partner?"

"Yes. We were working a thing down the street when we heard an explosion from down this way. Was that you guys?"

"It's this incident, but we didn't shoot the explosives. That was a couple of burglars."

Gail made herself look shocked. "Burglars with explosives? That can't be good." She hoped she didn't oversell it.

"I've been down here in the street since it started. Only been about fifteen minutes."

"Did you get them?"

"Not that I've heard. That's why we stopped you." His scowl deepened. "Why are you here again?"

"Some federal business down the way. We were just shutting it down."

"I didn't hear anything about that."

Gail offered a dramatic shrug. "Got no answer for you. I wasn't the agent in charge. Usually, we deal the locals in on the game, but not always. I don't know in this case."

Blake moved his hands away from his rifle and rested them on his Sam Browne belt, one on each hip. "I don't think you've got a role here, though."

Gail laughed. "Lord, I hope not. It's been a long day. If it's the same with you, I'd like to be on my way."

"Where do you live?"

"Not far. Just outside Colonial Beach. But first, I need to deliver Agent DuBois back to her car."

"Where's that?"

This interview was getting too chatty for Gail's liking. The more details you manufacture, the greater the chance of making a mistake the ruins everything.

"The Seven-Eleven," she said. "Can you make a hole for us?"

Something wasn't right with Blake's body language. Clearly, he wasn't buying some of what they were selling.

Gail decided to double down. "Is something wrong, officer?"

He took his time, but finally got around to it. "No, everything's fine. This isn't much of a car. You can probably sneak around the cruiser. If not, we can move out of the way."

It was tight, but yes, they could squeeze by. The Nissan's tires scraped the curb a little, but not enough to do any damage.

When they were on their way, Gail answered the question she knew was coming. "We established a record," she said. "If we get stopped between here and the Cove by cops looking for fleeing burglars, we'll identify our-selves again and use the ruse about being on a job up the road. By talking to the cop, we got ahead of any questions about why, as FBI agents, we didn't stop to lend aid."

In the pulsing glare of passing streetlights, she could see Venice staring back at her.

"I told you it took a different way of thinking," Gail said.

Chapter Eleven

The El Paso Police Department's Central Regional Command building at the corner of South Campbell and Overland was an architectural nod to the past. Its red-brick arched entryway flanked by old-school sconces with glass globes stenciled POLICE reminded Jonathan of urban station houses of the past. Sitting as it did in the middle of buildings of more modern design, he wondered if the neighbors considered it to be a gem or an eyesore.

Jonathan, Boxers, and Harry parked across the street in the massive garage, and as they entered, a patrolman named Carpenter was there to meet them and escort them past all the security screening devices. Doug Kramer had promised to request special courtesy, and clearly he had delivered. Jonathan wondered if the rank-and-file officers and administrative staff would have approved of the un-screened entry of armed visitors.

Officer Carpenter led Jonathan and the others to a conference room, where they were invited to sit. They de-
clined the offer for water or coffee.

"Do you work with the EPPD a lot?" Jonathan asked
Dawkins.

"Not really. Not the way you probably think of it. I
keep them informed of known bad guys and bad deeds,
and they do the same for us. The JTF is pretty much pure
feds, but it's always good to show a cooperative spirit."

They hadn't been seated for five minutes when a tall,
rail-thin man with a dark tan and a no-bullshit set to his
jaw rounded the corner into the conference room and
closed the door behind him. His smile looked genuine
enough, it just didn't look comfortable. "Special Agent
Dawkins," he said, extending his hand. "How nice to see
you."

"Back atcha, Chief," Dawkins said. "These are the
friends I told you about. Jonathan Grave and Brian Van
de Muelebroecke."

"Call me Digger," Jonathan said as he shook the
chief's hand.

"Chester Gill."

"Boxers," Big Guy said.

"Chester Gill." The chief's eyes flashed shock at Boxers' size, but he didn't say anything. "Please, have a
seat." EPPD uniforms consisted of a dark-blue shirt with
pocket flaps and epaulettes that matched light-blue pants.
Three stars lined both points of Gill's collar. "I'm the assistant chief in charge of the Investigations Bureau.
While I don't mean to be rude, I need to tell you that I
have a lot on my desk."

"That's fine, Chief," Jonathan said. "I'll get right
to it."

"You want me to move heaven and earth to find a missing boy and his girlfriend," Gill said. "Or maybe the other way around. Missing girl and her boyfriend."

Clearly, the guy had been briefed. "Yes, sir, that's it exactly. I understand that it's not protocol given the ages of the kids."

The chief's uncomfortable smile returned to his lips. "I'll do what I can, but you have to make me a promise."

Jonathan and Boxers exchanged looks. "Sure," Jonathan said.

"I've already told the supervisors to distribute pictures of the kids, so every patrol car will be able to pull it up on their computers. In return, I want you to do whatever you need to do to get that Alexander woman to stop terrorizing my officers."

"Terrorizing?"

"The nonstop telephone calls. The threats to report us to the media. The threats to have people come down here and beat people up."

Jonathan laughed. "I can't say I've ever seen that side of Venice before, but I'll talk to her."

"She's the boy's mother, right? Roman's mother."

"Yes."

"Well, she's not the one. She's called, but she's not the harasser. It's the other one. Florence?"

Boxers launched a guffaw. "Good luck with that, Dig."

The chief looked confused.

"You've been talking to Mama Alexander," Jonathan explained, fully aware that he wasn't explaining anything. "That's Venice's mother, Roman's grandmother."

"What am I missing?" Gill asked.

Jonathan explained, "You, me, the president of the

United States, or the pope in Rome have a better chance of stopping the tides from coming in than they do of keeping Mama from doing anything the hell she wants. Sorry, Chief, but you're on your own."

Chief Gill got the joke, and he joined the laughter.

"Did you get the information about the silver BMW?" Jonathan asked.

"We did. Courtesy of the other Alexander. Description and license number. But we couldn't do anything with it."

"Why not?"

"My detectives looked at security footage from the surrounding businesses, and while we saw a car pick up the kids, that car was a Ford. And the license plate was not the same. We can't even figure out why she is so certain that a BMW is involved."

"The Ford was a RoadRunner," Jonathan explained. He then filled the chief in on the details of the abduction.

Deep creases appeared in the chief's forehead. "Did you two by chance stop by the Shady Sun Water Park and beat up a ticket taker?"

Jonathan remained stone-faced. Neither confirm nor deny.

"Never mind," Gill said. "I heard the guy was very beat-upable. My cops heard nothing about an abduction, though."

"Trust us," Jonathan said. "It happened. And the silver BMW is the one you need to be looking for."

Chief Gill folded his arms across his tie. "It's not a matter of trust, Mr. Grave."

"Digger."

"I'll stipulate that you're right, but we cannot target a car for a crime when (a) we've seen no evidence of a crime, and (b) the only vehicular evidence we have features an entirely different vehicle. How can you be so sure?"

The question pushed Jonathan into a corner. "I can't answer that question," he said.

Gill's cop-sense piqued, and he sat a bit taller. "Can't?"

Jonathan's shoulder twitched a little, a noncommittal shrug. "Won't," he said. "Choose not to."

The chief smirked. "You didn't drive all the way to a police station to confess to a crime, did you?"

Jonathan returned the smirk with a smile. "I never share means and methods, Chief. Intelligence gathering is Security Solutions' special niche in the private investigation business. I can't share the hows."

"Then I can't act on the results," Gill said. "I'm sorry, but you know, Constitution, laws, and stuff."

Jonathan's mind was already racing ahead to how he was going to break the news to Venice that the EPPD's hands were tied.

"I'll tell you something interesting about all of this," Chief Gill said. "Again, I'll stipulate that the kids disappeared, and we can argue about the reasons behind the disappearance. But you know what? The only reason we've heard anything about this is because of you and your team."

"Well, that's why we're here."

"No, you're missing my point," Gill said. "The names and pictures we've put out are Roman Pennington and Ciara Kelly. Are those the right names?"

"Roman prefers Alexander, but Pennington is the actual name."

Gill made a sweeping motion with his fingers, wiping the detail aside. "Fine. Whatever. But while your team and, to a lesser degree, the headmaster have been melting our phones, we haven't heard a peep from the other side. From the Kellys."

Jonathan recoiled from the thought. Surely, Ciara's mom or dad or both had been notified by Dr. Washington.

"Nothing at all?"

"Nothing. Apparently, the Kellys are not concerned about the possibility of kidnapping. Digger, maybe your friend's son is out being made a man."

Jonathan felt a flash of anger. Not just because of the sentiment and the cliché of it, but because of the casual way in which the chief spoke the words.

Jonathan turned to his team. "You guys got anything?"

Neither did.

Jonathan stood and the others followed. "Okay, then, Chief. I thank you for your time and consideration."

They shook hands. "The longer Harry Dawkins is with you, the less time he spends hounding me and my officers." He sold it with a smile.

When Gail dropped Venice off at the mansion, they were both dead on their feet. They agreed to a three-hour break, after which they would reconvene in the War Room to wade through whatever they could find in the files they *stole*. Might as well be honest with the terminology. There was no way either of them was going to endure the risk of returning the file.

Right on time, Gail wandered back into the Cave to find Venice already in the War Room, images projected onto the screen.

"Did you sleep at all?" Gail asked.

"I'll sleep when Roman is back at home. How about you?"

"A little. What did you find out?"

"Get some coffee and have a seat. This is going to take a while."

Six minutes later, Gail had her caffeine and was settled into her seat. "Ready to go," she said.

"First of all, that was very scary last night."

"I tried to warn you—"

"I'd do it again in a heartbeat. Scary also means exciting. I've never seen you in action like that. You're pretty darned fast on your feet."

Gail felt her ears turning red.

"Now, look at the screen," Venice said. The left side of the screen filled with the ruddy face of the man Gail knew to be Patrick Kelly. Then the image flickered, and the right-hand side of the screen filled with a picture of the same man. This one was more serious than the first, reminding her of a photo you'd use for an ID badge.

"Two pictures of Patrick Kelly," Gail said.

"Yes," Venice said. "And no. More *no* than *yes*. The subdued face on the right is actually Toby Jackson, the sole owner of Toby Jackson Bail Bonding Company."

Gail twisted in her chair. "Twin brothers?"

"No. Same guy, according to their fingerprint records."

"How do you get fingerprint records?"

"Do you want to know the story or don't you?"

Gail backed off. It didn't matter. Venice knew stuff because she knew it. If Mother Hen ever got hit by a truck, Security Solutions would evaporate.

"Ciara Kelly's tuition is paid for by Toby Jackson. It seems that the bail bond company is the prime source of revenue for the family. Now before I go further, what do you know about the bail bond business?"

"Are you quizzing me, or do you really want to know?"

"You know I hate to admit ignorance," Venice said with a grin. "Pretend I don't know."

Gail smiled. "So long as we're only pretending. Here in Virginia, when a person is arrested for a crime, he's taken to the magistrate, who verifies that the arrest was in pursuit of a valid warrant and then sets bail, based on a number of factors. The most important factor is probably flight risk. If somebody's in the hoosegow for a first offense DUI charge, he's not likely to leave his job and his family and default on his mortgage to run away. So, his bail will be small in the grand scheme. Fifteen hundred to maybe five thousand dollars, depending on things like his ability to pay."

"Rich people pay higher bail than poor people?"

Gail considered that. "In general, yes, all things being equal. Not only do rich people have a greater ability to pay, they have more elaborate assets to finance a plan to make a break for it—financial and others. What does this have to do with Roman?"

"Please keep going," Venice said. "I want to make sure that my theory is plausible before I put it out there."

"What more do you need to know?"

"What does the bondsman do?"

"Ah. Okay." Gail looked up at the ceiling as she arranged her thoughts. It had been a while since she'd been through this. "Let's say a guy named Charlie has been arrested and his bail is set at ten thousand dollars. Charlie has a couple of choices. One is to pull the ten grand out of his account and hand it over to the court. The money is his promise to appear at his court dates and trial. If he does, then at the end of the line, whether he's acquitted or convicted, he'll get his money back, minus court costs.

"But let's be honest. The prisons are not filled with people who have an extra ten large in their checking account. If Charlie doesn't have the cash, he needs to go to a bail bondsman, who will charge him a fee—usually ten percent—to front him the amount of the bail."

Venice looked confused. "So, if Charlie runs away . . ."

"The bondsman will owe the court nine thousand dollars. Only, not really. The bail will be collateralized somehow. Cars, houses, jewelry, whatever."

"The Charlie in my head doesn't have anything like those kinds of assets."

Gail winced. "This is where the bail business gets uncomfortable. Charlie might not have anything, but I bet his gramma loves him. She's probably got a life insurance policy with cash value. Maybe his sister has equity in her home. Maybe his brother can pull the kids out of private school and write a check to hold in escrow."

"So, if Charlie runs, the bondsman screws his whole family."

"No, that's not fair. Everybody knows what the rules are. Charlie's the one who would be screwing his own family. And the collateral will naturally have to be more than the actual amount, right? Because it costs money to repossess all those things."

"So, the bondsman gets to keep the overflow?"

"That I don't know," Gail said. "I don't think so. Generally, that ten percent fee is the only money the bondsman makes, but that's nonrefundable. Seriously, where is this all going?"

Venice held up her hand. "Just a little more. Suppose

the bail is set not at ten thousand dollars but at one million dollars?"

Gail puffed out a laugh. "Then Charlie's probably going to rot in jail until his court date."

"No, play the game. Suppose the bond is a million."

Gail ran the scenario through her head. "It's the same thing. The bondsman gets a hundred grand up front, nonrefundable, and then he figures out a way to collateralize the rest of the money. Which is why Charlie is likely going to rot in jail."

"One last question. Is the bondsman on the hook if the collateral turns out to be fraudulent?"

"I would think so. There are insurance policies for those kinds of events, but not at that amount. I mean, seriously, million-dollar bonds just don't happen. Those amounts are intended specifically to keep suspects in jail."

Venice's lips pressed together as she considered it all. "Then I know what happened," she said. "Look back at the screen."

Roman hadn't seen Ciara since they were gathered in that filthy office near the water park. Nor had he heard a word of English spoken in his presence.

Whatever they had injected into his arm had knocked him out cold. When he woke up, he was inside an airplane, he thought, but then he fell asleep again. When he finally woke up for real, the airplane turned out to be an SUV and the surroundings were completely unfamiliar.

Hours ago, they'd cuffed his hands to the kind of belt he'd seen prisoners wear. His arms weren't bound behind his back. They just sort of dangled in front of him, near enough to his fly if he needed to pee, but with chains too short to let him scratch his nose.

Guzman was in the backseat with Roman, and when he noticed that he was awake, he wrapped duct tape around Roman's eyes and his mouth, but cut a slit in the mouth part so that he could breathe.

"For now, consider breathing to be a privilege," Guzman had told him as he cut that slit. "If you try to use that opening to shout out or cause trouble, I will tape it up and seal your nose." To prove his point, he clipped what felt like a wooden clothespin over his nostrils. The jaws squeezed hard, but Guzman removed them after a few seconds.

When Guzman finished taping him, he dropped something cold and heavy onto Roman's bare thigh.

"Go ahead and feel it," Guzman said. "Your chains are long enough. Tell me what you think it might be."

Roman got it right away. "That's a sledgehammer."

"*Exactamente.* So you know I was not bluffing. I love breaking bones, and I am very good at it."

Roman didn't say anything because he wasn't asked, but the weight and size of the steel head scared the crap out of him.

And those were the last words that had been addressed to him in what must have been five hours or more. Maybe twelve. How could he know?

After a while, the SUV stopped, and he felt himself being lifted and then shoved into what turned out to be another vehicle. In his mind, it was an ambulance, just because of all the moving parts, but again, how could he know?

They drove forever. For the most part, the roads were smooth, but the road sounds changed dozens of times. He heard regular pavement and then the *gallump-gallump* of expansion joints on concrete roads. At one point, they came to a stop and the driver spoke to someone, though Roman couldn't make out the words. Even if he had, he figured that he wouldn't have understood them. At another point, he thought he'd even fallen back to sleep.

Then at the end—for the last half hour or so, the roads got pretty awful. Lots of bumping and bouncing. The sound of gravel. Through it all, the air conditioning where he was stayed on, and he couldn't say that he was ever in pain or even horribly uncomfortable.

Still, the thought of that sledgehammer never fully went away. Combined with the empty look he'd seen in Guzman's eyes, Roman had no doubt that the man would follow through with his promise to break bones and enjoy every second while he was doing it.

When they finally came to a stop, the vehicle's doors opened again. The blast of heat startled him. He smelled horse shit. Or, maybe it was cow shit. They smelled the same, didn't they? People held his biceps on both sides as they escorted him across what felt like rough grass under his bare feet.

He wished he'd been counting steps so he'd have some notion of how far he'd walked. After several minutes of shuffling, the light beyond his blindfold dimmed and the walking surface changed to what felt like dirt.

The smell of shit intensified.

In the near distance, he heard the sound of chains being manipulated, and his heart rate tripled. There was no possible scenario where chains could be good. If fact, every scenario he could think of meant pain.

"Please don't hurt me," he said. If they heard him—if they understood him—they didn't answer.

They pushed him along the dirt for thirty-two steps before pulling him to a stop.

A man's voice said something to him in Spanish, and hands pushed him forward again. Still unable to see, he tried to move with baby steps to keep from stepping on something. And as he shuffled along, stuff that felt like hay gathered between his toes. Combined with the smell of animal shit, he decided that he had to be in a barn somewhere.

"*Alto,*" the man said after only five or six additional steps, and he pulled Roman to a stop. While that man's hands kept a grip on his shoulders, someone else fastened what felt like handcuffs around his ankles.

When that was done, the hands pressed down on his shoulders, and he carefully folded himself down into a sitting position.

Five seconds later, the duct tape was pulled roughly from his mouth, yanking what his mom called his practice whiskers from his upper lip and chin. He yelped, but upon his first inhalation, he realized how much he'd missed taking a full breath.

When they pulled the tape from his eyes, he wondered if they left any lashes or brows behind. As he blinked, he wondered if maybe he'd gone blind. The difference between being blindfolded and not was barely discernable.

The bright round beam of a powerful flashlight surrounded a five-gallon plastic paint bucket with a loose-fitting lid, with a roll of toilet paper on the ground next to it.

"*El baño,*" one of the captors said. Roman still hadn't gotten a look at them, but *bathroom* was one of the few Spanish words that he did know.

Behind him, he could hear at least two men leaving.

Curiosity notwithstanding, Roman forced himself not to look. If it was important to them for him to not see what they were doing, then who was he to do otherwise?

When the doors closed, the darkness became nearly absolute. Straining as best as he could against the short chains attaching his wrists to his belt, he tried to feel the shackles around his ankles, but there wasn't enough play. By scooting his butt against the floor, though, he could draw his feet in closer to his body till they were essentially crossed in front of him.

As his eyes adjusted to the darkness, he could see thin slivers of lighter darkness through horizontal stripes in the walls. It was enough light to outline the silhouette of the piss bucket, and if he used his imagination, he thought he could see the outlines of his legs and hands, too.

The cuffs around his ankles were attached to chains that ran to someplace along the floor. He thought maybe he was facing a thick pillar. In this light, all it was, was a black stripe in the darkness.

This was bad. Really, really bad.

But the police had to be looking for him, right? And Mr. Jonathan was a very rich man. Roman didn't know what kind of ransom his captors were going to ask for, but Mr. Jonathan wouldn't in a million years let anything happen to him.

Mr. Jonathan was like part of his family.

In the War Room, an image of a well-groomed young man blinked into the left-hand side of the screen. Late twenties, early thirties, the image could have been that of a fashion model. High cheekbones, thin but solid jaw, piercing brown eyes. The height chart in the background and the lack of a smile marked this as an arrest photo.

"Meet Fernando Pérez," Venice said. "Deep and long history of petty drug stuff, but recently arrested for *drug trafficking*. I didn't delve into the details of the charges, but I figure that means he went from selling a little to selling a lot." She looked to Gail for validation.

"Generally, you're right," Gail said. "Sometimes the nature of the substance itself can elevate dealing to trafficking, but the point is the same. Do you think he had something to do with Roman's disappearance?"

"I'm getting there."

It was a quirk of Venice's personality that irrespective of the ticking clock or the direness of circumstances, she loved to build to a big reveal. You could fight it, or you could learn to live with it. Either way, Venice was Venice, and she'd deal her hand at her own pace.

The screen blinked, and a new face appeared in the right-hand screen. This one looked more like a surveillance photo. A tall, thin Latino man climbing into the back of a Mercedes sedan.

"This picture comes from Mexico City," Venice explained. "This is Santiago Pérez, the father of our friend Fernando."

"Why do I recognize that name?"

"From a thousand classified reports that have flowed our way. Santiago is a senior lieutenant of some sort within the Cortez drug cartel. The U.S. has multiple warrants out for his arrest, on everything from drug trafficking to human trafficking to murder and arson. Not a nice man."

Gail thought she might see the dots beginning to connect. "So, Santiago has something to do with Roman's disappearance."

"Sort of."

Gail groaned and leaned back in her chair, determined just to remain quiet until the details were revealed.

"When Fernando was arrested, his bail was set at one million dollars," Venice explained. "He was released the following day. Toby Jackson Bail Bonding Company put up the money for the bond. That was three days ago. Now, look at this."

Venice tapped her keys, and numbers appeared on the screen. It looked like a bank statement.

"This is Toby Jackson Bail Bonding Company's bank account. What do you see?"

According to the statement, the company ran kind of lean, with only forty thousand dollars in cash on hand.

"What am I looking for?" Gail asked.

"What *don't* you see?"

"I really don't enjoy this game."

"Where's the hundred grand? The ten percent nonrefundable money?"

"I have no idea. Certainly not in the account, but maybe in a safe. Maybe he got the money in cash. I'm sure daddy the drug dealer could scare up a hundred thousand."

Venice made her eyebrows bounce a little. "Or, maybe he just made a phone call. Think about it. Toby Jackson has built an okay business out of backing minor bonds. Look, I did a search. It's amazing what you can find once you know where to look."

More clicking, and the screen changed again, this time to an official-looking list of names, charges, and case numbers.

"These are the cases Toby Jackson has been involved with over the past two years. Look at them. One thousand. Twenty-five hundred. Fifty-two hundred." She looked to Gail and scowled. "I wonder why such a random number?"

Gail didn't bother to answer.

"I could scroll through all of these, but I won't. If I did, you'd see a maximum bond amount of fifteen thousand dollars—only two of those—and about a dozen at ten grand. This guy doesn't do million-dollar bonds."

Venice paused in a way that gave Gail the sense that she was supposed to understand everything now. "Tell me you're not done."

"Come on, think about it, Gail. Patrick Kelly owns a ton of companies that appear to have little business and pay no taxes. The bail bond company isn't even in his name, and it has a record of petty, small-size bonds. Yet, when the time comes that the son of a drug kingpin needs a whole lot of cash, Patrick Kelly produces it. Or Toby Jackson does. Same person."

At last, Gail thought she saw the big picture. "All those companies exist to do work on this side of the border on behalf of the cartels?"

"Yes, I think so."

Gail held up a hand for silence. She needed a minute or two to force the pieces of the puzzle together. "What does this have to do with Roman?"

"I don't think it does," Gail said. "I think Digger might have been right. I think Roman was not the target of whatever happened. I think the target was Ciara Kelly."

"The cartel kidnapped Ciara Kelly?"

"The Cortez Cartel is the only constant through all of this," Venice said. "The guys who stopped the driver, Fernando and Santiago Pérez, and now Toby Jackson. Now, throw in the fact that they were snatched in El Paso, just an easy hike or wade from the border. That has to be it."

Gail thought it didn't *have* to be anything, but those pieces fell together pretty easily.

"Now, the question is *why*," Venice said.

"We've walked that road a thousand times," Gail said. "There are only a few reasons to kidnap someone. I think we can rule out random act of violence or the act of some serial killer. That leaves ransom or leverage."

"Santiago Pérez is a rich man."

"Yes, he is. So that leaves leverage."

"They're holding the kids till Patrick Kelly does something for them."

"That's what I think," Gail agreed.

"How do we find out what that something is?"

"I don't know," Gail confessed. "More to the point, I'm not sure we need to know that. It'd be nice, but only in the sense that knowing more is better than knowing less."

"I need to find out," Venice said.

"Then I'll help you."

Venice started to type again, but her fingers froze over the keyboard. When she pivoted her head around to face Gail, her eyes were rimmed with red.

"What is it?"

"This is about Ciara Kelly," Venice said, her voice catching in her throat. "I don't care about Ciara Kelly. I only care about Roman."

Gail was confused again.

"The cartel leaders are bad, bad people. God only knows what they'll do to that poor girl while she's in captivity, but at the very least, they'll have to keep her alive."

Gail saw it, but she didn't want to say it. Her stomach tightened, as if preparing to be punched.

"There's no reason to keep my little boy alive, is there?"

"You can't think that way, and you know it." Gail stood.

"Where are you going?"

"I'm going to pay a visit to Patrick Kelly and Toby Jackson."

"I'll go with you."

"No, you won't. You stay here and find that car. If we can pinpoint that location, we'll be halfway to bringing Roman home."

Venice clearly didn't like it, but she remained seated.

"And Ven? We are going to bring him home, and he *is* going to be healthy."

Venice chewed her lip and turned back to her computer screen.

Chapter Twelve

Daytime had arrived while Roman wasn't paying attention. He didn't remember falling asleep, but clearly, he had. As he lay on his back, looking up at a complex assortment of timbers fifteen or twenty feet overhead, he realized that his guess about being in a barn had been correct, as had his suspicion that he'd been tied to a heavy pillar. It was the tallest one, the one that went from the floor all the way to the highest peak of the roof.

Bright sunshine spilled through cracks in the walls and the ceiling to paint a complex matrix of stripes over everything.

As he sat up, he twisted his back to the left and right to crack out the stiffness. Now that he had some light, he could see that the three feet of chain that spanned the cuffs on his ankles had been attached to a longer, heavier chain that had been fastened to the pillar in such a way that he was stuck facing it. He had enough chain to travel to the piss bucket, but not enough to find a comfortable position that would allow him to lean up against the pillar unless he sat on the ankle cuffs, which would hurt like hell. Effectively, his choices were to sit up straight or to lie flat on his back. He could cross his ankles if we wanted, but that likewise put a lot of pressure on the metal rings. Overnight, they'd already worn rough, inflamed spots into the anklebone on his left leg and the Achilles tendon on his right.

Where the hell was Ciara? Was she somehow involved in all of this? Clearly, she knew the guy who'd confronted them on the street, but how? Equally clearly, Guzman's presence had unnerved her. She'd been surprised and she'd been frightened.

Roman wondered if he himself had made everything worse. He'd tried to protect her by fighting, but that was when everything went to shit, right? If he had just stayed out of the way, would everything have gone down with less violence? Should he be feeling guilty now?

He ran the conversation—if that's what you could call it—from the office through his head for the hundredth time, trying to figure out what was going on.

What was it that Cristos Silva had said to him? They were going to kill him and dump his body before Ciara saved his life by mentioning Mr. Jonathan.

Roman didn't know *exactly* what that meant, but one thing that was certain was that he wasn't supposed to be here. The kidnappers, whoever they were, hadn't been interested in him. They took him, he supposed, to get him off the street and to someplace where he'd make less noise. Had people started to gather at the fence to watch? He thought he'd seen that.

But maybe not. His balls were still tender from the kick they'd taken. That kind of pain pushed memories out of the way and made the ones left behind pretty fuzzy.

He should have done more.

Better to die in the street than get into the car.

That was the extent of Mr. Jonathan's stranger danger instructions. That, and never allow yourself to get tied up.

Once you were off the street, whatever advantage you might have had because of fighting skill or weapons reduced dramatically. Once you lost the use of your hands and feet, all advantage was transferred to the other guy. This was precisely why Roman had been so focused on his self-defense classes. To prepare for this moment.

And when the moment came, he completely screwed it up.

And how is this helping? Mama Alexander's voice asked that question inside his head with all the clarity of actually being there. He looked behind just to make sure he was still alone.

Mama had been through a lot in her life, and she'd overcome all of it. She'd never spoken of his grandfather, and he knew better than to ask. The one time he posed the question to his mom, the rebuff was short, stern, and nonnegotiable. Roman knew that Mama had been Mr. Jonathan's nanny when Mr. Jonathan was little and that Mom had given Mama some rough times. He also knew that people in Fisherman's Cove who never showed respect for anybody or anything showed respect for Mama.

Even Mr. Boxers seemed afraid of her.

Mama looked at the world as a problem to be dealt with. *The past stops mattering as soon as now happens.*

It made no sense for Roman to beat himself up over what happened in the street yesterday—that *was* yesterday, right? If it couldn't be undone, then it made no sense to worry.

So, if worrying wasn't working, what *could* work?

You'll never walk again.

Guzman's voice popped into his head with equal clarity.

Roman jumped when he heard the sound of the door opening behind him. "Good morning, Mr. Roman Alexander," a voice boomed from behind him.

He did his best to pivot around and twisted his body to see Cristos Silva striding toward him. Guzman was with him, a step behind, carrying a gym bag in one hand and the sledgehammer in the other. Now that Roman could see it, he realized that it was even bigger than he'd feared. The metal face looked dented and chipped. The wooden handle looked well used.

"I hope you slept well," Silva said.

"Not really," Roman said. "I can't move very well chained like this."

Silva walked around the boy to look him straight on, a smile on his face. "That is the point of using chains, don't you think?"

"Can I have something to eat?"

"In time," Silva said. "First, we have to make a movie."

Roman wasn't sure he understood.

"You look confused," Silva said. "It will make sense in a few minutes. Please stand."

It was a harder task than Roman had expected. The shortness of the chains, combined with limited use of his hands and the stiffness from being on the floor for however long that had been, got the best of him. By leaning forward and using the massive beam for support, he finally got his balance and stood facing Silva.

"Very well," Silva said. Smile still beaming, Silva launched a slap that drove the heel of his hand into the bone under Roman's left eye.

Roman saw a flash of light, then he was back on the ground, unaware that he'd fallen. He smelled blood in his sinuses. As his head cleared, he saw Guzman standing over him, squinting to get a better look at whatever he was trying to see on Roman's face. Guzman said something in Spanish, then he reached down to grab Roman under the collar of his T-shirt. He gave it a yank, and the fabric tore. From the neck ring to the middle of his chest.

Silva appeared in Roman's field of view next, and he at first looked concerned, and then he looked satisfied. He delivered a command in Spanish, and Guzman backed off.

"Sit up now, please," Silva said.

Roman didn't want to. What the hell had he done to deserve a punch?

"Would you prefer Guzman to convince you?"

That did the trick. Roman grunted through a sit-up to pull himself upright and he started to stand.

"No, stay seated for now," Silva said. "I want that blood to drip down your face."

Pain started to bloom before Roman was fully aware that he was injured. His left cheek felt numb and achy at the same time. It was getting harder to see through that eye, and his teeth weren't meeting quite right when he locked his jaw. When he leaned forward, he saw blood dripping onto his thighs before he felt it running off the angle of his jaw.

"Why did you do that?" he asked, and he leaned farther forward to explore the wound with his fingers.

"Stop!" Silva said. "Don't touch it. It looks great just as it is."

"What are you talking about?"

Silva ignored him and disappeared out of view. Roman thought about turning to watch him, but not moving his head was a good thing for now. When he heard the zipper on the gym bag opening, though, he figured he had a right to see what they were going to do to him next.

Guzman pulled a cheap camera tripod out of the bag. While he extended the legs and locked them in place, Silva busied himself with an expensive-looking digital camera.

We have to make a movie.

Now, at least, something finally made sense. But why did they have to hit him like that?

When the tripod was standing and ready to go, Silva said something to Guzman, who picked up his sledgehammer and walked over to Roman.

"No," Roman said, trying to scoot away. "I'm doing what you told me."

Guzman's lips twisted into an unnerving grin as he lifted the hammer high, head down, and let it drop.

* * *

Patrick Kelly entered Fair Oaks Mall on the upper level, via the entrance nearest the Cheesecake Factory. The stores hadn't opened yet, so the only other people to be seen were a few dozen intrepid souls who used the mall as an ersatz track, walking their rounds and racking up their strides. He wasn't from around here, so he didn't know the real numbers, but he imagined from the size of the place that if a walker caught all the nooks and crannies, he could cover at least a mile.

This cloak-and-dagger stuff unnerved him. On the one hand, it seemed silly—why on earth would anyone be following him?—but on the other, Cristos Silva was not a man to cross. They'd been friends for years, in a predatory sort of way, but Patrick had witnessed what the man was capable of when he felt that he'd been crossed.

Start with the fact that Silva had taken Ciara hostage. That was an unnecessary step, but classic Silva. Patrick was willing to go along with the fraudulent bail bond. It was good business for all of them, but Silva had decided that putting Ciara's life on the line was somehow necessary to get Patrick to do the job as he'd agreed to do it.

The plan all along had been for Fernando Pérez to bolt when he got out of jail, and in recompense for taking the risk and providing the bond, Santiago Pérez would pay him the cash value plus twenty percent more. But the $1.2 million that was supposed to be deposited in Patrick's account by Santiago Pérez had never materialized. A deal was a deal, and when Fernando failed to make his first court appointment, Patrick was going to be on the hook for that money.

As far as Patrick was concerned, that was what this clandestine meeting really was about.

The instructions he'd received for this meeting were both specific and complicated. Right turn at the end of the first hallway, then take the stairs down to the first floor. At the bottom of the stairs, he was to buttonhook to the left and walk to the unoccupied store whose front glass wall was covered with brown paper and whose glass door bore a white building permit.

Patrick didn't relish the notion of meeting a stranger in a strange place. He'd upgraded his carry gun from his usual Glock 42 to a much larger Glock 19. Nine-millimeter instead of .380, sixteen rounds instead of seven. If the morning included the throwing of lead, more was always better, but the bigger Glock was heavy and threatened to pull his pants down.

He made his way to the store, and as advertised, the door was unlocked. He checked over his shoulder to see if anyone was watching, then realized he was being stupid. Dozens of cameras were likely recording his every move, anyway.

He stepped inside the store under renovation and looked around. Either the place had been a shoe store and was going out of business or it would soon be a shoe store. Dusty display racks lined the walls. At the back of the room, in the center, in the spot designed for a cashier's station, a guy in an expensive business suit sat in a tall director's chair.

"Good morning, Toby," the man said.

"Good morning, Billy," Patrick said. "I didn't expect this meeting to be with you."

"Who did you think it would be?"

"I guess someone more used to getting construction dust on his clothing."

Billy Monroe was one of the local attorneys who made buttloads of money defending the interests of the cartels and their operators. His most recent client was Fernando Pérez. Within that world, Patrick preferred to be known simply as Toby Jackson, bail bondsman.

"Is this where you tell me that Señor Pérez has deposited a big check in my account?"

Monroe forced a smile. There was probably a time—maybe twenty years and fifty pounds ago—when he had been a handsome man. There was a ruggedness around his eyes and a sharpness to his jaw, but age and weight had softened all of that. Now, his ruddy nose and the puffiness under his eyes made him look just old and tired.

"I can see how that is what you would like to hear," Monroe said. "But, alas, the reality is far more complicated."

Roman yelled as the sledgehammer landed with a heavy thud on the dirt floor between his knees. There was no way it would not have broken a bone if it had landed on his leg.

Without saying a word, Guzman stooped at Roman's feet and removed the shackles from his ankles. As soon as he was free, Roman scooted backward, away from the pillar and the sledgehammer.

"Where are you going, *hijo*?" Silva asked. Roman could hear the smile in his voice.

Roman spun on his butt to look at him. "Nowhere," he said.

"Guzman is a scary man," Silva said. "You are wise to keep your distance from him. Come, you can stand now."

"Are you going to hit me again?"

Silva looked to his enforcer. "Guzman?"

"No!" Roman shouted. "I'm doing it. I'm getting up." He pulled his legs under him and worked hard to get his feet under him again. "Can I have a little help, please?"

"No," Silva said. He was preoccupied with some up-close detail of the camera or maybe the tripod.

Roman nearly pitched over onto his forehead as he struggled for balance, but he recovered. Why were they being so mean to him? He hadn't done anything wrong. Finally at his full height, he lifted his knees high, one at a time, in a marching motion, trying to work out some kinks and get blood flowing in his legs again.

The bleeding had all but stopped from the cut under his eye, but the vision there was almost entirely gone. He hoped it was because of swelling and not because the punch had knocked something loose inside of this head. Could he have been bit that hard?

Silva gave an instruction to Guzman, who wrapped his fist around Roman's biceps and pulled him forward, stooping for the gym bag as they passed it. Silva lifted the camera and tripod and led the way out of the barn and into the blistering sunshine.

Roman squinted against the light.

"Go over there," Silva said, pointing to nowhere, the middle of an empty yard.

Roman allowed himself to be guided to the spot that Guzman clearly recognized, dancing an awkward jig against the rocks that poked at the soles of his feet. It occurred to him at that moment that he had no idea when he'd lost his flip-flops. He knew he had them at the pool, but after that, he had no idea.

Guzman pulled him to a stop and then turned him around to face Silva and the barn behind him. It was pretty much the wreck of a structure that he had imagined, with a roof that looked far more dangerous than it had from the inside.

Silva took his time setting up the camera, pulling the view screen out from the side and making adjustments. Focus, maybe? Zoom? Whatever he saw did not please him. He waved a finger toward Roman and said something in Spanish.

From behind, Guzman swung his fist around and nailed Roman with a punch into the same spot on his eye. Maybe not as hard as Silva's slap, but it wobbled his legs. This time, the big man caught him before he could fall and stood him up again.

Roman's eye wound started bleeding again, and a second stream of crimson joined it from his nose. For the first time since this whole ordeal started, he started to cry.

"Why?" he sobbed. "Why do you keep hurting me?"

Silva seemed pleased. "That's good," he said. "That's very good." He reached into the gym bag, withdrew a few pieces of paper, and hurried them over to Roman. "Here. When I say *action* look into the camera and read this."

The boy's legs started to fold, but again, Guzman propped him up and whispered in his ear, "The sooner you get through this, the sooner the pain will stop." The man let go of him and stepped away.

Roman's left eye was swollen shut now and the vision in his right was blurred with tears. The words he'd been given to read had been drawn in block letters with a bold black marker. It was as if they knew ahead of time that he would have difficulty seeing.

"Look at the camera," Silva instructed, and Roman did his best.

Blood dripped over Roman's lips, and he tried to blow it away, creating a crimson spray.

"That's very good," Silva said. "Do it again when the camera is rolling." He carefully pushed a button.

"Action."

Chapter Thirteen

Jonathan felt an unlikely surge of pessimism—a surge of dread—when he pulled his phone from his pocket. Venice sounded terrible, clearly exhausted and on the verge of tears. As soon as he heard the emotion in her voice, his spirits fell even further.

"Tell me you have good news," he said. Always put a positive spin.

"I have awful news," Venice said, barely able to get the words out.

Jonathan's insides tightened. *Please don't let him be dead.*

"I watched the silver BMW—*the* silver BMW—cross the El Paso bridge into Mexico."

"Were the kids still in the car?" Jonathan and his team were crossing the street outside the police building, on the way to the towering parking lot.

"I couldn't tell," Venice said. "The angle was from too far away."

He tapped Boxers on the shoulder and indicated that he was stopping. "How are you sure it was the same car?"

"We'll get the truck," Boxers said. He and Dawkins left him and headed for the parking garage.

Venice explained, "I tapped into the ALPR database and was able to track their progress—"

"Stop. Which database?"

"Oh, sorry. Automated license plate readers. Those passive cameras on the back bumpers of cop cars?"

Jonathan was familiar with the cameras, but not the acronym for the database. ALPRs were part of the sweeping post 9/11 measures that started as a grand idea but had devolved into a critical element of Uncle Sam's ongoing efforts to spy on its citizens. The cameras collected thousands of license plates per hour and cross-checked them against criminal databases. When there was a hit on a plate number, that vehicle could be singled out and tracked. The grand idea was to catch bad guys. Now, overzealous prosecutors—a.k.a. politicians—had begun to use the data to track the travel habits of their opponents.

"So, I'm very sure," Venice said. "But there's even more, and it gets even worse." Her voice hitched in her throat again. "The last image I have of the BMW is from Abraham Gonzalez International Airport across the border in Juarez. It was purely by luck, but I found the vehicle parked on the tarmac, next to a private jet."

"Oh, shit."

"Yeah. My initial thought was to panic. I mean, starting from an airport, they could go anywhere in the world, right?"

The fact that she was not sobbing—in fact, that she sounded excited—told Jonathan that there was some silver behind the cloud.

Venice continued, "The image caught the aircraft's tail number. The plane landed at Mazatlán International Airport."

"That's in Sinaloa, right?"

"Correct. You guys need to get there."

Jonathan closed his eyes and leaned back against the warm brick wall of police headquarters. This was a horrible turn of events. As bad as the corruption was in the northern part of Mexico, along the U.S. border, it was many times worse in the state of Sinaloa.

"Yeah, okay," he said. He had no idea how he was going to pull that off, but it was the right thing to say.

"Have you spoken with the El Paso police yet?" Venice asked.

"Just leaving there now."

"I'm sure they told you that I called."

"Yes, they did."

"Now, do me a favor and go back in there and tell them that if they'd bothered to listen—if they'd bothered to do their jobs—my boy would have already been saved."

"We'll get him back, Ven. I promise. We'll get them both back."

"You can't know that."

"Focus, Venice." Jonathan made his tone a stern one. "We don't consider failure, remember?" This had been

Jonathan's mantra for as long as he'd been in the business he was in. People work toward their anticipated outcomes. He'd seen far too many soldiers die over the years because their fear allowed them to lose sight of the final victory.

"It's very hard."

"Of course it is. But you have to suck it up. We've got a job to do here, and you're an important part of it. Once I figure out how we're going to get into Sinaloa with all the shit we've got to bring, you're going to be a *very* important part of it."

"Whatever you need, of course."

"Of course. Now, what do we know about the guy in Alvarez's window?"

The question seemed to startle her. Jonathan figured her head was in a different place. "Oh, him. Give me a second." He could hear the clack of her keys and the click of her mouse as she worked her magic on the other end. "Okay, this is interesting. The man's name is Ernesto Guzman. He's a small-time thug but has a long arrest record. And as you've probably already guessed, he has ties to the Cortez Cartel in Mexico."

"No surprise there, I suppose."

"It's worse than you think," Venice said. She relayed what she and Gail had learned about Patrick Kelly.

"So, all roads lead to the cartels," Jonathan said.

"Is it possible that Roman wasn't their target at all?" He heard the lilt of hope in her voice.

"At this point, I think anything is possible."

"Would that be good news or bad news?"

Jonathan took his time answering. He understood that she was terrified and that she needed him to say something reassuring, but he also understood that none of what was happening could be seen as good news. Hope was one thing—everybody needed to have hope—but false expectations were dangerous.

"I don't know how to answer that, Ven. Let's focus on the best news of all—bringing Roman back home to you and Mama."

"Don't let me down, Digger."

Jonathan pivoted the topic to something else. "What's the next step on Patrick Kelly? We need to trace that to ground."

"Gunslinger is on her way over to talk with him."

"How long ago did she leave?"

"Ten, fifteen minutes."

The fact that Patrick Kelly hadn't reached out to the El Paso police bothered Jonathan. He didn't know why, exactly, but it was an inconsistency, and inconsistencies in cases like this were always problematic. People under stress acted in predictable ways, at least within certain bounds. Some panicked, some didn't. Some cried, some went quiet, and he'd even seen a few be overcome with inappropriate laughter. But the one thing that frightened parents always did when their kid was taken was reach out to the cops.

He shared that concern with Venice.

"That's really odd," she said.

"Remember the first rule," Jonathan said. "Everybody always acts in their best interests. At least, their perceived best interests. There's a reason why Kelly didn't call. Please reach out to Slinger and bring her up to speed."

*   *   *

"It's about more than just money now," Monroe said. "I'm afraid Señor Pérez has one more task for you to perform."

"Señor Pérez needs to make a deposit to my bank account. I'm on the hook for a million dollars."

"And a daughter, I'm afraid." The way Monroe uttered the words made Patrick feel cold.

"Has he harmed her?"

"I'm afraid I do not know her status," Monroe said. "And she is with Cristos Silva, not with Pérez. I have no reason to suspect that she's been harmed, but you know how . . . unstable those people can be. You know about his friend Guzman, of course."

Patrick closed his eyes. This couldn't be happening. Cristos Silva had been Pérez's right hand along the border for quite some time. As capable of violence as most of the cartel animals, Silva was nonetheless a reasonable man. A businessman. He saw situations and opportunities for what they were, and not every problem needed to be solved through bloodshed.

But Ernesto Guzman was the opposite of all of that. He was a true sociopath, a true torturer. When rivals needed to be brutalized and returned to their families literally in pieces, Guzman was the one to turn to. He especially liked to break bones with hammers. Those whom he allowed to live often wished that he had not. When certain important daily functions are no longer possible, many would say that life is no longer worth living.

Guzman was a killer without conscience.

Fear and anger welled up like a toxic bubble in Patrick's gut. "I swear to God, if a single hair on my daughter's head—"

"What, Patrick?" Monroe taunted. For the first time, his smile seemed genuine. "What are you going to do? Are going to invade Mexico? Are you going to swoop in and rescue your daughter from people who have made kidnapping and murder a profit center for decades? Pray, tell me how you will do any of those things."

"Then I will kill you."

The smile morphed to a laugh. "No, you won't. I am the remaining lifeline to Ciara. If I so much as get a cold—if I *forget* to call Señor Silva and relay the results of our conversation here—trust me, Ciara will learn many new life experiences."

All of it was too much for Patrick. He had done everything they'd asked of him. He'd fronted the money, he'd said nothing when he knew that they'd taken Ciara as collateral, but he also knew that *they* knew that those steps were unnecessary. Now, everything had changed, and for the first time, he found himself on the wrong side of Silva's sociopathy.

"What of my money?" Patrick pressed. "When the authorities find out that Fernando is gone, I'll lose everything."

"Then you'll need to work quickly to earn it back," Monroe said.

"Earn it back! It's my money!"

"Patrick. Toby. Do you want to scream, or do you want to save your daughter and your bank account?"

Patrick wanted to scream. To lash out. To do *something* to hurt this man. This man and his smugness.

"What is it?" Patrick asked.

"One more task needs to be done before you earn back the money," Monroe said. He pulled his phone from the inside pocket of his suit coat and scrolled through for the item he was looking for. "What does the name Angelina Garcia mean to you?"

"Absolutely nothing." A true statement.

"I will send you some pictures, along with her address and other particulars."

"Who is she?"

"She is a special agent with the FBI. She is the intrepid investigator who has made Fernando Pérez's life a living hell for these past few years."

Patrick's phone buzzed, and he pulled up the pictures. One was an official Bureau photo, the cliché with the famous shield in the background and the American flag off to the side. A second picture showed the same young lady—young, dark haired, could have been a lawyer more readily than a cop—playing in a park with two small children.

"Why are you showing me these?" Patrick asked.

"Because that is the woman you need to kill."

Patrick felt blood drain from his head. His vision sparkled around the edges, and he wondered if he was going to fall down.

"Whoa, Patrick," Monroe said. "Take a seat." He indicated one of the chairs in place to try on shoes.

Patrick sat. "You can't be serious."

"Oh yes I can."

"But I'm not a murderer. I don't even know how to go about killing someone."

"It's not all that difficult," Monroe said. "You walk up and you pop her. Now, getting away with it might be more of a problem."

"She's an FBI agent!"

"Then getting away and staying away may be a very big problem." Monroe smiled again.

"Why?"

"That is a not a wise question to ask to Santiago Pérez. But I imagine it's to deliver a message. Our federal agencies like to think that they are above retribution for the things they do. They sometimes need to be educated otherwise. That would be my guess."

"Then why doesn't he hire an assassin?"

"He doesn't need to," Monroe said. "He has you. Besides, assassins only work for money. You work for passion. For love. For Ciara."

Patrick's mind raced, but it produced nothing. No way out, no real comprehension.

"It would be good for you to work quickly," Monroe continued. "Señor Silva asked me to inform you that while young Ciara is safe and unmolested for now, he cannot guarantee her condition indefinitely."

"How long do I have?"

"How long do you want your pretty young daughter to be in the custody of Cristos Silva and his friend Guzman?"

Patrick's head felt full. Physically full, as if filled with cotton. Or concrete. This was all too much. "Don't look so devastated," Monroe said. "If you can pull it off—you know, just a walk-up and shoot—you've got a great chance of getting away with it. No one will suspect you because there is no real connection between you and Agent Garcia. Don't check out any library books on her, don't ask the neighbors any questions, and for God's sake, don't drive your own car. Wear a hoodie. If you've got one with the logo for a team you hate, so much the better."

"But you will know," Patrick said. It was weakness to show fear, but he saw no other way. "And through Silva, Pérez will know. He will own me forever. So can all of you."

"I assure you I have no interest in owning you. I have no interest in being involved in any of this. You are involved because of circumstance, but after this meeting and my report to Señor Silva, I am out of here."

"How do I do this, Billy?" There it was, the totality of his hopelessness.

"You've got a lot of information in what I sent you about her. Someone has done their research. You've got her address, and you've got her schedule. You've got where she drops her kids off before and after school, and you've got as much as Pérez knows about the kids themselves."

"Who did all this research? And why?"

"Way above my pay grade. I have no idea, and I don't want to know. My guess? They had a backup plan in case you screwed up on the business with the bail bond."

There had to be a way out of this. There *had* to be. If only he had time to think, he'd find it.

While Ciara suffered at the hands of Ernesto Guzman.

"That's all I have for you," Monroe said. He rose from his seat. "I know it's a lot, and for what it's worth, I think they're handing you a shitty deal. Good luck with it."

Patrick sat in his seat, unmoving, until he heard Monroe pull the door open. Then he spun around. "Hey, Billy, one more thing. If I do this thing—no, *when* I do this thing—you be sure to tell Cristos Silva that I'm definitely going to do this thing—do you think they'll really let Ciara go? Will they really put the money into my account?"

Monroe gave him a look that seemed genuinely sympathetic, but he didn't say anything before he disappeared back into the mall.

Chapter Fourteen

"**W**hy were you so mean to him?" Ciara asked in unaccented Spanish. "Roman is a nice boy. Why can't he be in here with me?" She sat comfortably on a sofa in the main salon of Silva's hacienda. She hadn't seen Roman since they were placed in separate compartments on the airplane.

Silva sat nearby at his computer, editing the video he had just shot. "He is lucky that he is alive." Guzman had been stupid enough to walk into the frame once, and that had to be cut. He also needed to edit the sound in a couple of places where Silva himself could be heard giving directions from behind the camera.

"But he didn't do anything to hurt you," Ciara said.

Her voice had a grating, whiny edge to it that caused Silva to grind his teeth. "My business is not your business, young lady."

"I want to go home."

"I am sure you do."

"Where is my father? You told me last night in the plane that he would be here."

Silva clicked the icon to render the video to make it easier to play back. Perhaps if he didn't answer the bitch, she would stop talking altogether.

"Did he really ask you to come and get me?"

You know that he did not, he thought. She hadn't believed it when he'd first told her that—he could see it in her eyes. But when people are frightened, they choose to believe the unbelievable. Knowing that there is a lie is often more comforting than knowing the reality of the truth.

"I asked you a question!" Ciara snapped.

That was it. The step too far.

Silva spun his padded desk chair away from the table he used to support his computer and addressed Ciara face-to-face. "Who do you think you are speaking to?" he asked.

He saw the fear return, and he suppressed a smile. He disliked children in general, and he *hated* those with disrespectful mouths. It was easy to hate every American child. Every American, for that matter.

"Don't just look at me, Ciara," he said, rolling his chair closer. "I asked you a question, and I expect an answer."

Confusion joined the look of fear in her face. "Who do I think you are? I think you are you. Uncle Cristos."

He allowed his smile to bloom. "And you know that that is a fiction, do you not? If you have an Uncle Cristos, I am not he. I am your father's employer."

"Yes, I know, but he told me—"

"He lied to you. I am not a close family friend. I am not even a friend. He does work for me and I pay him."

"But that time at the lake house—"

"That was business." Several years ago, Patrick Kelly'd needed to learn the lesson that he was never out of Silva's sight. Not really. He'd needed to know that even while on vacation, Silva could reach out and touch him. Patrick had concocted a story about them being old friends and had marveled at the coincidence of them running into each other at Deep Creek Lake. Kelly'd done a fine job of pretending to be happy as he invited Silva to stay in the cabin with the family.

"Do you want to know a secret?" Silva asked.

Ciara shook her head. The fear was beginning to overwhelm her now. He liked that. Frightened children were compliant children, and he needed her to stay alive and healthy until she'd served his purposes. Once that was done, he'd have choices.

"I watched you while you were sleeping in the cabin," he said. "You're very pretty when you sleep."

There it was, the flash of terror he'd been looking for. She curled her legs up and hugged herself. "W–why am I here?"

"That is business, too," Silva said. "You are here to help me convince your father to perform a task that perhaps he would otherwise not want to do."

"What kind of task?"

"Again, my business is not your concern."

"I want to go home." Ciara stood. "You can't keep me here."

Silva kicked out with his feet to roll his chair to block her path. "I assure you that I can," he said. "More importantly, I assure you that I will."

Ciara's eyes filled with tears.

"Oh, please," Silva said with a dismissive flick of his hand. "Weep if you must, but understand that I do not and will not care." He gave her a few seconds to absorb the words. "Now, please sit back down."

"Can't you just take me back?"

"That would not be fair to your friend, would it? After all, you are the reason why he is here in the first place." Another pause. "I will not ask nicely again for you to sit back in the sofa."

Ciara remained standing, not taking her eyes off of Silva.

And he would not be the first to break eye contact. Let her understand that he had complete control over her and everything she might do.

Finally, Ciara folded her legs and lowered herself back into the seat cushion, where she drew her legs up again and lowered her face into her hands.

How stupid was this girl? Silva wondered. How could it just now be occurring to her that she was in peril? Did she think that she had special status over Mr. Roman Alexander? Perhaps, since they had met each other in the past, but these dramatics seemed so . . . belated.

A courtesy knock at the front door pulled his attention away from the girl. Guzman entered and walked across the room to the high-top bar that dominated the center of Silva's main room. He placed his sledgehammer on the granite top, its handle pointing to the stamped copper ceiling.

"Is our house guest settled in?" Silva asked.

"Yes. And so you know, when I rechained him, I gave him some bales of hay that he can lean against. I can take them away if you want him to remain uncomfortable."

"No, that is fine. He performed well for us. He has earned a little comfort."

"Have you heard back from his people?"

"I have not yet sent them the video. I will do that soon." Silva heel-walked his chair back to his computer. "Unfortunately, Miss Ciara Kelly over there has been asking the wrong kinds of questions. I believe she has become a flight risk."

In his peripheral vision, he saw her head snap up from her hands. "Please don't hurt me."

"Please don't hurt her," Silva said in a mocking tone. "But do escort her to her bedroom and chain her to the bed."

Ciara gasped. "No! Please."

Guzman approached her, his hands out, and she clamored across the cushion to get away from him.

"Ciara!" Silva boomed. "Stop!"

He rose from his chair and approached her. He stared down at her, his fists on his hips. "If you wish to be treated in the same manner as your boyfriend in the barn, we can accommodate that. I do not wish for it to be so, but I will do what I must. It is up to you. Walk with my friend Guzman on healthy legs or be dragged by broken ones. Which is your choice?"

Gail Bonneville thought Patrick Kelly's house was nice, but nothing special. Nestled among other homes that looked more or less identical to his, the Kelly residence looked less cared for. Other lawns were greener, other flower beds better trimmed.

She drove a different pool car today. They'd already changed out the license plates on last night's vehicle, and by the day after tomorrow, it would be a whole new color and on its way to the car auction. The biggest mistake criminals made when they were breaking the law is that they kept with a pattern. That very pattern was the one that detectives were trained to recognize and follow.

She'd first met Jonathan Grave when she was a sheriff, pursuing him to arrest him, tracking the pattern he didn't even realize he'd established.

She took in as many details as she could as she approached the Kellys' front door. The yard held no toys, so there likely were no small children about. The walkway needed to be edged. Gardening tools and ancient outdoor furniture that clearly had not been used in months if not years cluttered the front porch, concealed from the street by a line of shrubs.

Gail saw no button for a doorbell, so the used the peeling brass knocker. Just three quick raps, nothing urgent. As a last second inspiration, she pulled her FBI credentials case out of her pocket and held it up where it could be seen.

She was reaching again for the knocker when the door opened a sliver and stopped against the chain. An eye appeared in the gap, but not a face.

Gail held up her creds. "Is this the Kelly residence?"

The door closed, the chain slid, and then the door opened again to reveal a woman in her forties who looked like she'd been crying. "Thank God you're here," she said. "Please, come in. Have a seat."

A stairway hugged the wall to Gail's left, and on the

right, the foyer opened up onto a living room, and beyond that, a dining room. The kitchen lay at the back of the house, a straight shot from the doorway. Gail was willing to bet that a family room lay to the left of the kitchen with doors that led to the backyard.

The furniture in the living room had an eclectic feel, and not in a good way. In an early marriage way, where she'd brought her stuff and he'd brought his, and they'd never replaced anything.

Gail headed across the living room to sit in an orange-patterned sofa that judging from the butt-feel had to be a foldout sleeper. She preferred this to the more comfortable-looking La-Z-Boy because this gave her the best view of the door. Never have your back turned to the door if you can avoid it.

"Can you tell me what is happening?" the woman asked.

The question startled Gail. She held up a finger. "First, is this the Kelly home?"

"Yes, of course it is."

"Home of Patrick and Ciara Kelly?"

"Yes."

"And who are you?"

The hostess looked surprised. "I'm Karen Kelly. Patrick's wife."

Karen Kelly was wrapped tighter than a square knot. She sat on the lounger, but on the first three inches, causing the whole chair to teeter forward. She wanted answers.

Gail wanted to know what the question was.

"Please tell me what is going on," Karen said.

"Is Patrick Kelly here?"

"He was, but he's not anymore. He left just a few minutes ago."

Of course he did. "Do you know where he went?"

"He was very upset."

"About what?"

"That's what I was hoping you could tell me. I don't know."

Gail settled herself with a breath. "Let's dial back the clock a little. Why do you think he's upset?"

"I already told you that."

"No, how do you know he's upset? What did he do? What did he say?"

Karen broke under the pressure. She brought her hands to her face and coughed out a sob. Then she got it back together. "We've been married for twenty years. I know when he's upset, and he was upset."

"Angry?"

"More scared, I think. He wouldn't tell me about anything. He just came in, grabbed a rifle and a pistol, and stormed back out to his car."

Gail recoiled. "That's it? He just stormed out with weapons? Was there a phone call first? An argument of some sort?"

"No. When I got up this morning around eight-thirty, he was already gone."

"Does he disappear often?"

"He's almost always out of the house before I get up. I don't have to be to work till one in the afternoon. I'm off today."

"So, when he came back . . ." Gail hoped the lead would inspire more story.

"I saw him pull into the driveway very fast. I thought maybe he was going to be sick or something. He came in through the garage and didn't say anything to me. You know, normally, there's a jokey *hi, honey, I'm home*, but not this time. He just stormed in, went upstairs, and then came down with guns. I asked him where he was going, and he didn't say anything. It was like he didn't even know I was there."

"He didn't mention any names? Didn't say—"

"Anything," Karen interrupted. "He didn't say *anything*."

Gail noticed that there'd been no mention of Ciara going missing. If you're going to be spun up this tight over an issue, that would be the lead one, right? She decided to go for it.

"Do you think this has anything to do with Ciara?"

Karen clearly hadn't been ready for the question. "Ciara? Why would this have anything to do with Ciara?"

Right away, Gail regretted bringing it up. Now she was trapped. You can't mention someone's child in conversation and then not expound.

Then Karen got it. "You're not here about Patrick, are you? Has something happened to Ciara? And who are you again?"

Gail smiled gently as she retrieved her creds case from her pocket. "Gerarda Culp. I'm a special agent with the FBI."

Karen pretended to look at the credentials, but she clearly did not read what she saw. "And what does anything have to do with Ciara? She's in Texas, for heaven's sake."

"I don't know that anything does," Gail said, though

everything had everything to do with everything else. "I'm just following up on a call we received that Ciara and a boy she was with didn't rejoin their group during their field trip."

Karen's eyes narrowed to slits. "She's still on her field trip. I told you that. She's in El Paso, Texas."

"Do your husband and your daughter get along, Mrs. Kelly?"

Panic and anger were forming a stew inside Karen. "Of course they get along. She's our daughter."

"So, she's biological kin?"

"Agent . . ."

"Culp."

"Agent Culp, you'd be wise to—"

"*You'd* be wise to answer my questions," Gail snapped. It was time to play the role of the cop all the way. "I'm not here for my own entertainment, ma'am. I am here hoping to help your husband and your daughter. I'll tell you what I can when it's time, but I'll ask you to dispense with the posturing and answer my questions. Can I be any clearer than this?"

Karen reared back in her chair. "Ask your question again."

"Are you and Mr. Kelly Ciara's biological parents?"

"Of course we are. Do you want to see the birthing pictures?"

"That won't be necessary. Before today, was Mr. Kelly acting strangely? Differently?"

"No."

"You answered too quickly," Gail admonished. "Please give that one some thought. Just for the last day or two. Has he been distracted? Disturbed?"

Karen looked at the ceiling as she considered the question. After thirty seconds or so, she said, "Maybe. I think it's fair to say that he has not been as talkative as usual."

"But not enough so that you were worried?"

"Right."

Gail pulled her notebook from her purse and opened it. "Bear with me for a little while longer, please. I'm going to run some names out, and I'd like you to tell me if they mean anything to you."

Karen answered by rolling her eyes.

"Roman Alexander."

She winced as she thought. "Yes, but give me a minute. Is he a boy from school?"

"Yes."

Karen smiled, as if she'd won a trivia challenge.

"Ernesto Guzman."

"No."

"How about Santiago or Fernando Pérez?"

Karen's jaw clenched. "Yes."

"Tell me."

"Santiago Pérez and Patrick are business associates. They've known each other for years. They don't deal with each other directly anymore, though. There's a middleman. His last name is Silva. He invited himself to our vacation house once."

Gail wasn't interested in hearing about their vacation. "And Fernando?"

"Santiago's son. A real piece of work. He's a nice enough young man, but he's not the sharpest knife in the drawer, if you know what I mean."

"Did you know that Fernando had been arrested?"

"I didn't know, but it doesn't surprise me." She tapped her temple with her forefinger. "Like I said, not a lot of brainpower there."

"You said that your husband and Santiago were business partners. What business were they in, exactly?"

Karen had to think for a few seconds. "Well, you know that Patrick owns several different companies, right?"

Gail said nothing. Sometimes it was best simply to stay out of the way and let people run on.

"Aces and Eights Distribution is an importer and exporter of various goods from down south."

"Down south?"

"South of the border. Our border. Mexico, Central America, South America."

"What kind of goods?"

Karen moved her hands as if balancing the air from one to the other as she searched for an answer. "All kinds, I guess. I always assumed it was the usual. Textiles, toys. You know, all the stuff that comes up from down there."

Gail jotted a note and crossed her legs, right over left. "I'm sorry, but I have to ask. Is your husband in the drug trade?"

"Are you going to tell me what any of this has to do with Ciara's field trip?"

Again, Gail waited for her answer.

"No!" Karen nearly shouted her reply. "My husband is not a drug dealer. How dare you even ask such a thing?"

"Did you know that Santiago Pérez is very much a drug dealer?"

"Bullshit." The word seemed to embarrass her.

"I assure you it is not," Gail said. She kept her tone reserved, almost flat. Matter-of-fact. "And that's not even a secret. Feel free to Google it on your phone if you'd like."

Karen looked stunned. She stared at Gail, speechless.

"He's a lieutenant in the Cortez Cartel out of Juarez and Sinaloa," Gail explained. "And he is not a nice man. In fact, he's very much a murderer."

Realization was beginning to dawn. "Are you connecting Ciara's alleged disappearance to the Mexican drug cartels?"

Gail decided to go for the kill. "Did you know that your husband owns Toby Jackson Bail Bonds, Incorporated?"

"I know he's an investor, but he does not own it."

"No, ma'am, I beg to differ. He owns it outright. That is the company that pays for Ciara's tuition at Northern Neck Academy."

Karen gaped. It was too much.

"A couple of days ago, your husband put up a million-dollar bond for Fernando Pérez, who'd been arrested for distribution of narcotics."

"I–I'm not sure I know what that even means."

"From what I can tell, that is not a sum that you and your family can afford. It is not a decision he would make under ordinary circumstances."

Karen still hadn't embraced what surely was obvious, but Gail felt she had to let her find her own way to the obvious conclusion.

"You're speaking in riddles, Agent Culp. What are ordinary—" Her eyes reddened. "Are you saying that Ciara was kidnapped to make Patrick front this money?"

"It's most definitely what I fear," Gail said.

"Is that why Patrick was so upset?"

"I don't know," Gail confessed. "That—whatever had

upset him—is not the reason why I am here. But in my experience, when two events happen in close proximity, they're almost always connected."

Karen brought her hands to the sides of her head, as if to keep it from exploding. "Oh, my God. What do I do?"

"If you want to find your daughter and maybe save her, you'll let me have your husband's phone number."

Chapter Fifteen

"I don't buy that they took the kids across the border," Boxers said after they'd reassembled in the rental Suburban. "When the cartels want revenge, they kill people. They don't kidnap them. They might drag them off the street for an evening of casual torture, but they're not going for ransom. Certainly, not across the border, with all the risks that come with that."

As Jonathan listened to Big Guy's words, he offered a silent prayer of thanks that Venice wasn't around to hear the torture talk.

"I have to agree," Dawkins said. "Don't get me wrong. The cartels cross the border all the time to kidnap Americans, but those cases are all business executives. Hell, most of the big companies along the border have a budget number for ransoms, and the cartels know it. It's a damned profitable business. Snatching a couple of kids off the street and dragging them across the Rio Grande is way outside the normal business model."

Jonathan nodded as he listened to their theories. They were right. In a twisted way, the cartel business was an honorable one. The rules were clear and they never changed. When the cartels kidnapped someone for ransom, they invariably released their hostage once the money was exchanged. Jonathan hadn't heard of a single case of a double-cross. It was that reliability that made kidnapping such a viable business.

And, on the darker side of the business, everyone knew that the penalty for crossing the cartels involved unspeakable torture and mutilation. And the rules were applied equally for cops and criminals alike.

"We also haven't received a ransom demand," Jonathan said.

Venice's computer dinged with an incoming email, and a notification in a yellow box popped up in the lower right corner of her screen.

EMAIL FROM ROMAN ALEXANDER

Her stomach cramped and her vision blurred as she clicked on the link. The email came in on a public server—not the secured server that they typically used for family business.

As the window opened, she saw that a video file had been attached. As she read the introductory email, her chest tightened, and she wondered if this was what a panic attack felt like.

"Mom,

This is really me and the video is really real.
Please do what they say. And don't worry too
much. It looks worse then it really is. They want
me to tell you that we are in Mexico and there
ready to hurt me really bad."

Her heart hammered against her breastbone as she
tried to open the video file, but her thumb was shaking
too violently against the track ball to get an accurate
click. She finally hit the target on the third try, and right
away, she brought her hands to her mouth to silence her
approaching sob.

He'd been beaten. His left eye was swollen shut, his
shirt was nearly torn off his body, and blood streamed in
heavy drops across his lips and off his chin. He appeared
to be standing in a field, surrounded by grass. The only
distinguishing feature of the terrain was a split rail fence
far in the distance.

As the video started, his gaze was focused off camera,
and then when he got his cue, he looked down at what
Venice assumed to be a script.

"My name is Roman Alexander, and I have been kidnapped. I am in Mexico now and unless you follow these
directions to the letter . . ."

His voice cracked and his lower lip trembled. Venice
hadn't seen him make that face in years. All of the encroaching manhood seemed to have given way to his
inner terrified little boy. She could barely make herself
watch.

Roman choked through the message with a trembling
voice. "Unless you follow these directions to the letter,

they will break my bones one at a time and send me home in pieces." He looked off screen and begged, "Please don't make me do this. I can't do this."

Someone clearly said something, but the audio dropped out for that part as a new terror flooded Roman's face. He shook his head as an emphatic *no*, and when he tried to put both hands out in front of him to ward off what might have been an incoming attack, Venice caught a quick glimpse of the shackles that pinioned his wrists to his waist.

"I–I'm sorry," he said as the sound returned, but it wasn't clear to Venice who he was speaking to. He sniffed, coughed, and spit a gob of blood onto the ground.

He returned his eyes to the script. "The price to get you back—I think that means to get *me* back—is two million dollars. You will receive more instructions soon. Do not call the police, and do not take long. Every hour you delay means more of this."

The camera blinked—a cut in the action—and an instant later, it showed Roman on the ground, his knees up and writing in pain. That image held as a freeze frame, then the screen went black.

Angelina Garcia lived in Old Town Alexandria, a neighborhood of homes that sold for over $700 per square foot, despite the fact that most had built in the era of George Washington. Patrick had visited similar homes a number of times over the years, and he couldn't wrap his head around how people lived every moment of every day in a place that creaked like it was going to break, and the concepts of being square or plumb were entirely alien.

According to the materials given to him by Billy Monroe, she shared the house with her widowed mother and her two children, five-year-old Linus and seven-year-old Paul. The older boy went to public school, while the younger one went to a private preschool during the day. Both ended their afternoons at a daycare program at the St. Agnes Church School, where Angelina would pick them up every day between five-thirty and six.

Patrick had decided that killing her in Alexandria was a nonstarter. Too many people and too many police. Too many cameras on every corner.

No, he'd have to take her out near her workplace at the FBI field office in Manassas, Virginia. The office was more of a campus, actually, located more or less by itself in a newly developed corner of western Prince William County. From the outside, the place looked visitor friendly, but he couldn't help but believe there was crushing security everywhere in and around the building. Certainly, there'd be a bajillion cameras.

He glanced at the sprawling complex as he drove by, but he kept going, never veering off of Prince William Parkway. He saw no reason to draw focus to himself.

Instead, he drove into the Historic District of Manassas City and found a parking spot there where he could wait outside the place he knew Angelina Garcia would soon be visiting.

According to the research, Angelina was a creature of habit, bordering on obsessive-compulsive. Every day of the week had a different lunch spot assigned. Today was Fat Freddie's Fabulous Bar-B-Q, located very near the railroad tracks that ran through the center of town—the very railroad tracks that had twice drawn the Union Army into Manassas during the Civil War, only to have their butts kicked both times.

Angelina would arrive between 12:15 and 12:30, driving her yellow Mini Cooper, and she would depart exactly forty-five minutes later.

Patrick planned to take her out with a rifle shot as she was on her way into the restaurant. Whether he could do this or not was yet to be determined. He told himself that if he lost his nerve as she was on her way in, he'd have a second shot—literally—when she was on her way out.

This was for Ciara, after all. He was *not* performing the dirty work for the Cortez Cartel. He was only trying to defend his family.

Trying to rescue his only child from the grip of a monster.

But first, he needed to bring his heart rate under control. He needed to modulate his breathing. And he needed to look like he wasn't scared out of his mind in case someone walked by.

Oh, shit. What if someone thought he was acting suspicious and they called the police to investigate? How would he explain why he was sitting in a parking lot with a rifle on the passenger seat and a pistol on his hip?

He told himself that he wouldn't have to explain anything. For the time being, this was still the land of the free, and in Virginia, he could have nearly any guns that he wanted.

But they'd see through it, wouldn't they? Patrick had never been a good liar. He'd learned that the hard way as a kid when he'd try to get one past the nuns. They had the most finely tuned bullshit detectors of any people he'd ever known—including his mother, who was also damned hard to fool. If a cop came to his window, he'd sweat and stammer and they'd pull him out of the car and handcuff him because they'd be crazy not to.

"Stop it!" His words were stern, and he'd said them aloud. "Don't borrow trouble. You can do this. You *have* to do this." The biggest danger of all was for him to get all in his head and overthink everything. He knew he was a good shot, and he knew that his scope was sited in at a hundred yards. This shot wouldn't be that far, but the shorter range would only affect the impact point of the bullet by a fraction of an inch.

He planned to go for a center-of-mass shot, so an inch here or an inch there wouldn't matter. Really, *six* inches wouldn't make that big a difference.

He'd brought his Bushmaster AR-15, chambered in .223 caliber. It was a tiny round, but it flew superfast. A quick triple-tap would take care of all the business he needed to transact, and then it would be time to drive off and hope no one saw him.

He'd considered an up-close shot with a pistol, but decided against it. As an FBI agent, Angelina Garcia would be trained in hand-to-hand combat, and that was something at which Patrick righteously sucked. Age and lifestyle, along with an affinity for pasta and beer, had taken away what little athletic prowess he had ever had.

Besides, he figured that someone in Angelina's line of work would be trained to be keenly aware of her surroundings. For a pistol shot to work reliably, he'd have to be within a few yards, and she'd almost certainly notice his approach.

No, the rifle shot would be his best bet. Maybe it was cowardly, but—

His phone rang from inside the cup holder where he'd placed it.

"Come on, Karen, give it break," he said as he reached to cancel the call. He knew that he'd scared her when he flew in and out of the house—the weaponry didn't help—but what was he going to talk to her about? This thing had to happen. They could talk about it later, but for the here and now, words couldn't do anything to help.

Only it wasn't Karen's number.

This one said, PVT NUMBER. Yeah, like he was going to deal with a spam call right now. He pressed the disconnect button.

Jesus, could things get any weirder?

Right away, he thought maybe he'd made a mistake. He'd never received spam calls on this phone before. Or, if he had, he hadn't received many of them. What if things had changed? What if Cristos Silva had come to his senses and changed the rules? Even if the call was coming from Billy Monroe—and that was the most likely scenario, wasn't it—he wouldn't call from his own phone, would he?

No, of course not. He'd use some kind of burner phone. And didn't burner phone numbers all come in as private? Come on, what would be the point of going through all the hassle of getting one if the party on the other end could just call you back?

The phone rang again, this time in his hand as he was watching the screen.

PVT NUMBER.

Shit, shit, shit.

In the end, what choice did he have? He pressed the connect button. "Hello?"

"Is this Patrick Kelly?"

"Who wants to know?"

"This is Special Agent Gerarda Culp with the FBI, and I need—"

He pressed the disconnect button and tossed the phone back into the cup holder as if it had bitten him.

How could they know? He hadn't even done anything yet.

Was this about the bail money, maybe? Had the feds already figured out that Fernando Pérez had bolted from the country? Did they know that he'd cooked the books so that—

The phone rang again.

Let it go to voicemail.

No, you moron. You don't want that shit on your voice-mail.

He snatched the phone up again and pressed the disconnect button without connecting first.

Ciara.

Could this be about Ciara? The FBI was the agency charged with investigating kidnappings. Could it be that they had information about Ciara? Maybe the whole Agent Garcia thing was just a bizarre coincidence.

The phone range again.

Goddammit.

"Ah, screw it." He pressed the connect button.

"Yes, this is Patrick Kelly."

"Don't hang up on me again, Patrick. I can do this all day, but I need your help. It's about Ciara."

"Have you found her?" The question was out before he knew he'd thought it.

"No, but I intend to," the voice said.

"What's your name again?"

"Agent Culp." Her tone sounded reasonable. Helpful. "Tell me what you know."

Patrick opened his mouth to speak, but he couldn't make the words form. To answer her question, he'd have to confess what he'd done.

"Mr. Kelly, I know about the bail money for Fernando Pérez, and I'll tell you right now that I don't care. That is not my case and not my job. My only job is to find your daughter and bring her back home. We have reason now to believe that she has been transported across the border to Mexico. Once there, things get much more difficult and time becomes an infinitely more valuable commodity. Now, what can you tell me?"

Patrick felt as if his brain had cramped. What *could* he tell her? Oh, God, where to even start? What could he *bring* himself to tell her? He didn't know.

"I've spoken with your wife," Agent Culp said. "I know that you and Santiago Pérez are friends and business partners. I know that you were in the import/export business with him, and I promise you that I won't ask anything about the commodities you dealt with. I don't care about them. I care only about Ciara."

Patrick closed his eyes and steeled himself with a deep breath. He knew that cops were liars. He knew that the Supreme Court had ruled it perfectly legal for police officers of all stripes to lie outright to suspects in order to get them to confess to crimes. He *knew* that sharing details with this lady on the phone could get him put away for a long time. At a minimum, he would lose his business and his income. With that, he would also lose his wife.

But if it can help Ciara . . .

Patrick had no choice but to roll the dice. To trust this Agent Culp.

"There's a man," Patrick began. "His name is Cristos Silva. He is an associate of Santiago Pérez, who I imagine you already know is highly placed in the organization known as the Cortez Cartel. He is the man who has Ciara."

He paused, expecting a question or a comment, but driven by silence, he continued.

"Ciara knows Cristos. He has been to our vacation house in the past."

"So, she's with a friend?" He could hear the relief in her voice.

"No. Well, she might think so, but he is not a friend. There's another man. At least one other man. His name is Ernesto Guzman. He is a terrifying man. A murderer. A hit man."

"Whom Ciara does not know?"

"Well, she has met him. Silva and Guzman are rarely far apart."

"You're not being clear, Mr. Kelly. Do you believe she is safe or not?"

"No, she is definitely not safe. I'm sorry I sound so jumbled, but this has been a very difficult day. Let me explain . . ."

Jonathan listened to Gail's conversation with Patrick on his muted phone, along with Boxers and Dawkins. They'd just finished loading the toys into the Hawker when Gail called with the news of her interview with Karen Kelly. They decided together that she should be the one to reach out to Kelly to see what she could find out. Boxers had paired the aircraft's Bluetooth to Jonathan's burner so they could listen on the Hawker's speakers.

Patrick Kelly sounded desperate. Maybe there was some anger in his tone, but it had been pushed away by fear and sadness. Jonathan couldn't help but feel sorry for the guy.

". . . but then they changed the rules on me," Kelly said. "Now it makes sense why they took her. It never was about the bail money. They knew I'd do that. It's this other thing I have to do that they're holding her for."

"Other thing?" Gail asked.

"Yes, but I can't get into that."

"This other thing," Gail pressed. "Does it have to do with the guns you took out of the house?"

Kelly went silent.

"Gotcha, you son of a bitch," Boxers said.

"I–I don't want to get into it."

"Who are you going to kill, Patrick?"

Gail was good, Jonathan thought. Very good. She showed a level of patience in this call that he would have a hard time mustering. He for sure didn't think he'd be able to keep the tone so . . . conciliatory. Kelly had known his daughter was in the grasp of a cartel operator, and he had let it happen. For money. With that kind of information in hand, he could have stirred the El Paso PD into action despite the kids' ages.

"Who said I'm going to kill anyone?" Kelly said.

"He sucks at the phone game," Dawkins said.

"Come on, Patrick," Gail coaxed. "Remember the stakes. This is Ciara we're talking about. Your only child."

"That's exactly my point. That's exactly why I have to do what I have to do."

"Who is it?" Gail pressed. "Who do you need the guns for?"

"I've given you plenty to start hunting Ciara down," Kelly said. "If that's really your intent, you're wasting time on the phone with me right now."

"What happens if you just go home?" Gail asked. "Think about that. Suppose you just go home, go back to your wife? Go back to Karen. Let us work on getting Ciara back. If you kill someone, that will be murder. That will ruin everything for you and your family. It will ruin everything *forever*."

"I never said I was going to kill anyone."

"Come on, Patrick. Don't be obtuse. It's obvious. This Silva guy wants you to kill one of his enemies, and he's leveraging Ciara to make that happen. He's using you."

"He's *allowing* himself to be used," Boxers said. "*Choosing* to be a victim."

"I have no choice," Kelly said. His voice trembled. "If I don't do this . . ." Then his voice faded away entirely.

"Is there a deadline, Patrick? This person you have to . . . This thing you have to do. Does it have to happen before a certain time?"

"Goddammit, didn't you listen?" Kelly's verbal explosion made Jonathan jump. "Guzman is an animal. It doesn't matter what the deadline is. There doesn't have to be a deadline. Every moment with a beast like Ernesto Guzman is a potential death sentence."

"Okay, Patrick, calm—"

"Don't you dare tell me to calm down, Agent Culp. You don't know. You don't have kids, do you?"

Gail said nothing, exactly the right play. Once the interview was rolling, information could only flow in one direction.

"Sledgehammers, Agent Culp."

"Excuse me?"

"That is Ernesto Guzman's implement of choice when he's angry."

"Holy shit," Boxers grumbled.

Jonathan closed his eyes against the image that was forming in his head.

"I've seen him do it, Agent Culp. Have you ever seen what a sledgehammer does to knees and toes? His specialty is not to kill, you know. His specialty is hurting, and he doesn't need a reason to do it."

"But surely your friend can rein him in."

"My *friend* is the one who took Ciara away in the first place. According to Billy Monroe, Cristos Silva is impatient. He wants this to happen, and he wants it to happen soon."

As Gail continued to try to pull information out of Kelly, Jonathan addressed his team. "Are y'all hearing what I'm hearing? That is, Kelly doesn't kill whoever he's supposed to kill, Ciara is toast?"

Nods all around.

"Do we know who Billy Monroe is?" Dawkins asked.

Jonathan and Boxers answered together: "Nope."

"Surely you have a few hours," Gail said. "Just take a step back from the edge and reassess."

A long moment of silence drew them all to look at the speaker. Had they been disconnected?

"Patrick?"

"There's something about me that you need to understand," Patrick said. He had nothing left in his spirit. He sounded utterly defeated. "Agent Culp, I am a coward. And I am selfish. I know these things, and I know that you agree. How could you not? I mean, my God, I talked myself into endangering my daughter for the sake of a little business."

Jonathan expected Gail to intervene, to tell him he wasn't such a bad guy, and was pleased when she did not.

"If I don't do this thing now—if I go home and sit with my wife and have a beer and say a prayer that you guys can get her back—I'll find a way to talk myself out of it."

"Just a few hours," Gail said.

"Do your best," Patrick said. "And I'll do mine."

The line went dead.

After a few seconds, Gail said, "He's gone."

Jonathan unmuted his phone. "Nice job, Gunslinger," he said. "Did you ever consider a career in law enforcement?"

"He's going to kill someone," Gail said. She wasn't in the mood for humor.

"Yeah, I believe he is," Jonathan agreed.

"Maybe it's time to take this to the real cops again," Gail said.

"Absolutely," Boxers said. "Perfect chain of evidence. The facial recognition software that it's a felony to possess led us to a name that's linked to an operation we were able to confirm by burglarizing a school and assaulting a cop after setting off explosives in the parking lot. I'm sure the local prosecutors would be thrilled, but not for the right reasons."

Jonathan saw this conversation heading off the rails, so he moved to intervene. "There was no mention of Roman through any of this, right?"

"Not from me," Gail said.

"What do you think?" Dawkins asked. "Is Roman still—"

"Don't," Jonathan warned.

"Ease up, Scorpion," Dawkins said. "I know the rules. I was going to ask if we think Roman is still with the girl."

"We have to assume that," Jonathan said. "Otherwise, we've got nothing."

Boxers gave Jonathan a look that spoke too many thoughts, and it pissed him off.

"Look," Jonathan said. "I know what y'all are thinking, so let's just get it out in the open, okay? If this isn't about Roman, then there's no reason to keep Roman around. And yeah, that's a way to look at it. But it's *not* the way we're going to look at it. Here's how we're heading forward, and if you disagree, keep your silly-ass opinions to yourselves.

"If they didn't want Roman, they didn't have to take him. They could have left him on the street, or they could have popped him on the spot. They didn't do either of those things.

"And maybe the reason they took him along was to keep him quiet long enough for them all to get away. They didn't want him calling the police and spoiling every friggin' thing.

"So, maybe they took him someplace else and killed him there. Because they're cartel monsters and that's what they do. Have I covered it all so far? Have I missed any permutations?"

Jonathan glared directly at Big Guy, who couldn't hold his gaze.

"Okay, then. We've talked it out. Now, here's the reality. Roman Pennington Alexander is healthy. He's scared shitless, and we're going to bring him home. And I know this to be a fact because I have known him since the day he was born, and I am not going to his mother and tell her that he's dead."

He felt tears pressing behind his eyes, and he swiped them away with an angry flourish. He shifted his glare to Dawkins, who was already engaged in the study of something on the floor.

"And why are you still here?" Jonathan asked.

Dawkins looked startled. "Me?"

"Yeah. You made your introductions, you gave us a place to crash—thanks for that—but what are your intentions from here?"

Dawkins's face pinched up. "I'm still here because I'm going with you. At least I thought I was."

"I thought you had a job," Boxers said.

"Are you trying to get rid of me?"

"No," Jonathan said. "I just don't—"

"Call it revenge," Dawkins said. "I've seen these sonsabitches from a whole different angle than you. My fingertips still hurt on cold days from when they pulled out my fingernails."

"That was a different cartel," Jonathan reminded.

"Different pockets on the same suit," Dawkins replied. "Yeah, I've got job, and it's a damn good one. I get to help Uncle Sam move at a glacial pace to bring justice to those assholes in a court of law where they'll probably never show up. Working with you guys is more . . . satisfying."

"Hey," Gail said over the speaker. "I'm outta here. I've got to go knock on some doors."

The line went dead, and Jonathan kept his eyes on Dawkins. They'd worked together before and he was a good operator. But the more times they tapped that well, the more Thor learned of their operations. And the more he knew, the more vulnerable they could all be.

"I don't know what this hesitation is all about, and I'm not going to beg for the chance to risk getting shot up, but if you're heading to Mexico—especially if you're heading to Sinaloa—I know people who can help flatten the discovery curve. It's your call."

Roman's clock was ticking faster and faster. If Dawkins could help them move farther faster, then there really wasn't much of a decision to be made.

"Okay," Jonathan said. "Welcome aboard. Again."

Chapter Sixteen

Less than a minute after they'd disconnected from Gail, Jonathan's phone buzzed with an incoming text message from Venice. "*Check your email and get back to me ASAP.*"

"Uh-oh," Jonathan said. This was odd at two levels. One, Mother Hen rarely texted him unless it was directions for his GPS. She preferred phone calls, as did he. And two, she rarely deployed urgent pleas like "ASAP."

"What's up?" Boxers asked.

"I don't know yet." The message from Venice was essentially a forwarded email from Roman. "Roman found a computer. Maybe this isn't as bad as we thought."

After reading the introduction, all three of them shared a look of dread.

When the video was over, Boxers said, "We're not

going to Mexico anymore. We're friggin' *invading* Mexico."

The video changed everything. Any lingering doubt about the stakes had just been obliterated.

Roman's script had mentioned nothing of the cartels, but the language and the imagery—breaking bones and sending the body home in pieces—were dark with cartel fingerprints. And since the cartels were involved, there was no way in hell that Mexican law enforcement officers would lift a finger. Not an effective finger, anyway. They had their own families to think about. God knew they couldn't make ends meet on their salaries alone, and they wouldn't want to give up that lucrative second income they earned by simply not seeing anything illegal going on.

"Are you going to pay the ransom?" Boxers asked.

"If it comes to that, sure," Jonathan said. A million here, a million there, Jonathan couldn't outlive his money in three lifetimes.

"Be careful," Dawkins said. "A lot of this does not fit the cartel model. First of all, Roman was not the target of the hit. That was Ciara Kelly, and the purpose was not money. It was influence. That's the first departure."

"The cartels are terrible people," Jonathan said. "But they always pay their bills."

"Who's to say these guys who have Roman are even with the cartel?" Dawkins asked.

Jonathan's phone buzzed again, this time with a call from Venice. He put it on speaker. "Hi, Ven. How're you holding up?"

"What are you going to do?" As blunt and direct a question as he'd ever heard from her.

"The mission hasn't changed," Jonathan said. "We're getting him back."

"Are you paying the ransom?"

"I will if it comes to that," Jonathan said.

"How can it not come to that?"

"Have you gotten the terms yet?" he asked. He wanted to push the conversation back to current action, not hypothetical decisions.

"Not yet."

"Okay, then, for the time being, we stay on the course we've charted," Jonathan said.

Venice fell silent on the other end of the line.

"Mother Hen? Are you there?"

"It occurs to me," she said in a heavy tone, "that you've always said it was a mistake to pay the ransom."

Jonathan's breath caught in his chest. He had, indeed, always said that.

"You said that once a ransom is paid, all the advantage goes to the bad guy. You said that when the reason to keep people alive goes away, so do people's lives. I believe that that is your pithy quote."

Jonathan glanced at Boxers and got a silent *Don't pull me into this*.

"I don't know what you're looking for, Ven."

"Let's start with an honest assessment," she said. "The rules don't change just because he's my son."

"Actually, they kinda do," Jonathan said. "I've known you both since you were born."

"Then pass command to someone else," Venice said. "I need you to think clearly."

"I think I'm thinking as clearly as I can with as little information as we have," Jonathan said.

"I know you have a plan," she said. "You always have a plan."

How could she read his mind like that? "I think it might be too generous to call it a plan," he said. "Think of it more as a template."

He explained that he'd done similar operations in the past. The weakest moment for the bad guys in any ransom exchange was the exchange itself. Transferring money could be done remotely and at the speed of light. The physical transfer of a person, on the other hand, required someone to show themselves, if only it was the hostage.

Then there was the timing of events. When a hostage transaction was truly about money and not some international political bullshit, the deposit of the funds and the transfer of the hostage had to happen simultaneously if they were going to happen at all. The kidnapping industry among the cartels had put a whole new spin on the meaning of "Mexican standoff."

Jonathan's play in the past had been to take positions at the handoff location well ahead of the scheduled transfer. If everyone played by the rules, the bad guys got rich on ill-gotten gains and the hostage got to go home to his or her family. If the bad guys broke the rules, it came down to marksmanship to make sure that the hostages were not killed in the crossfire.

"This is a high-risk game," he concluded. "A dangerous game."

Venice asked, "Suppose the rules of the transfer don't meet your criteria?"

"Sooner or later, they always meet the criteria," Jonathan said. "We're talking lots of money, and these dickheads love their money. There might be some negotiation in the middle, but sooner or later, we'll get what we need."

"Meanwhile, Roman continues to suffer." Venice's voice cracked again.

Jonathan hated speaking to frightened parents. It was never his strong suit. Now that the frightened parent was essentially family, he hated it even more. But she had a right to know the facts for what they were.

"This is a shit sandwich, Ven," he said. "There's no good way to eat it, and it's going to be damned unpleasant. But we need to face some basics. First, that beating they laid on Roman? That was for the benefit of the camera. We know that because the blood was still flowing."

"And they said they'd keep beating him until they got the ransom."

"That doesn't make sense," Boxers said, earning an angry look from Jonathan.

"I've got this, Big Guy."

"I'm just sayin'," Boxers continued. "For now, he's an important asset to them. Makes no sense for them to bust him up so long as he doesn't try to get away or pull some other stupid shit."

Dawkins added, "And from the brief glimpse we got of his shackles, that's not likely."

On the other end of the phone, Venice snuffled.

"We've never lost a PC," Jonathan said, referring to *precious cargo,* the hostages they'd rescued over the years. "We're sure as hell not starting now. The instant you hear from them again, let me know. Do *not* respond on your own, and do not get the police involved."

"Suppose they can help?" she asked.

"Think it through. We've walked this walk dozens of

times. Now that this is an international incident, not only are federal law dogs gonna want in on it, we'll have to deal with State Department pukes, too. Chances are good that we're going to have to break some things and hurt some feelings before this is all over. We don't need that kind of paper trail. And Roman doesn't need that kind of delay."

"What do I do if they call?"

Interesting question. Jonathan couldn't imagine that happening under the circumstances, but this was a bizarre op already. What's a little more bizarreness?

"I can't tell them that we'll call them back," Venice pushed when he didn't say anything for a few seconds.

"No," Jonathan agreed. "I don't suppose you can. If it comes to that, tell them that you don't know where I am at the moment and that you're tearing up the world trying to find me. Obviously, you're going to record the call and do everything you can to track it down, but they won't know what your skills are. Treat the contact as a research opportunity. Gather every bit of data you can find.

"If he dumps out a lot of information on where to make the pickup, trace all that down and give us as much info as you can. Here is the key element, and you cannot forget this: No boy, no money. Hard stop. They need to provide real-time proof of life. The instant they do that is the instant that we get Roman back."

It was Venice's turn to be silent.

"Talk to me, Mother Hen. Are we on the same page?"

More silence. Then: "Yes."

"Okay, I gotta go. Remember, don't let thirty seconds pass between the ransom details and getting in touch with me."

He clicked off.

"A little abrupt there, don't you think, Boss?" Boxers asked.

"We've got shit to do," Jonathan said. "Holding her hand is not even on the list." He turned to Boxers. "Your turn, Big Guy. We've got to get fly a thousand miles or so into Mexico, and we've got to get there with guns and ammo."

"Whoa," Dawkins said. "Then what? Knowing what airport they flew into hours and hours ago is a big step from knowing where they are. It's a big country. How are you going to find two people who may or may not even be there?"

"I don't have an answer for that yet," Jonathan said. "But we do have names. We have Ernesto Guzman, the guy who stopped Alvarez, the RoadRunner driver. We've got his boss, Cristos Silva, and we've got somebody named . . . What was it?"

"Billy Monroe," Dawkins reminded. "And I know the names Guzman and Silva. Maybe there's a way to track them down."

"These are names," Big Guy said. "More one-offs. It's a big country, remember?"

"Not necessarily," Dawkins said. "This Guzman dude has some connection to the Cortez Cartel, right? By definition, if we stay consistent with our assumptions, that means he's got to be dialed into the bad-guy network south of the border. DEA is not completely blind in that network. Just the opposite, in fact. We've been infiltrating with various levels of success for years. That means he's not just another random guy." Dawkins seemed excited. "He's a bad guy with connections that I might be able to leverage."

"You tellin' us you have a key to the front door of the Bad Guy Club?" Boxers asked.

"If not to the front door, then certainly to a window. A good friend of mine runs a watering hole down at Mazatlán, not far from the airport. If she doesn't know Ernesto Guzman, she can probably point us in the direction of someone who will."

"How good a friend is she?" Jonathan asked.

Dawkins smiled and winked. "Good enough to make sure the blade is sharp if she has to cut my throat."

"Hell, I have relatives I don't like that much," Boxers said.

"Back to you, Big Guy," Jonathan said. "What do we have to do to go across the border?" Jonathan asked.

Angelina Garcia loved her car, though she took a lot of heat for it. Most of her colleagues preferred SUVs, and those who didn't mostly seemed to go for tree-hugging hybrids. Her Mini Cooper was neither large nor especially fuel efficient, but it was as cute as could be. She'd fallen in love with the brand after the first of the Bourne movies with Matt Damon, and she'd owned three since then. She considered it to be a dachshund of a car—you wanted to laugh at the looks until you realized what a hearty beast it really was.

Today, she was running later than she'd like, but her boss had bombarded her with a thousand questions about the Pérez case, and he was not a man to walk out on just to feed your face with barbecue. Although that's exactly what she was about to do.

She only had forty-five minutes. She had a conference call with Washington at 1:30, and that was something to be very, very prepared for. In truth, she probably should have just eaten on campus today, but to hell with that. This was Fat Freddie day, and come hell or high water, she was not turning away from his Carolina-style pulled pork. It was really that wonderful.

Ray Jacobs, her boss, had his Jockeys in a knot over the fact that Fernando Pérez made bail. They needed his testimony, or they needed him to rot in jail. Preferably both. Having him run around free—even on a million-dollar bond—was nobody's preference, and the U.S. attorney's office had made that clear to the judge.

It wasn't Angelina's fault that judges don't always listen to prosecutors, but Ray Jacobs was the kind of guy who had to hold someone under him responsible for any shit that might flow down on him. Ray was a special leader that way.

She prayed every night that she'd get her transfer to Salt Lake City. One of the many quirks that separated her from most of her fellow agents was the fact that she had no desire to one day become a special agent in charge of anything. And she certainly did not aspire to any job in any corner of headquarters in Washington. The Northern Virginia Resident Agency was close enough, thank you very much.

Like any other bureaucracy as vast as the FBI, climbing the ladder meant crawling up your own ass while kissing the asses of others. The brass had somehow lost touch with the real world, and Angelina didn't want that to happen to her. She got into this business for all the recruitment poster reasons. Truth, justice, the American way. All that sappy stuff.

She'd done damn good work so far with the Pérez case. She'd ridden Fernando like the cowgirl she once was—and would be once again, when she settled on the spread she'd bought in Utah. She was the one who made Fernando break, made him lose focus and drop his guard. His father never would have discussed the details that Fernando had. He'd thought he was among friends, and he was pissed that Angelina had left him so little room for error.

He should have known that every breath he'd taken in the past six months had been watched, recorded, and cataloged. Such was the price for bringing poison across the border for distribution to little kids. Such was the price for financing the trafficking of children across the border, only to then rent them out an hour at a time to American psychos.

Angelina was doing God's work on earth, and she was proud of it.

But she was ready for a change. Everything about Washington, DC, and its suburbs was bad for kids. Raised in overprivileged and self-important affluence, Northern Virginia kids learned not to respect anything but their own feelings and priorities. Raised so close to politics, they learned that there's nothing wrong with lying, so long as the lies served to benefit themselves and their friends. It was a toxic place, and she was ready to punch out.

Fat Freddie's took up both floors of an ancient building that sat within fifty yards of the railroad tracks. Famous not just for his barbecue and beer, Fat Freddie Franklin had built a reputation in Prince William County as a philanthropist. Every week, he sponsored a fundraiser for one cause or another. He had a special warm spot for first responders and military, so that made the mega-calories go down a little easier.

The fifteen-minute delay in her arrival had made a difference. The lot was way more full than it normally was.

She spied a spot reasonably close to the building, but closer to the Dumpster than she liked. *Better to walk a little farther than inhale the stink of grease and garbage*, she thought. She kept looking.

Patrick Kelly saw the Mini Cooper the instant it turned the corner a block away. How could he not? It was a shade of yellow that just shouldn't happen. Having nearly given up on her, he felt real relief that she'd finally arrived.

As she approached, though, the relief turned to dread. *You can walk away from this.*

Was that the smart thing to do or the cowardly thing? *It's for Ciara.*

If he didn't go through with this—if he didn't commit *murder*—then wouldn't he be causing the murder of his only child?

None of this was right. None of it was fair. This wasn't what he'd signed on for when he agreed to help Pérez and Silva. It was outrageous for them to put him in this position.

The Mini Cooper slowed as it entered the parking lot, which was crowded with many times the number of cars he'd expected to see in a town so small in the middle of the day.

He could do this. The key was to not hesitate. Not even for an instant.

As he leaned to his right, his hand found the pistol grip for his AR-15. He'd only shot it a few times at the range, but he knew how it worked. The magazine was in place in the well, but the dust cover was closed. He didn't know if the bolt was closed or not. He didn't know if there was a round in the chamber, for that matter.

The Mini Cooper appeared to veer toward a close-in parking spot, but then the driver changed her mind at the last second and turned away. Now she was headed toward Patrick's car.

"Oh, shit," he said aloud. He was counting on a long shot—the longer the better, as far as he was concerned. Scanning the lot himself, the only slots he saw for her were along the back row. His back row. That would put his prey only twenty or thirty feet away from him.

He needed to move quickly. Keeping the rifle out of view, below window level, he wrapped his left thumb and forefinger around the charging handle and cycled it. He jumped when a bullet leapt from the breach and twirled into the passenger side window.

The gun had been chambered the whole time.

He reseated the charging handle and pressed the bolt release. At first, he was concerned that the bolt didn't snap closed, but then he realized that it already was. He needed to settle himself down. Needed to breathe.

Patrick could see Angelina's face now. She looked just like the pictures from the research packet Monroe had emailed him.

Only now she was three-dimensional. Now she was real flesh, and her hair showed movement. Her eyes blinked.

She had two little boys to raise, and her husband was dead. Killed by an IED in some town in Afghanistan that Patrick couldn't pronounce when he read it.

Patrick took comfort in the fact that the boys would

have each other after their mother was gone. And they'd have their grandmother. He knew they all lived together. He knew the neighborhood where they lived, and they clearly had money. The boys would be fine.

Ciara, on the other hand, would be ravaged and beaten if he did not go through with this. God only knew the tortures she would endure.

"Stop thinking about it," he told himself. "Stopthinkingstopthinkingstopthinking . . ."

Angelina swung her tiny car wider than she needed to get it lined up with the parking spot she'd chosen. As she eased in, her head turned, and she looked right at him.

It was as if she knew. Perhaps the intensity of his glare had drawn her attention. He'd heard of things like that happening. That supernatural stuff. That supernatural *bullshit*.

Timing would be everything. She had to be standing, and she had to be looking elsewhere when he slid out of his seat, shouldered his rifle and pumped rounds into her until she fell.

He wished now that he'd had the presence of mind to back into his parking space to make his getaway easier, but it was to late to worry about that now.

Why was she taking so long?

Angelina didn't like the way that guy in the Ford was looking at her. It wasn't an ogle or anything remotely flirty. Not really predatory, either. Frightened, maybe?

She'd picked up his gaze right after she'd abandoned the parking space by the Dumpster. First, she noticed that he was sitting in the car in the first place. Why would someone be sitting alone in a car in a restaurant parking lot? She supposed he could be waiting for someone, but how would that someone even be able to find him way back here?

At first, she decided that it was none of her business, but then she saw the cast of his eyes. They really were following her.

As she got closer, she noted how he was listing in his seat to his right. He appeared to be trying to hide something.

It was damned suspicious behavior, for sure. When she got inside, maybe she'd place a call to the Prince William cops to have them cruise through the lot and check him out. From what Angelina could tell, there was no reason to suspect a federal crime in progress, so she had no jurisdiction to investigate.

And if he was hanging out to mess with her, well, it hadn't yet been forty-eight hours since she'd kicked the ass of her regular sparring partner. One of the conditions she'd set for herself for her return to real fieldwork was to sharpen her ground fighting skills. Most agents never dealt with any of that stuff after the academy—and certainly not after their thirtieth birthday, give or take—but she wanted to be the agent she'd always dreamed of being.

As she shoved the gearshift into PARK, she paused for a moment and peered through the windows of the adjacent car to see if the guy in the Ford was posing any kind of threat.

He was looking straight out through his windshield. Listening to the radio, maybe? Talking on the phone? His lips weren't moving, but that didn't mean he wasn't listening to the other end of a conversation.

To hell with it. Fat Freddie's barbecue was only fifty yards away, and her clock was ticking.

The rifle lay across Patrick's lap. He held it by the barrel shroud, the grip hovering on the far side of the center console. With the Mini Cooper so near and with its driver looking at him as she was, there was no way for him to position the weapon properly without it being seen.

That was okay, though. He had a plan. As he slid out to his left, he would drag the rifle across and get a proper grip. By the time he positioned himself for the shot, everything would be fine.

What was happening? The Mini Cooper had been stopped for probably thirty seconds now. Why wasn't she getting out? He knew better than to look because his gut told him that she was watching him.

Was it getting hard to breathe, or was that his imagination?

Movement.

She was out of the car. This was it. This was his moment. He waited until she was clear of her vehicle.

She closed her door. She stretched her back. She turned away from him.

He pulled the latch on his.

In a few seconds, this would be over.

Angelina glanced at the Ford as she climbed out of her car, disguising the glance as an extended stretch of her back. The guy hadn't moved. He just continued to stare.

She followed his eyeline. There wasn't anything out

there. Certainly, nothing that would rate such intense examination. Could it be that he was avoiding her gaze? Could it be that she'd embarrassed him when she looked at him, and now, he just wanted her to go away?

Surely, that was it.

Or, was she being surveilled?

She settled herself. One of the complications of being in her line of work was a strong streak of paranoia. With the various shake-ups the Bureau had seen in the past few years, it was hard not to feel jumpy. The director's own bodyguard had betrayed her, for God's sake. At least, that was the rumor that no one spoke of aloud.

This was stupid.

She started for the restaurant, even though her appetite had dimmed.

Behind her, her left channel picked up the click of a door opening.

It had to be her guy because there wasn't anyone else out there.

Just ignore it, she told herself. The guy was probably harmless.

But her Spidey-sense wouldn't let her. She pivoted her head for a nonthreatening peripheral view, and right away, she knew something was wrong.

It was the way he moved. It was too fast. Too . . . sideways.

Holy shit, did he have a rifle?

Patrick knew he'd been made as soon as she started walking. Her stride wasn't right. She was watching him without wanting him to know.

He had to move now. If he didn't move *right now*, he'd lose his nerve entirely. Besides, she knew. Made no sense to go back now.

He opened his door and slid out of his seat, pulling the rifle with him, but the sling caught on the shift lever.

"Goddammit," he muttered. He leaned back in and freed it. Only cost him a couple of seconds. He moved his hand to the AR-15's pistol grip and stepped clear of the door.

Just like being at the range, he swung the stock up to his shoulder, settled the reticle of this scope on his target.

But the target was ducking for cover.

"Shit! Oh, goddamn!" Angelina heard the words out of her mouth before she knew she'd said them.

It *was* a rifle! What the hell?

She squatted low and went for cover.

Amazing what you can notice in the time of a shutter flash. Black rifle. AR15 of some sort. Glass scope.

Angelina knew from a dozen different training classes that cars made miserable sources of cover under any circumstances, but they were particularly useless against any kind of rifle. Especially when the rifle was only twenty feet away.

Her only chance was to put an engine block between her and the shooter. She squatted in front of a high-end Mercedes, vaguely aware of how much the emblem on the hood resembled a target.

When the shooter opened up, it was perhaps the loudest noise she'd ever heard. He fired over and over again, and with each report, she felt the impact reverberate through the frame of the vehicle and into the Mercedes's engine.

Somehow, her SIG-Sauer nine-millimeter had materialized in her hand. Honest to God, she didn't remember drawing it.

She needed to shoot back. He'd be advancing on her, and if she wasn't prepared, she'd die cowering in the parking lot of a place named Fat Freddie's. That was not the obituary she'd dreamed of.

The shooting went on seemingly without end.

Angelina belly-crawled back toward her own vehicle—the direction she figured the shooter would not anticipate.

She popped up for her shot probably before she should have, before she'd re-established effective cover, and there he was, pounding away at the spot where she no longer was.

She brought her SIG up to a shooting position just as he saw her. He pivoted his rifle to shoot.

Angelina did a mag dump on the guy. Her pistol bucked over and over in her hand, and she could see her rounds tear into her assailant. The first two tore into his hands. Such a cliché. They say that in a gunfight, people always shoot the thing that scares them, and the gun is always in the hands. As the shooter dropped the rifle, she saw his shirt and suit coat dimple with impacts, and then he was gone from sight.

Never breaking her aim, Angelina dropped her spent magazine onto the asphalt parking lot and replaced it with one from her belt.

Her hearing was gone. Her vision was blurred, and she didn't think it was possible for her heart to hammer any harder. Her eyes never left the front sight of her pistol. If this guy had somehow survived and he stood up, she was going to cut him in half.

With the pistol at high-ready and her elbows locked, Angelina sidestepped back in front of the Mercedes with its shredded hood, and when she cleared its side, she got her first good look at her shooter. He lay on his back, wedged between his opened door and a blue Chevy parked next to him. His head was propped up by the Chevy's tire, his chin resting on his chest as blood pooled around him.

Angelina still approached carefully. Call it horror movie syndrome, but if he sat up now, she knew that she would shit herself on the spot.

But he didn't move.

His eyes were open, pupils fixed.

Angelina kicked his rifle away with her right foot and holstered her pistol. Protocol called for cuffing the body, just in case, but she didn't have any cuffs on her.

As the sound of sirens crescendoed around her, she double-checked to make sure her badge was visible. The local cops were going to be spun up pretty tight.

As she pulled out her phone to call her boss, she sent up a prayer of thanks that voice dial was a thing. No way would she be able to dial with her hands shaking like this.

Chapter Seventeen

Jonathan and Boxers had spent the bulk of their Army careers as operators for the First Special Forces Operational Detachment-Delta, or the Unit, engaged in missions that never officially happened. Before the 9/11 attacks changed everything, many of those missions took them to Mexico and Central America to harass drug lords and bring justice for people who so rarely saw it from their own leaders.

For decades, the state of Sinaloa had been the epicenter of drug smuggling, providing much of the infrastructure necessary to transport raw product produced in Central America up to the southern border of the United States, and from there to be distributed across the Fruited Plain.

Over the years, that mission had transitioned from the military to the Drug Enforcement Administration, where enforcement and interdiction was uneven at best and entirely dependent upon whose butt sat in the big chair in the Oval Office. Under the Darmond administration, no one seemed to care all that much about porous borders and the streams of poison and damaged children that flowed into American commerce.

Still, the infrastructure that supported the days of strong enforcement survived, ready for the inevitable return to sanity.

Boxers had a good memory for individual elements of that infrastructure, and a phone call to Papa Smurf, an old friend who still toiled in the shadows, confirmed that a runway cut into the forest a long time ago was still functional and was capable—though barely—of handling the needs of their Hawker 500.

They approached in the dark, flying as low and as slow as possible to mimic the flight characteristics of the much smaller airplane that approach radars had been fooled into believing they were. Papa Smurf had marked the runway for them with infrared strobes, allowing them to land without lights, using night vision instead.

The old barracks building was still there, though it provided shelter for every species of animal other than human. Jonathan was not interested in exploring that.

Papa Smurf had even delivered on his promise to have a locally registered Dodge Durango waiting for them.

Favors in this part of the world always came with a hefty price tag—made even heftier by the shortened time frame—but with cash came reliable results.

On Jonathan's order, they stayed in the aircraft until after sunrise so that they could all get some sleep. Besides, transporting all the gear from the Hawker to the

Durango in the middle of the night, using only night vision, was an invitation for trouble.

"How often do you DEA boys come this far south to play?" Jonathan asked as they were loading toys into the Durango.

"Not as often as we should," Dawkins said. "Not as often as we're going to, once the big boss is voted out of the Oval. Maybe even sooner, if word of the tourist abductions leaks out."

In recent months, even the high-dollar tourist attractions had become hotbeds for criminal activity. For Americans in particular, kidnapping was the most significant risk, but those abductions were often accompanied by other violence. When victims resisted, they died at an alarming rate. The U.S. State Department had had a travel advisory in place against most of the northern half of Mexico for the better part of a year now.

Local gun laws were so draconian that possession of even a single bullet could get you put away for most of a lifetime, so no one was able to defend themselves against the gangsters who terrorized the country. The cartels owned the cops and the politicians, who cooperated by making sure that the populace was unable to resist or defend themselves.

"I thought drug raids were picking up," Boxers said. "I read that somewhere."

"Staged for the cameras," Dawkins said. "Every now and then, President Darmond makes noises about Mexican corruption, and the politicos down here do their little dance. The press takes pictures and then loses interest."

Jonathan hated all of it. "When I'm elected king, I'm going to make hypocrisy a capital crime," he said. "I don't care if some asshat politician swings for the fences and whiffs the shot, so long as it was an honest swing."

"I've got my money on pigs flying before politicians stop lying," Dawkins said.

Boxers laughed. "Mine's on pigs flying before Digger is elected anything."

Once they were loaded up and ready to go, Jonathan turned to Dawkins. "Tell me more about this contact of yours."

"Not much to tell, really. She's talented at working all sides against each other and always coming out on top in the end. You'll get it when you meet her."

"Has she got a name?" Boxers asked.

"Sofia Reyes. And before you ask, I have no idea if that's real or a pseudonym."

Dawkins directed them to a place called La Lagartija. Calling it a dive bar would be generous. Barely one story tall, the place appeared to be constructed of recycled siding, with random splashes of pastel blues, greens, and oranges. A covered porch wrapped around the entire exterior, furnished with an eclectic collection of once-abandoned furniture. Everything from overstuffed loungers to folding card table chairs. About half the chairs were occupied, and of those, about half of the occupants were passed out.

"La Lagartija," Jonathan said. "The lizard?"

"The *little* lizard," Dawkins corrected.

Jonathan pointed through the windshield as they cruised the parking lot. "Is that a cop car?"

"Of course," Dawkins said. "It's a cop bar. But it's also a bad guy bar. Fees have to be negotiated somewhere, and with listening technology improving the way it is, the old-fashioned text messages and phone calls are too risky anymore."

"So, the cartel guys are brazen enough just to do business face-to-face?" Boxers asked.

"We can't even call it an open secret anymore," Dawkins said. "The secret part doesn't even exist. But if anyone can point us in the direction of Silva and Guzman, Sofia's the one."

"Isn't it going to be a bit awkward for her to give us information in front of her customer base?" Jonathan asked.

"Oh, they won't stick around when we enter," Dawkins said. "Believe it or not, the cartels are still a little bit afraid of us. The DEA and FBI still make them nervous. I always thought it was my good looks, but I think the badge has something to do with it."

"Why be afraid of Americans?" Boxers asked. "We don't have jurisdiction down here."

"No, but we can make their lives uncomfortable. Nobody likes to look up and see a drone watching them."

"Do you actually do anything with the drone footage?" Jonathan asked.

"I don't know. Whether headquarters does or not is above my pay grade. All I know is nothing changes. The bad guys get richer and more people keep dying. Good times."

Boxers nosed the Durango into a spot between a '70s-era Harley and a fairly new S-Class Mercedes. "I've been to worse places," he said.

Dawkins said, "If you're packing, you'd better keep 'em covered up."

"Oh, we're packing," Boxers said. "And I'll do my best."

Jonathan said, "Historically, attempts to disarm Big Guy have not gone well for the disarmers."

"Remember, there are cops in here."

"Crooked ones," Jonathan said.

"They still look after their own."

"I promise we'll do our best to be good," Jonathan said. "But let's not lose sight of the stakes, okay? There's a terrified boy out there somewhere whose fuse is burning very short very fast."

Jonathan's first thought as they crossed the threshold into the bar was that it smelled like Mexico. Old food, stale sweat, and booze. He'd stipulate that there were probably better places—there'd almost have to be—but in his line of work, he never got to spend any time in them. Three seconds in, he could feel the sweat blooming on his back. It had to be eighty-five degrees in here. Perhaps as an accommodation to the heat, perhaps for privacy, the light was way too dim, lending a sepia tone to all of the pastels on the walls.

"Opening a window might help," Boxers grumbled.

"Don't want to let the flies out," Jonathan said.

"Please behave yourselves," Dawkins said.

As they took a couple more steps inside, conversation stopped and heads turned. Tough to tell whether it was because they were gringos, as Dawkins had predicted, or because Big Guy's head nearly brushed the low ceiling. "*Hola*," Jonathan said.

Back in their days in the Unit, Jonathan and Boxers had spent far too many years on deployment in Central America, taking care of business that Uncle Sam officially had no hand in. Both of them spoke fluent Spanish, albeit with accents. Jonathan's words had a Colombian flare to them, while Boxers' carried a trace of South Carolina.

Saying *hello* had the effect of hastening the departure of about half of the dozen or so people in the bar. Behind the bar, a large woman with hard features pushed a rag in large circles across the chipped and ring-stained surface.

"*Hola*, Sofia," Dawkins said with a little wave.

The barkeep's face showed a flash of recognition, but she remained silent as she watched them.

All but one of the customers were men, and the one who wasn't looked like she wanted to go to sleep. Maybe seventeen years old, her eyes looked at once empty and frightened.

"Excuse me," Jonathan said to his team, and he walked toward the exhausted girl.

"Hello, Miss," he said in Spanish.

The man she was with stood up and went chest-to-chest with Jonathan, maybe twelve inches separating them. "Get away from us," he said, also in Spanish.

"I don't want any trouble," Jonathan said.

"Then go away."

"In a second," Jonathan said. He stepped to the side to see past the guy he would bet money was her pimp. "Miss, you don't look well. Are you—"

The protector planted a hand on Jonathan's chest. "I already told you—"

Jonathan fired a piston of a punch from down low into the pimp's gut, driving all the wind out of his lungs. The guy collapsed back toward his chair, only he missed it and ended up doing a butt-plant on the sticky tile floor. To anyone watching, it would appear that the guy had had a seizure.

Jonathan stepped around to get closer to the girl, while Big Guy moved closer to the pimp. The guy wouldn't be getting up for a minute or two—until he could breathe again—and the towering presence of Boxers might encourage him to fake injury for a while longer.

The girl scooted her chair back to pull away from Jonathan.

He held up his hands. A gesture of friendship. "I mean no harm," he said. "Mind if I sit down?"

She clearly didn't know what to say, and it wouldn't have mattered. He grabbed the chair that used to belong to the pimp and lifted it over the guy, turning it backward as he sat and hugged the seatback. Ordinarily, it would be a mistake to turn his back on the room, but he knew that Big Guy and Thor would be his eyes.

"My name is Neil," he said. "What's yours?"

The girl cast a terrified look at the man on the floor.

Jonathan looked up at Boxers. "Take him outside, will you?"

"Be a pleasure," Boxers said. He bent down and wrapped his arms around the pimp's middle and lifted him like a dog, arms and legs dangling, struggling to fight. Maybe pretending to struggle to fight.

Somewhere in all the excitement, the place had emptied out. All except for Sofia.

"Now," Jonathan said to the girl. "It's just us. What's your name?"

"*Me llamo Erica,*" she said. "My name is Erica," but the accent was wrong. Spanish was not her native language.

Jonathan switched back to English. "Where are you from, Erica?"

The new language startled her. "Who are you?" The native accent was clear as crystal in her English.

"Australia or New Zealand?" he asked with a smile. "I can never tell the two apart."

"New Zealand. Korokoro, a little town outside of Wellington. You're American?"

"Guilty as charged. Now, tell me the truth. Who is that guy you were with?"

She dropped her gaze to the floor and brought her hands to her eyes. Her shoulders shook, but she made no noise.

"Look," Jonathan said. "Things happen, and there's no shame in bad stuff. If that's the case here—if that guy is bad news to you—I can make him go away. I promise. Would you like me to do that?"

She kept her face buried in her hands.

Jonathan turned to get Sofia's attention, but found he already had it. In Spanish, he asked, "Could you bring a glass of water, please?"

Then, to Erica: "Was he hurting you?"

Moving very slowly, Erica brought her hands down. As she did, the water arrived. To the bartender, Jonathan said, "Are you Sofia Reyes?"

The bartender's head twitched. A *yes* perhaps?

"Pleased to meet you, Sofia," Jonathan said in Spanish. "We need to talk."

Sofia ignored him as she handed the glass to Erica. "Here you go, little girl," she said in Spanish. Up at the front of the bar, the door opened as Big Guy reentered.

Erica's hands were shaking as she took a sip. Looking back at the dirty floor, she said, "He . . . raped me. Said he was going to sell me." She spoke in a monotone, as if something inside her had died.

Back at the front, Big Guy said, "I'll be back," and he stormed outside.

"You won't have to worry about him anymore," Jonathan said. "Are you alone with him? Or are there . . . others?"

She shook her head and looked away again. "There were five of us last time I was there."

"Last time you were where?" Jonathan beckoned for Dawkins to join them.

"At the house," Erica said. "You know, where . . ."

She couldn't finish the sentence, and Jonathan didn't need her to. He was missing Gail's presence. This kind of thing was out of his depth. He had it on good authority that he didn't do *sensitive* well.

"Where is this place?" he asked.

"I don't know."

"I do," Sofia said. "Why do you want to go?"

Jonathan regarded Sofia with suspicion. What could he safely share? "Tell me how reliable she is, Thor," he said in English.

"Not a single tire track on my back," Dawkins replied. She hadn't thrown him under the bus. Yet, anyway.

"Two children were kidnapped from El Paso a day or two ago," Jonathan explained to Sofia in Spanish. "We're here to bring them home."

"El Paso is a long way," Sofia said.

"We have reason to believe they were brought here to Sinaloa."

Sofia made a face that Jonathan had a hard time interpreting. *Feel free to be as stupid as you wish,* was one thought that came to mind.

Jonathan turned his attention back to Erica, switching back to English. "This place . . ."

"It's a whorehouse," Erica said.

"You never have to go back there," Jonathan said.

"But what about Esteban?"

"Is that the man my friend just carried out of here?"

A little nod. The thought of him terrified her.

"You won't have to worry about him again."

"You can't know that."

The door opened again, and Boxers entered. He gave a thumbs-up. Jonathan saw blood on his shirt.

"Yes," Jonathan said. "I really can."

"This whorehouse," Sofia told him in Spanish, "is a place where kidnapped children are often brought. It is a terrible business and a violent place."

"I want to go back to my family," Erica said.

"Where are they?" Jonathan asked.

"Last time I saw them, they were in Puerto Vallarta. We were on holiday there. And then . . ."

Jonathan leaned in. "Please finish that story. As much as you can tell me."

Boxers locked the door and stepped closer to listen.

Erica thought for a long time before starting her answer. During that minute or so, she seemed to grow smaller in her seat. Her eyes unfocused as her mind returned to the night when she and a boy she'd met—Alejo, she thought, but wasn't sure—decided to step off the grounds of the resort and take in the local nightlife. They'd stopped in a bar they'd noticed from the bus on the way in. It looked like it had a mechanical bull on the inside, and that was something Erica had always wanted to try.

After about an hour of hanging out and a single go at the bull, which didn't end well for her at all, they decided to leave. The night was darker than she liked, but the resort was only about a half mile away. They hadn't gone very far when the attackers struck.

Erica sobbed as she told of the machete strike that cleaved Alejo's skull. How she could see the glimmer of the blood in the moonlight. They'd cut off her attempt to scream by clamping hands around her throat, and then they put something over her head, threw her into a vehicle, and the nightmare had begun.

As Erica spoke, Jonathan felt his blood pressure rising. Behind him, Boxers literally was growling. He did that as he got angry.

"How long ago was that?" Sofia asked. That she spoke English surprised him.

"I don't know," Erica said. "Weeks. Maybe months."

"At the house," Dawkins said. "Among the people who entertain the clients—"

"Among the whores," Erica said. "If I can be one, you can at least say it."

Dawkins blushed. "Yes, of course. Among the . . . among you, are there any boys?"

Jonathan's teeth clenched.

"Boys who are whores?"

"That's what he means," Jonathan said. He dreaded the answer. "Are there any?"

"Come one, come all," Erica said, snickering bitterly at her own double entendre. "There's no end to what perverts like to do, or who they want to do it with."

"Have you had any new whores arrive in the past couple of days?" Boxers asked.

"They come in and out. All the time."

Boxers stayed on point, unswayed by issues of sensitivity. "We're looking for two kids, about fourteen years

old. A black boy and a white girl. Does that sound familiar to you?"

Erica seemed frightened by the physical presence of
Boxers. "I–I haven't been there much in the past few
days. Esteban called me his special girl. I was . . . exclu-
sive . . ." She looked to Sofia for guidance.

"Okay," Jonathan said. "You don't have to say any
more." He looked first to Big Guy and then to Thor before concentrating his gaze back on Sofia. "Ma'am, can
you take care of Erica? Give her shelter for a while?"

"Of course," Sofia said. "What are you planning to do?"

Jonathan said nothing, let her connect the dots on her
own.

"These are not people to anger," Sofia said.

Jonathan forced a smile. "Neither are we."

Chapter Eighteen

Venice listened to the address that Jonathan read to her and entered it into her computer. "Is this it?" she asked. "Is this where they took Roman?"

"I hope not," Jonathan said. "I deeply hope not. But maybe. It's a place where kidnapped children are often brought. I need you to work your magic and make sure to take down any security cameras they might have."

"Why? What are your plans?"

"My plan is to bring Roman back if he's there."

"And if he's not?" Venice asked.

"I'm not sure what you're asking me. If he's not, he's not. We can't know until we look. It's the only lead we have so far unless they've come through with the ransom details. Have they?"

"No." She couldn't put her finger on why, but this mission to the whorehouse felt irresponsible to her. Unjustified. A thread of possibility that didn't seem enough to justify the risk. What if Digger got himself killed in this thing? Where would that leave Roman? Where would that leave her little boy?

The plan was to wait for the details of the ransom demand and then move on that. In that case, at least they'd have *something*. This felt too much like a wild guess.

"Think about what happens to the children in that place," Jonathan said, as if reading her mind. "Maybe it's Roman, and maybe it's not, but this is a thing that needs to be done, Mother Hen. You know that, even if you don't want to."

"What makes you think that I can even hack into Mexican databases?" she asked. "I mean, they're in Spanish, right?"

"Since when do ones and zeroes have accents? Isn't computer code just computer code?"

Digger had no idea what he was talking about, and she was too worried to explain it to him. "Look, I'll do my best."

Her computer dinged with an alert.

"I've got to go."

The ping from her computer likely was important. In the aftermath of the 9/11 attacks, the federal government sprayed money as if it were so much water through a fire hose. Half the police departments in the country got some form of armored personnel carrier, every cop got new body armor, and the emergency response community became buried in firearms and bullets. It made sense at the time, and it immeasurably advanced the sophistication of even small departments.

Among the monies spent was an open secret of a program known as the Interstate Crime Information System, or ICIS. Pronounced *EYE-sis*, the acronym predated the homophone associated with Al Qaeda in Iraq, and apparently, no one was inclined to change either of them. The purpose of the program was to provide a secure information mechanism by which law enforcement agencies could be informed of ongoing operations from other agencies, more or less in real time. Thus, if a car was stolen in one state and a child was abducted in a different state, investigators in both jurisdictions would be able to deduce whether or not the two incidents were related.

The feds exonerated themselves from contributing, of course, but they were more than willing to monitor the traffic and cherry-pick the cases that intrigued them.

To Venice's eye, ICIS was one of the few acts of federal largesse that provided exactly the service it was designed to provide, and it did it in a way that helped frontline emergency responders. It also proved to be invaluable to looky-loos like Venice when she wanted to peek into ongoing criminal activity.

Proactive alerts were one of the most valuable elements of the ICIS program. With a little bit of easy programming, the system would let her know right away when a person she'd designated as a target broke any law.

Today, she'd loaded the system with as many names as she could think of who might be associated with Roman and/or his disappearance, plus she'd entered Patrick Kelly's license plate into the ALPR network. When a name popped up, or when a significant event occurred in a geographical area she targeted, her computer would ping.

She changed screens and saw an item from Prince William County, Virginia. That's where Patrick Kelly's Ford last passed a camera, and it was now the place where police were responding to multiple reports of a shooting in a restaurant parking lot.

When multiple reports were lodged on a single incident, that almost always meant that it was real. And because reporters of all stripes monitored emergency traffic on their radio scanners, dozens of them would be racing to the scene with as much zeal as the police and fire and rescue personnel. Often as not, the reporters arrived first.

Knowing that it would be a few minutes before the police named names, she opened up another screen that would allow her to search for unofficial reports from bloggers and amateur journalists. Citizen journalists were one of the primary drivers behind the cratering of journalistic standards around the world. A scoop was a scoop, after all, and clicks paid the bills—whether for a major network or daily paper or a guy living in his mom's basement. No one needed the so-called facts to actually be true anymore, when a story that was nearly true got the clicks. You could always apologize later. Or settle the defamation suit.

For Venice's purposes, though, rumormongering meant more raw data to analyze on her own. She'd learned a long time ago not to trust the analysis of *experts*. In her experience, the higher the profile of an expert, the more likely he was to make the data fit whatever agenda or book he was selling.

It took a few minutes, but she finally found a group of bloggers and internet news mavens who trolled the southern and western regions of Northern Virginia.

Almost instantly, she was rewarded with a blurry photo of a bullet-riddled Mercedes with the caption:

"Dud shit in pkg litof ft frddy"

Perhaps one downside of being first was to be scared enough for your hands to shake. Venice's instinct was to translate that to *Dude shot in parking lot of Fort . . .* Something. Assuming, of course, that the incident did not involve outdoor defecation.

She clicked back to the ICIS site for an update, but found nothing new—although she had an address to reference. After a few clacks of the keys, she saw that Fort Something was actually Fat Freddie's.

Another picture of the shot-up Mercedes was up, and this one showed the license plate.

She ran the number and got a name she'd never heard of—a guy who lived in Hampton Roads, Virginia. She fought the urge to look him up because he wasn't one of her targets.

ICIS dinged again with an update on the shooting. No real details, but a name jumped off the screen. *Angelina Garcia.* Venice knew that name. A recent reference.

Then it dawned on her. "Oh, God, no." The name came from Gail's research on the Pérez case and the Toby Jackson Bail Bondsman thing. The U.S. attorney didn't want any bail set, and he quoted an FBI agent who was working the case. Venice remembered less about the specific quote than noting the irony that the agent had a Hispanic name. Angelina Garcia.

ICIS dinged again. "*LEOs ok. Suspect dead.*"

Venice started to hyperventilate. This information

could mean only one thing—that Patrick Kelly's mission—the one he wouldn't talk about—was all about killing the agent in charge of the Pérez investigation. That was the price he needed to pay to get his little girl back.

Right away, Venice saw Angelina Garcia's reprieve from death was in fact a tragedy.

God bless Agent Garcia for still being alive, but with Kelly dead, there was no reason to keep Ciara alive. Certainly, there was no reason to keep her safe. And with Ciara no longer an asset, was the promise of money still enough to keep Roman out of danger? The cartels had more than enough money. What was two million dollars more?

What was it the Digger had called this? A shit sandwich? The leaders of the Cortez Cartel would know all too well the risks of the physical handoff of their hostage. If they didn't already have the *real* prize they were after—a dead FBI agent—why would they go ahead with such a risk?

Venice needed to do something. She had no idea what that something might be, but she had to figure it out.

Now.

An idea formed in her mind, and she knew the instant it arrived that it was stupid. Unworkable.

It required her to violate long-standing protocol with the Security Solutions team, and it required her to make a phone call that was going to piss everyone off.

But she had no choice.

It took her less than a minute to cloak her phone, to make it appear that she was Digger. Then she dug into a deeply encrypted file to recover the phone number that she had no right to know but had stolen nonetheless.

She pressed the buttons and clicked SEND.

FBI Director Irene Rivers answered on the third ring. "Hello, Mother Hen," she said.

Venice's heart skipped. "Um . . . how . . ."

"Your boss doesn't use this number anymore," Irene explained. "And he told me a long time ago that if you ever called it, it would be a huge emergency. So, talk to me."

The house Sofia Reyes sent them to wasn't visible from the main road. Rather, it sat at the end of a half-mile long driveway that itself was shielded by a line of trees and tall shrubs. According to the satellite map Jonathan had pulled up, the house sat in a field, among a few scattered outbuildings.

"Pretty high-end for a brothel," Jonathan said.

"Did you see the guards stationed out front as we drove by?" Dawkins asked.

"Two of them," Jonathan said.

"Looked like MP5s to me," Boxers said, a reference to their armament.

"Not the worst news," Jonathan said. While the Heckler and Koch MP5 had a blistering-fast cycling rate, it was a pistol-caliber carbine, packing no more firepower per bullet than a nine-millimeter pistol. Translation: Body armor was a more effective defense than it would be with hotter rounds.

"I've heard better," Dawkins said. "What's our plan here?"

"Ask me when I have one," Jonathan said. "For right now, all I have is a goal. We're looking for our precious cargoes."

"And if they're not there?" Dawkins pressed.

"If they're not there, we say some bad words and rescue whoever else we can. We're not leaving any of them behind."

Dawkins took a deep breath, started to speak, and then stopped himself.

"Don't be a pussy," Boxers said. "Say what's on your mind."

"You're poking a hornet's nest," Dawkins said. "We're about to trigger a shitstorm. It'll be worth it for Roman and Ciara. But if they're not there . . ." His voice dropped away.

"What?" Jonathan said. "Just leave them there? You saw that girl. You saw Erica."

"And after we shoot this place up and take away whoever's in there, do you really think there won't be others to take their places?" Dawkins pressed. He was building a head of steam. "You think you're going to wipe out prostitution in this cesspool?"

"God grant me the serenity," Jonathan said. "The system is a thing I cannot change. These kids in that hacienda? They are in a situation that I *can* change, whether our PCs are there or not."

"Regardless of the collateral damage?" Dawkins asked. "Do you believe for a moment that there won't be some form of retaliation?"

"That is not my problem," Jonathan said. "We'll be long gone."

"But the locals—"

"The locals shouldn't frequent whorehouses staffed with children," Boxers said.

"I'm not going to fight you on this," Dawkins said. "It's all so soul-stealing. Going in there and rescuing those kids is like building a mile-long wall on a five-hundred-mile beach. The flooding won't stop."

"Roman or no Roman, a handful of lucky kids get to go home to their families," Boxers said. "And if the bad guys cause trouble, we get to kill some child abusers. How could a day get any better?"

Dawkins smiled.

"Tell me you haven't dreamed of doing something like this," Jonathan said.

"We have no authority."

"All the better," Jonathan said.

Dawkins shook his head as if he were tired. "I surrender. Here's hoping this is our final stop."

"But for the right reasons," Jonathan said with a wink.

"By the way," Dawkins said. "I never heard what happened to that guy from La Lagartija. Esteban was his name?"

"Was that his name?" Boxers asked. "Good for him. And you didn't hear what happened to him because I didn't tell you."

"And?"

Jonathan said, "Are you sure you want to know? Wouldn't you rather just suspect?"

Thirty minutes later, they had a plan. Boxers parked the Durango behind a patch of trees about a mile from the hacienda. Once there, they kitted up in body armor and did a weapons check. Jonathan's long gun would be an

M27, the Marine Corps' version of the Heckler and Koch 416 assault rifle. An improved version of the stalwart M4 rifle, the M27 was chambered in 5.56 millimeter. He carried eight spare thirty-round magazines, along with the one in the mag well, so that should give him all the firepower he needed. His CQB weapon—close-quarters battle—was an HK MP7, which he carried in a holster on his right thigh. Barely bigger than the Colt 1911 he carried on his belt, the MP7 fired a wicked 4.6-millimeter round that was lightning fast.

Boxers was similarly kitted out, but he preferred the HK 417 as his long gun. Physically a close cousin to Jonathan's M27, the 417 was chambered in 7.62 millimeter. It made much bigger holes at much longer distances. An HK45 pistol adorned his hip.

For his part, Dawkins preferred the old-school M4 with a Glock 19 on his hip. At Digger's suggestion, Dawkins switched out his G-man DEA vest for one of Jonathan's generic black ones.

"No Policía gear?" Boxers asked. The team had an assortment of Velcro patches to attach to their body armor. The one they used most frequently proclaimed them to be FBI, but they also had Policía patches when they wanted to masquerade as cops south of the border. Even the baddest of bad guys hesitated a second or two before shooting law enforcement officials. When bullets travel at 2,300 feet per second, a second or two was the only advantage you needed.

"Not today," Jonathan said. "We're gonna be sideways with Wolverine over this no matter how it turns out. No sense launching her to Mars." While the FBI didn't have much of an official role in quelling the cartels south of the border, Irene Rivers worked closely with the agencies that did. No one at her level enjoyed surprises, and Jonathan had supplied more than his share over the years.

Once they were geared up, Boxers launched Roxie, the latest in civilian drone technology. This Roxie was the fourth or fifth in his collection, which was constantly updated to include new toys. Size was a limiting factor, of course, but even the smaller drones had great photographic and listening capabilities. The last few iterations came equipped with great tracking and hovering capabilities, as well, but Jonathan drew the line at Boxers' dream of being able to drop munitions from the air.

Roxie provided the kind of intel that they used to depend on satellites to give them—and satellite time was a pain in the ass to arrange. Not only was Roxie easier to use, the quality of the intel was far better than what they could expect from civilian satellite systems. With Roxie at two hundred feet, they could count individual rocks on the ground if they wanted to.

Under the cover of the trees along the side of the road, Jonathan and his team gathered around the hood of the Durango, where Boxers had propped his laptop and flight controller. "Let's start out far and then move closer," Jonathan said. "What kind of perimeter security do they have?"

The house sat on what appeared to be about two acres of unremarkable land, its boundaries defined by a garden-variety chain-link fence. "Okay," Jonathan said. "Let's go around front and take a look at the guards at the entrance."

The image swooped in a blurred transition that finally settled on the gravel driveway and then advanced to a faded green Beefeater guard shack where two young men lazed in the shade.

"Want to hear their conversation?" Boxers asked.

"Nah," Jonathan said. "I just wanted to get an idea of what we'll be up against."

"Are you sure you don't want to wait till dark for this?" Dawkins asked.

"Ordinarily, yes," Jonathan said. "But dark is a long time from now. That's a lot of extra raping." He pointed to the screen. "Do we agree there are only two guys and the only visible weapons are MP5s?"

"That's what I see," Dawkins said.

"Yup. Time to look at the house?"

"Yeah," Jonathan said.

The ground dropped away and rotated 180 degrees. In a few seconds, they were looking down on a red tiled roof supported by beige stucco walls. The building itself was T-shaped, with the top cross defining the front of the house and the vertical portion of the T represented by an annex that extended out into the backyard, or the black side. Eight vehicles were parked at random angles in the patchy lawn in front of the front door.

"Can you get us a better ground-level view?" Jonathan asked.

"Easy-peasy." The computer brain that made Roxie so expensive was able to transform overhead views into lateral views, enabling them to observe details as if they were standing on the ground. Some finer details got lost in the translation, depending on the steepness of the angle, but for now there was enough to suit their purposes. If they were doing this at night, they could bring Roxie right up to a window to peer inside, but that move was too risky in daylight.

"Look how all the windows are open in the front," Jonathan said, tapping the screen to show all the casements gaping wide.

"You say that like it's important," Boxers said.

"I think it is," Jonathan said. "Now, take us around back."

The image shifted violently, and then they were in the backyard, looking at the building.

"It's all buttoned up back here," Jonathan pointed out. "Only a couple of windows. They're small and they're closed."

"Must be hot as shit in there," Dawkins said.

The image shifted again as Boxers piloted his toy around to the left side—the green side. "Nope," Big Guy said. "That's an air conditioner compressor." The boxy air handler sat on a concrete pad close to the building. The image zoomed in, and they could see the blades spinning at the top of the unit. "And it's working."

"I think that's where the victims are," Jonathan said. "Kept in a prison in the dark. No windows, so they can't run away."

"That's a lot of speculation, Scorpion," Dawkins said.

"It makes sense, though," Boxers said. "Reception area in the front, business in the back."

"Go back higher," Dawkins said. "There was something in the backyard I want to get a closer look at."

The ground fell away again, and they had a broad view of the scruffy back lawn.

"What are we looking for?" Jonathan asked.

"That thing there at the top of the screen," Dawkins said. "Looks like a clothesline."

Two posts had been sunk into the ground, about fifty feet apart, with a wire five feet off the ground spanning the distance.

"That's not a clothesline," Jonathan said.

"Looks like a dog run to me," Boxers said. He zoomed in closer, revealing a worn path that ran parallel to the strung wire. "Those are footprints, Boss."

Once you knew what they were, it was obvious.

"I think it *is* a run," Dawkins said. "But not for a dog."

"Jesus," Jonathan said. "Their version of an exercise yard?"

"I think so," Dawkins said. "Look how the footprints run strictly parallel to the wire. I think they must be shackled to the wire to keep them from running away."

"This is why we don't wait till the sun goes down," Boxers said.

"Go back to the rear annex," Jonathan said. "Is there a door?"

As the image spun again, Boxers said, "Yeah, I saw one. There it is. Looks like steel to me."

"Is that our breaching point?" Dawkins asked.

In most circumstances, that would be the perfect spot. Close to the hostages and likely unguarded. In this case, though, it wouldn't work. "We don't know what's on the other side," Jonathan said. "The only reliable way to breach it would be with explosives, and that's too risky."

"So, we're going to go in through the front door?"

Jonathan and Boxers exchanged glances. In unison, "Yes." Digger added, "But fast and violently."

"What are the rules of engagement?" Dawkins asked.

Boxers said, "Whatever it takes to rescue those kids and get them out healthy."

"I meant with the johns."

"Same thing," Jonathan said. "Whatever it takes to rescue the victims. I'm not here to punish those perverts, but I'm not going to shed a tear if they get hurt."

Chapter Nineteen

The shakes always come later. Not the mild, immediate post-shooting shakes, but the whole-body temblor-quality convulsive shakes. Angelina Garcia had felt perfectly fine until the local cops arrived. She greeted them with her hands in the air, her left palm displaying her gold FBI shield. But when one of the first-arriving officers approached her—a young guy named LePew, according to his nametag—her body started to seize.

"I–I'm FBI," she said. "That man tried to shoot me. I returned fire. He's . . . he's dead. I secured his weapon in my vehicle."

Officer LePew looked nearly as unnerved as she. "Are you hurt?" he asked.

"I don't think so."

"Here, sit in my car," he said.

"I didn't do anything wrong."

"You're not under arrest, Agent . . . What's your name?"

"Garcia. Special Agent Angelina Garcia."

"Ma'am, you're not in trouble, so far as I can see, but you really need to sit down. Before you fall down. You don't look good."

As more emergency vehicles arrived at the scene, Officer LePew escorted Angelina to the backseat of his cruiser and opened the door.

"I don't want to be sitting in the back of a police car like a criminal," she objected.

"Ma'am, you don't have to do anything you don't want to do. But it's cool and it's safe."

"The press will see it and take pictures. You can't undo that kind of narrative."

LePew thought for a few seconds, then shrugged. "Suit yourself." He withdrew a notepad from his back pocket and flipped it open. "Tell me what went down here."

The first step for Digger and his team would be to get past the guards out front. Jonathan knew better than most about the danger of underestimating your opposition, but these sentries were just boys, fifteen, sixteen years old, and they were working for pennies and maybe some stash on the side. He didn't relish the idea of shooting them. Even beyond their relative innocence, there was the noise factor. If the fighting started so far from the front door, the rest of the bad guys would have too much time to prepare.

Jonathan was hopeful for a peaceful solution out here. From what he'd seen through Roxie's eyes, he thought there was a way to keep things from getting violent at the guard shack. His plan hinged on scaring the shit out of them.

Boxers piloted the Durango past the guards, then pulled over twenty yards later, where they were barely out of sight. They pulled balaclavas down over their faces.

All three of them got out of the truck together, and with their weapons up to their shoulders, they rushed back to the guard station.

Jonathan arrived first, but he became invisible to the kids as soon as they saw Boxers.

"Hands up!" Jonathan said in Spanish. He kept his M27 leveled at the chest of the guard on the left. He assumed that Boxers was covering the other one. Dawkins's job was to keep security at the mouth of the driveway to make sure they didn't get sneaked up on.

"Don't shoot!" Jonathan's guard said.

"What's your name?"

The question startled the kid. His voice trembled as he said, "My name is Juan. Why are you—"

"What's yours?" Jonathan asked the other one.

The second guard's face had turned into a series of near-perfect circles as he stared at Big Guy. It reminded Jonathan of a jack-o'-lantern.

"Hey!"

The kid jumped and shifted his head to face Jonathan.

"Name."

"Carlos."

Still in Spanish, Jonathan said, "You don't want to die here, do you?"

Their whole bodies pivoted as they shook their heads *no*.

"Then you keep your hands away from those guns. Understand?"

Their bodies shook the other way. Yes, they understood.

"Thor," Jonathan called. "Come in here and grab their weapons."

Both MP5s were propped against the wall of the guard shack, muzzles up. As Dawkins ducked in and took custody of them, Jonathan said, "Okay, Juan and Carlos, I need you to take your clothes off."

The thought seemed to horrify them even more than the prospect of getting shot.

"Just down to your underwear," Jonathan said.

"Why?" Carlos had finally found his vocal cords.

"So I don't shoot you," Boxers said. When he wanted to deeply frighten people, he could make his voice sound like a combination of thunder and an earthquake.

"We can't have you making phone calls, can we?" Jonathan said.

The kids' hands trembled as they worked on their clothes. Both wore shorts. Juan wore a Nike T-shirt, and Carlos sported a green button-down cotton shirt that hadn't been washed in a very long time.

Keeping his rifle at his shoulder, Jonathan took a step back and gestured with his head. "Toss those out into the road."

The boys complied.

"Shoes and socks, too. Don't want you running off, either."

Juan pulled his low-top black canvas tennis shoes off by anchoring the heels with his toes and pulling his feet out, but Carlos sat back in the folding chair to undo the laces of his Jordans and pulled them off one at a time. Neither were wearing socks, and the stench of feet hit hard.

"Toss them out, too."

"These cost me a lot of money," Carlos said.

"You can have them back when we are done," Jonathan said. "I promise. Now, throw them out into the street."

They did as they were told, and Dawkins picked up the clothes and shoes and took them to the Durango. A few seconds later, the truck appeared at the head of the driveway.

"Are your cars parked up there?" Jonathan asked, pointing toward the house.

"Yes," Carlos said.

"I ride a bicycle," Juan said.

"Here's what we're going to do," Jonathan said. "We're going to go up to the house for a little while. I want you boys to stay here and keep any other people from coming in. When we're done, if you've done your job, we'll stop on the way out and leave your stuff. Nobody has to get hurt."

Hope seemed to bloom where before there'd only been dread.

"But remember that we know where you live," Boxers menaced. "If you cross me, I swear to God that I will hunt you down and kill you. After I kill your families."

The hope vanished, run off by sheer terror.

"Okay," Jonathan said in English. "Let's mount up and get this done."

As Angelina relayed the details of the attack and her attacker, she was reminded of several lectures she'd received at the Academy. How eyewitness accounts were essentially worthless. Trying to think back now, she remembered the fact that the guy had been staring at her, but she couldn't relay the color of his eyes. As for his clothes, she was pretty sure he was wearing a sport coat, but again, nothing in the way of color.

Except for the redness of the blood and how it somehow looked even redder against the black pavement.

She had no recollection of how his hair was cut or what his nationality might have been. But she knew precisely what kind of rifle he had, and she relayed within millimeters where each of the bullets she'd fired had pierced his body.

Officer LePew had asked her four times during the past fifteen minutes if she was okay, and each time, she assured him that she was. In fact, the act of talking about it made things a little easier. Her heart still pounded in her chest, but she didn't feel sick anymore, and her hands had stopped shaking.

LePew never stepped away from her, though he acknowledged his fellow officers several times with a cursory nod.

"You know, you don't need to babysit me," Angelina said.

"I kinda do, actually," LePew replied. "You've, you know, been involved in a shooting, and even though I'm sure you've done nothing wrong, it's in everybody's best interest—"

"To be babysat," she said, finishing his sentence for him. Call that Crime Scene 101. For innocent people, it's always useful to have witnesses who can account for all of your movements. On the other hand, for guilty people, there's no better time to alter evidence or sneak away than when they're left alone, even for a few minutes.

"Uh-oh," LePew said as something caught his eye over Angelina's shoulder.

She turned to see a police Suburban pulling into the lot. "Who's that?"

"That's Chief Rendel," LePew said. "She's chief of the department, and she almost never wanders into the field."

"Sort of a carpet cop?" Angelina guessed.

"You didn't hear that from me."

"Didn't hear what?" She winked.

"Exactly."

If Angelina had been in LePew's shoes and her boss was arriving at the scene, she would have done everything she could to avoid eye contact, but this cop's eyeballs were locked on the approaching Suburban.

"What is she doing?" he asked, probably to himself.

The answer arrived with the SUV as it pulled to a stop within ten feet of them.

"Oh, this can't be good," LePew mumbled.

The electric window in the backseat lowered to reveal a tough-as-nails sun-worn face above a white shirt and gold collar hardware. "Agent Garcia?"

Angelina scowled. "I am."

"Chief Rendel. I need you to get in here with me." The urgency of her tone was unnerving.

"Why?"

"I'll explain once you're inside."

The resistance against climbing into a vehicle occupied by a stranger must be hardwired. It didn't matter that the vehicle bore the decals of the police department. "Am I under arrest?"

"I don't think so," the chief said. "Officer LePew?"

"Ma'am?"

"Is Agent Garcia under arrest?"

"No, ma'am."

"Okay, then. I need you to get in the car. Both of you, actually."

This didn't feel right at all, but there was no reason to refuse. Angelina had, after all, just shot a guy.

"Pepé, you climb all the way into the backseat," Rendel instructed. "Agent Garcia, you sit here with me. Please move quickly."

LePew worked the latch to release the near side of the bench seat, thus allowing him to climb into the back. Angelina reset the latch and then climbed in next to the chief.

"I'd like to know what's going on, Chief."

"So would I," Rendel said. "Please, don't panic when you hear the next part." To the driver she added, "Take us to the jail, to the sally port."

Angelina recoiled. "Whoa, whoa, whoa. I want a lawyer." She reached for her cell phone.

"Don't," Rendel commanded as the Suburban started to move. "Just don't. You're not under arrest, and as far as I know, you're not even in any trouble."

"So, I'm free to go?"

They were nearly up to speed as the Suburban hit the parking lot exit. The driver hit the lights and siren.

"Not exactly," Rendel explained. "Look, I'm being straight with you when I tell you I don't really know what's going on. I got an urgent phone call from a very important person who told me to do exactly what we're doing."

"Important person? What does that mean?"

"It means Irene Rivers."

Angelina felt her jaw drop. "As in *Director* Irene Rivers?"

"Of the FBI. I believe you would call her your boss."

"Holy shit," LePew said. "Me, too?"

"Yep. And I'm in the mix, too."

Angelina asked, "Are you aware that you're not making any sense?"

"I'm aware that I'm following directions," Rendel said, her voice showing an edge of annoyance.

"But you don't work for her."

"A fact of which I am fully aware," Rendel said. "She indicated that it was of the utmost importance to bring you to safety ASAP."

Angelina found herself gaping. "Me? You mean, by name?"

"Exactly that."

"She literally told you to get *me*. Not just the random person who was in a shoot-out."

"Your name's Angelina Garcia, is it not?"

She waited for the rest.

"How would I know that unless she had told me?"

Angelina waved the chief off. "I'm not suggesting that you're lying, Chief. I just don't understand how she would know about any of this. There's only like a hundred thirty layers of bureaucracy between me and her."

"Did she mention me by name, too?" LePew asked.

"No, of course not," Rendel snapped. "How would she know your name?"

He seemed to deflate a little. "Then why am I here?"

"Because the director asked for everyone who knows about Agent Garcia being involved in the shooting."

"Isn't that a lot of people?" Angelina asked. "Every cop on the ground out there? The nine-one-one call taker? Witnesses?"

"I checked the tape on the way over," Rendel said. "None of the callers into the dispatch center mentioned that you were a fed."

"But they saw *me*."

"Look," Rendel said, "you're wanting me to explain things that I don't understand myself."

Angelina tried to make the pieces fit. This was wrong at so many levels, not the least of which was, why she was in the company of Chief Rendel rather than her boss, Ray Jacobs? "Why are we going to the jail?" she asked.

"Security," Rendel replied. "Too many eyes in the station. Too many people to see you."

That detail didn't help her nerves a bit. In fact, it made them even rawer. "Am I being disappeared somehow?"

"Again, I don't know. I was told to get you to a tele-conference room with the fewest possible number of people seeing you. The jail has a sally port. The deputies who see you won't have any idea who you are. I've arranged with the sheriff to get a secure room. In short order, I presume we will all learn together what the hell is going on."

Angelina decided that it no longer made sense to ask questions, at least not out loud. Silently, though, where the hell was Ray Jacobs? She'd called him in the immediate aftermath of the shooting. The office wasn't that far away. He could have made it down if he'd made it a priority, but he never showed up.

Was that what was going on here? Had Ray called Director Rivers to tell her about the shooting? Was this a disciplinary thing?

Surely not. Ray wasn't a guy to sub out a good tongue-lashing. Ruining careers was one of his specialties. One of his best things. He liked to shout loudly enough to be heard through the walls. No, this was something else. Still, where the hell was he?

The ride to the jail was only four or five miles. The chief's driver piloted the big beast around to the back of the building and down the ramp into the pit that was the sally port—the transfer location for prisoners in custody to be moved from the transport vehicle into the jail itself. They stopped at the bottom of the ramp to let an overhead door rumble open. When the way was cleared, they pulled into an overlit concrete cave and the door rumbled down again.

"This is it," Rendel said. "Let's see what's up."

Angelina pulled the door latch on the passenger side, climbed out, then lifted the seat to allow LePew to climb out. Chief Rendel waited for them on the driver's side, then led the way to the heavy steel door that separated freedom from incarceration for so many.

Cameras high on the walls and all over the ceiling no doubt documented every move they made. As they arrived at the door, the lock buzzed, and they entered a concrete mantrap that was equipped with even more cameras. The next lock buzzed, and they stepped into misery.

Angelina had always hated this end of the law enforcement business. There was something utterly soul-stealing about the concrete and steel of a jail. Perhaps literally soul-stealing. For those who were under arrest, that step she'd just taken defined the end of anything that resembled happiness and reset the future to survival, at least for the short term.

"Please tell me there's no strip search," Angelina said, an attempt at humor that fell flat.

She imagined that there'd been a time when the walls and bars had been painted white, but those times were long gone. The walls had faded to a dingy, filthy cream color, and the bars had been largely chipped away to the bare brown steel.

Three strides in, a deputy in a crisp brown uniform stepped out to greet them from a room to the right that was sealed off by another solid steel door.

"Afternoon, Chief," he said. "Do you have any idea what this is all about?"

"Hi, Grant," Rendel said. "Everybody, this is Deputy Sergeant Grant Harper. And no, I have no idea."

"You must be Angelina Garcia," Harper said, extending his hand.

"I suppose I must," she said. "Pleased to meet you. What's the next step?"

"If you are armed, I need you to put your firearms in the safe over there."

Angelina reached to her holster out of habit, only to feel her shoulders sag when she remembered that it was empty. As far as she knew, her SIG sat unattended in an evidence bag in the back of Officer LePew's cruiser.

"Don't worry about it," LePew said, as if reading her mind. "I texted another officer and had him take custody of your weapon."

She nodded a curt thank-you. All the rationalization in the world, and all the calm explanation, could do nothing to reduce the sense of dread brought by being in this terrible place. It was, after all, the very same spot she'd have been if she'd been charged with murdering that man.

He was shooting at her, goddammit. She had every right—

"This way," Harper said, pointing back to the steel door. It buzzed, triggered by an unseen guard. Harper pushed the panel open to reveal a hallway that was every bit as unpleasant as the previous room. Same ugly paint, same dingy lighting. Angelina wondered how people could spend a career working here and still preserve their sanity.

In this hallway, the interior doors were made of wood rather than steel, and Harper stopped at the first one on the right. He pushed it open, and they were greeted with a plain vanilla long conference table with eight leather swivel chairs arranged around it.

"Take a seat, any seat," Harper said. He lowered himself into the chair at the end, farthest from a big flat-screen television. He pushed a button on the remote and brought the screen to life. It showed the image of a county sheriff's badge. Then he called someone on his cell and said, "Everybody's in place."

He clicked off, yet nothing changed on the wall.

"Has anyone told you what to expect, Sergeant?" Rendel asked.

"No one, Chief. I gotta say we don't do a lot of cloak-and-dagger—"

The screen blinked, and the sheriff's emblem was replaced by the famous gold-edged red, white, and blue FBI shield. Ten seconds later, the frame cleared to reveal an empty chair in a conference room that looked no fancier than the one they were in.

Irene Rivers served as an inspiration to law enforcement officers around the world. The Bureau's first female director, she was also the real deal. She'd kicked doors as a member of the Hostage Rescue Team, closed hundreds of cases as a field agent, and, if rumors were true, early in her career, she'd shot and killed a corrupt assistant director.

When she entered the frame and set herself in the empty chair on the other end of the call, Angelina found herself wanting to stand.

"Thank you all for gathering on such short notice," Director Rivers said. She looked up over her glasses, presumably at a video monitor and said, "Which one of you is Angelina Garcia?"

Angelina raised her hand. "Right here, ma'am."

Director Rivers smiled. "How are you doing, Agent Garcia? Shootings can have bad consequences for the shooter." She chuckled. "Okay, perhaps not as bad as for the shot, but still. Are you well?"

"Yes, ma'am, I'm fine."

"No, you're not," the director said. "I've been in your shoes. You think you're fine, but trust me, you're not. Your SAC will make arrangements for you to talk to someone. Be sure that you do."

"Yes, ma'am." There was no way in the world that she was going to talk to a shrink. Not with Jacobs staring down at her.

"If anyone gives you shit about that, you are to call me," Rivers said.

"Yes, ma'am."

Rivers pulled her glasses off and leaned forward. Her gaze shifted from the monitor to the camera lens. To the center of Angelina's soul.

"This is the twenty-first century, Agent Garcia. Angelina. It is one my personal goals as director to smoke out the remaining dinosaurs in the Bureau and replace them with a new breed of manager. Do not blow this off, and do not blow sunshine up my skirt. Do we understand each other?"

"Perfectly, Director Rivers."

"Good. Now, who else is in the room. Introduce yourselves."

They did exactly that, one by one.

"What's your role in this, Officer LePew?" Director Rivers asked.

"I was early on the scene. I did the first interview with Agent Garcia. I have no idea why I'm here. Ma'am."

"And Sergeant Harper? Your role?"

"It's my conference room. I know how to work the electronics."

Rivers threw her head back and launched a throaty laugh. "Well, again, I thank you all for coming together for such an odd meeting. I'll get right to it. You cannot release Patrick Kelly's name to the public."

"Who's Patrick Kelly?" several asked in unison.

"He's the dead man in the parking lot," Rivers said.

"How do you know his name?" Chief Rendel asked. "Even I don't know his name yet."

"Sure you do. I just gave it to you. I need you to keep it quiet. And how I know this is irrelevant. Suffice to say that it's a matter of life and death."

"This went down in a parking lot in the middle of the day," Angelina said, shocked at the sound of her own voice that she'd spoken up at all. "God knows how many people saw the exchange of gunfire. He—Patrick Kelly, I guess—must have fired twenty, thirty rounds of five-five-six at me. A mag dump. And I emptied my service weapon in return. We can't keep that kind of thing off the news."

Rivers listened with what appeared to be a feigned smile. "Are you finished, Agent Garcia?"

Angelina looked at the others and noted that they were all staring down at the table. "Yes, ma'am," she said. "I think so."

"Good. And I hope you feel better. Because this next part is going to blow your mind."

That brought all the heads up.

"Agent Garcia, I need you to disappear for a day or two," Rivers explained. "I have agents on the way down from DC to take you to a safe house."

"Oh, my God," Angelina said. "Why?"

"Because we've got a complicated situation on our hands." Rivers sat back in her chair and chewed on the stem of her glasses as she weighed something that was clearly troublesome to her. When she'd made up her mind on whatever the dilemma was, she put her specs back on and leaned forward till her forearms were on the table.

"Chief Rendel," Rivers said. "Please take whatever action you need to take to lock down that name and to keep Agent Garcia's name out of the news. I know that you have a thousand questions, and I'll be happy to address them later, but right now, that one thing is of critical importance. And the clock is ticking."

"The press will already be on the scene," Rendel objected. "I'm not sure I can get the genie back in the bottle."

"Make it happen," Rivers said. "If you fail, one child will be tortured and killed and a second will likely be sold into the sex trade, to be tortured and killed later. If that happens, I will use the not-insignificant power of my office to hang that around your neck. Have I made myself clear?"

"Director Rivers," Rendel said. "All due respect—"

"I'm fully aware of how much respect I am due," Rivers snapped. "Find a way to quarantine this story for forty-eight hours. It may take less time than that, but that's the number to plan on."

Angelina watched as Chief Rendel's jaw worked like

she was chewing gum. She was *pissed*. Clearly, it had been a while since she'd had her ass chewed.

"I look forward to your formal complaint," Rivers said. "But for now, I'd like to be left alone with Special Agent Garcia. Alas, Sergeant Harper, that means that I'd like you to entrust the electronics to Uncle Sam for just a few minutes."

Harper rose, looking relieved not to be needed.

"One other thing," Rivers said, causing them to freeze at the door. "Not a word of what you've heard is to be uttered outside of this room. Whatever stories you tell about the whats and the whys cannot reflect the truth."

They all gaped, unsure what to say.

"It's the nature of a secret," Rivers said with a smile. "Truth is the first casualty. Welcome to your first taste of federal law enforcement. Thank you all."

Angelina stayed in her seat as the others left. When the door closed, Director Rivers asked, "Are we alone now?"

"Yes, ma'am."

"First things first, relax a little, okay? No one thinks you did anything wrong. Your career is not in danger, and I'm well aware of the unique pressures you face at the hands of your immediate supervisor."

Angelina recoiled in her chair. The director *knew* that Jacobs was an asshole?

"The Bureau seems much larger than it actually is," Rivers said. "I won't elaborate, but rest easy that I outrank Special Agent in Charge Jacobs, and anything I say trumps anything he says."

Angelina couldn't suppress her smile. "That's good to hear, ma'am. Now, why—"

"About the safe house," Rivers interrupted. "Here's

the deal. Patrick Kelly's fourteen-year-old daughter was kidnapped, and the ransom was for you to be killed."

Angelina rattled her head. Surely, she had not heard correctly. "Who would do that? And who is Patrick Kelly?"

"He is the owner of Toby Jackson Bail Bonding Company."

Angelina felt a jolt of electricity in her spine. "Fernando Pérez."

"The one and only," Rivers confirmed. "The Cortez Cartel is coming for you."

"They're not sending their A-team, then. Kelly's rifle was in charge of him, not the other way around."

Director Rivers chuckled. "That was only their first try."

"Look, Director Rivers, I appreciate your concern, but I'm an FBI agent. I piss off a lot of people, many of whom would love to see me dead. That's true of every agent in the Bureau. If we sent all of them to safe houses—"

"That has nothing to do with why you're going to the safe house," Rivers interrupted. "You're going there because, meaning no offense, you're dead now."

Okay, there went the brain cells again. "I, um . . ."

"And Patrick Kelly is still alive. At the very least, he's not officially dead."

"Ma'am, with all due . . ." She stopped herself, remembering that the director already knew how much respect she was due. "This isn't making any freaking sense. Ma'am."

"Sure it does. Pull your investigator hat a little tighter. The only thing keeping Patrick Kelly's daughter, Ciara, alive is the anticipation of your murder. If your murderer is known to be dead, then all of that leverage goes away. You know the cartels. The Cortez Cartel in particular. They'll sell her off to the highest bidder without two seconds' thought."

Angelina ran the data through her head. "So, you're buying time?"

"Exactly."

"Do you know where she is? Is HRT looking for her?"

"We do not know yet where she is, but yes, people are looking for her."

"You mentioned a second person," Angelina remembered. "Someone who would be killed."

"Yes," Rivers said. "Another young teen. A boy. Ciara's boyfriend, apparently. He's being held for a monetary ransom, but sort of as an afterthought. Smart money says that if there's no reason to keep Ciara, then the boy becomes more of a liability than an opportunity."

"Do you even know where to look for them?" Angelina asked. "You told the chief that you only needed forty-eight hours. That's not a lot of time. Implies that you have reliable leads."

Rivers smiled. "There you go. The investigator's hat is fitting well again. Let's just say that we have a pretty good idea."

"Ma'am, permission to be blunt?"

"Oh, hell, yes. Consider that to be an open invitation. I'll knock you down if you cross a line."

"It makes no sense for me to go into hiding if we're keeping the shooter's identity a secret. If he's not officially dead, then I don't need to be, either. I'm a big girl. I'm pretty good at this self-defense thing. I don't want to hide from these asshats."

"Call it an abundance of caution," Rivers said. "If word leaks out that Kelly is dead, we'll build a narrative that you shot each other."

The ease with which Director Rivers launched the already formed cover story caught Angelina off guard. Startled her, actually. "And the witnesses?"

"You didn't know you were shot. You were on your way back to RA when you started to bleed out internally."

Angelina found herself without words.

"You're going to take a few days off, Agent Garcia. You're going to take one for the team. And if it comes down to it, you're going to accept your fake death with dignity."

Chapter Twenty

Jonathan and his team went in hard and fast, with their feet propping open the Durango's doors so they would be able to peel out of the vehicle quickly. It had been a very long time since Jonathan had run a daytime op like this. Normally, at night, they could kill power to the building and own the darkness with night vision, but in daylight, everyone could see everything, thus eliminating that one big advantage.

In the absence of night vision, the ability to intimidate the enemy became paramount.

As soon as the big SUV slid to a halt, the team was out. Jonathan led the way, with Dawkins right on his tail and Big Guy bringing up the rear. At his size and girth, Boxers always needed to be last in the room, if only to give the others in the stack a chance to see anything.

The front door was closed, but it wasn't latched. When

Jonathan kicked it with the sole of his boot, it exploded inward and rebounded off the interior wall. He caught the bounce with his left shoulder and pivoted to his left. Dawkins would pivot right, and Big Guy would cover them all.

The place looked like a trailer park gentleman's club. A dozen or so overstuffed club chairs were arranged in conversation groups on top of shiny pine floors. None were occupied. On the left in the rear of the room, a man in a stained business suit literally jumped out of his desk chair as they exploded through the door.

"Hands in the air," Jonathan said in Spanish.

The man complied without complaint.

"Cuff him, Thor," Jonathan said. He pointed toward the closed door at the far side of the long wall. "Is that door locked?"

The guard (receptionist?) stared back.

"I asked you if the door is locked."

The guy was petrified. "He wet himself, Scorpion," Dawkins said.

"Won't matter," Boxers said. He rarely used knobs anyway.

The door to the back was hinged on the inside, and it was, indeed, locked. That meant it opened inward. It took three slams with the sole of Big Guy's shoe to break the tongue of the lock from its steel keeper, each one of them shaking the entire building. Both Jonathan and Dawkins had their long guns shouldered.

As that door slammed open, they were confronted by a guard of the same age as the ones outside and armed with the same model of MP5.

Jonathan tried to tell him to put his weapon down, but the muzzle had already lifted up past the neutral line. He shot the guard in the pelvis to knock him down and to direct any overpenetration into the floor, away from the walls. As the kid collapsed, Jonathan sealed the deal with a bullet to his forehead.

This section of the building resembled a low-rent hotel with curtains hanging where doors should have been along the hallway. Six rooms per side. The sound of the gunshots provoked a lot of yelling from behind those curtains, both from males and females.

"Everybody step out right now with your hands up!" Jonathan shouted in Spanish. He didn't shout for Roman specifically because if the boy wasn't here, Jonathan didn't want a direct connection between him and the raid.

At the far end of the hallway, a naked man stormed out of a room with a badge in one hand and a pistol in the other. He started to shout something, but Boxers shot him dead.

"No one else has to get hurt!" Jonathan said.

"Don't tell them that," Boxers grumbled in English.

Jonathan ignored him. "Let's clear the rooms."

Jonathan started with the first room on the left. With his rifle pressed against his right shoulder, he used his left hand to pull the curtain aside. A naked man in his twenties sat on the floor, apparently in the spot where he'd fallen. His hands were in the air, and his face showed utter terror. The girl on the bed was far too young to be there.

"Cover her up," Jonathan said.

"W–who are you?"

"The man who hasn't killed you yet. Now, cover her up and lie facedown on the floor."

The rapist reached for his clothes.

"No," Jonathan said. "You stay naked. Cover the girl.

If you try to run, I will kill you. If you hurt her any more, I will kill you slowly."

Beyond this first room, bedlam grew. Another gunshot rattled the shoddy construction. Unless someone else had brought in a portable cannon, the shot had come from Boxers. And if he had fired the shot, someone had just died.

"Everybody step out into the hallway!" Jonathan shouted again, but no one complied. Who knows, maybe that was the smart move under the circumstances.

Thor arrived in the doorway. "Where do you want me?"

In English, Jonathan said, "Keep the rapists facedown on the floor as I pull them out. If any of them tries to run, kill them."

Jonathan moved to the next room, and as he pulled back the curtain, he was startled by a man on the other side, knife raised in his hand, ready to defend himself. Jonathan yelled a curse and shot the guy in the chin even as the blade was coming down. The point of the knife caught Jonathan's left shoulder, just at the margin of his vest, but the blow didn't have much behind it. It didn't hurt much yet, but he'd been stabbed before and knew that the real discomfort would come in the next couple of days.

Across the hall, Boxers' 417 boomed again.

Big Guy yelled, "Give up, you sonsabitches! Or I will kill every friggin' one of you!" His warning came in English, but even if the people in this place could not understand the words, there was no denying their meaning.

Jonathan wanted to help the second girl, but she would have to wait.

As Jonathan approached the third room on his side of

the hallway, a fat guy in his fifties tumbled through the curtains and damn near collided with him.

"I'm getting down," he said in Spanish. "Please don't shoot me." He lay facedown on the filthy indoor-outdoor carpet.

When Jonathan peeked in, he saw a young boy on the bed. Maybe fourteen years old, his eye was swelling shut from a recent blow to his cheek. "You're okay, now," Jonathan said. "I'll be right back." Based on what he saw, he offered a silent prayer of thanks that the boy was not Roman.

Turning back into the hallway, Jonathan saw Big Guy smash a john in the bridge of his nose with the buttstock of his rifle. The man's face erupted in blood, and his legs folded.

The fourth room on Jonathan's side of the hallway was empty. As he scanned the interior, a john from the fifth room crawled out from behind his curtain and lay face-down on the floor, just as he'd been instructed. Apparently, he didn't realize that he was within the halo of the dead cop's spreading gore until he hit it. He tried to lift himself away from it, but Jonathan forced him back down into the blood by stomping on the space between his shoulder blades.

"Take a taste," Jonathan said in Spanish. "Be happy it's not your own."

"Put your guns down, or I will kill this boy!" a man's voice yelled in broken English from behind the last curtain on the left. "I am a police officer. You are all under arrest."

Jonathan looked back at his partners and placed his gloved forefinger across his lips. *Say nothing.*

"Do you hear me? I know you are Americans!"

Jonathan remained silent. Who might the boy be?

The fifty-something said, "They're still standing—"

Jonathan kicked him in the head, and he fell silent.

"I am not bluffing!" the cop said. "Drop your weapons, or I will kill him."

But he *was* bluffing, whether he realized it or not. There were only a few ways for this to play out. In scenario one, he came out with a gun to the kid's head, and either Jonathan or Boxers would kill him. In scenario two, he'd follow through with his threat and kill the kid (*please God, no*), and Jonathan would kill him. In scenario three, he was in there by himself—the hostage being a true bluff—and he would have to show himself sooner or later.

If he was armed, he would die.

If his hands were empty, Boxers would probably kill him anyway.

"Say something!" the cop yelled. Then he yelled it again in Spanish.

"Please don't let him shoot me," the boy said. There went scenario three. And Jonathan did not recognize the voice.

The other johns on the floor had begun to stir, but none of them said anything. Lessons well learned.

"How many of you are there?" The hostage taker had switched back to Spanish.

Jonathan gestured again for silence.

"Say something, or I will shoot this boy!"

They'd crossed a tipping point. They had to assume that the bad guy was thoroughly committed to his cause by now, with his finger on the trigger and his fear levels through the roof. Even if Jonathan swooped around the corner and took him out, chances were good that the cop would get off a shot out of reflex.

They needed to play this out.

Jonathan heard movement behind the sixth curtain. It was a shuffling sound, but he couldn't determine what it was. Were they on the way out?

Jonathan let his M27 fall against its sling, and he unholstered his Colt. His thumb found the safety and pressed it off. This had the feel of a confrontation that was going to play out at bad-breath distance, and wielding a longer barrel—even as short as that of the MP7—presented an opportunity for the bad guy to swipe at it and ruin his aim.

Behind and to his right, Jonathan more sensed than saw Boxers moving around him to get a better angle on the doorway.

Then he heard the sound of a phone being dialed.

Shit! The guy had played for enough time to get to his cell phone. This thing had to go down now. Maybe his distraction would play to their favor. Maybe—

"Hey!" A naked child bolted through the curtain and dove for the floor just as the cop fired his gun.

Scorpion moved with speed that gave credit to his radio handle. With the hostage no longer in play, this would go down easy. As the kid flew out into the hallway, the curtain parted far enough to for Jonathan to get a flash of the fat cop standing against the far wall before the fabric fell back into place.

Jonathan fired three rounds through the curtain at the image that was still retained by his retinas. To his right, Boxers pounded the same spot with five rounds from his 417.

"Go!" Big Guy yelled.

Pistol up, Jonathan squirted in past the curtain to finish the job. The cop lay very dead on the floor, his jiggly body punctured with holes and his bottom jaw sheared from his face.

"We're clear!" Jonathan called. Then he shot the phone that the cop still clutched in his fist.

That done, he returned to the hallway, where he checked his watch. So far, not counting the business with the kids at the guard shack, they were three minutes into this operation.

"We've got two minutes," Jonathan announced to his team. "Thor, get these assholes zipped and dragged outside."

"Let 'em get dressed?"

"Absolutely not. Let them explain that to their families. Big Guy, find a way to burn this place to the ground."

"Pleasure."

In Spanish, Jonathan said, "Boys and girls, please get dressed and go outside. We are taking you back to safety. Taking you back home."

The boy from the sixth room still lay facedown on the disgusting carpet. When Jonathan stooped and touched his shoulder, the boy yelled and tried to run. Jonathan caught him with an arm around his chest.

"No, no, no," Jonathan said. "We're here to rescue you."

"*No hablo Español,*" the boy said. His accent sounded Texan.

"Are you American?" Jonathan asked in English.

That seemed to settle the kid. A little.

"We're here to rescue you, son. We're here to take you home."

He seemed confused. Terrified. He cast a nervous look back toward the room he'd just escaped from.

"You don't have to worry about him," Jonathan said. "Not ever again. Go get dressed."

The boy continued to stare. He said nothing as he twitched his head *no*.

"How old are you?" Jonathan asked. Truth be told, he didn't think he wanted to know.

The boy looked at the floor. "Almost twelve."

"Your name?"

"Number Seven."

Jonathan's stomach turned. What the hell had they done to these kids? He didn't really want to know that, either. "What's your *real* name?"

"Cameron. Cameron Porter."

"I need you to get dressed, Cameron. We need to get you out of here."

He cast a nervous glance back at the curtained room. Clearly, he was afraid to go back inside. Jonathan understood that. "Are your clothes in there?"

A nod.

Up toward the front of the annex, several of the victims had stepped out into the hallway. They all wore an identical garment, a cross between a dress and a nightshirt. None of them had shoes.

Jesus.

Jonathan stepped back into what he now thought of as Room Six and scanned the walls for a dresser or a closet. Then he saw what he was looking for. This nightshirt might have been older than Cameron. Threadbare and stained, it was hung on a nail in the wall. As he plucked it off, the temperature of his blood dropped ten degrees as he noticed the leg shackles that were attached to the steel footboard of the bed. The chain separating the cuffs was perhaps six feet long and it passed through a loop that had been welded to the face of the footboard.

As he took the nightshirt out to Cameron, he noted the red irritations around his ankles.

Upon closer inspection, each of the children's legs bore similar markings. "Here you go, Cameron," he said. "Let's get you out of here."

Jonathan thought back to the wire and posts in the backyard as he dropped the partially spent magazine from his pistol into his palm and replaced it with another from his belt.

Then he did the same with the M27, switching the partially empty magazine out with a new one from a pouch in his vest.

Two minutes turned out to be an unreasonable time frame, but he still felt the press of time. What he'd done— and what he was about to do—was going to piss off a lot of people, and the more time they spent here on-site, the worse things were going to be.

"Hey, Scorpion," Dawkins asked as he stood from zip-tying his third john and headed for the one in the back who hadn't moved from the puddle of cop-gore. "What are we going to do with these guys?"

"I haven't decided yet." His first choice was to kill every one of them. As an alternative, maybe he could shoot their balls off. He'd dealt with difficult stuff before, but nothing that rose to this level of awfulness. They were all *kids*.

"You know this happens every day, right?" Dawkins said. "They even have a name for it. They call it sex tourism."

Jonathan had heard of it. He knew it existed. But this

was the first time he'd been this close to it. He wondered how many of these assholes were Americans. Yeah, this stuff was illegal even in Mexico, but no one had the stones to stand up to any industry run by the cartels.

"For the time being, just haul their asses outside. We'll figure it out from there. Wait till we get the kids out of here, though."

Jonathan had heard stories over the years of what it was like when the allies liberated concentration camps at the end of the Second World War, where despite being free of the immediate hazards of murder and torture, there was an utter lack of joy. The misery of what the prisoners had endured surpassed the wonder of being free.

He thought of those stories here at the brothel. These kids had endured tortures that Jonathan couldn't begin to understand—didn't want to understand. A pall hung over the place as the boys and girls padded out through the front room and then into the yard. Perhaps they understood that they would never truly recover from this. They would never be the same again. They would always and forever be wounded.

Jonathan led them out through the sunshine, well past the parked vehicles, and stopped about halfway to the guardhouse. "Sit down in the grass," he said. He couldn't help but notice that Juan and Carlos had left their post.

The liberated children complied, each sitting in identical postures, their feet folded under their thighs. None of them had said a word.

"You can talk among yourselves," he said, but they didn't appear to be interested. "We'll get you to safety very soon." He repeated the words in English for Cameron and for any of the others who might not understand

Spanish. Hell, for all he knew, some of these kids might have been vacationing from Europe when they were taken.

When Jonathan turned back to the house, he saw Dawkins, who looked disgusted as he escorted four trussed and naked men outside. With them was the receptionist, who was also trussed but clothed. Jonathan pointed to a spot far away. "Plant them over there."

Boxers then appeared from behind the house with what looked to be a can of gasoline. Jonathan joined him at the front door. "Here's the plan," he said.

"We're going to kill those shitheads, right?"

"No," Jonathan said.

"You saw what they were doing."

"Yes."

"They have to die."

"We promised Thor."

"I didn't promise shit," Boxers objected.

"We need to stay focused, Big Guy."

"I *am* focused. Those assholes need to suffer."

"We're going to set fire to the building," Jonathan said. "We're going to burn this place to the ground. And while it's burning, we're going to set fire to their clothes, and we're going to drive away and leave every one of them trussed and stranded."

Boxers looked at his boss with a slight smile.

"Maybe coyotes will come and feed on them," Jonathan said.

Big Guy's smile grew larger. "It's not as good as killing them," he said. "Not even close."

"But it will do?"

Big Guy took his time answering. "Yeah, it'll do."

While Dawkins kept an eye on the kids and held guard over the rapists, Jonathan and Boxers made quick work of stacking mattresses, bedding, clothing, and furniture into two enormous piles, one in the torture chamber and another in the front room. Every bed frame had been affixed with the same shackles as the ones Jonathan had found on Cameron's bed.

"Want to pull out IDs or anything?" Boxers asked as he slung men's clothing onto the pile. "We can figure out who they are?"

"I don't care who they are," Jonathan said.

"You know what we should do?" Big Guy asked. "We should chain each one of those sunsabitches to a bed and then torch the place. Burn 'em alive."

For reasons that Jonathan didn't understand—and about which he'd never inquired—Boxers had a particularly homicidal intolerance for anyone who harmed children. Jonathan had seen him kill kid touchers with his bare hands. The last one they'd encountered, Big Guy had slashed the guy's eyes with a knife before breaking his body one bone at a time.

Boxers didn't reach that frenzied stage very often, but when he did, it was a frightening thing to witness.

"Tell you what," Jonathan said. "We'll stack the bodies onto the pile and burn them with the rest of the trash."

Boxers smirked and winked. He liked the idea. "You know, Boss, I've never found you to be this sexy before."

Less than three minutes later, they were ready to go. Boxers sloshed about a third of the gasoline in the can onto the stacked clothes and bodies in the torture room and lit it with his Zippo lighter.

With the fire burning in the back room, they needed to move more quickly to ignite the pile in the front room with another pour of the gas.

The fire in the back room grew from small to raging

with startling speed. The pile in the front started as smoky, but then after thirty seconds or so, it found its momentum. Soon, the entire structure was ablaze.

Their final stop was out at the parked vehicles. Jonathan used an ASP collapsible wand to break out windows, and Boxers added splashes of gasoline. While they let the vapors expand, Jonathan shot holes into the gas tanks. When they got rolling, he didn't want just to gut the interiors. He wanted it all to go up.

Because Big Guy considered himself an artist whose medium was destruction, he'd daisy-chained the vehicles together with a trail of gasoline so he could light the whole thing with a single flip of the Zippo.

They were rewarded with a satisfying *whump* as they all lit at once.

"Is that a pretty sight or what?" Boxers asked with a grin.

"Our work here is done," Jonathan said. "Thor! Load 'em up, and let's get on the road."

"What about us?" the fifty-something fat guy yelled from his spot on the ground. "You can't just leave us here like this."

Boxers stopped, pivoted, and headed toward the trussed rapists.

"Big Guy," Jonathan said, following behind. "Easy."

"They couldn'ta just kept their mouths shut."

"We're done here, Big Guy. Leave it alone."

But Boxers was focused. He walked in long strides, and his eyes showed murder.

"Goddammit, Big Guy, listen to me!" Jonathan yelled.

"Leave you here like this?" Boxers growled in Spanish. "You don't want to be left here *like this*?" He drew his HK45 pistol from his holster on his hip and, in one quick motion, shot the guy in the ankle. "You like this way better?"

The man howled, and the others tried to get their legs under them to run.

"Stop!" Big Guy yelled. "Or I swear to God that I will cripple all of you." As he spoke, he swept the pistol's muzzle past each of their faces. Jonathan noted that his finger was on the trigger. That was Big Guy's tell that he was a half-pull away from blasting these guys apart.

Jonathan stepped in closer, hoping to defuse the situation some.

"Yes, we can leave you here like this," Jonathan said. "And yes, you're lucky that you're still alive."

The guy who'd been manning the desk—the only one whose dick wasn't hanging out—said, "Just who—"

Jonathan cut him off. "Do you really think this is a good time to be running your mouth? You see that hole in your friend's ankle, right? Just shut up. It doesn't matter who we are, and I don't care what happens to any of you. Given the size of those fires, I'd say somebody's got to notice and come by to do something. I just wish I could be here to listen to your stories."

He looked up to Boxers. "Big Guy, we've got to go."

Chapter Twenty-one

Jonathan and Dawkins rode in the cargo area on the way back to La Lagartija, leaving the seats for the children. They still had not spoken, and they still looked terrified. Not surprising, Jonathan supposed, given what they'd been through—compounded by the violence surrounding their rescue—but he hoped that freedom would bring some happiness into their faces.

When they were still ten minutes out, Dawkins called Sofia Reyes to tell her they were on their way to her. He listened carefully and then held up a finger. "Wait," he said as he looked to Jonathan. "You have something to write with?"

Jonathan pulled a pen from a pocket on his vest and then a tiny notebook. He offered them to Dawkins, who shook his head.

"Write this down for me," he said. Then, into the phone

he said, "Go ahead." He repeated an address to Jonathan, who wrote it down. "Okay, Sofia, we'll see you in a few minutes." As he clicked off, he said to Jonathan, "That's our new destination."

"What is it?"

"Not a bar with a bunch of cops and bad guys hanging around."

"I didn't ask what it's *not*," Jonathan said.

"She said it's a safe place."

"She said." Jonathan's skepticism was front and center.

"Best I can do," Dawkins said. "Look, I've dealt with Sofia for years."

"And you trust her?"

"Didn't we have this discussion already? Sofia is a survivor and a quiet spy. Those two identities are almost impossible to juggle down here. She pretends to be the local Switzerland, totally neutral. She knows who the dirty cops are, and she knows who pays them off. I've heard rumors that both sides actually trust her to hold the money."

"What's the nature of your interactions with her?" Jonathan asked.

"Intel, mostly. We're building cases against a number of the players—working our way up to the big guys. She walks a line where she keeps us on the right track—never misleads us—but also never cuts her own throat by handing us exactly what we need."

"Your own Deep Throat," Boxers said. "Pardon the pun."

Dawkins feigned a shiver at the thought. "But here's where she really stepped up. Two, two-and-a-half years ago, one of our informants got burned, and Sofia sheltered him for long enough for us to get him out. That takes real guts."

Jonathan still didn't like the change. He hated surprises. Every surprise on an op provided one more way for things to go wrong.

"Well, shit," he said. "I guess a friend of yours is a friend of ours." Shouting past the kids, he yelled, "Hey, Big Guy, we've got a change in location. I'll send it to your GPS."

Twenty-five minutes later, they arrived at a tall adobe structure with an orange tile roof. A peak in the center of the front wall gave the impression of a church. Old-school functioning shutters framed tall casement windows, all of which stood open. As they approached, Sofia Reyes stepped out of the front door in the company of a nun who wore the kind of habit that is rarely seen in the United States anymore, complete with black tunic and white wimple.

"Children, stay in the truck," Jonathan said as Boxers released the tailgate to let Dawkins and him out. "Thor, Big Guy, come with me."

They hadn't yet disarmed, and Jonathan was well aware that they projected menace to the ladies, but that was part of the point. Sofia Reyes may be a friend of Dawkins's, but she was nobody to him, and in his line of work, trust needed to be earned.

As they approached, Jonathan said, "You guys check out the interior. Make sure it's safe."

"I already told you," Dawkins protested.

"Then it shouldn't take very long, should it?"

Jonathan slid his M27 around to the side and extended his hand to address the nun. "Neil Bonner."

"I am Sister Katherine," she said in Spanish as she

shook his hand. With so much of her body covered, it was difficult to make out her age, but Jonathan pegged her at around thirty. Thirty-five at most, and she had the kind of smile you wanted to see from a lady of the Church. "Thank you so much for rescuing the children. I will take care of them now."

"Did you find who you were looking for?" Sofia asked.

"Not yet," Jonathan said. Then, to Sister Katherine: "Regarding the children in the truck. I don't mean to insult, but an hour ago, they were living in hell. And I mean that as literally as it can be meant. My friends are checking out the inside to make sure that, well, you know."

"I understand."

"What is this place?" Jonathan asked.

Sister Katherine said, "This church used to be home to the parish of St. Ignatius."

"Used to be?"

Her eyes hardened. "The cartels. They do not like people to gather in churches. Especially in churches like this one, in so rural a location."

It was a classic power play. Governments learned centuries ago that congregations of worshipers were likely to discuss topics that were not a part of the approved talking points. The closings were always sold to the people as actions designed for their own good, but the very fact that the people involved had no say laid bare the truth.

Sofia explained, "Sister Katherine and the other sisters have turned this place into a safe house for children who manage to escape."

His interest piqued, Jonathan hooked his thumbs into his vest and shifted his weight to one foot. "How do the children find out that you are here?"

"We get help from people like my dear friend Sofia," Sister Katherine said.

"Mexico is a fine country, Mr. Bonner," Sofia said. "It happens to be run by very bad people, but the citizens are good people. Most of them, anyway. Many of us who run taverns, restaurants, hotels, and even gasoline stations are very aware of what you in America call child trafficking. Frankly, I think that's too clean a word for what actually happens."

"Excuse me," Sister Katherine said, "I am going to see to the children." She pressed past Jonathan and headed for the Durango.

"So, you are part of a modern-day underground railroad?" Jonathan asked.

Sofia clearly did not understand the reference. "We try to spread the word to places where escaped children are likely to go first. From there, contacts are made with the sisters. They are not the only group that is concerned, but they are the most organized."

"And all of those children come here?"

"No, of course not. This is just one of what I assume are many safe houses. This is the only one that I know of personally."

Jonathan turned to watch as Sister Katherine opened the passenger side door and addressed the children. Her demeanor seemed easy and friendly. Motherly. "What happens next with the children?"

"I believe they are reconnected with their families," Sofia said. "That is most certainly the goal."

The children started climbing out of the Durango, and they followed Sister Katherine as she led them away from Jonathan, toward the side of the building.

"Wait!" Jonathan said, and he started to follow.

Sofia grabbed his arm. "No," she said. "They will be fine."

"Where is she taking them?"

"Somewhere else," Sofia replied. "I do not know where, but if I did, I would not tell you. It would not be safe for the children. The fewer people who know, the better."

Jonathan didn't know what to do. He'd taken all those risks, hurt all those people, done all that damage, and now he was supposed to—

"Trust the sister," Sofia said. "You have my word. And while you don't know me, you need to trust me, too. It would be foolish to keep the children here for more than a few minutes. The cartels have spies, and they have money. It would be equally foolish to assume that some of the people entrusted with knowledge of these efforts would not betray us all for money."

Boxers and Dawkins emerged from the front door. "It's all clean," Big Guy said.

At that moment, a minivan with heavily tinted windows emerged from behind the church and rumbled past the Durango on the way to the road.

Boxers raised his rifle. "What the hell—"

Jonathan pushed the muzzle down. "Whoa, there, cowboy."

"Are those the kids?" Dawkins asked.

Jonathan explained, "Our friend, Sofia Reyes, arranged for them to be transported to safety."

"You're gonna explain that later, right?" Boxers asked.

"Absolutely. Now, Sofia, can we talk about our original topic?"

Sofia led the way into the empty church, where they all slid into pews. The interior showed signs of structural cancer, the kind of disrepair that evolves so quickly when a building sits unused for too long a time. Mold—or maybe moss—had begun to climb the corners of the concrete block walls where the floors and walls met. The air smelled like an old sponge.

When they settled, Sofia said, "How much damage did you cause, and how many people did you hurt?" Everything about her had changed. Anger had replaced that easygoing persona from a minute ago.

"Trust me when I tell you it was a worthwhile trade," Jonathan said. "You saw those kids."

"Answer my question."

Dawkins said, "We burned the building down, left the . . . customers tied naked in the front yard."

"Did you hurt any police officers?"

Jonathan shifted uncomfortably. "We killed a couple of child rapists who tried to kill us," he said. He regretted not having the opportunity to interview at least one of the cops.

Sofia moaned and lowered her head. "I wish you hadn't done that."

"I guess I do, too," Jonathan said.

"I don't," Boxers added. "And while we're sharing details, I shot one of the customers in the ankle, just to be nasty."

Sofia brought her hand to her face and pinched her forehead. "What did you do with the bodies?"

"Burned them with the rest of the trash," Big Guy said. He sounded proud.

"What does that mean?"

He told her.

"Oh, my God, what have you done?"

"We made the world a safer place," Jonathan said.

"You are dead men. What happens to people who kill and defile the bodies of police officers in the United States?"

"No one will know it was us," Jonathan said. "We had our faces covered, and, well, you might say that we are untraceable."

"Look at the size of this man!" Sofia said, pointing at Boxers. "Do you really think that his face is the first thing people notice?"

"It's my personality," Boxers said.

"This is not funny!"

"No, it's not," Boxers said, and he stood, as if to prove her point. "It has never been funny to do the things the people in that whorehouse were doing to those children. It's not funny that everybody in the whole goddamn neighborhood—hell, in the whole goddamn *country*— knows that they're doing it, and yet you just choose to look the other way."

"You don't live here," Sofia said.

"Oh, hell, no, I don't live here. I'd rather set my eyes on fire than live in this cesspool, but you do! Every goddamn day, you face a choice to do the right thing or the wrong thing, and every goddamn day, you choose to do nothing. How can you live like that?"

"Easy, Big Guy," Jonathan said. He took a minute to explain the underground railroad for the child victims.

It didn't help. "What the hell, Scorpion? You think that changes anything? Those poor kids—those victims— does anyone know or care how many of them just friggin' die?" He thrust a finger at Sofia. "You think that hell is gonna be any cooler for you because you accept them after they've figured out all by themselves a way to escape on their own? You really think that means anything to them?"

Sofia's eyes were growing red and hot.

Big Guy still wasn't done. "Don't you dare take up a position on Morality Mountain and lecture us for killing people who should have been killed a long friggin' time ago. Who the *hell* do you think you are?"

Jonathan hadn't seen Boxers' genie this far out of the bottle in a very long time. He wasn't sure he knew how to put it back in.

And Boxers was still on a roll. "What you should be doing is learning from our example. We showed you how to take care of business. If there's another one of these godforsaken brothels left in the country at the end of tomorrow, it's because *you* let them stay."

"Big Guy!" Jonathan shouted it. "Step away, dude!"

"Why?"

"Because you have to! This is what Thor was trying to tell us. We're throwing rocks in the pond and leaving just as big a hole."

"God damn!" Boxers boomed, making the walls move. "Not you, too! I won't accept that from you. Not *you*! Not after all the shit we've done together. You can't surrender, too."

"Screw you!" Jonathan shouted back. "Surrender? *Surrender?* If you want to have that out right now, I'd be happy to go for it. But it is not *surrender* to keep at least one eye on our mission. Now, let this go. At least for now, let this go."

Jonathan understood exactly where Big Guy was coming from on this. History was littered with societies who willingly and willfully looked away from the very thing that ultimately destroyed them. People whose hearts were still beating could tell stories of European atrocities that everyone knew needed to be ignored unless they wanted to join the misery of the camps. Each of those people chose to put their own comfort and prosperity—whatever that meant to them—ahead of other people's basic right to live. If you pretended not to smell the stench of the pyres, you could tell yourself that it was something completely different than what you knew it to be.

That's the way it was with the cartels, too, and it wasn't just the Mexicans and the Central and South Americans. Politicians in the United States were hip deep in the subornation of human trafficking. In all of the political bickering over the porousness of the U.S. southern border, where accusations of racism and xenophobia and socialist economics were thrown like beer bottles in a street rumble, no one shined the spotlight on the plight of the real victims—the children.

"I'm sorry, Sofia," Jonathan said. "Tempers are running hot. The things we saw—"

"Should never be seen," she said. "Should never happen. Yes, I know." She settled herself with a heavy breath. "Can I assume that these people you are looking for—these children—are close to you?"

"Yes," Jonathan said. "Okay, to be honest, one of them is. The other is a stranger. We're worried about both of their safety."

"As you should be. How can I help?"

Jonathan fished his phone from his pocket and flipped through to the picture of the man who'd stopped the driver, Alvarez, after he'd dropped the kids off at the water park. "Do you recognize this man?"

"I do," Sofia said. "He is a regular in my bar. I believe

he commutes back and forth across the border. His name is Ernesto Guzman. He frequents the building you burned. Was he there?"

"No, he was not. What does he do for a living?" Jonathan asked.

"I do not know. I mean, I hear him talk of a *pupusería* in El Paso, but given the cars he drives, I do not believe that to be his prime source of income."

Jonathan recognized a pupusería to be a restaurant or roadside stand that sold *pupusas*, corn tortillas stuffed with pretty much anything you could stuff into a corn tortilla. Jonathan didn't care for them. "What do you think his primary source of income is?"

She gave him a look. *Duh.*

"The cartels."

"Yes," she said. "At least, I believe that to be the case. He's one of many messengers and smugglers who deal with contacts across the border. Because he runs a business in the U.S., no one questions his presence."

"Is he the kind of man who would kidnap children?"

"He is the kind of man to be very cruel," Sofia said. "There are stories that he enjoys torturing people. If I may ask, what was his involvement in the kidnappings you speak of?"

"We're not entirely sure," Jonathan admitted. "We know that he intimidated a driver in El Paso into giving up the location of the children. He'd taken them to a water park."

"Was it the Shady Sun?"

Jonathan cocked his head. "It was."

Sofia's shoulders sagged. "Oh, my," she said. "The children may be in very bad trouble, then." She stood and walked to the altar, where she turned back and sat on the step in front of the rail. "Does the name Cristos Silva mean anything to you?"

Jonathan sat taller. "Yes."

"I'm sorry to hear that," Sofia said. "I believe that Silva uses a warehouse very near that park."

"Uses it for what?" Boxers asked.

She gave him an angry glare. Apparently, her wounds were still raw.

"Don't do that," Jonathan said. "The stakes are too high, and the clock is running too fast."

"I do not know what he uses the warehouse for. Not specifically. But the fact that it is so close to the spot where your children were taken should not be ignored."

"Does he own a place here in Sinaloa?" Jonathan asked.

"Oh, my God, Mr. Bonner," Sofia said with a gasp. "You do not want to encounter him. Not after what you just did with his gentleman's club."

Boxers growled at the sound of that phrase, and Jonathan moved quickly to avert another explosion.

"Please call that shithole anything other than that," Jonathan said.

"That's what he called it, like it or not. If you left anyone alive up there, Mr. Silva will soon know what happened. He will be very angry. He has an army of enforcers who defend him, fight for him."

"We've faced armies before," Jonathan said, though he didn't relish the idea of doing it again.

"I told you we shoulda killed them all," Boxers said.

"Can you tell me where Cristos Silva lives?" Jonathan asked.

"He has a vast hacienda," Sofia explained. "Not near, but not far. It is very well guarded."

"You've been there?" Dawkins asked.

"No, but I have heard from those who have." She approached from the altar and took Jonathan's hands in her own. "I like you, Mr. Bonner. I do not want to see you die that way."

Jonathan blushed. "I appreciate the words, Sofia. Now, please tell us how to find Silva."

"I do not know that he is even there."

He waited for it.

"All right, then," she said through a heavy sigh. "And when you leave here, I will say a prayer for you."

Chapter Twenty-two

Alberto Bris did not look nearly frightened enough as he sat in the parlor of Cristos Silva's hacienda. Sure, he trembled and there were tears in his eyes, but given what he had allowed to happen, Silva wanted more.

"Y–you don't understand," Alberto stammered. "They came from nowhere. I could not have stopped them."

"You pay guards to stop them, do you not?" Silva said. He wanted to keep his tone quiet, calm. He'd found over the years that people are more intimidated by measured words and tone than they are by shouting.

"They could not stop the likes of these men. I think they are American soldiers. They wore masks over their faces, and each of them had many guns. One of them must have been over two meters tall. The largest man I have ever seen."

"That makes him a better target," Silva said. "You were a coward, Alberto. You did *nothing* as they burned down my club."

"But they tied—"

"You are paid to run the club. Part of running the club is protecting it from damage." He leaned in very close. "Do you think that you did your job well today?"

"Mr. Silva, please."

Silva walked back to his worktable and sat in his rolling chair. He crossed his legs and straightened the crisp seam in his chinos. "Please what?"

"Please do not hurt me."

"You allowed them to burn my club to the ground, Alberto. You allowed them to steal my property. You let them walk away with eight of my best workers. Do you have any idea how much you have cost me?"

He waved two fingers at Guzman, who stepped forward out of the corner. As Guzman passed the stools that were pressed up against the chest-high bar, he snagged the handle of his sledgehammer in his right hand and smiled.

Silva continued, "After all of that, what do you think I should do with you?"

"No, please, Mr. Silva. Please, sir. I swear that this is not my fault." He spat saliva as he spoke and moved to rise out of the hardbacked chair he'd been assigned.

"Stay seated," Silva said.

Alberto stood anyway—how could he not?—and Guzman struck like a snake to grab the man by his tie and jerk him back down into the chair.

Silva said, "Sit."

"P–please," Alberto begged. "Please look at the security video. You'll see. We had no chance against those men."

Silva couldn't stand the sight of this sniveling creature. "Show some self-respect—that is, if you can find any after that spectacle out in the yard. Tied to a bunch of naked men. None of you should show your faces again. When you make a laughingstock out of my business, you make a laughingstock out of *me*. And when people are laughing at me, they are not respecting me. When they are not respecting me, that is when I am in danger. Alberto, you put me in danger."

Silva nodded to Guzman, who reacted instantly. With a grand underhand rotation of his arm, he swung the sledgehammer full force into the point of Alberto's kneecap. The bone splintered like a pistol shot. Alberto shrieked in pain as the leg of his suit pants became wet with blood.

"Take him outside," Silva said. "Finish it in the barn. Do not kill him. I want him to be an example to my rivals for many years to come. Let him be an example for our young guest, as well."

Alberto howled as Guzman lifted him by his tie. As soon as he was vertical, he collapsed, launching another agonized scream.

"Carry him," Silva said. "I do not want a blood trail through my home."

Guzman had to put the hammer down for a few seconds, but after he'd hefted the screaming man onto his shoulder, he picked it up again. Silva watched them exit through the kitchen door, then turned to his laptop.

A message awaited him. He clicked on the icon to open the window and was met with an unintelligible scattering of letters and numbers. He ran them through the decryption protocol to reveal a message from Billy Monroe, one of his lawyers in the United States. Normally, his usefulness was limited to keeping politicians in check on Capitol Hill and making sure that selected headquarters personnel at DEA and ATF were well compensated and always contented with their stations.

Because of this business with Fernando Pérez, though, and its proximity to Washington, Silva had been forced to elevate Monroe to a more trusted position, at least for a short time. Not trusting of lawyers in general, Silva had special trepidations about Monroe that he couldn't fully explain. Perhaps it was because they'd always been at arm's length before.

The text of the encrypted message was both short and direct. *"Media reports that an FBI agent was killed by a gunman this afternoon. No identities released for either the agent or the shooter, but confidence is high that PK did his job."*

Silva felt his face redden as he saw the inclusion of the initials. In this business, at this level, monograms were as good as names. They provided one more search vector for people who were hell-bent on knowing Silva's business. Monroe should have known better.

Silva settled himself. This probably did not matter in the grand scheme. Still, sloppiness got people killed.

He presumed that Monroe's conclusion was correct. How many FBI agents would be killed in a small Virginia town on any given day?

Now that the agent was dead, it would be up to Santiago Pérez to decide whether or not to pay Patrick Kelly. As for the return of the girl, that would be Silva's decision, just as it had been his decision to take her as collateral. He believed that maximum leverage led to most reliable results. Unfortunately, repatriation posed serious risk.

He shook it off. All of that could wait until Monroe closed the loop on the ransom for the Alexander boy.

In the end, the boy had to die. At this point, he was an unacceptable liability. While Ciara came from a family who understood the importance of holding secrets, the Alexander kid posed nothing but problems. It made no sense to release him back into the arms of that friend of his—his father figure—who makes his living investigating others. It was one thing to ransom the children of business executives who would fold quickly, pay promptly, and be reimbursed by their companies. It was something else entirely to deal with the children of anyone even distantly related to American law enforcement authorities. And Silva had no choice but to assume that this Jonathan Grave had such connections. After all, he was the chief executive officer of one of the United States' most respected private investigation firms. It was one thing to poke the sleeping bear that was Security Solutions, but it was something else entirely to hand them an eyewitness.

Already, Silva regretted making the ransom request in the first place. He did not need the money, and he certainly did not need the hassle. But at this point, with the money no doubt on the way, it was foolish to turn away from it.

The only reason the boy still breathed was in anticipation of a proof-of-life demand from his people. After that, he would die. Killing him was the only sensible thing to do.

As for Ciara, well, she had significant market value to him. Having lost his stable of workers to the raiders on his club, he needed to backfill with others. It took time to lure vacationers away from their hotels and party spots, and each time involved risk. Suppose they fought back? Suppose the local beat cop was new and hadn't yet learned the rules?

He winced as a shriek of pain from Alberto passed through the walls of his hacienda. His was a terrible business in so many ways. It was a shame that so many people had to suffer, but it was equally shameful that people didn't listen, that they didn't simply obey the rules and do their jobs.

How could Alberto imagine even for a moment that he would escape punishment for what had happened on his watch? Alberto had only two jobs to worry about. He had to make sure that customers paid and then make sure that everyone else did their jobs. Silva had told him that he should have hired older, stronger security guards, but he'd allowed the man to convince him otherwise. Alberto had argued that the community's fear of the Cortez Cartel in general and of Silva in particular would render any guards unnecessary—that the mere presence of armed men, irrespective of their ages, would be enough.

And for many years, it had been.

Silva clicked his laptop to life and navigated over to the video security files that Alberto referred to. It was concerning that on the day after Roman Alexander, loved one of a private investigator, was taken, his gentleman's club was attacked and burned by strangers. Alberto called them American military, but that was not possible. As long as the feckless Tony Darmond sat in the White House, U.S. armed forces would never dream of following through on the threats they so often made.

He clicked the security feed icon to open it, then dragged the status bar back a few hours. The screen showed three feeds—outside the front door, inside the reception area, and then inside the service hallway. Each of the bays had its own camera, but the cameras only ran at night to make sure the girls and boys behaved themselves. He linked the three main feeds to the system's clock so they simultaneously displayed the same action.

He watched as a Dodge Durango raced from the driveway and slid to a stop in front of the club. As Alberto had attested, one of the men from the vehicle's right side was enormous. Beyond enormous. At least two meters tall, with the girth of a competitive weight lifter. The other two men looked puny by comparison, though he was certain they were not.

They were dressed completely in black, including the cloths that covered their faces, and they were heavily armed with rifles and pistols. They moved as a team, as if in rehearsed motions.

Once they stormed through the front door, Silva closed that feed to increase the sizes of the remaining two.

The way Alberto Bris surrendered without so much as a threat disgusted him. The security feed had no audio, so he could not hear what was said, but the words clearly terrified Alberto, who immediately fell to his knees and presented his hands to be zip-tied.

As one of the terrorists tended to Alberto, the other two, including the enormous one, charged into the service bays. They shot without hesitation as some of the customers fought back, and one room at a time, they stole Silva's children.

The whole operation took less than three minutes, and five minutes after that, the building was on fire.

Silva clicked PAUSE, then backed up to the best frame he could find of the three terrorists. The featureless men clearly were professionals. It was in their stances and in the way they moved. The way they held their weapons.

The big one seemed important to Silva. It was as if he knew of that guy. He'd heard of him before, but from whom? He didn't remember the details, but he knew that it involved violence. It involved ruining someone else's business.

Antonio Filho. The name popped into Silva's head, seemingly from nowhere. Filho had been a cocaine producer in Colombia—one of Cortez's prime suppliers—until a paramilitary group like this one had attacked and set everything on fire. Unlike today, where most people had survived, Filho had lost just about everyone. Children were involved there, too, as he recalled, though they were his workforce in the field.

It had been a long time since Silva and Filho had discussed this, but if he wasn't mistaken, that attack had involved rescuing someone who had been kidnapped. Rescuing a child.

Silva saved the photo of the terrorists, then closed the security footage. He'd seen all that he cared to see. He saw no point in watching till the camera lenses melted.

He opened his encrypted list of email addresses and searched to see if he had anything for Filho.

He feared no interference in his business from local officials, but if the bottom fell out of the world and they did come after him, they would find no contacts to anyone.

He found Filho's address, attached the photo, and asked if these people looked familiar. He clicked SEND and leaned back in his chair. Now he just needed to wait.

Venice's computer dinged with an incoming email to one of her many covert email addresses—the one that she had given to the kidnapper. This would be the incoming ransom instructions.

She reached to her landline and called Gail, who answered after the first ring.

"Yes?" One of the internal security requirements within the team was to never give anything away with a telephone greeting. A simple *yes* or Digger's favorite, *yup*, established the connection and forced the other party to commit to the conversation first. As spoofing increased—the masking of numbers to make them appear as if they belong to someone you know—even caller ID wasn't enough.

"Slinger, it's here," Venice said. "Can you come—"

"I'm on my way."

The email could not have been less complicated. It merely instructed the recipient to call a number with a Saskatchewan area code within the next ten minutes. Three minutes had passed since the time stamp on the notification. Outside, the sun had dipped below the trees.

"That's gonna be a burner," Gail said.

"Really?" Venice snapped. "You don't think he'd use his home phone?"

Gail stepped back and sat in one of the chairs around the conference table.

"Sorry," Venice said.

"Stressful time," Gail said. "Can you put the call on speaker?"

"I'll record it, too," Venice said. She called through her computer. She considered spoofing the number to read as CORTEZ CARTEL, but decided it was a bad idea to poke the bear. Instead, she coded it as WORRIED MOM. She didn't think Jonathan would approve of showing weakness like that, but she didn't care. If these monsters took pleasure in her misery, then what was the harm in giving them a little more of a good time?

She clicked the button and the call connected. "Six three four seven," a male voice said, reciting the last four digits of the phone number.

"You know who this is," Venice said. Her voice would sound entirely different to the man on the other end. Not one of those patently electronic monster voices from the movies, but one that sounded very real and with a slight Maryland twang. "You called me."

"Tell me when you're ready to write," the man said.

"How is my boy?" Venice asked. "Why did you have to hurt him like that?"

"We're not here to chat," the voice said. "I'm going to send you a routing number in five seconds. You'll get it or you won't, but I will not repeat it. You've had time to gather the funds, so the transfer should go easily."

He started to read the number, but Venice interrupted him. "We need proof," she said.

"You're not is a position to want anything but your son back."

"It's not my money," Venice said. It was the cover story they'd agreed upon. "The man whose money it is demands that we see proof that he is alive."

"You've seen the video," the man said.

"That was hours ago. Mr. Grave is not going to hand over two million dollars unless he knows that Roman is still alive."

"If he does not, then Roman will surely die."

"I understand that," Venice said. Her voice cracked. "But I am not in charge of this part."

"I will arrange something," the man said. "After the money is deposited."

"It has to happen simultaneously," Venice said. She only hoped that the terror she felt in her heart did not show through in her voice.

"Excuse me?"

"We will transfer the money when you hand over my son. Not one before the other, but at the same time."

"You are not in a position to bargain here."

"I wish it wasn't like this," Venice said. "But my instructions are very clear. You can drop him off in a parking lot somewhere. When we see him alive and well, we will transfer the funds."

The man fell silent for a few seconds. Venice read that as a positive sign. Had she won him over to her side?

"I have my instructions, too," the man said. "They are explicit and exactly as I have presented them to you. My instructions are also to inform you that failure to comply will result in young Roman being dismembered. As a personal aside, I would like to emphasize that the people involved do not exaggerate and they do not hesitate. Now, copy down this number."

He read it, and both Venice and Gail wrote it down.

Venice read it back to confirm, then said, "You really must tell your boss what my boss said."

The line went dead.

Venice looked to Gail, whose form was only a blur through tears. Suddenly, there wasn't enough air in the room. As her hands began to tremble, her mind went to the kind of dark place where a mother's mind should never go. She saw Roman in pain, saw him bloody and screaming out for her.

In that instant, she hated Jonathan Grave. She hated Security Solutions, Fisherman's Cove, and everything about this life she'd chosen to lead. How many people had to suffer because of her and because of what she and her team did before it all collapsed under the weight of its own tragedy? How many lives could they crush before Karma finally retaliated?

What kind of hubris had she embraced by claiming to be on the side of the angels when the results of their actions were so awful? Derek Halstrom, the love she'd finally found, had been killed inside her home during an attack. She herself had been attacked in this very office. God only knew what was the real truth of the violence that Digger brought with him while acquiring his own injuries.

"Stop!" She shouted it while slamming her hands down on the table, startling the shit out of Gail.

"What?" Gail shouted back.

It took a few seconds for Venice to reel it all back in. "I was having a panic attack," she said. "I was seeing failure." As she locked eyes with Gunslinger, a weird sense of calm floated over her. A hard resolve. "We have to win. There is no other option."

"I know that," Gail said. "And you're strong enough to plow through this."

"Yes, I am," she said. An idea formed in her head. "I think I know how to do it."

She entered the routing number into her computer and went to work.

Chapter Twenty-three

Roman watched in horror as the animal who was Guzman tortured the man only ten feet away. Guzman had stripped the victim of his clothes, down to his underwear, deaf to his screams as the fabric pulled on the leg that looked all wrong. It hung kind of sideways, and as the pants pulled away, Roman thought he might barf at the sight of a bright white protrusion that could only be a shard of bone.

The abuse unfolded directly in front of where Roman sat against a stable wall, his bound hands having gone numb a long time ago. He should have closed his eyes to make the images disappear, but he couldn't bring himself to do it. Not until after he'd seen the blows delivered, then he would look away, as if that would erase the awfulness from the files in his brain.

It went on forever, it seemed. Until the sun was beginning to disappear. As darkness spread around them, the images of the torture became somehow more awful in the shadows.

Roman's vision sparkled as he watched Guzman's hammer turned the poor prisoner's elbow inside out. He thought he might pass out, but he had no such luck.

The screams were unearthly. Inhuman. Stomach-wrenching. He couldn't tell if the man was screaming for mercy or merely screaming. Roman found himself wishing that Guzman would just kill the man. Make the suffering stop.

But the blows continued. Guzman was wet with perspiration and spattered blood by the time the prisoner fell unconscious. The poor man's torso collapsed backward, his head thudding against the filthy floor.

Guzman stood over his victim, his chest heaving from the effort of it all. As he looked up, he seemed surprised to see Roman still sitting there. In the encroaching darkness, the man's eyes were indiscernible disks of shadow, but the set of his mouth and jaw were clearly visible.

He pointed at Roman with the head of the sledge, lifting it as if it weighed nothing. "I told you, didn't I?" he said in heavily accented English.

Roman drew up his legs to push himself away, but there was no place to go.

Guzman stepped closer, the hammer still extended.

"Please don't," Roman said.

"Let us dance a little," Guzman menaced.

Angelina Garcia felt as if she were under arrest. The safe house sat on a wooded lot in Oakton, Virginia, an old-growth hamlet of million-dollar homes nestled in Fairfax County. She'd been locked out of her Bureau accounts and had been forbidden to contact anyone about anything. She was to be totally invisible while the official apparatus told the press that an FBI agent had been killed in Manassas and that a man bearing a withheld name was being sought in connection with the murder. As for the identity of the murdered agent, the Bureau would release that once the next of kin had been notified.

It had been a stupid plan from the beginning, but Angelina didn't have the courage to reveal her thoughts to Director Rivers personally. The Manassas RA was a small community, a wildly dysfunctional family whose members gossiped more than soccer moms. The headquarters carpet cops thought they could control agents' activities out in the real world, but they'd lost touch with reality.

When word spread that an agent had been killed, three things would happen simultaneously.

First, every office would do an inventory of who was present and who was missing. Second, all the reporters within a thousand miles would start working their sources to find out what had happened, and third, every parent, spouse, sibling, and friend of every agent in every office would burn up the switchboards to determine whether their loved one was safe.

By now, Angelina figured that Jacobs had filled her closest associates in on what the reality was and, perhaps, the reason why, presuming Director Rivers had chosen to trust him. From there, the odds were fifty-fifty whether or not the secret could be kept. If recent history has proven anything, it was that the most efficient way of getting a secret exposed on the front page of the *New York Times* was to share it with an FBI agent. The prospect of sinking ships with loose lips didn't seem to be that much of a deterrent anymore.

On the positive side, the secret only had to be kept for a couple of days at most. But on the vastly larger negative side, that was a couple of days of real worry that her mom would have to endure. Through her, the kids would worry, too.

That was the element of this plan that Angelina would not tolerate, even if it meant losing her job. This bullshit might end up being her last straw, anyway. In flagrant violation of her quarantine, she texted her mom that she was fine and unhurt. She would be away for a couple of days, but Mom shouldn't worry. Angelina was not the agent who was killed.

Then it all went to shit.

Apparently, the geniuses who concocted this plan had forgotten about social media—how everybody was their own cinematographer. God only knew how many people had flooded that parking lot by the time the official investigation had started. Agents from the Bureau would have been instructed to collect all the phones from people as evidence—with a promise to be returned, of course—but that only worked for the ones who stuck around long enough to be noticed *and* were foolish enough to confess that they'd taken pictures.

The first image to go viral was that of Patrick Kelly's corpse crumpled on the ground, surrounded by piles of spent brass. Blood smeared the vehicles on either side. The caption accompanying the photo read, *"This is the man the FBI is seeking as a 'person of interest.' I think they can stop searching."*

One video, clearly shot from behind cover, seemed to

show Angelina as the aggressor, as the only person shooting. A lot.

Another, a photograph likewise taken from behind
cover, showed a better perspective of her engaging with
the other shooter. That one came with the caption, *"Correct me if I'm wrong, but this FBI agent looks very much
alive to me."*

At this point, the whole thing was just silly. The secret
had leaked, and maybe that little girl wasn't going to survive, and that was a shame. For her part, all Angelina
wanted to do was get back to work.

Silva listened with feigned interest as Billy Monroe relayed the demands of the Alexander family.

"Who are they to make demands?" Silva asked. "Does
she think that I am bluffing? Does she for a moment believe that I would not kill her son?"

"I tried to relay that to her, sir, but she insisted. She
said that this was the requirement of her boss—the man
with the money. If it were left to her, she would just pay,
but she says that this Jonathan Grave guy is a hard-ass."

Silva considered this. From the way Ciara spoke, and
later the way that the boy spoke, this Grave fellow seemed
like a father to him.

"This is a bluff," Silva said. "They won't let the boy
die for the sake of a couple of million dollars that Mr.
Grave can obviously afford."

"Businessmen can be funny about their money here in
the United States," Monroe said. "I don't know this man,
but I know others who would think the same way. Yes,
they would pay anything for the return of their child, but
not merely on the chance."

"I will kill the boy."

"All the more reason to make the promise," Monroe pressed. "From your own words, it is reasonable for Mr. Grave to suspect that such are your plans, irrespective of what actions they take."

Silva felt his blood pressure rising. He hadn't wanted to get involved in this kidnapping to begin with. He didn't need the money, and he didn't need this show of disrespect.

Monroe went on, "Perhaps if you lower the ransom amount to a number that the mother could manage herself—"

"This is *not* a negotiation, Mr. Monroe. We are not auctioning off car parts. We are charging a ransom for the return of a human being."

"Whom you have no intention of returning," Monroe said.

Something about the way the lawyer delivered those words angered Silva. "Be careful how you speak to me."

"Mr. Silva, I am your attorney. My job is to present you with the facts as they are. My job is to make sure that you make decisions based upon the most factually accurate information that I can supply. The decision itself is up to you, sir."

Silva sensed that the lawyer wasn't done yet, so he waited him out.

"Of course, I do have something for you to consider," Monroe said. His tone sounded less cocky.

"I am listening."

"All right, then. Why don't we come up with a plan to drop the boy off at a specific location? We arrange the timing to be such that the other side cannot have assets in place to attend the handoff, but we can provide live video evidence of you letting the boy go. With that imagery done, they will make the wire transfer. When that's done, you can do whatever you'd like with the boy."

Silva continued to listen without comment.

"Are you there?"

"Is that your entire plan?"

"For my part of it, yes. As I said, the final decision is yours, but if I were in your position, I would think that a reasonable chance of two million dollars in your bank account is better than no chance at all."

"So, what is my next step?"

"We arrange a place for the drop-off to be made. I pass that along to the kid's mother, and then we're good to go. They'll want it to be a public place."

"Of course they will. More demands."

"I have an idea," Monroe said. "The reason I've been so long getting back to you with all of this is because I wanted to do the legwork for you. There's a shopping district . . ." He went on to describe a place that Silva had visited many times. "I know it's kind of far away, but I figured that you would not want the place to be very close to you. When there's very little time left, I will contact the family with the means to monitor a camera I will have someone set up on their behalf. When they see the boy, they'll transfer the money and you can kill the camera feed. After that, you have nothing but options."

"Since you are suggesting a ruse, why not just set up a camera nearby and save myself the trouble of a long drive?"

"You're not going to go yourself, are you?" Monroe sounded mildly panicked by the thought.

"Of course not. But *someone* will have to make the drive. Why have them do that when it is not necessary?"

"There's a concerning level of sophistication to your hostage's mother," Monroe said. "I sense that she has advanced computer skills. She will no doubt be able to trace the actual location of the camera we use. The drop-off needs to be at the place we say it will be."

"Fine," Silva said. "Tell them whatever you want. I will follow through on my end. What happens, happens. Are we finished here?"

"Um . . . No, sir, we're not." Monroe's tone turned dreadful. "About Patrick Kelly's final mission. He, uh, failed, sir. The agent is still alive, and Kelly is dead."

Gail Bonneville parked near the roll-up garage doors, in the center of Billy Monroe's driveway, effectively blocking egress by automobile. He lived in a nice house in a rapidly developing part of Haymarket, Virginia, in Prince William County. Nothing in the neighborhood appeared to be more than ten years old. This was a place of new money and young professionals. It was a place of nosy neighbors and rumor mills, both of which could work for or against Gail's purposes.

Monroe lived in one of the larger models among similar brick-and-vinyl-siding homes. The front façade featured a towering Palladian window over the door. The shrubs in the front appeared to be newly planted and hearty, but barely as tall as the front windows. It was dark enough for the lights to be on. As Gail approached the door, she saw Monroe in his office, which was located off the front foyer. She'd seen the interior in a thousand other houses, and in her mind saw the soaring ceilings inside the door and the sweeping staircase that led to a bridge across the second floor.

She watched Monroe through the window as he hung up from a cell phone call.

"Mother Hen, are you there?" she asked the air. A bud in her left ear connected her to Security Solutions headquarters via a radio clipped to her belt.

"I'm here. You're loud and clear."

"All right, I'm going to VOX," Gail said. Without looking, she reached behind her back and toggled the switch on her radio. "Still there?"

"Affirmative."

"Okay, you should know that Monroe just now finished a phone call and now he's smashing the screen into the corner of his desk." After that, he broke the phone in half and removed what must have been the SIM card, which he then put somewhere behind him and near the floor.

"I think he just shredded the SIM card."

"That means whoever he was talking to, it was via a burner phone," Venice said. "Shredding the card is a wise thing for him to do."

Gail had a pretty good guess as to who might have been on the other end of the call. In a perfect world, this was not a visit she should be making on her own, but backup was hard to come by when the rest of the team was a thousand miles away. On the positive side, Billy Monroe had no history of violence. Seeing his portly form through the window made her feel a little more confident that he wasn't much of a fighter.

But she'd been wrong before. And she had the limp and the hospital record to prove it. Prudence trumped bravado every time. If only she could convince Digger of that.

Once again, Venice had blown Gail away with her

computer skills. The offshore account that the mysterious caller had given them traced to a shell company called Three Seas, LLC, which apparently did nothing other than occupy space on the internet. The ownership of the company was murky, at best. Venice could no doubt track it to ground if she'd wanted to—and maybe that's what she was doing now. The real find, though—the one that sent Gail here to Billy Monroe's house—was the name of Three Seas' registered agent, William Belmont Monroe, a.k.a. Billy.

The same Billy Monroe who was counsel of record for Fernando Pérez, son of Santiago Pérez.

It wasn't exactly a smoking gun, but it was close enough to warrant further investigation. Now, she needed to decide her approach. Since Monroe was a lawyer, she decided to become Agent Culp again.

"Are you ready for this, Gunslinger?" Mother Hen asked.

"We're about to find out," Gail replied.

She attached her badge to her belt, withdrew her ersatz credentials from her pocket, and knocked on the door. When Monroe hadn't answered after thirty seconds, she pounded on the door. "William Monroe! Open the door! This is the FBI!"

Perhaps he was a criminal, perhaps he was not, but he was a resident of this suburban oasis and that kind of noise was sure to draw attention and spin up the rumor mill.

Ten seconds later, the door opened and there he stood. Taller than she'd expected, he was also older and more disheveled. Perhaps it had something to do with the sub-stantialness of his gut. She'd noticed many times that large men with large bellies have difficulty keeping neat.

He still wore his suit pants and dress shirt, but his collar was open and he'd loosened his tie to the second button.

"Jesus, lady!" he exclaimed. "You'll wake everyone!" Exactly the reaction she was going for.

"William Monroe?" she asked, louder than was necessary.

"Yes. Obviously. What the hell is this?"

Gail presented him with her creds case. "I am Agent Gerarda Culp with the FBI. I need to speak with you."

Monroe craned his neck and pivoted his head left to right to see if people were watching. Then, he seemed to realize what he was doing, and he pulled back. "Come in, please," he said. He never even looked at the credentials. People rarely did.

"Thank you," Gail said, and she stepped into the foyer. It was exactly as she had expected. "Are we alone? Anyone else in the house?"

"No. Just me."

"Your wife?"

"We've separated. This time next year, I suppose this will either be hers or we'll have had to sell it in a settlement."

Gail didn't care. She led Monroe into the dining room on the left-hand side of the foyer—away from his office. Desk drawers all too frequently contained firearms and other weaponry that she didn't care to deal with.

"Have a seat," she said, indicating one of the chairs around the rectangular table that was disproportionately short for the room.

"What is all this about? What are you doing here?"

"Sit."

Monroe lowered himself into the chair at the head of the

table, his back to the front window. Gail walked around him and chose the chair at the angle, facing the foyer.

"You are the registered agent for Three Seas, LLC," she said. It was an accusation rather than a question.

Monroe's eyes widened, but he otherwise made no response.

"I understand that you're expecting a large payment soon," Gail pressed.

Beads of perspiration blossomed just under his hairline.

"Now, disrespect me again by asking why I'm here. See how that goes."

Monroe tried to hold her gaze, but he couldn't pull it off.

"Who were you on the phone with right before I arrived?"

"I want a lawyer," Monroe said.

"And I want to reunite a couple of children with their families," Gail replied. She kept her tone even yet intense.

"I don't know what you're talking about. Lawyer."

"Yeah, well, that's not going to happen." Gail had anticipated this moment and planned for it. From the right pocket of her sports jacket, she withdrew a Ruger SR 22 outfitted with a threaded barrel, and from the left, she withdrew a can suppressor, which she made a show of screwing onto the muzzle.

"This is bullshit," Monroe said. He issued a nervous laugh. "You're not going to shoot me."

With the suppressor set, Gail fired a shot past Monroe's left ear. The sound of the action was louder than the gunshot itself, as was the sound of the shattering of the glass speaker's trophy on the bookshelf on the far end of his office. Monroe slammed his hand up against his ear.

"Shit!"

"I was sitting next to Ms. Alexander when you two spoke," Gail explained. She stood from her chair and, never breaking her aim at his chest, twisted closed the venetian blinds on the dining room windows.

When she caught him casting a quick glance to the ceiling behind her, she said, "Global Protection Security Company. I know. We've had their system hacked for a very long time. I assure you that your system is down."

"You can't do this!"

"Evidence to the contrary notwithstanding. I need you to tell me where Roman Alexander is, Billy."

"I demand to see a lawyer!" As he spoke, he slammed his right hand down on the tabletop.

She shot his thumb, nearly severing it at the root.

"Ow!" he shouted. "God *damn* it!" The digit flopped as he hugged it to his chest.

Gail's heart pounded as if to bruise itself. Never in a million millennia would she have imagined a time when she'd descend to this level of depravity.

"Billy, you need to understand that I am not the sort of person who does this kind of thing. You need to understand that Roman Alexander is very, very important to me. You are not."

"I–I don't even know what you're talking about."

Her next shot relieved him of the tip of his right elbow, causing his arm to jerk and slam the thumb into the table. He howled in pain.

Gail fought the urge to vomit. "It's too late to deny," she said. "Your face shows everything."

"You bitch! I'll have you put in prison for the rest—"

"Just stop!" Gail yelled. "You're going to do nothing but suffer and bleed, Billy. I can plink away at you all night, and the only way to limit how crippled you'll be tomorrow morning is to tell me what the arrangements are for delivering Roman Alexander and Ciara Kelly back to their homes."

"When the police get ahold of you—"

Gail coughed out a laugh. Genuine amusement. "You do that," she said. "I can't wait to hear the recording of the phone call." She did finger quotes with her free hand. "*I let a crazed assassin into my home, and she tortured me until I gave up the details of the kidnappings I suborned.* That will play well in the media, counselor."

"I'm taking you down," Monroe seethed.

She shot a trench into the flesh of his right shoulder. "Look at what I'm doing to you," Gail said. Her voice caught in her throat, and she swiped tears from her eyes. "How can you possibly take me farther down than these depths where I already am?"

She let her words hang in the air, felt encouraged when Monroe looked away. The flesh of his face had taken on a gray hue. It couldn't have been from blood loss, because she hadn't hit any major vessels, but the pain must have been nearly unbearable.

"Make no mistake, Billy," she said, hoping that this would seal the deal and allow this horror show to stop. "I will continue to shoot chunks off of you all night long if I have to. For both our sakes, please don't make me do that."

Monroe's eyes reddened, and his lower lip began to tremble. "It wasn't supposed to be like this," he said. "I was a good lawyer once. An honest lawyer."

"I'm not your priest," Gail said. "Every second is precious to those young people. I need to know where they are and what the plan is to trade them off."

"I–I don't know where they are," he said. The pain had started to take hold, and his tone had turned desperate, pleading. "I swear to you."

She believed him. "Are they with Cristos Silva?"

Instant confirmation in his face. "How can you know that?"

"Tell me the plan," Gail said. She owed him no information, and she sure as hell was not going to waste time answering his questions.

She listened for the better part of ten minutes as Monroe relayed details of the drop-off. When he was done, Venice said into her ear, "I got it all. Ask him what number he called before you arrived."

"It's safe to assume that you were speaking to Cristos Silva when I arrived, right?" Gail asked.

Monroe considered lying, then changed his mind. "Yes."

"I need that number."

Horror. "I–I . . ."

"Stammering is not answering," Gail pressed.

"I don't have it memorized."

"It's written down, then?"

He again wrestled with the thought of lying. Finally, he nodded. "It's over at my desk."

Gail took a step back and motioned for him to stand. "Go get it."

"I'm not sure I can get up."

"There's nothing wrong with your legs," Gail said. "Yet."

Clearly in agony and listing to his right, Monroe struggled out of his chair and steadied himself before taking tentative steps toward the foyer. Blood dropped in heavy spatters from his wounds, and he moaned with each step.

"God *damn* this hurts," he said.

Gail said nothing. As they passed from the area of closed blinds to open ones, she lowered her pistol down to her side but remained on point, fully aware that he was crossing into new territory. Whereas the dining room table was clear and every corner could be assessed with a glance, the first floor office was a study in clutter.

As he hobbled across the wooden floor, he cast a glance backward, as if to make sure that she was still following.

"Still here," she said. "Just be careful. Be mindful of your hands. When you give me what I need, I can be on my way. This is all about to be over."

Not a superstitious person, Gail didn't believe in angels and devils on your shoulders or in the importance of hairs standing up on the nape of your neck, but she sensed that something was wrong here. Perhaps it was the speed and ease with which Monroe had shifted from aggression to remorse. This effort at cooperation didn't sit well at all.

The phone number was important, but it wasn't critical. With it, Venice could find the phone among the cell phone towers in Mazatlán, but mostly as a means to verify that Jonathan and his team were in the right place. Also, with the phone number, they could block Monroe from doubling back with a warning to Silva. That warning could spell disaster.

But Gail had a plan for that, too. This house had a basement, and Venice had been able to find through a popular real estate app how the developer had laid them out. She knew exactly where the water heater was—and the furnace. By the time Gail left this place, Monroe would be securely chained to one or the other.

"I'm going to have to reach inside one of the drawers," Monroe said.

"I don't think you do," Gail countered. "That doesn't even make sense. No one uses pen and paper anymore. Open up your encrypted file instead, and pull up the number."

Another look of shock.

"We're very good at what we do, Billy," Gail said. "We know about the files. We know your password to your machine, and we know that you have a thing for the kind of online porn that could get you put away for a long time."

Utter shock.

She didn't see a reason to tell him that they intended to share the kiddie porn link with the real FBI when this all settled out. If the Cortez Cartel didn't execute him outright for dropping this ball, they would have adequate opportunity to off him during his inevitable long prison term.

This was Gail's first experience with flat-out vengeance, and as much as she knew it was well-earned, it all made her uncomfortable. Made her feel dirty. This was not what she'd signed on for.

Monroe hadn't moved for ten seconds or more.

"The file isn't going to open itself," Gail reminded.

"Of course." Monroe made it to his desk, then stopped. He turned. His color was awful. "If I may ask, what is the rest of your plan for tonight? Are you going to kill me?"

"Not if you don't make me. You're of no use to me dead."

"I don't see how you can walk away," he said. "If our roles were reversed, I would kill you. I would have to."

"I hope that is but one of many ways in which we are entirely different," Gail said.

"I want you to kill me."

"No."

"I don't want to die at the hands of Silva and his henchmen."

"I need the phone number," Gail said.

"If I give it to you, will you promise to shoot me?"

Gail knew there was a right answer. She believed that he meant what he was saying—at least for now—and she also knew that the words were driven more by pain and fear than by true belief. If she promised to kill him, she could always renege at the end, but that somehow made things only worse.

"I can't do that," Gail said. "I am many things, and many of those things are shameful. But I am not a murderer." As she spoke, she realized that she'd heard Digger speak nearly the same words. Were they merely the ultimate in rationalization?

Gail saw the determination set into Monroe's eyes. He was going to force the issue. Despite his wounds, he moved with startling speed to jerk open the top drawer of his desk, and even in the dim light of the desk lamp she could make out the grip of a chrome-colored revolver.

As Monroe reached for the gun with his good hand, Gail lashed out with a kick that she hoped would break his wrist between the drawer and its slot, but he'd moved too fast. Instead, the door closed against the cylinder of the revolver.

Off balance now, Gail dropped to one knee as she watched the gun come around on her.

"Don't!" she shouted, but he never slowed. Her finger jerked on the trigger, and she nailed him twice in the forehead, then once in the chest as he collapsed to the floor.

"Goddammit!" she yelled.

"What?" Venice asked in her ear. "What happened?"

"I had to shoot him. He pulled a gun and made me kill him."

"You need to get out of the house, Gunslinger."

"He had a gun! Why didn't he just shoot himself? Why did he make me do it?"

"Slinger, listen to me," Venice said. She'd engaged her motherly tone. "We got the confirmation we needed, and we got the plan. Call it a win and get out."

Gail stared at the body. Monroe wasn't the first man she'd killed, not by a large margin, but each one seemed to carve a larger divot out of her soul.

"Are you moving?" Venice asked.

Gail closed her eyes and settled herself with a deep breath.

"You did nothing wrong," Venice said. "You're saving Roman's—"

"I know what I'm doing, Mother Hen," she snapped. "I know all too well what I'm doing."

Before heading back toward the foyer and on to the front door, she separated the suppressor from the pistol and slipped them back into their respective pockets.

"You're going to need to take the car directly to the scrapyard," Venice instructed.

"Yeah, I know," Gail said.

"I'll make sure to have another car waiting for you."

Gail took the bud out of her ear and slipped that back into her pocket, too. Then she switched her radio off

VOX. She didn't need voices in her head right now, not even friendly ones.

As she closed the door behind her, she scanned the surrounding homes, wondering how many video doorbells and security cameras were taking her picture right now. In the end, it wouldn't matter because Venice would be able to wipe every record clear with a single swipe at the cloud.

Gail and her team could do anything now, she thought wryly. They could crush constitutional rights, invade privacy, and even commit murder without consequence.

All in the quest to save a life.

Chapter Twenty-four

Silva closed his eyes and leaned far back into his chair, tilting the seat until the joint at the base cracked. Nothing about this plan had gone right. No, that wasn't right. *Everything* about this plan had gone *wrong*.

Santiago Pérez was going to be furious when he found out that the FBI bitch was still alive. God only knew what he would order as a result. His son, Fernando, would never be able to rest peacefully again, now that the once-greatest law enforcement agency in the world was going to be 100 percent committed to bringing the kid to justice because of the threat to their agent.

This strategy had been stupid from the outset, but one did not live long by telling Pérez that he'd made a mistake.

Ciara Kelly's worth had diminished to zero now. In fact, she'd transitioned over to the liability column. He supposed that she could prove her worth in one of his other clubs, but he worried about the fact that she knew him in a context outside of the flesh trade. He worried that she knew him at all, for that matter. None of the other workers did.

Still, the notion of killing her unsettled him. Again, it was the fact of the relationship. And her youth. Her father had proven himself to be a loyal employee for more than a few years. In retrospect, he should have trusted Patrick to do his best to do what was expected of him. He'd never said *no* in the past.

On the other hand, he'd never been asked to commit so grievous a crime.

So, the stupid decision to murder the FBI bitch was on Pérez, but the stupid decision to take Ciara as collateral was all on him. Silva was a big enough man to take that responsibility onto himself.

But what about Roman Alexander? What the hell had be been thinking?

Silva studied the photo of the terrorists from the gentleman's club. Though faceless, they certainly were recognizable. Especially the tall one. The huge one. These people had hurt the cartel before, he was certain of it. Multiple times, perhaps.

There were stories from the Jungle Tigers up north near the Gulf coast about a suspected military intervention that left a dozen or more members of the cartel dead, including its leader, Orlando Azul. Rumor had it that the mysterious American team escaped by sea after an epic shoot-out at a seaside mansion.

Later, as they were about to be arrested by a Mexican navy patrol boat, a helicopter from the United States intervened.

Other rumors had swirled through Silva's world about similar operations. Not just with the Jungle Tigers and Antonio Filho's production operations, but elsewhere, as well. As often happens, these attacks took on a mythical status as they were repeated over and over. Among Silva's associates, the group had become known as *Los Raders Sigliosos*—the Stealth Raiders.

Now that he thought about it in earnest, it occurred to him that in each of the no doubt apocryphal stories, an element of rescue figured prominently. In the raid that killed Orlando Azul, the residents of an entire orphanage were escorted out of the country. In Colombia, as Filho's production facilities were destroyed, several of the juvenile workers were also taken away.

If Silva remembered correctly, one of the children taken from Filho was an American.

The orphans taken from the Jungle Tigers were not, however, so he needed to be careful not to draw conclusions that would not be supported by the facts.

The workers stolen from the gentleman's club weren't Americans, so far as Silva knew, but they were of a certain age, and their nationalities were from all over the globe.

And they were stolen in a hail of gunfire. By Americans.

Ciara Kelly was American. And Roman Alexander was most definitely from the United States.

The coincidence was beyond troubling.

Standing from his table, Silva slipped his paddle-holstered Glock 43 into the waistband of his trousers and walked to the door. Outside, night had nearly fallen on this long, difficult day.

He strolled across the yard toward the barn. The screaming had stopped, thank God, and he wanted to make sure that Guzman hadn't gone too far with Alberto, who would serve a far better purpose as a crippled example to others than he'd ever served as a manager of Silva's business. He had no value as a corpse, however, and sometimes Guzman couldn't stop himself. That man enjoyed his job far too much.

As he crossed the threshold of the barn's large double doors, he slapped the switch on the wall, bringing to life a line of three dangling incandescent lightbulbs. The artist in him admired the pattern of shadows that the dim yellow light created, a patchwork of geometric shapes and slashes.

Even in the dimness, Alberto's blood trail stood out in high relief in the dust and grit of the barn floor.

Alberto himself lay in a heap on the far end. He was not moving.

Guzman was standing over Roman, who was chained nearby. He spun around as the lights came on, his face a mask of worry, as if he'd done something wrong. Silva locked him with a glare and strolled closer to Alberto. The man was a mess. Both arms appeared to be broken, along with both ankles. His hands had been crushed.

"Dammit, Guzman, what have you done?"

He noted the look that transpired between Guzman and the boy, and he didn't like what he saw.

"He is not dead," Guzman said defensively.

"He might as well be," Silva said. "Look at him. He will never heal from this."

"Was that not the point?"

Silva had to laugh. Such was the simple nature of Guzman's world. "Yes, I suppose it was. Are you sure he is still alive?"

Guzman pointed with the head of the hammer. "His chest is moving. He is breathing. He is alive."

Silva pointed at Roman with his forehead. "What did you do to the boy?"

"Nothing," Guzman said, a little too quickly, Silva thought. "Not a thing."

"Why were you standing there so close to him when I came in?"

"We were talking."

"Uh-huh." Silva walked around the other man and approached Roman. In English, he asked, "Are you all right?"

"No, I'm not all right!" the boy shouted. His eyes were red and wet, and he looked terrified.

"Did my friend hurt you?"

"Yes! You were there."

Silva smiled. He admired the boy's spirit. "I do not mean from before. I mean did he hurt you within the last thirty minutes?"

"I can't feel my hands."

Silva thought about that. Not being able to feel is, after all, the very opposite of pain. The kid had too much attitude and energy to have been hurt. Perhaps later.

He looked at his watch. Billy Monroe should be reaching out to the frightened family any minute now, if he hadn't done so already.

"Guzman," he said, summoning the man to join him at his side. In Spanish, he said, "I am concerned by the co-incidence of the club being burned at the same time we are managing this other business."

"What do you think might be happening?"

"That does not matter," he said. "But I want you to

bring in more of the boys. I want a triple guard here around the clock until further notice."

"Starting when?"

"Five minutes ago. Make it happen."

Guzman seemed relieved not to be scolded or disciplined for whatever he was planning to do to this boy.

When Guzman was gone and he and Roman were alone, Silva sat on the ground across from the lad, who at least seemed more comfortable now that he had a stable rail to lean against. Roman sat with his knees drawn up to his chest. Was it possible to lose weight in twenty-four hours? Roman Alexander seemed drawn, much thinner somehow than he'd been yesterday and this morning.

"Are you unwell, Roman?" he asked.

Roman gave him the kind of look that only adolescent children can muster on command. The silent, *Don't be stupid.*

Silva strained to peer over to the piss bucket they'd left for him. It was empty. "Have you been drinking the water we've been giving you?"

Roman stared back, saying nothing.

"It's important not to let yourself become dehydrated," Silva said. He reached out and patted the top of the young man's bare foot. "This will be over for you soon."

Roman jerked his foot away, and Silva raised his hands in surrender. "It was a gesture of reassurance," he said. "Nothing more, I promise."

"Where is Ciara?"

"She is resting inside."

"What have you done with her?"

"Young man, I am trying to be friendly with you, but you make it very difficult."

"Yeah, sorry about that," Roman said.

Such insolence. Silva reached out for Roman's foot again, but this time, he grabbed it in a vicelike grip, and he yanked it straight, eliciting a startled yelp. "There's a reason I never fathered children," he said as calmly as he could. It took real effort to not show violence. "I don't like them. They are not cute. They are not entertaining. They are burdens to be carried or business options to be exploited. Nothing more. You would be wise to consider your words before you speak them."

The boy's face had changed. The insolence had morphed to fear, and Silva found solace in that. "I think I sent you the wrong message when I pressed Guzman about harming you. I fear you might have interpreted that as an interest in your well-being. Perhaps you think we might become friends."

Silva squeezed Roman's ankle tighter and twisted it to its limit. The boy shifted to the side to ease the pressure. He let go, and Roman instantly retracted the leg and tucked his ankles under his thighs.

"Look at that man," Silva went on, pointing to Alberto Bris, who was just now beginning to stir. "The only thing keeping you from looking like him is a single command from me. I say this not to frighten you, though clearly you are frightened. I say this so that you understand the reality of your situation. When I clashed with Guzman a few minutes ago, it had nothing to do with *you*. I had given him orders not to deal with you. Yet. If that time comes, then let it come. Do you understand me? Understand what I am trying to communicate to you?"

Roman's head jerked quickly, spasmed, really.

"If that was a nod, I would prefer to hear you say it."

"I understand," he said.

"Very well." Silva forced himself to smile. "Now, moving on, what happens to young Ciara is none of your concern. Do you understand me?"

"Yes. Sir."

"Much, much better, Roman. Truly, your life here will be so much easier if you think about your words before you state them. And showing respect to me is always important."

"I understand, sir."

"Very, *very* good." Silva folded his own ankles under his thighs, mirroring Roman. "Tell me more about your friend, Mr. Grave. What is his first name again?"

"Jonathan."

"Of course. Tell me more about Jonathan Grave."

The boy looked genuinely confused. "I–I don't know what else you want to know."

"For example, does he travel a lot?"

"I suppose," Roman said with a noncommittal movement of his shoulders. "I don't know what a lot means."

"Fair enough. Your mother works for him, is that correct?"

"Yessir."

Silva could see that the boy had swallowed words he wanted to say. Probably something like, *I already told you that*. He considered it a good sign that Roman was thinking now. That his *head was right*, as the Americans liked to say.

"Do you know any of his friends?"

"Some, I guess. It's a small town."

"Is he in the military?"

"Not anymore," Roman said. "He used to be."

"Does he talk about that?"

"Not with me." Roman seemed to grow uncomfortable with the topic. "To be honest, Mr. Jonathan doesn't talk to me very much about anything."

"But he must talk with your mother."

"Of course."

"What does she tell you about his military service?"

"Not much. I mean, I don't ask. There's not a lot of talking about anything in our house, to be honest with you."

Silva considered that. Such must be the case in many households with teenagers, he supposed.

"Does your friend, your Mr. Jonathan, have any friends who are very large people?"

The flash of recognition could not have been more obvious. It didn't present itself for long, but it was there.

"Before I ask my next question, I want you to take another good look at my friend, Alberto Bris," he said, pointing. He waited while Roman got a good, long drink of the image.

"He is in that state because he works for me and he failed to do his job. He ran one of my business interests. Until earlier today, when some men burned the place down, stole my property, and killed some of my customers."

Silva enjoyed the aura of fear that enveloped the boy. "In retrospect, I worry that Guzman was perhaps too harsh with him. Alberto merely failed to stop the harm from happening. He didn't cause it himself."

Silva leaned to the side to get better access to his back pocket and the folded paper he'd placed there.

"I'm about to show you something, and your only chance of coming through this experience without being a cripple for the rest of your life is to be honest with me. If you lie, I will see it in your eyes."

He unfolded the paper. "These are the men who did all that harm to me and my business." He presented the photo of the terrorists to the boy. "Take a good look. Do you recognize these people?"

Jonathan and Dawkins pressed in close as Big Guy launched Roxie on a mission to scope out the hacienda Sofia had told them belonged to Cristos Silva. Night was falling fast, but Roxie could provide both low-light and infrared imagery. The issue now was the light of the computer screen. Boxers had parked the Durango well off the road, in a wooded area, but there weren't many artificial lights illuminated in this patch of the world, so any glow posed a potential problem.

To compensate, Boxers had draped an emergency blanket over the screen, the corners of which were held up by Jonathan and Dawkins, creating a kind of tent. It wasn't a perfect solution, but it would do.

As before, Big Guy had Roxie take them on a relatively high-altitude orientation tour of the property. The place looked like a ranch that could have been any other ranch of its kind. The main house was the most obvious structure, a one-story affair that seemed well appointed, at least from the outside. The heat signatures coming from the house indicated that it was occupied, though Roxie's detection capabilities at that level were rudimentary at best.

Roving guards, armed with what appeared to be MP5s, walked in pairs along the fence line, chatting like chums, their awareness levels hovering near cluelessness. The main gate, nearest the house, was equipped with the same kind of Beefeater shack that they'd seen at the rape house they'd burned.

"Same architect," Boxers quipped.

Sofia had said the hacienda sat on hundreds of acres, and Jonathan had no reason to doubt that assessment. All of it appeared to be fenced by tall chain-link barriers.

Other buildings on the property included pole barns for heavy equipment and stables for critters. The structure closest to the main house, about fifty yards distant, was a large barn that seemed in ill repair. Roxie detected cracks in the roof, and through those cracks, they could see the glow of a dim light inside.

"What are we looking for?" Dawkins asked.

"If you see it, let us know," Boxers said.

"See what?"

"Exactly."

"Don't listen to him," Jonathan said. "We're exploring. Ideally, we'll see a sign with Silva's name on it."

"No," Big Guy said. "*Ideally*, the sign would say *Roman is in here*."

"Is it your intent to hit this place?" Dawkins asked.

"Again, we're just gathering intel at this point. What we see will determine what we'll do next."

"So, we're winging it," Dawkins concluded.

"You're not new to our little family," Boxers said. "I miss the days when we would actually plan an op, but winging it seems to be our new normal."

Jonathan tapped Dawkins's arm. "Do me a favor and pull up the ransom video Roman shot."

Dawkins pulled his phone from his pocket, tapped it a few times, and turned it so Jonathan could see.

"Hey, Big Guy," Jonathan said. "Take a look at Thor's screen."

Boxers clicked a button to cause Roxie to hover in place, then straightened. "Whatcha got?"

"Look at the background behind Roman," Jonathan said. "Zoom past him, Thor. I want to see the fence rail behind him."

Dawkins took the phone back, used his thumb and forefinger to stretch the image, then held it out again for everyone to see.

"Okay," Jonathan said. "Take Roxie a little lower." On Roxie's image, he pointed to the corral fence on the far side of the barn. "I think that fence is the same one in the background of the ransom video."

Boxers leaned into the computer screen, then shifted over to the image on the phone. "A fence is a fence, Scorpion. Yeah, it could be the same one, but I think you could say that about the fence at your compound in Charlottesville."

"Look at the alignment of the trees in the background," Jonathan said.

Dawkins said, "Jeez, Scorpion, I see what you're talking about, but is it the same, or do you just want it to be?"

"Two things can be correct simultaneously," Jonathan said. He knew what he saw. He understood the dangers of overcommitting to a hypothesis, but he also knew that not every good thing had to have a dark side.

"Take her up and see if we can peek through the cracks in the roof," Jonathan instructed.

His earbud popped to life. "Scorpion, Mother Hen." The suddenness of the interruption startled them all.

Jonathan keyed his mic. "Go ahead."

"I have the transfer location. Gunslinger paid a visit to the middleman, and he shared it with her. It's going to happen at midnight."

Shit like this always happens at midnight, Jonathan thought. "Can you download the location to my GPS?"

"Already done."

"Who was the middleman?"

"Doesn't matter," Venice said. "It didn't end well for him."

"Is Slinger okay?"

"Physically, I believe so."

Jonathan knew what that meant. Gail's tolerance of moral ambiguity was less generous than his own. He didn't pursue it further.

"We've also verified that Cristos Silva is the kidnapper," Venice said.

Jonathan turned to the others. "We've got 'em," he said off the air. He keyed his mic again. "I think we're getting close, Mother Hen."

"Have you seen him?"

"No eyes on yet, but other signs are good. I need to go."

"Please keep me in the loop," Venice said.

"Of course. Scorpion out." He turned to the others. "Soldier up, gents. Plates, lids, the whole shebang." The ballistic armor they'd worn earlier was fine for stopping pistol bullets, but a rifle round would pass right through as if it were a T-shirt. By slipping ceramic plates into the vests, they gained protection against all but the largest caliber rifle rounds. The lids—helmets—would also deflect most rifle rounds. It'd be a helluva a bell ringing, but at least their brain would stay encased between their ears.

Kitting out for combat was an exercise in tradeoffs. The extra weight and armor could only be achieved at the expense of greater energy expended and less mobility and flexibility of motion. Sometimes, you had to roll the dice and hope for the best, but this time, given the fact that they were here to bring Roman home, Jonathan opted for maximum protection.

Nothing damages a rescue attempt as quickly or thoroughly as losing a rescuer in the process.

They moved the computer around to the tailgate so they could continue to watch the feed as they geared up. The light was still a problem, but the extra illumination allowed them to kit up more quickly. Jonathan and Dawkins went first so Big Guy could continue to pilot Roxie around the hacienda, looking for solid confirmation that Roman was, in fact, present. The cracks in the roof were too narrow to reveal anything useful, but shifting shadows made it clear that people were moving around inside.

Jonathan had just rested his vest onto his shoulders when the air filled with the sound of fast-moving vehicles. "The hell is that?"

On the computer screen, the ground dropped away as Roxie zipped up to a hundred feet, and they observed a line of vehicles streaming through the front gate. Four of them flooded in during a first wave, and then, two minutes later, a second wave of eight more screamed through.

The men who exited the vehicles looked armed for war. They carried many varieties of long guns, and most had pistols strapped to their waists and thighs.

"What do you think this means, Boss?" Boxers asked.

"I think it means I'm glad we didn't dawdle," Jonathan

said. He pointed to the screen at a man who was striding from the main house toward the barn. "Wait. Who's that? Is that Cristos Silva?"

Dawkins leaned in and squinted. "No, it's not," he said. He leaned in closer still and then stood tall again. "Oh, shit. It's way worse than Silva."

Chapter Twenty-five

Silva listened with satisfaction as his reinforcements arrived outside. Guzman had understood his orders. The men that he'd summoned were among the toughest, most ruthless operators that Silva had ever known. Buoyed by the authority they wielded courtesy of the Cortez family, they had evolved into a useful level of thuggery that kept them well feared and even better compensated.

When notified that they were needed, they came without question. When they were told to kill or maim, they performed without hesitation.

If Roman Alexander's friend, Mr. Jonathan, tried to pull the kind of shit here that he'd pulled elsewhere, he wouldn't live to see the top of the next hour.

Guzman pushed the double doors open and strode into the barn. His smile showed his pleasure at coming through on his mission. The ever-present sledgehammer dangled loosely from his hand.

"They came quickly," Guzman said in Spanish.

"Yes, they did," Silva agreed. "Thank you for your prompt attention. Now, I have some unpleasant business for you to take care of."

As if reading his boss's mind, Guzman shifted his gaze to Roman.

"Go and get Ciara from her quarters. Bind her hands and bring her out here."

"May I ask why?"

"Her father failed in his task," Silva explained. "Now, she is merely a liability."

"But a very pretty one," Guzman observed. "Could you not get top dollar for her services?"

"Perhaps. But she knows too much about me. About us. She needs to be disposed of."

"And the boy?" Guzman's lips twisted into a smile.

"After the show-and-tell for the ransom."

"Do you want me to do them together?"

Silva gave a noncommittal shrug. "I suppose that makes the most sense." He raised a forefinger and pointed it to Guzman's face. "Make it fast and painless," he said.

Some of the smile went away.

"I'm serious about this," Silva said. "Certainly, with the girl. Her father used to be one of us."

"And the boy?"

"Why do you hate him so?" Silva asked.

"He fought me," Guzman said. "He hit me. No one hits me."

Silva understood what Guzman was thinking. As a man whose reputation was built on pure fear, he stood to lose a great deal if word got out that anyone, let alone a boy, had landed a punch without consequence, and the results could be dire.

"All right, then," Silva said. "Just be sure to get rid of the bodies."

"We're not mailing the parts home?" More disappointment.

"Not for this one. Roman's mother is performing her role, and Ciara's mother is not involved at all. I do not want to be cruel. Now, go get the girl."

"That's Guzman," Dawkins explained.

"If we reposition, we can take him out," Boxers said.

"Not yet," Jonathan instructed. "Too many people. Too much return fire. And if Roman is, in fact, down there, we might as well shoot him directly."

"So, your plan is to wait?" Boxers asked. "How's that working for us so far? While we've been twiddling our thumbs, a whole world of reinforcements has arrived. Are we planning to wait for more?"

Jonathan bristled. "Personally, I think it's better they arrived before we were committed to some balls-out strike than in the middle of one." He keyed his mic. "Mother Hen, Scorpion. You still there?"

"Are you going hot?" In normal times, when she asked that question, her tone was hesitant. Now it was more akin to a kid at Christmas.

"Not sure yet. What can you tell me about the electrical grid around Cristos Silva's hacienda?"

He heard typing in the background. "Is that where you're pinging from now?"

"Affirmative."

"Stand by one." Venice clicked off the channel for

thirty seconds and then returned. "He's on public utilities, and he seems to pay his bills on time. The electric bill seems low to me, though. He must either get a special rate or supplement his electricity from somewhere."

"Can you locate the transformers for me?" Jonathan asked.

"Sure sounds like you're going hot," she said. She clicked off again.

"Mother Hen is amazing," Dawkins said. "How does she access all this stuff?"

"I know I wouldn't understand it if she told me, so I don't ask."

"I always think of her as a cyber door-kicker," Boxers said. While he and Venice had not always gotten along all that well, the tensions had eased recently. The mutual respect had always been there.

Jonathan's earbud popped. "Scorpion, Mother Hen."

"Go."

"There are three electrical transformers within two hundred yards of your location. I'm sending the coordinates to your phone."

His pocket buzzed with an incoming message. "Stand-by one." He pulled his phone from his pocket, clicked on the link, and showed it to Boxers, who copied the coordinates into his laptop. With a bit of finagling, he transferred them as red dots onto the map that Roxie had been creating as she flew.

"Shit," he said. "One of them's just on the other side of the trees." He leaned into his screen. "The others are an easy rifle shot."

"So, we've got a good chance that we can bring darkness to the compound," Jonathan said.

"If he's got this much money, he's got backup generators," Dawkins said.

Jonathan keyed his mic. "Mother Hen, let's stretch the boundaries of the impossible. Can you find out whether or not Silva has backup generators?"

"He bought two of them in the past three years," Venice said without dropping a beat.

"How do you know that so fast?"

"I already told you," she said. "The bills seemed low, so I searched purchase records from local suppliers and saw that he bought two generators. One for twelve thousand dollars and another for about eight thousand."

"The twelve grand would be for a whole-house generator," Jonathan said over the air. "The eight grand unit would be smaller, less capable." He looked to Boxers. "Find them."

The ground dropped away again as Roxie climbed high.

"I imagine the big one would be close to the house, right?" Big Guy asked, perhaps to himself. Roxie flew over the roof of the main house and into the backyard, where a squatty shed sat by itself on the far side. "I think that's it." He took the drone nearly into the grass and edged her forward for a better look. Sure enough, the shed was a lean-to that provided shelter to the generator.

"We can't hit that from here," Dawkins observed. "The house is in the way."

"I told you I wanted munitions capability," Boxers bitched. "But nooo . . ."

"If you could use Roxie to shoot people, the streets of your neighborhood would be littered with bodies," Jonathan said.

Boxers grinned. "I don't understand the problem."

The second generator sat in a similar but smaller shed tucked in behind the crumbling barn. If they could get just a little elevation, that one would be in view and in range.

"All right," Jonathan said. "If we need to take them out, at least we know where they are. Let's hope that the transformers will help out some." Boxers returned Roxie to her orbit over the main yard.

"Uh-oh," Dawkins said. "There's Guzman again. And he's got company."

"Shit," Jonathan spat. "That's Ciara Kelly. Mount up, folks. We need to get into position. You can leave Roxie hovering where she is, right?"

"I can have her do whatever you'd like," Boxers said with what could only be described as a tone of paternal pride. Big Guy leaned into the Durango's bed and pulled the gear bag a little closer. He pulled out the pistol case for their Ruger SR22 and can suppressor. Useful for close-in work, it was one of the few firearm combos that truly were silenced by their "silencers."

"Whatcha doin', Big Guy?" Jonathan asked.

"Killing the closest transformer. Might as well take care of it now."

"Please don't do that," Jonathan said. "Not yet."

"Why wait for a long shot when you take a close one?"

"Transformers blow up after you shoot them," Jonathan observed. "Let's wait till we're in position and ready to charge."

Boxers' hands hovered in the air, then he put the gun case back into the bag. "Charge?" he said with a derisive chuckle. "Did you really just say *charge*? If I knew we were gonna play cavalry, I'd have brought my friggin' bugle."

Roman's stomach flipped when they brought Ciara into the barn. She didn't look beaten, but she looked thoroughly whipped. Her eyes looked scarlet in the dim light, and she was somehow thinner than before. She walked awkwardly, shuffled really, with her head down and her gaze unfocused. Her hands had been bound behind her back. The brute Guzman ushered her over to where Roman was trussed and ordered her to sit.

"Are you okay?" he asked.

Her look seared his brain.

"I mean, are you hurt? Did they—" He didn't know how to phrase the question, so he stopped asking.

"Nobody touched me," she said. No eye contact at all. "They've had me chained to a bed in a bedroom like an animal. I kept expecting someone to come in and, well, you know. But no one did."

Roman felt relief, but it was not as profound as it probably should have been. At least she got a bed.

"How about you?" she asked, though she didn't seem really to care.

"Better than him." Roman gestured with his forehead to the broken man on the ground. He'd been moaning for quite a while now, but he never quite woke up.

"I'm sorry for getting you involved with this," Ciara said.

"I don't even know what *this* is," Roman said. "Beyond the obvious. Why did they take you in the first place?"

"Something about my father," she said. "But he's not rich."

"I thought that guy was your friend."

"I did, too. My father's friend, anyway." Her eyes grew wet again. "What do you think—"

"I don't know," Roman interrupted. For whatever reason, he didn't want to hear the question. One thing he knew for sure was that Mr. Jonathan would pay the ransom if he could. He had no idea how much that was, but from what he could tell and from what he'd heard, Mr. Jonathan had more money than God.

"But I think we're going to be okay."

"My parents don't have any money," Ciara said. "They can't pay anything for me."

Roman didn't reply. What could he say? He'd lost track of the number of times Mr. Jonathan had told him that as long as you never gave up, there always was hope.

Guzman had walked back to Mr. Silva and was talking quietly about something. Roman didn't like the way the killer kept looking back at him.

"Can you understand what they're saying?" Roman asked.

"I can't hear a word."

"Can you lip read?"

"I'm not that good with Spanish," she said, not bothering to look at them at all.

"Can you at least *try*?"

She drilled him with another glare. "What difference does it make, Roman? They're going to do whatever the hell they want to do. We can't stop them."

"It's better to know than not know."

"I'm not sure that's right," Ciara said.

"Here is the plan," Silva explained to Guzman. "We need to load the boy and the girl into a car, and we're going to head for Ahome. At midnight, once the family has seen their precious little boy and the money is in the account, we'll push them both back into the car and then you will be on your way into the jungle with them."

"What about Alberto?"

Silva sighed and swallowed his anger as he looked at the broken man on the floor.

"I'm sorry I went too far with him," Guzman said.

"I know you are."

"He will never recover."

"Fine," Silva said. "Dispose of him, as well. But next time . . ." He let his words trail off because it made no sense to complete the thought.

"I know. I'm sorry."

"Right. Get to work."

"Why leave so early?" Guzman asked. "We have hours before the drop-off."

"I want them out of here," Silva said. He didn't want to go into the details, but the sooner he had these kids off his land, the better they all were going to be.

"Are you expecting trouble here?" Guzman asked. "Is that why you summoned all the men?"

"I have concerns, yes. I have an idea that Mr. Roman's Mr. Jonathan may be the same man who burned down the club earlier today."

Guzman's brow showed concern, but he knew better than to press for details.

"Take most of the others with you," Silva instructed. "Leave me with five. Travel as a motorcade, then stop somewhere at least five kilometers from the drop-off point. Wait there in silence until midnight approaches."

"Do you want us to leave now?"

"Right now," Silva said.

"How will I know when it is okay to leave the drop-off site?"

"I will call you when I get confirmation that the ransom money has been placed in the proper account."

Guzman turned to the children and flipped the hammer in the air and caught it, as if it weighed nothing.

"I'll be with you two soon," he said.

Roman felt the panic building as Guzman approached. This was it. He wasn't sure what that meant, exactly, but he somehow knew that this was the beginning of the end. There'd been too many glances, too many secretive conversations.

The fact that after all these hours—or was it days—they'd finally brought Ciara out to join him meant that something major had changed.

Guzman walked first to the broken man on the floor. He'd stopped moaning a while ago, about the same time as he'd stopped moving. Guzman tapped the man's ribs with the toe of his boot. When he didn't move, he tapped a little harder. Then he kicked.

"Oh, my God!" Ciara cried.

Guzman whirled at the sound of her voice and lifted

his hammer. He was too far away to cause her harm, but the message was clear.

"You need to be quiet," Roman whispered. "This guy is crazy."

"Not crazy!" Guzman yelled in English. "Thorough!"

Silva had nearly exited the barn when the outburst brought him back. The two men discussed something in Spanish. As they did, Guzman looked troubled. Embarrassed, maybe. It ended with Silva shouting something and storming away.

"What did he say?" Roman whispered.

"He said to just leave him there. That he—Mr. Silva— will take care of the body. He also said something about not getting carried away again."

Guzman didn't move for a long time, maybe thirty seconds. He stood with his head bowed, his shoulders slumped. In a weird way, he reminded Roman of a dog who'd been scolded.

When Guzman straightened again and turned, he was as scary as ever, even more as he smiled. "Now, children," he said in English. "It is time for us to take a ride."

Oh, shit.

"W–where are we going?" Roman asked. His voice sounded reedy and whiny.

Guzman's smile spread. "Someplace other than here."

"Did Mr. Jonathan pay my ransom?" Roman asked.

Guzman said nothing. Instead, he pulled the boy's body forward till his head nearly touched his knees and worked on the chain that held him in place in front of the stable wall. The lock clicked, and Guzman pulled Roman's head back up by his hair.

"Stand," Guzman commanded. "Both of you."

When Roman had difficulty getting his feet under him, Guzman pulled harder on his hair. It helped with his balance, but it hurt like hell. He didn't yell this time, though.

"Can you uncuff my hands?" Roman asked.

"So that you can fight me again? Do not insult me, boy."

"What about me?"

"You have only been in them for a short time," Guzman said. "You will be out of them before you need to get used to them."

"Are we being set free?" Ciara asked.

"He won't give you the satisfaction of an answer," Roman said, earning a hard shove that made him stumble over the dead man on the floor. This time, he got his feet under him quickly, and he turned away from the corpse. He told himself that he didn't really see those broken bones move the way he knew he had. His stomach tumbled, but whatever was in there stayed down.

"Now," Guzman said. "You will keep your mouth shut, and you will walk out through those doors and stand until I join you."

Ciara waited for Roman to join her, then they stepped shoulder to shoulder out into the night.

Chapter Twenty-six

"**H**oly shit," Dawkins called from the backseat. "That's them! They just stepped out of the barn. Both of them. Roman and Ciara."

They'd just climbed into the Durango, and Boxers was easing the vehicle back out onto the road. At the sound of Dawkins's words, Big Guy hit the gas and launched them all into their seats.

"Big Guy, stop!" Jonathan commanded. He whirled in his seat and beckoned for Dawkins to hand over the laptop. When he got it, he handed it to Boxers. Together, they watched their precious cargo being led to one of four SUVs, all of them lined up nose to tail. The kids walked like prisoners on their way to their executions. Heads low, Roman's arms bound to his sides, Ciara's behind her back.

"Why are we waiting here?" Boxers demanded.

"Because they have all the advantages," Jonathan said. "Even if we got there before they all drove off, there's no way to protect the kids if a firefight breaks out. It's too risky."

"So, we do nothing?"

"Hell, no," Jonathan said.

Dawkins said, "We know where they're going. We get there first and lie in wait."

"That's not all true," Jonathan cautioned. "We know where they *say* they're going. That doesn't mean they'll actually go there. Can you imprint the kids' vehicle on Roxie so she'll track them wherever they go?"

Boxers clacked a few keys. "Already done," he said.

As Silva watched the caravan of vehicles snake through his main gate, a sense of calm settled over him. This whole mess had dragged him and his business in directions they never should have gone. The damage caused by the terrorists at his gentleman's club was only now beginning to clarify for him.

Two police officers numbered among the dead. Their demise was going to cause ripples through all of his businesses as word spread among politicians that the cartel's armor was not as impenetrable as everyone believed. Sooner than later, Silva was going to have to brief Señor Cortez himself on the scope of the disaster. That was something that could wait until tomorrow—until he had final news to report on the Kelly girl. Cortez had no need to know this business with Roman Alexander, however. That was all on Silva, as were the profits flowing therefrom.

He turned to walk back into his home—and a fine

glass of scotch—when his phone buzzed in his pocket. The caller ID showed PRIVATE NUMBER. Ordinarily, Silva would have ignored it, but he thought he might know who this was.

He pressed CONNECT. "Yes?"

"Is this Cristos?"

"Antonio Filho?"

"No one other."

"Yes, this is Cristos. It has been a long time." He continued his stroll toward the scotch.

"Those pictures," Filho said. "When were they taken?"

"Earlier today."

"Do you know where those sons of whores are?"

"Not exactly. But I believe they are nearby. They torched one of my businesses today. Are they American military?"

"I do not know who they work for," Filho said. "But I want their heads separated from their shoulders. I want to turn them into lamps for my nightstand." Antonia Filho was not a man of emotion. He was not one to easily spin up into anger, but even from a thousand miles away, Silva could hear the emotion in his voice.

"Why are they there in your business?" Filho asked.

"That is a long and complicated story," Silva said. "I will not bore you with the details. What it boils down to is the fact that I somehow ended up with his . . . Let's say I had custody of his adopted son. As we were negotiating a ransom, this Jonathan Grave found his way to Mexico. It seems he does not respect the way business is conducted here."

"Did you say you have his son in custody?"

Silva saw no reason to complicate the conversation with the confusing details of Roman's relationship. "Yes.

Well, I did. They demanded proof of life before they would deposit the ransom. He is on the way to the agreed-upon place as we speak."

"You're giving the boy back?" Filho sounded horrified.

"Of course not. The boy will be . . . taken care of."

"I want him," Filho said.

"Excuse me?"

"The boy. I want him."

This was not what Silva had been expecting. "I don't understand."

"It is not a complicated statement, Cristos. I want the boy. I will pay you for the boy."

"For what purpose?" Even as he asked the question, Silva realized that he had no right to do so.

"That man—what did you say his name was?"

"Jonathan Grave."

"That Jonathan Grave set my operations back two years. He cost me millions of dollars. I want to put his boy to work for me in the coca fields."

Silva issued a low whistle. Working the Colombian coca fields was torturous work from which few people emerged alive. Those fields marked the first step in the production chain that fed the world's demand for cocaine. Silva had visited only one such production field, and he still marveled at the efficiency of production even as the children's hands bled from the effort of picking, and their backs bleeding from the flogging scars if they did not work hard enough.

"Tony, I understand your anger, but I have already negotiated an amount with his father. At this point, we are talking a business transaction."

"How much?"

"How much what?" Silva thought he knew what Filho was implying, but he wanted to hear the words.

"What do I need to pay you for the boy to be sent to me instead of being sent home with his father?"

"It is a large number, Tony. Please do not be offended when I tell you. The family will be paying me two million U.S. dollars."

"For one boy?"

"Their only boy," Silva corrected. "They are wealthy people."

"I will pay three for the boy to be sent to me."

Even for cocaine farmers, three million dollars was a *lot* of money. The desperation in Filho's voice told Silva that there was room for negotiation, but he opted not to. That extra million dollars, offered so quickly and without hesitation, told him that Filho was speaking from the heart. He would honor the offer he made.

"Can you do a transfer directly from your account to mine?" Silva asked.

"I can," Filho said. "It is a ridiculous amount of money to spend, but I cannot think of a better way to spend it."

"All right, then," Silva said. "May I ask a favor as well?"

"I am already paying you three million dollars for a child who cannot possibly earn his keep in three lifetimes," Filho said. "Is that not a favor already?"

Silva shrugged his phone into the crook of his neck as he uncorked the bottle of Balvenie scotch and poured two fingers into a crystal whisky glass. "There is another child involved in this mess," he said. He lifted the glass and took a sip. "I don't want to go into the details, but she is the daughter of a friend. Unfortunately, if she stays here, I must kill her. Can you take her, as well?"

"For how much?"

"No charge. Of course, no charge. She is fourteen years old and quite beautiful."

"Ah," Filho said. "Can you not earn a lot of money from her?"

"I could," Silva replied, "but there is the matter that she knows me. That complicates things."

"I see. Very well, then. Who can say no to a beautiful fourteen-year-old young lady?"

"Thank you, Tony."

"Don't thank me yet," Filho said. "There are some difficult details for you to deal with. Are you familiar with El Colorado, along the coast?"

"I am."

"A boat will be leaving shortly from just off the coast," Filho said. "Write down these coordinates." He spouted a string of map coordinates.

Silva jotted them down.

"Don't bother even looking at a map. Use your GPS system. This place is the middle of nowhere. Tender boats will make trips from the shore to my vessel, beginning in forty-three minutes."

"Is this boat for . . . product?" It was none of Silva's business, but why not ask?

"The boat is my property," Filho snapped. "It's too big to come in close to the shore, which is why we supply it via tenders. Have your guests on that boat. When they are on board my vessel, you will get paid. The vessel will not wait for you."

"When does the vessel leave?"

"Precisely at ten o'clock."

Silva looked at his watch. Eight-fifteen. If he remembered properly, the drive to El Colorado would take about an hour. As the crow flies, it was less than twenty miles away, but the roads out here could be a challenge, especially at night.

"All right," Silva said. "I will make that happen. Thank you, Tony."

The phone clicked off, and Silva made another call.

Guzman picked up on the second ring.

"Change in plans," Silva said.

In this part of Sinaloa, the only roadway of note was Los Mochis Higuera de Zaragoza. Running roughly east to west, the highway terminated at the Pacific Ocean to the west and just sort of died out in the east. Every other right-of-way, it seemed, was a narrow country road that threatened the side-view mirrors of every vehicle that traveled down them. The kidnappers had chosen an all-night bar in Ahome for the location of the proof-of-life transfer. If the bad guys came through on their end and released Roman and Ciara, there'd be no violence. It'd be too risky with the kids in the mix.

If, on the other hand, they reneged on the deal, no one but the kids would be safe from harm.

The kidnapper's four-vehicle motorcade traveled bumper-to-bumper at a consistent forty miles per hour, making Jonathan think that they'd done this before. Perhaps they were the security team for Cristos Silva and his deputies.

While Roxie kept them in view and continually broadcast Roman's coordinates, Jonathan was concerned about her battery life, so they stayed as close to the motorcade as they could.

"I counted ten bad guys," Boxers said from the driver's seat.

"Sounds about right," Jonathan said.

"I didn't bother to count," Dawkins said. From the backseat, his job was to monitor the Roxie feed. "I want to know why they started out so early."

"To catch us setting up early," Jonathan said. "They figure we might be setting a trap." He chuckled. "Which is only reasonable, I suppose, because that's what we're going to do."

"Maybe we should take them while they're cooling their heels," Boxers said. "Their guards will be down."

Big Guy had raised an interesting point. Depending on where they set up to while away the hours between now and the handoff, maybe that would, indeed, be the best time to get the kids. "If they separate the kids from the adults," Jonathan mused aloud, "or if they cover them with just a guard or two, you might have a point. We'll keep the option open."

Boxers filled out the rest of the plan that was forming in his head. "They're not going to want to wait around in a very public place. Too much chance for the kids to make a fuss or for them to be seen."

"The cops wouldn't dream of interfering," Dawkins observed.

"Still, a crowd is a crowd. I could be wrong, but we'll see. We'd go in dark, using night vision. *Pop-pop-pop*, all done."

"I think you might have skipped a couple of steps there, Big Guy, but if they're kind enough to do exactly what we'd like them to do, we're all set."

"Oh, shit!" Dawkins yelled from the backseat. "Stop, stop, stop. Pull off the road."

"God *damn* it!" Boxers spat as he leaned on the brakes. "What the hell!"

"They're turning around," Dawkins said. They're coming back at us. Maybe a half-mile out."

"Kill your lights and pull off the road, Big Guy," Jonathan commanded.

Boxers cut the headlights, and Dawkins slammed the laptop shut. As their world went dark, the glow of headlights bloomed on the horizon, the only headlights they'd seen since setting out fifteen minutes ago.

"Thor, pull the NVGs out of the bag. Big Guy, duck down." Jonathan and Boxers nearly bumped heads as they both bent toward the center. This was not a contingency Jonathan had anticipated.

As the motorcade approached, the lights on the lead car flashed bright, beaming sharp shadows against the headliner.

"They're checking us out," Boxers said.

"At least they didn't stop," Jonathan said. "We were defenseless."

"And we were made," Boxers said. "They'll be keeping an eye out for us."

"Think it was a trap of their own?" Dawkins asked. "Trying to draw us out and show ourselves?"

"If so, then it worked," Jonathan said. "Pass out the NVGs, Thor. We're going to go dark for a while. Is Roxie still on them?"

"Affirmative." He handed up the night vision goggles, then reopened the laptop and toggled down the brightness of the screen.

Jonathan and Big Guy settled the arrays over their heads, and the darkness turned green. Without a word,

Boxers yanked the wheel to the left and U-turned to head west.

Jonathan's earbud popped. "Scorpion, Mother Hen."

"Jesus," Boxers said. "How does she know?"

Venice had a bizarre sixth sense for when operations took an odd turn. "Go ahead, Mother Hen."

"Sitrep, please."

Jonathan had deliberately not told her that they'd had eyes on Roman. It wasn't pessimism, exactly, but he worried about getting her hopes up too high, only to have something go terribly wrong in the end.

Jonathan keyed his mic. "It's a little complicated at the moment, but we think we know where the PC is." At this stage, Jonathan didn't like using real names—particularly when he'd formed a bond. Again, it traced to the possibility of things going bad. When an op went hot, the identities of the players didn't matter. All that mattered was the plan, execution, and outcome. To make any of that personal only muddied everything.

"His name is *Roman*. And you *think* you know, or you *know*?"

Jonathan felt his cheeks flush as anger flashed. "Scorpion out," he said.

"Wait!" she pleaded. "Don't shut me out. Please don't do that."

Jonathan took a deep breath and looked to Boxers for help. "Oh, hell, no," Big Guy said. "You're on your own for this fight."

Jonathan keyed his mic. "Just the facts, right? You're too emotional. Of course you are. You *have* to be emotional. And if you want us to do our jobs, you need to accept that we don't have the luxury of emotion. I am not going to give you a real-time blow-by-blow, Mother Hen.

I will reach out if I need info or intel from you, but other than that, you need to trust us. You need to trust me. Now, get off the net and stay off unless you've got news I need to hear. Scorpion out."

He expected pushback but was pleased when it didn't come.

"Mama Alexander's going to give you a spanking for the way you spoke to her daughter," Boxers said.

"Won't be the first time," Jonathan said, thinking back to his childhood. "That woman has mad skills with a hairbrush."

Chapter Twenty-seven

"Roxie's dying," Dawkins reported from the backseat. "Power level down to five percent."

"She'll be heading back to us, then," Boxers advised. "She's programmed to come home when she gets below five percent power."

"Will she find the truck?" Dawkins asked.

"Yeah, she'll find it," Boxers replied. There was real sadness in his tone. "She'll try to land next to the computer controlling her, but no one anticipated that computer to be going forty miles per hour. She'll kill herself."

"Hey, Big Guy," Jonathan said. "It's a machine. You talk about it like—" The look he got from Boxers froze his words. There were times when it was okay to poke the bear, but this was not one of them. And what the hell? People often said the Boxers was a machine. Maybe it was true love.

At this point, they didn't really need her anymore. Driving blacked out, they'd been able to pull back up to within a quarter mile of the motorcade. The road was very flat, though curvy. With NVGs in place, the headlights and taillights of the four SUVs were easily followed.

"I think they're headed for the beach, Boss," Boxers said.

"And then what?" Dawkins asked.

"The Pacific is big and deep," Boxers said. "I can't think of a better place to dump a couple of bodies." His head twitched around to Jonathan, as if he'd just heard the words he'd uttered. "Sorry, Scorpion."

"Don't be," Jonathan said. "Never apologize for stating the obvious."

"So, they're just going to walk away from a couple million bucks?" Dawkins asked. He seemed shocked.

"These guys don't need money," Jonathan said. "Not at their level. Shit, they get a spiff off of every business transaction in the country. It's about the power. Something spooked them."

"Must've been something big," Boxers said.

"What worries me," Jonathan said, "is that it's more complicated than just killing the kids and dumping their bodies. They could have done that anywhere. They could've shot them in the barn and driven them in the morning if they didn't want to simply bury them on-site."

"It could be to ship them to somebody else," Dawkins said. "Smugglers cruise these waters like no one even cares. Because they don't. Maybe they've sold the kids to a higher bidder."

"Nobody's going to pay millions of bucks for a couple of juvie prostitutes," Boxers said.

"Doesn't matter," Jonathan said. "The reason is unim-

portant. What's scary is the possibility that they're joining a larger group of bad guys. That'll be a lot more guns
and a lot more unknowns."

Something heavy hit the roof of the Durango, startling
the shit out of all of them.

They said it together: "Roxie."

For the last mile or so, the road had narrowed considerably, and they seemed to be following the bank of a me-
andering river. The air smelled of salt and diesel fuel. The
motorcade had slowed to under twenty miles per hour,
then it stopped, only to start again and stop again.

"I think they're lost," Boxers said.

"I say they're looking for something," Jonathan countered. "Either way, I think it's all about to come to a
head." As he spoke, he shrugged into the sling of his
M27. "Here's how I want to do this. Radios on VOX, set
to tach channel two."

"You don't want Mother Hen to listen in?" Boxers
asked.

"Not to this one, no. That would be torture for everyone. If we need her, we can switch back." Unlike their
main channel, the tactical channels were not tuned to any
satellite or repeater signal. That limited their range to just
a couple of miles, maybe less if the terrain didn't cooperate.

"I'm not sure what we're getting into," Jonathan continued, "but don't lose sight of the mission. We're here to
get Roman. He is the mission. Ciara Kelly, too, but she is
a hard second priority. Are we clear on that?"

"You're going to leave a little girl behind?" Dawkins
asked. "I don't think I can do that."

"Listen to the words, Thor," Jonathan said. "If we can rescue her, then, yes, absolutely we will. But we will not sacrifice Roman to make that happen." Every operation needed to have a clear purpose. Once the shooting started—and how could it not in this case—it was too easy to get distracted. You get angry at the guy who's shooting at you. You see or hear something that needs attention. If those things need to be resolved in order to move forward the mission objectives, then you had to do what you had to do. But you never let those things get in the way of rescuing the precious cargo.

"Maximum load-out," Jonathan continued. "Whatever you can carry. And each of us brings an extra vest with plates. When we get the kids, we cover them up and get the hell out. Thor, pull those out of the bag now, please. When the cars stop, we want to be ready to go."

"What's the exfil plan?" Boxers asked. Getting their hands on the kids wouldn't mean much if they couldn't get away.

"We're riding in it unless you have a better idea," Jonathan said. "If not this vehicle, then one of the others. We throw the kids in and haul ass out of here."

Boxers made a growling sound. "Whatever happened to the times when we spent days planning this shit?"

Jonathan wasn't done. "Here's the thing. We can't afford a running gunfight on the way out."

"What are you suggesting?" Dawkins asked.

"I'm suggesting that we settle all bets right here."

"Just kill them all?"

"Kill 'em or cuff 'em," Boxers said.

"Think about who they are and what they intend to do," Jonathan pressed. "What they've done. Either we take care of business here, or you and your fellow agents have to deal with it all later."

He let that sink in before continuing. "We work as a single team, certainly at the beginning. Once we have eyes on Roman, we move hard and fast to rescue him. Anybody with a weapon in their hands dies. Even with suppressors, they're going to hear pops and see that their buddies are going down. Word is going to spread fast, and we'll need to move faster. Focus, focus, focus."

Up ahead, the night sky was bright with artificial light. In the distance, a diesel generator churned. The motorcade stopped and doors opened.

"That's our cue," Jonathan said. "The balloon just went up." He turned the channel selector on his radio to channel two and toggled to VOX. "Radio check."

Boxers and Dawkins answered in unison.

Now, they could whisper.

They climbed out of the Durango, and Dawkins held out the extra vests. "We only have two extras," he said.

Jonathan took one of them. "Just the right number," he said. He pulled off his ballistic helmet long enough to drop the spare over his head to rest atop his own vest, but he didn't fasten it. He wanted quick access for when he got to Roman. "Big Guy wears custom armor," he pointed out. "No way he can shrug into that."

"Got it," Dawkins said, and he donned the other spare.

"Let's try to stay along the tree line until we can turn out the lights," Jonathan said. He led the way toward the river.

Up ahead, people were climbing out of vehicles. Beyond those vehicles, a work crew of five or six men were offloading cardboard boxes of stuff from two small watercraft that looked more suitable for bass fishing than smuggling operations. Rifles had been teepee'd a few feet away, presumably to keep sand out of the actions.

"I think you were right," Jonathan whispered. "There must be a vessel offshore." The cardboard boxes were being carried to waiting trucks. The whole thing looked like a bucket brigade, with one worker handing off to another until the boxes were finally deposited into an open flatbed.

"I've never actually seen this unfolding in real time," Boxers whispered.

"Where's PC One?" Jonathan asked, referring to Roman.

"Looking from behind, I'm not sure I'd know him if I saw him," Dawkins confessed.

That was a damned interesting point, Jonathan thought. He wasn't sure he'd recognize him, either.

"I see PC Two," Boxers said, pointing.

Sure enough, Ciara was flanked between two of the henchmen from the hacienda. Her wrists were cuffed behind her back, and her stooped posture showed terror. Her presence drew leers from the workers along the water.

"Every one of these assholes is armed," Boxers said. "We need to start shooting soon."

"Negative," Jonathan said. "Not until we have eyes on PC One." He pulled binoculars out of their pouch on his vest and searched the crowd. These guys were hustling, working hard. They had a rhythm to their efforts, a kind of choreography. Solid focus.

Then the rhythm faltered. Far to the left of the ongoing operations, there seemed to be some kind of disturbance. A discussion had started between two of the laborers and one of the henchmen. But the angle was bad. Jonathan couldn't make out the faces of the players.

There he was. Truthfully, Jonathan recognized the clothes before he noticed the face, but that was definitely Roman. His hands were still pinioned to his sides, and workers were helping him board the second motorboat—the one that apparently had already been offloaded. There was more discussion among the men, then a worker fired up the motor and wheeled the small craft around to the west to head into the Pacific.

"Shit," Jonathan said. "They're taking him out to sea. Big Guy, take out the generator."

Boxers already had his HK 417 pressed into his shoulder. Before Jonathan finished the command, he'd fired two suppressed .30 caliber bullets through the guts of the generator. The machine sparked, then belched flame, and darkness fell over everything.

"Weapons free," Jonathan said. He snapped his NVGs over his eyes, and the darkness transformed to shades of green. The air seemed alive with a lattice of infrared laser sights from his team's firearms as the three of them lit up targets that were both blind and terrified.

Jonathan settled on one of the workers offloading the remaining small craft—maybe a hundred yards away—and dropped him with two to the chest. To Jonathan's left, the others on his team pounded at their own targets.

"I'm going after the PC-One," Jonathan said. "Get a vest on PC Two."

Even in the blackness, the cartel crowd knew they were under attack, but they clearly did not know from where or by whom. They moved in random motions and meaningless directions, reminding Jonathan of activity from a ruptured anthill. Some tried to take cover, some tried to run. A few shot back, but into the darkness, wasting ammunition on trees and humidity.

Jonathan focused on getting to the boat at the shore before it had a chance to escape into the open ocean to follow its mate.

His NVGs gave him the additional advantage of advancing on his enemies in a straight line, rather than zigzagging his steps. That made aiming downrange a much simpler task.

"Easy, Scorpion," Boxers said in his ear. "You're getting too far ahead."

"PC-Two is yours," Jonathan said. "I'm going for One."

He double-tapped two people who ran toward the boat and then a third as he scrambled to pull a rifle from the teepee.

He'd closed the distance by half when a bad guy logged a lucky shot that glanced off Jonathan's chest plate. Had it been full-on, it might have taken him out of the fight. As it was, it spun him to his left and knocked him to his knees.

"Scorpion down!" Boxers yelled.

Jonathan sat back on his heels and leveled his M27 at the shooter who'd nailed him. He shot him in the throat and the chin, and the man dropped into the sand. "I am not down!" Jonathan replied.

"Then quit relaxing and get to work," Boxers said.

Close behind him, Jonathan heard a heavy *thwop* and a grunt just before a bad guy he'd never seen dropped dead.

"You're welcome," Boxers said.

The targets were thinning out quickly now, as was the pace of return fire. Jonathan saw an unimpeded path now to the transport boat, but he fought the urge to charge toward it. The fact that he was in a hurry didn't change the fact that he was also in the middle of a battle. He had himself and his team to be concerned about.

"I got her!" Dawkins exclaimed over the air. "I got PC-Two. She appears unhurt yet terrified."

"Package her up and get her to safety," Jonathan said. He never paused in his forward progress. "Take our vehicle and *di di mao* like a madman." He'd invoked a Vietnamese phrase from back in the day that translated roughly to "run like a burning bunny rabbit." "Lights out, pedal to the metal. Can you find your way back to the Underground Railroad?"

"Affirmative."

"Git."

Finally, Jonathan arrived at water's edge and the waiting boat. Two corpses littered the sand while a third oscillated in the tide. The boat was still packed with boxes of product, but there was ample room for him. He'd just begun to push off when he heard heavy footsteps approaching.

He whirled to see Big Guy sprinting toward him. It always amazed Jonathan that a man of his size could move with such speed.

"Can't let you go alone," Boxers said. "I know how you hate boats."

Through his earbud, Jonathan heard Dawkins soothing Ciara. It was okay that she had a name again.

"Thor, Scorpion," he said. "Switch to papa-tango-tango." Push-to-talk. "Godspeed. Monitor channel one for further traffic."

"Roger, Scorpion. Good hunting."

The radio clicked, and it was just Jonathan and Boxers on the net. As always, Big Guy drove. He settled into the back of the boat and pulled the starter cord while Jonathan pushed them away from the shore. When he was knee-deep in the Pacific, he pressed hard against the gunwale to leverage himself up and over.

Boxers twisted the throttle, and they were on their way.

"Where are we going?" Big Guy asked.

Jonathan pointed into the night. "That way."

Chapter Twenty-eight

Using a box on the bow as a seat, Jonathan peered out into the night. To avoid detection, smugglers had for generations plied their trade on moonless nights. Even with night vision, the blackness of the Pacific was absolute.

"Do you see any watercraft?" Boxers whispered.

"Negative. But those guys have to be navigating somehow."

"They probably have a GPS coordinate to aim for."

This was how smugglers were able to do what they did. Jonathan had no idea how sophisticated the Mexican shore monitoring capabilities were, but those probably didn't matter, anyway. The cartels got to do whatever they wanted.

"Kill the engine," Jonathan whispered.

Boxers complied, and the night went silent, save for the slapping and rippling of the water against the sides of their boat.

Their prey had no doubt heard the battle that had raged on the shore, so what would their reaction be? Would they understand that this was a rescue mission? If so, what would they do with Roman? It made as much sense to kill him and drop him overboard as it did to bring him aboard. Furthermore, they understood the advantage of darkness, so would they cut their engines, too, and float for a while? Or would they book it out to their vessel and get underway as quickly as possible?

Maybe they'd stick around until they thought the danger was over and go back to complete their mission to drop off product. No, that one didn't make sense. With their cover blown and people dead, they'd consider speed to be of the essence.

"Starboard bow," Boxers whispered.

As Big Guy spoke, Jonathan heard it, too. The definite, discernible hum of an outboard motor. They had no choice but to roll the dice that this was the right one. After all, how many boats would there be out on the sea at this hour?

"Fire it back up," Jonathan ordered.

Their motor jumped back to life, and Boxers' quick acceleration damn near tossed Jonathan overboard. He recovered and sat lower, bracing himself against the gunwales. He changed his NVGs from light magnification to infrared, and there it was, the glow of a working motor, its heat signature a stark contrast to the night.

"I see him," Jonathan said. "Speed up."

"It's wide open. How far?"

"Can't tell," Jonathan whispered into his mic. "No perspective." As he spoke, though, the distance closed considerably. "Pull back, pull back. They must be slowing."

As they approached, he could see three people aboard the motorboat. They glowed as white images in the night, almost like photographic negatives.

"I've got three souls," Jonathan said.

"I confirm," Boxers agreed. "I can't make out the PC from the bad guys, though."

The problem with IR imaging as opposed to light enhancement was a significant loss in visual detail. You could see that they were human and you could make out short from tall, but that was about it.

"I'm switching back to light enhancement," Jonathan said. Now that he knew where to look and what he was looking for, he could see his target, but it was still were too far out. They continued to close the distance.

"Cut it back," Jonathan commanded. He wanted them to be dead before they had a chance to see him.

They coasted in silence for fifteen or twenty seconds before he got enough detail to make out what he was looking for. "I see PC-One in the center, between two tangos," Boxers observed. Terrorists. His voice was inaudible in the atmosphere, but perfectly amplified through Jonathan's earbud.

"Why are they stopped?" Jonathan mused aloud.

"Why do we care?"

"We're missing something. This feels like a trap. Where were they headed, and why have they stopped now?"

"Where's the smuggling ship, you mean?"

"Exactly."

"What kind of trap could it be?" Boxers asked. "Even

if they figured out that we were chasing them, they can't know where we are. It's too dark."

As Big Guy spoke, Jonathan watched his IR laser sight settle on the man on the right, the one at the bow.

"Still too far out," Jonathan said. "Too much bobbing. Hold your fire."

"I know I have a shot now," Boxers said. "I don't know if I'll have a shot in thirty seconds."

"Hold your fire." His words notwithstanding, Jonathan settled his own laser beam on the centerline of the man on the left.

As they glided closer still, they could hear the puttering of the idling outboard on the target vessel. Their motor noise had deafened them to the sound of Jonathan's approach.

Then, without warning or apparent cause, they abruptly cut their motor, leaving Jonathan's the only sound on the water.

Roman's captors reacted instantly, reaching down onto the deck and retrieving automatic rifles.

"Fire!" Jonathan said, but Boxers' target had already pirouetted into the water. Jonathan dropped his with three to the chest.

"Sorry, Boss, were you saying something?"

Roman yelled and struggled to remain steady in the oscillating boat, unable to move his hands.

"Roman Alexander!" Jonathan yelled. "You are safe! We're here to take you home!"

The boy looked equal parts startled and terrified. "Who are you?" he called to the night.

"Stay still!" Jonathan called. "It's almost over."

Roman's boat continued to rock precipitously from

side to side. If he fell overboard, he'd drown with his arms pinioned the way they were.

"Sit!" Jonathan commanded. "Sit straight down. In fifteen seconds, this is over."

"Mr. Jonathan?" In the glow of the night vision, his wide eyes printed as comically large and he folded his legs under him.

Jonathan reached into a pocket of his vest and withdrew a glow stick. He broke it, shook it, and Roman's world filled with green light, too. "It's just a light stick, Roman. I'm tossing it onto your deck so you have vision."

Despite the warning, Roman jumped when the stick thumped onto the wooden deck.

"Mr. Jonathan, is that you? Mr. Boxers?"

"It's us, Roman. We're gonna bump your boat here in a few seconds."

Boxers worked the throttle carefully to bring their boat alongside Roman's. Jonathan reached across the gap and pulled them together until they touched.

"Which boat do you want to go back in?" Boxers asked.

"His," Jonathan replied. "More room. Roman, hang tight. We're coming over." Boxers held the boat steady while Jonathan rolled across both gunwales and landed on the deck of Roman's boat.

"Mr. Jonathan?" Roman looked frightened when he saw his rescuers up close, and Jonathan instantly understood why. Their ballistic gear—especially the four-tube NVG array—made them look more like sea creatures from a horror movie than men.

"It's us, I promise." Jonathan shrugged out of his spare

vest, made his way over to Roman, and dropped the neck hole down over the boy's head. "I need you to wear this."

"My hands . . ."

"We'll get to those." Jonathan turned back to the other boat to see Boxers light a flare and jam it under the remaining cargo. The fire lit instantly and grew quickly.

"Shit," Boxers said as he scurried across the gunwales to join the others in Roman's boat. "That caught faster than I thought." He pushed the boat away, and a few seconds later, something popped inside the boxes of cargo—it sounded like an aerosol can. The fire flared up, and within a few seconds, the whole boat was ablaze.

"Holy shit," Roman said. "What is happening?"

"Kinda cool, isn't it?" Boxers asked.

Jonathan said, "There's a lot you're going to want to know, Roman, and only a few things we can explain. The headline here is that you're going home."

Boxers pulled the starter cord for the outboard. An instant later, the water beside them began to churn. White foam boiled to the surface, luminescing in the light of the glow stick, made even brighter through his NVGs.

"What did you do?" Jonathan asked.

"It's a trick I learned from Moses," Boxers said, not dropping a beat. "I'm parting the Sea. I didn't do anything."

Before more words could be spoken, the ocean did appear to part. From it emerged the squatty superstructure of a submarine.

"You're shitting me," Boxers said.

"Who knew the cartel had a navy?" Jonathan asked.

Boxers twisted the throttle on the outboard and lurched them away from the breaching boat, back toward shore.

"No," Jonathan commanded. "Stay put."

"You're not serious."

"Serious as a heart attack."

"Our mission's accomplished, Boss. He's right next to you."

"You heard me," Jonathan said. "If we run, we're an easy target. We take the fight to them."

"A motorboat against a submarine," Boxers said. His voice dripped disbelief. "Just making sure we're on the same page."

There was more to Jonathan's logic, but it would take too long to explain, and he didn't want to argue. He'd heard of the narco navy, and he'd heard that they'd commissioned the construction of submarines for their smuggling operations between Colombia and Mexico, but he'd never seen one. He'd never even talked to anyone who'd seen one. But they had to cost a bundle of money, and how often did you get a chance to hurt the bad guys that bad?

Jonathan spoke quickly. "Here's how we work it. Big Guy, you bring me up to the sub as soon as it stops breaching. You stay with the PC while I engage the crew and scuttle the boat."

"You're shitting me."

"Bring us back," Jonathan said.

He'd expected the submarine to rise farther out of the water than it did, more akin to the breaching of a military submarine, but this one stopped with its deck barely above the surface—below the gunwales of the motorboat.

"Scorpion, this is a mistake."

"Duly noted." He reached over to Roman, put a hand on the back of his head, and pressed him down into the deck. "You stay low till this is over. Kiss the deck." Jonathan then took the glow stick and flung it out into the ocean.

Roman complied without complaint. His expression showed total overload.

Boxers worked the motor like a master, sliding their boat into the submarine's starboard side just as a hatch opened on the forward end of deck.

"Oh, shit, here we go," Boxers said. He raised his rifle to his shoulder.

"Hold your fire," Jonathan said. He wasn't in position yet. He wanted the crewman to be as clear of the hatch as possible before engaging him. The point here was to sink the sub and rid the world of smugglers. If they guy lived and returned below deck, it would become a whole new battle.

Jonathan hauled himself onto the aft end of the deck, on the other side of a four-foot-high superstructure, next to the heavy-duty fill cap for the fuel tanks.

On the forward end, a beam of dull red light preceded the emergence of a crew member who carried a slung AK47 in a way that showed he had no intention of using it.

"Hello, friends!" the crew member said in Spanish. He appeared to be addressing no one in particular. "What is this about human cargo?"

Jonathan settled the beam of his IR sight on the man's right ear and blew his brains out his left ear. The dead man dropped vertically, back into the open hatch. Instantly, from inside the sub, Jonathan heard commotion, the realization that a crewmate had been shot.

As Jonathan pulled himself up and over the superstructure, another crewman's head and shoulders emerged from the hatch to reach for the lid. Before Jonathan could react, Boxers killed the man with a single shot.

As that man dropped, the hatch nearly dropped with him, but Jonathan cleared the forward edge of the superstructure just in time to hook-slide into the hatch and prop it up with his foot.

Gunshots were fired somewhere inside the vessel, but Jonathan didn't know by whom or at whom they were aimed. All he knew was that he wasn't hit. And that it was a foolish idea to fire randomly inside a steel tube. Fragments would ricochet everywhere.

With the hatch lid standing vertical, Jonathan let his M27 fall against its sling while he pulled a fragmentation grenade from its pouch on his vest. He pulled the pin, let the spoon fly, and dropped it into the opening, and then slammed the hatch shut. The deck vibrated with the detonation, but the sub maintained its structural integrity.

As explosive devices went, hand grenades weren't all that powerful. They were designed to kill and maim people, not to break things.

He pulled the hatch open to repeat the process and was greeted with a plume of smoke that smelled of nitrates and burning plastic. He dropped in another grenade and slammed the hatch again.

Call him twisted, but there was something deeply satisfying in the subquake that the detonation triggered.

"That oughta do it," Jonathan said.

"Try this," Boxers said, holding up another grenade. He tossed it to Jonathan. "A little thermite for good luck."

Jonathan couldn't help but smile. "Well, this should send everything to the bottom." Thermite grenades were incendiary devices that burned at about four thousand degrees Fahrenheit. In the past, Jonathan had used them to destroy artillery guns and to take out electrical installations. This would be his first time using one to sink a ship.

His first thought was to drop the grenade through the same hatch and let it burn through the hull, but then he had a better idea. He hauled himself back over the top of the superstructure to the afterdeck, where he'd boarded the vessel. He pulled the pin, placed the grenade atop the filler cap for the fuel tanks, and hopped back aboard the motorboat.

"Full speed ahead, please," he said.

"Aye, aye." Boxers throttled in power, and they accelerated back toward shore.

Behind them, the thermite flashed with brilliant white light. A few seconds later, after it had melted the steel and dropped into the vapor space of the fuel tank, a *whump* rippled through the air, and a gout of orange flame seemed to rise directly out of the sea. Within a minute, that flame went away as the dead vessel disappeared below the surface, leaving the dark night illuminated only by the smoldering remains of the other rowboat. Soon, it would disappear below the waves, as well.

Chapter Twenty-nine

Every modern handcuff assembly in the United States can be opened by the same key. Jonathan had never looked into the official reasoning, but he supposed it made sense that one cop could free the hands and ankles of another cop's prisoner. Thus, a handcuff key was a standard part of Jonathan's everyday carry ensemble. Even when he wasn't kitted out for battle as he was today, he carried handcuff keys inside slits that he'd cut into his belt on the front side and in the rear. Given the collection of enemies he'd acquired over the years, it didn't seem unreasonable that one day someone might want to stuff him into the trunk of a car.

While Boxers drove the boat toward shore, Jonathan used one of his keys to free Roman's hands.

"I . . . I really don't . . ."

"And you shouldn't," Jonathan said. "It's a long and

complicated story, and you'll never hear the whole thing."
A few seconds passed. "It's good to see your face again,
kid."

"So, am I . . . are we safe now?"

"You're safer than you were a little while ago," Jonathan said, "but real safety is an hour or two away."

"How did you find me? Where did you get all this
stuff?"

Jonathan issued a loud sigh. This was why it was always a bad idea to deal with people you knew—*children*
you knew. "Roman, I'm really not trying to be difficult,
but most of the questions you ask will have to go unan-
swered."

"Does my mom know you're here?"

This was dangerous territory. He decided to roll the
dice on the truth. "Yes, she does. And she'll be thrilled to
know that you're safe."

"Can we call her?"

"Not yet. Not until we know for sure." Behind him, he
could hear Boxers chuckling. "How hurt are you?"
Jonathan asked. "I saw the ransom video."

"I'm okay. It hurt at the time, but not so much now.
Where is Ciara?"

"She's been rescued by someone else," Jonathan explained.

"Will I see her?"

Another awkward question. And once again, he went
for the truth. "Probably not." If only to change the sub-
ject, he turned to Boxers. "How far out are we?"

"Couple of minutes."

"Is Ciara okay?"

The kid wasn't going to let it go. "She was fine the last
time I saw her. How else did they hurt you?"

"When was that? When did you see her?"

"A few seconds after you last saw her. Now please, Roman, I need to know. How else did the people who kidnapped you hurt you?"

"If you saw the video, you saw most of it. There was a guy named Guzman who had this big hammer."

"I heard about him," Jonathan said.

Roman's shoulders sagged. "I saw him beat a man to pieces with it. I saw him kill him with it. He threatened to do it to me, but he never did."

As with Erica back in the bar, Jonathan didn't know how to form the question he really wanted to ask—the one about touching—but he decided it didn't matter. That was territory for Father Dom and Venice to explore. Jonathan would have made the world's worst psychologist.

Up ahead, someone turned on a bright white light and pointed it at them. The glare flared Jonathan's NVGs, rendering him momentarily blind. He snapped the NVGs out of the way as he heard the whizzing cracks of two bullets passing way too close.

Jonathan pulled Roman down to the deck and fell on top of him as Boxers wheeled the motorboat hard to the right and poured on the power. A bullet excised a chunk from the gunwale, and five seconds later, it was done.

"Anybody hurt?" Boxers asked.

Jonathan said, "I'm good, I think." He sat up and pulled Roman back upright onto his butt. "You okay, kid?"

"No! Why did you do that?"

The adolescent pique told Jonathan everything he needed to know. The kid was bruised, but functional. Not shot.

Jonathan brought his NVGs back down and saw that the beach had turned into a line of woods. They weren't getting shot at anymore because they couldn't be seen.

"Call the ball, Boss," Boxers said. "Are we fighting or fleeing?"

"You already know the answer," Jonathan said. They had no choice but to finish this fight. They were too deep into enemy territory and too dependent upon cartel rolling stock as their exfil plan to try to make a run for it via the water. And they'd never stand a chance if they tried to hoof it out through the wilds of Sinaloa.

"Bring us to shore," Jonathan ordered. "Okay, Roman, listen to me." As he spoke, he detached his NVG array from his helmet and handed the helmet to the boy. "Put this on and keep it on." He found the head suspension bracket inside the large pocket on the back side of his vest and attached the NVGs to that. "There's going to be more shooting, and you need to do exactly what I say, as I say it. Do you understand?"

In the dark, Roman struggled with the helmet straps. "Here, let me," Jonathan said. He settled the lid on the kid's head and cinched the chin strap tight.

"Did you hear what I told you?"

"There's going to be more shooting."

"Right. What was the rest?"

"I need to do what you say."

"Exactly."

"Who's going to be shooting at who?"

The question took Jonathan off guard. Wasn't it obvious? "Didn't you see those people shooting at us from the shore?"

Roman looked shocked. "They were *shooting*? I didn't hear any gunshots."

That explained his surprise at being thrown to the bottom of the boat. "Too far away to hear the shots. But they're definitely there. And we have to engage them."

"Why?"

"Okay, those rules about not asking questions and doing what you're told have just sort of come together."

"Can't I just stay here?"

"Absolutely not," Jonathan said. "Everything we need is up on that beach. We need to move forward. You need to stay with us."

"But what if—"

"And you need to stop asking questions. Right now."

Boxers beached the motorboat, killed the engine. "You know, Boss, the kid's got a point," he whispered. "Moonless nights, woods, and no night vision for Roman aren't a good mix."

Jonathan heard but did not acknowledge. He understood the point from a logical perspective but not from an emotional one. They'd come *this close* to repatriating Roman to his family. If they kept him close, they could defend him. But if they got separated, he would be on his own, however unlikely that scenario might be.

"We can move faster with fewer distractions," Boxers pressed.

"Fine." Jonathan grabbed Roman under his armpit and helped him out of the boat. "Follow along," he said. "I won't let you fall."

They walked across the short strip of sand to the edge of the forest.

"Put your hands out straight," Jonathan instructed.

Roman complied, and Jonathan led him to the trunk of a stout tree.

"This is your tree, Roman. This is where you stay until

I come back here and get you. No matter what you hear, you stay put. Do you understand?"

The boy nodded vigorously. "Yes, I understand. Can I have a flashlight?"

"No, you want to stay in the dark."

"I promise I won't turn it on. I just . . . You know, in case."

Again, the kid had a point. *In case* covered a lot of ground, a lot of possibilities, and many of those would be mitigated with light instead of dark. Jonathan pulled his Mini Maglite from the pouch on his belt.

"Hold out your hands," he said.

When Roman extended his arms, Jonathan pressed the aluminum tube into his palm. "I do this with your promise to keep it off unless there's no other choice."

"I promise."

"We'll be back when we can."

After Mr. Jonathan and Mr. Boxers walked away, the silence around Roman became oppressive. Terrifying. Within seconds of them walking away, he found himself wishing that he'd gone along.

In the silence and the dark, he wondered if maybe all of this was a dream. Maybe he was still in that awful barn, asleep and unable to wake up. Even better, maybe he was at home in Fisherman's Cove, sound asleep in the mansion, surrounded by security teams with a safe room nearby.

None of that was true, of course. He really had been kidnapped, and he really had been beaten. He'd been tied up and threatened and forced to watch a man be beaten to death with a hammer.

And if all of that was true, then this part about being rescued must be true, as well.

But by Mr. Jonathan? By Mom's boss? How the hell could that—

In the distance, the forest erupted in the staccato chatter of gunfire. He heard shouting, much of it in Spanish, so he couldn't make out the words, but it all seemed far away. Long strings of machine gun fire split the night. Twice, three times. Four times. But then it stopped.

Silence returned, but now the silence was bothered with a ringing sound in his ears. Maybe the shooting had been closer than he'd thought.

Had people been killed? He hoped they had. He hoped that all those bastards had been killed. The way that Guzman killed that man in the barn.

And he prayed that Mr. Jonathan and Mr. Boxers were both fine.

Oh, my God, what if they're the ones who got killed?

The thought terrified him. He hadn't been prepared for that. If they got killed, what was Roman going to do? Where was he going to run to? There'd be no more ransom requests, that was for sure—not if this is what became of ransom requests. God only knew what Mr. Guzman would do to him when he found out about the fight.

Maybe Guzman was already dead. This was the second time there'd been shooting coming from the beach, the first coming right after they'd thrown him in the boat and pushed away from shore.

Maybe—

He heard something in the woods. Footsteps. Someone was coming.

Roman sat as still as he could, squeezing the flashlight

in his hand so tightly that the pocket clip dug into his flesh. In his mind, he could see it leaving a stripe in the skin across his knuckles, but the pain felt good somehow. Felt necessary.

He tried to make his heart stop so it wouldn't hammer so loudly.

The footsteps approached closer.

Then they stopped.

Roman's eyes strained to see through the blackness, but they saw nothing.

Maybe it was Mr. Jonathan coming to look for him. Maybe they'd forgotten where they'd stashed him. If he called out quietly to remind them . . .

A brilliant white light exploded in front of him, blasting his eyes and causing him to roll to his side to look away.

A man's voice made an animal sound, and the light lunged closer.

Roman rolled to his stomach, and his feet found traction in the sand. He bolted blindly away from the light just as something heavy impacted the ground behind him, at the base of the tree where he'd just been sitting.

Roman's karate training kicked in. He fought the urge to run because there was nowhere to run to. If he turned his back on his attacker, God only knew what the attacker could do, so Roman dipped his body into a widened fighting stance, weight equally distributed, hands up in front to block an incoming blow. From this stance, he could run away if he had to, or he could duck and jink or defend himself.

As the light came around again, Roman caught a glimpse of a sledgehammer. He also caught a glimpse of red wetness on the front of the man's shirt. It wasn't until the man spoke that he could confirm that it was Guzman.

"So, we get to dance our dance after all," Guzman said in slurred English. "We—"

Roman launched himself at the man. Plowing his shoulder into Guzman's gut with everything he had. Together, they drilled themselves into the trunk of the tree that was to be Roman's shelter and tumbled onto the ground.

Guzman's flashlight pirouetted into the sand, its beam illuminating them both as they clamored on the ground.

Roman heard screaming, a guttural, awful cry of pure anger as he rose to his feet and dropped his knee into the bloody spot on Guzman's shirt. He realized when Guzman howled in agony that the scream he'd been hearing was his own.

Guzman reached for his sledgehammer, but Roman kneed him again and the man's hands jerked back to his belly.

Roman dropped the Mini Maglite and grabbed the handle of the sledge.

"You killed that man!" he yelled. "He begged for help, and you killed him! You were going to kill me!"

Roman felt rage and sadness and hopelessness pour out of him. Suddenly, the sledgehammer felt as if it weighed nothing, but he knew the power it held. He knew the agony it could bring.

He wanted to see Guzman's bones break. He wanted to hear the animal beg for mercy. He wanted—

Guzman's head burst apart at the same instant a sharp *pop* from very close by.

Roman whirled, ready to kill whoever it was.

He saw the silhouette of a man against the dark sky.

"Roman, it's me. It's Mr. Jonathan." He'd taken off the night vision stuff, and it really was him. Even in the dim glow from Guzman's flashlight, Roman could make out the blue eyes. The smile.

"He . . . he tried to kill me." Roman heard his voice catch in his throat. "He was . . . he killed that man."

"I know," Mr. Jonathan said. "It's over. He'll never hurt anyone again." He approached Roman softly and slipped the sledgehammer out of his grasp. "You're safe now."

Roman didn't know what to do. He didn't really know what had just happened. Could it really be true that he was safe?

"It's really okay," Mr. Jonathan said. He held out his arms and embraced Roman as he sobbed into the rough surface of his equipment vest.

Three hours later, after they were joined by a man they called Thor, Roman was airborne, wrapped in a blanket and strapped into the leather seat of the fanciest airplane he'd ever seen. They'd just taken off when Mr. Jonathan said, "Roman, I have one more thing for you to do."

"Yes, sir?"

He handed Roman a portable radio. "Okay, I want you to key that mic there and say exactly what's written on this piece of paper."

Roman looked at it, but he didn't get it.

Mr. Jonathan winked, and then he did get it.

"Just make sure to wait for the other side to acknowledge you."

Roman keyed the mic. "Mother Hen, PC-One."

Seconds passed in silence. Jonathan nodded for him to do it again, but just as he was about to key the mic again, his mom's voice jumped out of the speaker. "Go ahead, PC-One. Oh, my God." She was crying.

Roman's voice cracked, too, as he said, "Mother Hen, PC-One is secure. I'm coming home."

Chapter Thirty

Jonathan Grave sat behind his massive mahogany desk, oblivious to the swaying masts in the harbor behind him, yet very aware of the snoring and ever-flatulent Labrador retriever at his feet. JoeDog didn't really belong to anyone, but she split much of her time between Jonathan and Doug Kramer. She had official immunity from Fisherman's Cove's leash laws, so it wasn't unusual to see her soliciting tummy rubs from anyone who would offer.

He'd been back from Mexico for nearly a week now, and the breaking news on his computer screen amused him. Apparently, the U.S. Drug Enforcement Administration had broken up a major operation of the Sinaloa arm of the Cortez Cartel. A team of unnamed operators had intercepted and destroyed over three hundred kilos of cocaine and methamphetamine as the product was being brought ashore. Officials were astonished yet pleased that the operation also sank a submarine used by the cartels to ferry imported product from the manufacturing fields in Colombia.

Apparently as part of the fallout from the collapse of the cartel in the region, one of the known lieutenants of Santiago Pérez, a rancher named Cristos Silva, had been found murdered in his home, his dismembered limbs scattered throughout his property.

A spokesman for the FBI would neither confirm nor deny that the Bureau was in any way involved in the operation.

For his part, President Tony Darmond publicly praised the leaders of his administration for their tireless dedication to ridding the world of the scourge of illegal drugs.

A knock at Jonathan's door brought his head up to see Venice walking in. She covered her nose. "Oh, my God, is that you?"

He laughed. "JoeDog's under the desk."

Venice helped herself to one of his guest chairs. "You've been watching the news, I suppose?"

"I have. Words cannot express how thrilled I am with the aggressive way that federal law enforcement protects us all."

"Is it safe to say you had something to do with spinning the story?"

Jonathan gave a wry smile. "I might have made a few suggestions to Wolfie. This administration needs a few victories, and it seems the attorney general was easily sold. I understand that Harry Dawkins got a career bump, too."

Venice's expression turned serious. "How long do plan to keep doing this?"

"Sit in a cloud of doggie gas?" He had an idea where this was going, and he really didn't want to travel there.

"You know what I mean, Dig. This cut way too close to home."

"Close, but no cigar. We won, Ven. That's all there is. We won and the bad guys lost. The world is in balance."

"And my son is under guard," she said. Her eyes glistened and she wiped at them.

"He is not. He's going to school at RezHouse. Which, I hasten to add, scores higher on every test than any private or public school within a hundred miles. Including that intellectual prison, Northern Neck Academy."

"But that's where he wants to be. Especially now that Ciara is finally back."

Jonathan had thought it a bad idea to bring Ciara back with the rescue team and Roman. Dawkins had left her in the care of Sister Katherine at St. Ignatius, who'd worked her magic to repatriate the girl via her underground resources.

"Is she *really* back?" Jonathan pressed. "Or has she been expelled?"

Venice's eyes narrowed. "Did you have anything to do with that?"

"Absolutely not." A statement more true than not. As a member of the Board of Regents, he had abstained from casting the vote that would have kept her from being expelled. "The Board felt that she had made a very poor and dangerous decision. And as I told you before, I recused myself entirely from the vote on Roman."

That last part, while true, was deliberately misleading. Offline, he'd pushed Dr. Washington pretty hard to terminate Roman's enrollment in the Neck. The cartels were going to be apoplectic about all that had transpired, and he thought the boy would be much safer in the secure environment of RezHouse.

"Look, Ven, I think that as time passes—"

He stopped himself as he saw Gail entering the Cave with Doug Kramer in tow. This was a massive violation of their security protocols. As Jonathan rose to greet them at his office door, JoeDog scrabbled to her feet and beat him to it. She galloped out to meet Doug, swinging her tail with leg-breaking force.

"To what do I owe the pleasure?" Jonathan said, extending a hand.

Kramer rubbed a dog ear with one hand and greeted Jonathan with the other.

"Actually, I'm here to see Venice and Gail," he said.

Jonathan cast a glance, but neither would make eye contact. "Do I need to step out?"

Doug asked Gail, "Do you mind if he stays?"

"Well," she replied sheepishly, "it *is* his office."

Jonathan indicated the leather conversation group near the fireplace. "Take a seat," he said. "Save the rocker for me."

Ever fickle, JoeDog chose to sit with Kramer at the feet of the club chair.

"Is this official business?" Jonathan asked.

Kramer took a deep breath and scowled. "Okay, I'll get right to it. I saw some interesting bodycam footage from one of the county officers. It was taken about a week ago up near Northern Neck Academy. You heard the place was broken into, right?"

Jonathan shifted his gaze to Venice and Gail, who each remained expressionless.

Kramer continued, "You know, it's the damnedest thing. It appears that there are two FBI agents in our area that look very much like you two." He paused.

"Huh," Gail said. "What are the odds?"

"I know, right?" Kramer said. "And you know what's even stranger? As a favor—you know, so you could know the names of your local lookalikes—I ran their names and faces through the databases we have, and I found the oddest thing. Both of those agents are real people." His eyes narrowed. "Seriously, if you saw these ladies, you'd swear you were looking in a mirror."

Jonathan cleared his throat. "So, these agents," he said. "Are they suspected of any wrongdoing?"

Kramer reached down and gave JoeDog the tummy rub she was begging for. "No, not that I know of. I mean, we never did catch those burglars at the school, but I don't think that will ever be a big priority for us." As he petted the dog, his eyes never wandered from Venice and Gail.

"I appreciate you letting us know about those doppelgängers," Gail said. "With identity theft being as rampant as it is these days."

Kramer laughed. "Exactly." He stood, and the rest of the room stood with him. "I'd show you the footage, but this whole thing seems snakebit. Fumble-fingered as I am, I somehow erased the digital record as I was watching it."

"What a shame," Venice said. She put her hands behind her back when she noticed that they were trembling.

"I don't even remember what the agents' names were."

Kramer held out his hand to Jonathan, who accepted it. "One day," Kramer said, "after we're retired and don't care anymore, you really must fill me in on just what you do here."

Jonathan smiled. "One day."

JoeDog followed as Kramer headed for the office door. "I'm really glad you got your boy back, Ven. No price is too high to pay for that kind of reward."

ACKNOWLEDGMENTS

If I've counted correctly, *Stealth Attack* is my twenty-third book, making this the twenty-third round of acknowledgments. Think about that for a second. When I was a kid, I dreamed of one day having one book published, but I would have felt greedy even praying for this honor to be bestowed so many times. Thank you all so much for being a part of the journey.

My lovely bride, Joy, is the one who really makes any of this possible. I have heard rumors—all of them unsubstantiated, as far as I'm concerned—that I can be difficult to be around as I dive more deeply into a story. Without stipulating to anything, I am blessed that she's tolerated me for so long and continues to love me as much as I love her.

My technical support team continues to keep me from digging holes for myself in things related to weaponry. Thanks to Jeff Gonzales, Rick McMahan, and Steve Tarani for their guidance in tactics and weapons. Thanks also to Robbie Reidsma, my go-to expert at Heckler and Koch.

Thanks to Chris Thomas for his aviation expertise.

Chris Shaw is a member of the FBI's Hostage Rescue

Team, and I am forever thankful that he returns my texts quickly and cheerfully.

Steve Thompson is the proprietor of After-Hours Bail Bonds in Martinsburg, West Virginia. Thanks, Steve for your patient guidance through that fascinating corner of the law enforcement world.

As always, I am indebted to Art Taylor, Donna Andrews, Ellen Crosby, and Alan Orloff for their wisdom and guidance as I wrote *Stealth Attack*. Ditto the wise counsel of my buddies Jeffery Deaver and Reavis Wortham.

This has been a challenging year on many fronts. The fellowship and support shown by my Masonic brethren and fellow nobles of the Kena Shrine kept sanity alive in my world. Thank you so much, brothers.

Kensington Publishing has been my home for many years now, and I hope for many more. My editor, Michaela Hamilton, showed special patience with me this year, as did Lynn Cully and Steve Zacharius. Somehow, in spite of everything, Crystal McCoy, along with Vida Engstrand, Lauren Jernigan, and Alexandra Nicholajsen kept the train on the tracks for me. There's a real sense of family at Kensington, and I am proud to be a part of it.

Last but never least—far from it—is a thank-you to my longtime friend, mentor, agent, and fellow martini lover Anne Hawkins of John Hawkins & Associates in New York.

Don't miss the next exciting Jonathan Grave thriller

LETHAL PREY

Coming soon from Kensington Publishing Corp.

Keep reading to enjoy a gripping sample chapter . . .

Chapter One

Jonathan Grave hadn't moved in nearly three hours. He sat at the base of a towering cedar tree, his knees pulled up to his chest, his rifle draped across his lap as he scanned the sloped bank on the other side of the river for any sign of his prey. The November Montana air felt clear and sweet. Not yet cold by local standards, but weather reports said that the mercury would dance around fifteen degrees after dark—about where it was when he'd started out this morning.

Somewhere in the woods on Jonathan's left, his giant friend, coworker, and Army buddy Brian Van de Muelebroecke—a.k.a. Boxers—was presumably scanning the horizon on his own.

Jonathan was certain he'd seen a bull elk along the far side, but by the time he'd settled into position for a shot, the beast had disappeared into the trees. He hadn't run, though. Jonathan took that as evidence that he hadn't been spooked. If he was correct, then he figured there was a good chance that the bull—or one of the cows he was no doubt trying to impress with his big rack of antlers—might follow the same trail back this way. Jonathan had allotted five days for this hunt, and this was only the first. He had the time to show patience.

This was his favorite part about hunting, anyway. He didn't get enough silence in his life these days. Sometimes solitude worked against him, dredging up images and events that he'd rather forget, but so far, the demons had all stayed away. He considered those demons to be a form of occupational hazard, having spent so much time in nasty places doing nasty chores to protect innocents from nasty people.

In many ways, on a hunt like this, pulling the trigger and dropping the animal was a kind of letdown. Not that he felt guilty about filling his freezer with seven hundred pounds of deliciousness, but because the gunshot marked the end of the silence.

The transceiver in his left ear popped as it broke squelch. "Scorpion, Big Guy."

He and Boxers had had those radio handles since their days back with the Unit, and old times died hard.

Jonathan reached under the blaze orange vest he wore over a camo'd chest carrier and keyed the radio that resided in its pouch on his shoulder. "Go ahead," he whispered. God had blessed elk with amazing ears and an even better nose. He didn't want to waste these last hours by spooking his prey.

"Gotta take a break, Boss," Boxers said. "We got a visitor. We're coming your way."

Boxers knew better than to break a moment like this,

so whoever the visitor was, Jonathan knew it had to be important. Smart money said it was a game warden. He muttered a curse under his breath as he flexed his knees, straightened his back, and stood. He let his Vortex Viper binoculars fall against his chest by their lanyard and slung his rifle. "Are you coming to me or are we meeting in the middle?"

"We'll come to you."

As he waited, Jonathan brought his binoculars back up to his eyes and scanned the opposite bank again. Believing with all his soul that Murphy and his law ruled the universe, he knew that if Mr. Elk were going to make a surprise midday appearance, it would be now, when Jonathan was out of position, or in a few minutes when he'd be locked in conversation with somebody.

Rustling leaves and heavy footsteps preceded Boxers' arrival with exactly the person Jonathan had been expecting. The game warden looked to be little more than a kid—maybe twenty-five—and he carried himself with the stern authority of a street cop. Topped with a wide-brimmed cowboy hat, the warden wore the standard uniform of a khaki shirt and blue jeans, along with Sam Browne belt packed with a big Glock, handcuffs, and enough spare mags to engage a militia single-handed.

Jonathan adjusted his rifle on his shoulder, put a smile on his face, and walked toward the others. "We can't be in trouble yet," he said, offering his hand. "We haven't been here long enough."

The warden looked at Jonathan's hand, then tucked his thumbs into the arm holes for his ballistic armor. The name SIMONSEN was stitched into a patch that was Velcro'd onto the vest.

Jonathan didn't appreciate being dissed by a child, but

he also didn't want to get sideways with the one agency in Montana that could turn this adventure into something very unpleasant. He decided to roll with it and see what the guy wanted.

"Are you from DC, too?" Simonsen asked.

"Nope. Virginia."

"You two are hunting together, then?"

"We traveled together," Jonathan said. "Not sure we're exactly hunting together, with him being a couple hundred yards away. Have we done something wrong?"

"I don't know," Simonsen said. "Have you?"

Boxers made a sound and rolled his eyes.

Simonsen turned on him. "Did you just growl at me? Get around with your friend, where I can see both of you. Let me see some identification."

Jonathan reached around to his back pocket for his wallet. "I've got my nonresident hunting permit, too," he said as fished out his driver's license and handed it over. "But it's on my phone."

Simonsen held the license with two fingers on his left hand while he jotted the information into a skinny, lined reporter's notebook. "Won the permit lottery, did you?" he asked as he wrote.

"Been trying for years and finally struck. Both of us did." Elk licenses were distributed by lottery every April 1, and they cost nearly $1,000 to get.

"How'd you get here?"

"We flew."

"What airline?"

Jonathan hesitated. There was no inoffensive way to say the next part. "My own. I have my own plane."

"How many stops between home and here?"

"None."

"Not even a fuel stop?"

This was all beginning to sound strangely intrusive. "Not even," Jonathan said. "My plane has the range."

"And a lot more," Boxers said. As the designated pilot for their team and the man who specked out the two planes that comprised Jonathan's fleet, he showed a certain parental pride.

Simonsen handed back the driver's license. "I'll see your permit now."

Jonathan returned his license and wallet to his back pocket and pushed his hand into his left front pocket for his phone.

Simonsen pointed at the binoculars hanging from the strap around Jonathan's neck. "I guess that a man who can afford his own plane has plenty of scratch for those eight-hundred-dollar field glasses."

They were only six hundred, but Jonathan let it go. He pulled up the electronic image of his permit, but Simonsen barely looked at it. "Put it away," Simonsen said. "I figure if you were that ready to show me, I got no reason to look." He nodded to Jonathan's slung rifle. "What're you shooting?"

"MR-seven-six-two," Jonathan said. "It's the civilian version of—"

"The Heckler and Koch four-seventeen. Yeah, I know. Same as your tall buddy." Simonsen's mood lightened as he spoke of weaponry. "I carried the four-sixteen over in the shit pile." He glanced at Jonathan, then gave Boxers a long look. "You guys serve?"

"A long time," Jonathan said. "Been out for a few years, though."

"Why are you wearing body armor?"

"We're not," Jonathan said. "Just the plate carrier. Easiest way to keep the essentials at hand."

Simonsen pointed to the camo-patterned rucksack that rested against the base of a tree. "You and your buddy dress together every morning?"

"That was the best Uncle Sam could buy," Jonathan said. "Why try to improve on it." This whole interview didn't seem right. It felt two clicks too adversarial.

"What would I find if I opened it?"

"Socks, shirts, some underwear. Can I ask why you're so curious about Boxers and me?"

"You guys are drivin' a Suburban, right? A rental?"

"Yup."

"The way you parked it up there," Simonsen said. "Most people when they hunt, they just pull off to the side of the road and go at it. You folks tried to hide your vehicle. Pulling it into the trees, well off the road." His eyes narrowed. "Mind tellin' me why?"

Jonathan had no idea why. It was just the way they'd parked. He looked to Big Guy for help.

"Old habits die hard, I guess," Boxers said. "I never like leaving a vehicle too close to the road."

"It's the way poachers behave," Simonsen said. "I didn't have a lot else to do, so I thought I'd seek you out and find you." He pointed briefly to Boxers' boots. "Them size fifties make tracking pretty easy. I saw where you guys split from each other, so I followed the easy one first."

Now it made sense. Sort of. "You walked all this way just to ask a question?" Jonathan said. "That must be two miles."

"Every bit of three," Simonsen corrected. "And it's my

job. It might not surprise you to know that not everyone has the patience to wait the years it can take to win the permit lottery."

Jonathan had grown tired of the jaw flapping. "Are we free to go?"

"As far as I'm concerned. Unless you need to confess to something."

Jonathan chuckled. If only the warden knew what Jonathan could confess about the last many years. "I've got a question for you about elk. This is my first time with game this big. Is this spot—"

Simonsen's vest dimpled, and he made a burping sound as he sat down hard. He was still moving when the sound of a gunshot reached them.

"Shit!" Jonathan and Boxers said it together. They reacted instantly—instinctively—by likewise dropping to the ground and crawling for cover. Jonathan had just dived behind another cedar when a bullet tore through it at what would have been the level of his head if he hadn't ducked. The report reached them about a second later.

"You okay, Boss?" Boxers asked.

"Fine. You?"

"Peachy. Who'd you piss off this time?"

Simonsen had been hit hard, drilled through his center of mass. He'd collapsed onto his back, staring up at the blue sky. Jonathan had no idea whether he was dead or alive, but he knew he was unacceptably exposed.

"Cover me," Jonathan said. "I'm going to pull him to cover."

"He's dead."

"We don't know that."

Jonathan watched as Boxers shifted his butt around so

he could better stabilize his rifle. "You do what you want," Big Guy said, "but I don't think Ranger Rick is the shooter's target."

"Why?"

"Watch. Keep an eye on the slope on the other side of the river." Without any warning, Boxers darted back into the clear for half a second and then ducked back behind cover. Two bullets tore into the trees behind where he would have been, accentuated after the fact by the sound of two reports.

"Big Guy!" Jonathan yelled. "What the hell?"

Boxers had made himself small—as if that were possible—behind his tree. "Did you see muzzle flashes?"

"Seriously?"

"I told you to watch the other side."

Jonathan settled in deeper behind his cover and thought things through. The fact that the shooter had not anchored his kill of the game warden with another shot made it clear—well, mostly clear—that Simonsen was not his intended target. That left the only two men who were left.

"What do you figure the time delay between the impact and the report?" he asked Boxers.

"I give it about a second."

"That's what I got. Speed of sound is three hundred forty meters per second, right?"

"Three forty-three," Boxers corrected

"What's that, three hundred seventy-five yards?"

"Give or take."

Jonathan pulled his laser range finder from its pocket on his vest and scanned the other slope. The trees were thick, and the hill was steep. At the three-fifty- to three-seventy-five-yard mark, the woods were especially thick.

"I don't see a spot at that range where he could get a shot off without hitting another tree," he observed aloud. This was not a long shot for a talented sniper, but it was a challenging range for a hunter. Even twigs and leaves can make a difference in the flight path of the bullet.

Maybe that's what happened.

"Hey, Boss," Boxers said. "Take a look at the rock ledge about ten meters to the left of the massive red tree."

Jonathan pulled the range finder away to locate the landmark with his bare eyes, then brought it up again. An outcropping of rocks rose from the trees. From it, a shooter could have a clear field of fire. Mother Nature had built a perfect sniper's nest—an elevated platform for taking the shot and lots of cover in the event of return fire. And it was at the right distance.

"Okay," Jonathan said. "Now that I know where to look, jump out again and I'll watch for the muzzle flash."

"I already rode that horse once," Boxers said. "I believe it is your turn."

It was hard to argue the logic. Besides, since Big Guy's stunt had clearly been a ruse to get the guy to show himself, the shooter would be foolish to fall for the same trick a second time. "He's probably moved on to get a different angle," Jonathan said.

"Definitely," Boxers agreed. Neither of them moved.

"You're still going to make me do this, aren't you? After all the good times we've had together."

"Nah," Big Guy said. "I'm not making you do anything. I don't mind sittin' here till dark. It'll get damned cold, though."

Jonathan peered through the range finder again. He supposed there were other options. They could just pound the outcropping with a shit-ton of ammo, but if they did that and the bad guy wasn't there, that would just reduce the bullets available to them to fight off the real attacker.

"Well, shit," Jonathan said. "I'm gonna do this thing, okay?"

"If you insist."

"But I'm not going to just duck in and out, okay? I'm going to make a dash for that thick oak on the other side of the marshal." He was betting on the fact that the shooter wasn't good enough to lead his target effectively.

"Want me to keep his head down?" Big Guy asked.

"That'd defeat the purpose, wouldn't it? I mean, the whole point is to get him to show himself."

"You're right," Boxers said. "I was just testing your commitment. What about that orange vest?"

"I'll keep it on for the mad dash. It'll add to his temptation to shoot."

"Good thinking," Boxers said. "I'd hustle, though, if I were you. Sometimes you run like a girl when you're scared."

"I hate you."

Boxers answered with a loud smooching sound.

"I'm counting it down," Jonathan said. "Three . . . two . . . one . . ." He launched himself into the opening at what would have been *zero* if he'd continued with the cadence. He sprinted out into the clearing, bent low at the waist to create as small a target as possible, and beelined to cover behind a stout hardwood. As he passed Simonsen, a quick glance showed that his eyes were fixed and lifeless.

As Jonathan slid into place, Boxers opened up with a sustained barrage of ten shots.

"Did he shoot at me?" Jonathan shouted after Big Guy was done.

"Negative, but I saw a flash. I figured it for the lens of a rifle scope."

"Game warden's dead," Jonathan said.

"I figured he would be."

Now that they could eyeball each other across the clearing, Jonathan tugged at the lapel of his blaze orange vest and unzipped it. This was not a time for high visibility. As he shrugged out of it, Boxers did the same.

"Well, this is exciting," Big Guy said. "What do you want to do next?"

Connect with  Us

Visit us online at
KensingtonBooks.com
to read more from your favorite authors, see books
by series, view reading group guides, and more.

 Join us on social media

for sneak peeks, chances to win books and prize packs,
and to share your thoughts with other readers.

facebook.com/kensingtonpublishing
twitter.com/kensingtonbooks

Tell us what you think!

To share your thoughts, submit a review,
or sign up for our eNewsletters, please visit:
KensingtonBooks.com/TellUs.